The Oath of the Vayuputras

Amish is a 1974-born, IIM (Kolkata)-educated banker-turned-author. The success of his debut book, *The Immortals of Meluha* (Book 1 of the Shiva Trilogy), encouraged him to give up his career in financial services to focus on writing. Besides being an author, he is also an Indian-government diplomat, a host for TV documentaries, and a film producer.

Amish is passionate about history, mythology and philosophy, finding beauty and meaning in all world religions. His books have sold more than 6 million copies and have been translated into over 20 languages. His Shiva Trilogy is the fastest selling and his Ram Chandra Series the second fastest selling book series in Indian publishing history. You can connect with Amish here:

- www.facebook.com/authoramish
- www.instagram.com/authoramish
- www.twitter.com/authoramish

Celebrating
30 Years of Publishing
in India

Other Titles by Amish

SHIVA TRILOGY

The fastest-selling book series in the history of Indian publishing

The Immortals of Meluha (Book 1 of the Trilogy)

The Secret of the Nagas (Book 2 of the Trilogy)

RAM CHANDRA SERIES

The second fastest-selling book series in the history of Indian publishing

Ram – Scion of Ikshvaku (Book 1 of the Series)

Sita – Warrior of Mithila (Book 2 of the Series)

Raavan – Enemy of Aryavarta (Book 3 of the Series)

War of Lanka (Book 4 in the Series)

INDIC CHRONICLES

Legend of Suheldev

NON-FICTION

Immortal India: Young Country, Timeless Civilisation

Dharma: Decoding the Epics for a Meaningful Life

www.authoramish.com

'{Amish's} writings have generated immense curiosity about India's rich past and culture.'

– Narendra Modi

(Honourable Prime Minister, India)

'{Amish's} writing introduces the youth to ancient value systems while pricking and satisfying their curiosity…'

– Sri Sri Ravi Shankar

(Spiritual Leader & Founder, Art of Living Foundation)

'{Amish's writing is} riveting, absorbing and informative.'

– Amitabh Bachchan

(Actor & Living Legend)

'Amish is one of India's greatest storytellers, creative, imaginative, so you have to turn the page.'

– Lord Jeffrey Archer

(One of the highest-selling authors of all time)

'{Amish's writing is} a fine blend of history and myth...gripping and unputdownable.'

– BBC

'Thoughtful and deep, Amish, more than any author, represents the New India.'

– Vir Sanghvi

(Senior Journalist & Columnist)

'Amish's mythical imagination mines the past and taps into the possibilities of the future. His book series, archetypal and stirring, unfolds the deepest recesses of the soul as well as our collective consciousness.'

– Deepak Chopra

(World-renowned spiritual guru and bestselling author)

'{Amish is} one of the most original thinkers of his generation.'

– Arnab Goswami

(Senior Journalist & MD, Republic TV)

'Amish has a fine eye for detail and a compelling narrative style.'

– Dr. Shashi Tharoor

(Member of Parliament & Author)

'{Amish has} a deeply thoughtful mind with an unusual, original, and fascinating view of the past.'

– Shekhar Gupta

(Senior Journalist & Columnist)

'To understand the New India, you need to read Amish.'

– Swapan Dasgupta

(Member of Parliament & Senior Journalist)

'Through all of Amish's books flows a current of liberal progressive ideology: about gender, about caste, about discrimination of any kind… He is the only Indian bestselling writer with true philosophical depth – his books are all backed by tremendous research and deep thought.'

– Sandipan Deb

(Senior Journalist & Editorial Director, Swarajya)

'Amish's influence goes beyond his books, his books go beyond literature, his literature is steeped in philosophy, which is anchored in bhakti, which powers his love for India.'

– Gautam Chikermane

(Senior Journalist & Author)

'Amish is a literary phenomenon.'

– Anil Dharker

(Senior Journalist & Author)

www.authoramish.com

The Oath of the Vayuputras

Book 3
of the
Shiva Trilogy

Amish

HarperCollins *Publishers* India

www.authoramish.com

First published in 2013

This edition published in India by HarperCollins *Publishers* 2022
4th Floor, Tower A, Building No. 10, Phase II, DLF Cyber City,
Gurugram, Haryana – 122002
www.harpercollins.co.in

2 4 6 8 10 9 7 5 3 1

P-ISBN: 978-93-5699-013-5
E-ISBN: 978-93-5699-001-2

Original cover image by Rashmi Pusalkar
Map on page X illustrated by ATLASkeeda

Typeset in Garamond by Ram Das Lal

Printed and bound at
Thomson Press (India) Ltd

This book is produced from independently certified FSC® paper
to ensure responsible forest management.

To the late Dr Manoj Vyas, my father-in-law

Great men never die

They live on in the hearts of their followers

www.authoramish.com

Har Har Mahadev

All of us are Mahadevs, All of us are Gods

For His most magnificent temple, finest mosque and greatest church exist within our souls

www.authoramish.com

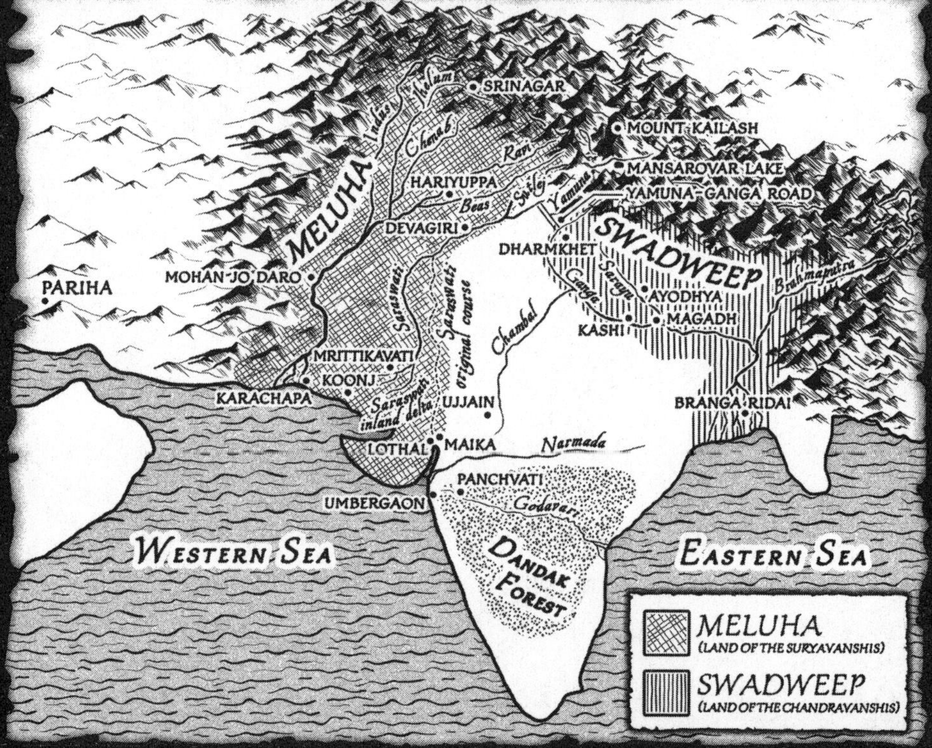

India, 1900 to 1850 BCE

Contents

		Acknowledgements	*xv*
		The Shiva Trilogy	*xix*
		List of Characters	*xxi*
Chapter	1:	The Return of a Friend	1
Chapter	2:	What is Evil?	11
Chapter	3:	The Kings Have Chosen	32
Chapter	4:	A Frog Homily	50
Chapter	5:	The Shorter Route	66
Chapter	6:	The City that Conquers Pride	80
Chapter	7:	An Eternal Partnership	90
Chapter	8:	Who is Shiva?	103
Chapter	9:	The Love-struck Barbarian	115
Chapter	10:	His Name Alone Strikes Fear	128
Chapter	11:	The Branga Alliance	137
Chapter	12:	Troubled Waters	147
Chapter	13:	Escape of the Gunas	156
Chapter	14:	The Reader of Minds	166
Chapter	15:	The Magadhan Issue	176
Chapter	16:	Secrets Revealed	187

Chapter	17:	Honour Imprisoned	195
Chapter	18:	Honour or Victory?	204
Chapter	19:	Proclamation of the Blue Lord	214
Chapter	20:	The Fire Song	222
Chapter	21:	Siege of Ayodhya	230
Chapter	22:	Magadh Mobilises	241
Chapter	23:	Battle of Bal-Atibal Kund	250
Chapter	24:	The Age of Violence	261
Chapter	25:	God or Country?	270
Chapter	26:	Battle of Mrittikavati	279
Chapter	27:	The Neelkanth Speaks	289
Chapter	28:	Meluha Stunned	301
Chapter	29:	Every Army Has a Traitor	311
Chapter	30:	Battle of Devagiri	321
Chapter	31:	Stalemate	332
Chapter	32:	The Last Resort	342
Chapter	33:	The Conspiracy Deepens	351
Chapter	34:	With the Help of Umbergaon	357
Chapter	35:	Journey to Pariha	367
Chapter	36:	The Land of Fairies	373
Chapter	37:	Unexpected Help	382
Chapter	38:	The Friend of God	394
Chapter	39:	He is One of Us	404
Chapter	40:	Ambush on the Narmada	415
Chapter	41:	An Invitation for Peace	422

Chapter	42:	Kanakhala's Choice	432
Chapter	43:	A Civil Revolt	441
Chapter	44:	A Princess Returns	450
Chapter	45:	The Final Kill	463
Chapter	46:	Lament of the Blue Lord	481
Chapter	47:	A Mother's Message	488
Chapter	48:	The Great Debate	494
Chapter	49:	Debt to the Neelkanth	506
Chapter	50:	Saving a Legacy	516
Chapter	51:	Live On, Do Your Karma	523
Chapter	52:	The Banyan Tree	531
Chapter	53:	The Destroyer of Evil	540
Chapter	54:	By the Holy Lake	551
		Glossary	566

Acknowledgements

The acknowledgments written below were composed when the book was published in 2013. I must also acknowledge those that are publishing this edition of **The Oath of the Vayuputras**. *The team at HarperCollins: Swati, Shabnam, Akriti, Gokul, Vikas, Rahul, and Udayan, led by the brilliant Ananth. Looking forward to this new journey with them.*

***

I hadn't imagined I would ever become an author. The life that I live now, a life spent in pursuits like writing, praying, reading, debating and travelling, actually feels surreal at times. There are many who have made this dream possible and I'd like to thank them.

Lord Shiva, my God, for bringing me back to a spiritual life. It is the biggest high possible.

Neel, my son, a rejuvenating elixir, who would regularly come and ask me while I was obsessively writing this book, *'Dad, aapka ho gaya kya?'*

Preeti, my wife; Bhavna, my sister; Himanshu, my brother-in-law; Anish and Ashish, my brothers; Donetta, my sister-in-law. They have worked so closely with me, that many times I feel that it isn't just my book, but a joint project, which just happens to have my name on it.

The rest of my family: Usha, Vinay, Meeta, Shernaz, Smita, Anuj and Ruta. For always being there for me.

Sharvani Pandit, my editor. She has battled severe health troubles, without asking for any sympathy. And despite the trying times she went through, she helped me fulfil my karma. I'm lucky to have her.

Rashmi Pusalkar, the designer of this book's cover. She's been a partner from the first book. In my humble opinion, she's one of the best book-cover designers in Indian publishing.

Gautam Padmanabhan, Satish Sundaram, Anushree Banerjee, Paul Vinay Kumar, Vipin Vijay, Renuka Chatterjee, Deepthi Talwar, Krishna Kumar Nair and the fantastic team at Westland, my publishers. They have shown commitment and understanding that very few publishers show towards their authors.

Anuj Bahri, my agent, a typically large-hearted, boisterous Punjabi. A man brought to me by fate, to help me achieve my dreams.

Sangram Surve, Shalini Iyer and the team at Think Why Not, the advertising and digital marketing agency for the book. I have worked with many advertising agencies in my career, including some of the biggest multinationals. Think Why Not ranks right up there, amongst the best.

Chandan Kowli, the photographer for the cover. He did a brilliant job as always. Also, Atul Pargaonkar, for fabricating the bow and arrow; Vinay Salunkhe, for the make-up; Ketan Karande, the model; Japheth Bautista, for the concept art for the background; the Little Red Zombies team and Shing Lei Chua for support on 3D elements and scene set-up; Sagar Pusalkar and team for the post processing work on the images; Julien Dubois for coordinating production. I hope you like the cover they have created. I loved it!

Omendu Prakash, Biju Gopal and Swapnil Patil for my photograph that has been printed in this book. Their composition was exceptional; the model, regrettably, left a lot to be desired!

Chandramauli Upadhyay, Shakuntala Upadhyay and Vedshree Upadhyay from Benaras; Santanu Ghoshroy and Shweta Basu Ghoshroy from Singapore. For their hospitality while I wrote this book.

Mohan Vijayan, a friend, whose advice on media matters is something I always treasure.

Rajesh Lalwani and the Blogworks team, a digital agency which works with my publisher, for their strong support in an area I don't understand too well.

Anuja Choudhary and the Wizspk team, the PR agency of my publisher, for the effective campaigns they've implemented.

Dr Ramiyar Karanjia, for his immense help in understanding the philosophies of Zoroastrianism.

Purnima, an old friend, for her impeccable legal advice. Caleb, for working with me on my film deals. Raajeev, for working with me on the music album created for the Shiva Trilogy.

And last, but certainly not the least, you the reader. Thank you from the depths of my being for the support you've given to the first two books of the Shiva Trilogy. I hope I can give you a sense of completion with this concluding book.

www.authoramish.com

The Shiva Trilogy

Shiva! The Mahadev. The God of Gods. Destroyer of Evil. Passionate lover. Fierce warrior. Consummate dancer. Charismatic leader. All-powerful, yet incorruptible. Quick of wit – and of temper.

No foreigner who came to India – be he conqueror, merchant, scholar, ruler, traveller – believed that such a great man could ever have existed in reality. They assumed he must have been a mythical God, a fantasy conjured within the realms of human imagination. And over time, sadly, this belief became our received wisdom.

But what if we are wrong? What if Lord Shiva was not simply a figment of a rich imagination but a person of flesh-and-blood like you and me? A man who rose to become God-like as a result of his karma. That is the premise of the Shiva Trilogy, which attempts to interpret the rich mythological heritage of ancient India, blending fiction with historical fact.

The Immortals of Meluha was the first book in a trilogy that chronicles the journey of this extraordinary hero. The story was continued in the second book, *The Secret of the Nagas*. And it will all end in the book that you are holding: *The Oath of the Vayuputras*.

This is a fictional series that is a tribute to my God; I found Him after spending many years in the wilderness of atheism.

www.authoramish.com

I hope you find your God as well. It doesn't matter in what form we find Him, so long as we do find Him eventually. Whether He comes to us as Shiva or Vishnu or Shakti Maa or Allah or Jesus Christ or Buddha or any other of His myriad forms, He wants to help us. Let us allow Him to do so.

Yadyatkarma karomi tattadakhilam shambho tavaaraadhanam
My Lord Shambo, My Lord Shiva, every act of mine is a prayer in your honour

List of Characters

Anandamayi: Ayodhyan princess, daughter of Emperor Dilipa, married to General Parvateshwar.
Athithigva: King of Kashi.
Ayurvati: The chief of medicine at Meluha.
Bappiraj: Prime minister of Branga.
Bhadra a.k.a. Veerbhadra: A childhood friend and a confidant of Shiva, married to Krittika.
Bhagirath: Prince of Ayodhya, son of Emperor Dilipa.
Bharat: An ancient emperor of the Chandravanshi dynasty married to a Suryavanshi princess.
Bhoomidevi: A revered non-Naga lady who established the present way of life of the Nagas a long time ago.
Bhrigu: A Saptrishi Uttradhikari (successor of the Saptarshis), rajguru of Meluha.
Brahaspati: Chief Meluhan scientist; belonged to the swantribe of Brahmins.
Brahmanayak: Father of Daksha, previous emperor of Meluha.
Chandraketu: King of Branga.
Chenardhwaj: Governor of Maika and Lothal; earlier the governor of Kashmir.
Daksha: Emperor of the Suryavanshi Empire of Meluha, married to Veerini and father of Sati and Kali.

Dilipa: Emperor of Swadweep, king of Ayodhya and chief of the Chandravanshis; father of Bhagirath and Anandamayi.
Divodas: The leader of the Brangas who live in Kashi.
Ganesh: Sati's first child, one of the Naga leaders.
Gopal: Chief of the Vasudevs.
Kali: Sati's twin sister and queen of the Nagas.
Kanakhala: The prime minister of Meluha, she is in charge of administrative, revenue and protocol matters.
Karkotak: Prime minister of the Nagas.
Kartik: Son of Shiva and Sati, named after Krittika, Sati's best friend and attendant.
Krittika: A close friend and attendant to Sati; wife of Veerbhadra.
Manobhu: Shiva's maternal uncle and teacher.
Manu: Founder of the Vedic way of life; he lived many millennia ago.
Mitra: Chief of the Vayuputras.
Mohini: An associate of Lord Rudra; respected by some as a Vishnu.
Nandi: A captain in the Meluhan army.
Parshuram: A dacoit in Branga; he was named after the sixth Vishnu.
Parvateshwar: Head of Meluhan armed forces, he was in charge of army, navy, special forces and police; married to Princess Anandamayi.
Ram: The seventh Vishnu, who lived centuries ago. He established the empire of Meluha.
Rudra: The earlier Mahadev, the Destroyer of Evil, who lived some millennia ago.
Sati: The royal princess of Meluha, daughter of King Daksha and Queen Veerini, married to Shiva, mother of Kartik and Ganesh.

Satyadhwaj: Grandfather of Parvateshwar.
Shiva: The chief of the Guna tribe; Neelkanth, the saviour of the land. Married to Sati, father of Kartik and Ganesh.
Siamantak: Prime minister of Swadweep.
Surapadman: Prince of Magadh.
Swuth: Chief of a tribe of Egyptian assassins.
Tara: A pupil of Bhrigu.
Vasudev pandits: Advisers to Shiva, tribe left behind by the previous Vishnu, Lord Ram.
Veerini: Queen of Meluha, wife of Emperor Daksha and mother of Sati and Kali.
Vidyunmali: Brigadier in the Meluhan army.
Vishwadyumna: A close associate of Ganesh.

Chapter 1

The Return of a Friend

Before the Beginning.

Blood dribbled into the water, creating unhurried ripples which expanded slowly to the edges of the cistern. Shiva bent over the container as he watched the rippling water distort his reflection. He dipped his hands in the water and splashed some on his face, washing off the blood and gore. Recently appointed Chief of the Gunas, he was in a mountain village far from the comforts of the Mansarovar Lake. It had taken his tribe three weeks to get there despite the punishing pace he had set. The cold was bone-chilling, but Shiva didn't even notice. Not because of the heat that emanated from the Pakrati huts that were being gutted by gigantic flames, but because of the fire that burnt within.

Shiva wiped his eyes and stared at his reflection in the water. Raw fury gripped him. Yakhya, the Pakrati chieftain, had escaped. Shiva controlled his breathing, still recovering from the exhaustion of combat.

He thought he saw his uncle, Manobhu's bloodied body in the water. Shiva reached out below the surface of the water with his hand. 'Uncle!'

The mirage vanished. Shiva squeezed his eyes shut.

The macabre moment when he had found his uncle's body replayed in his mind. Manobhu had gone to discuss a peace treaty with Yakhya, hoping the Pakratis and Gunas would end their incessant warmongering. When he hadn't returned at the appointed time,

Shiva had sent out a search party. Manobhu's mutilated body, along with those of his bodyguards, had been found next to a goat trail on the way to the Pakrati village.

A message had been written in blood; on a rock next to where Manobhu had breathed his last.

'Shiva. Forgive them. Forget them. Your only true enemy is Evil.'

All that his uncle wanted was peace and this is how they had repaid him.

'Where's Yakhya?' Bhadra's scream broke Shiva's chain of thoughts.

Shiva turned. The entire Pakrati village was up in flames. Some thirty dead bodies lay strewn across the clearing; brutally hacked by the enraged Gunas seeking vengeance for their former chief's death. Five Pakrati men knelt on the ground, tied together, a continuous rope binding their wrists and feet. Both ends of the rope had been hammered into the ground. The fierce Bhadra, bloodied sword in hand, led the twenty Guna guards. It was impossible for the Pakratis to escape.

At a distance, another contingent of Guna warriors guarded the shackled Pakrati women and children; unharmed thus far. The Gunas never killed or even hurt women and children. Never.

'Where is Yakhya?' repeated Bhadra, pointing his sword menacingly at a Pakrati.

'We don't know,' the Pakrati answered. 'I swear we don't know.'

Bhadra dug his sword point into the man's chest, drawing blood. 'Answer and you shall have mercy. All we want is Yakhya. He will pay for killing Manobhu.'

'We didn't kill Manobhu. I swear on all the mountain Gods, we didn't kill him.'

Bhadra kicked the Pakrati hard. 'Don't lie to me, you stinking arsehole of a yak!'

Shiva turned away as his eyes scanned the forests beyond the clearing. He closed his eyes. He could still hear his uncle Manobhu's words echo in his ears. 'Anger is your enemy. Control it! Control it!'

Shiva took deep breaths as he tried to slow down his furiously pounding heart.

'If you kill us, Yakhya will come back and kill all of you,' screamed a Pakrati at the end of the rope line. 'You will never know peace! We shall have the final vengeance!'

'Shut up, Kayna,' shouted another Pakrati, before turning to Bhadra. 'Release us. We had nothing to do with it.'

But the Pakrati seemed to have come unhinged. 'Shiva!' shouted Kayna.

Shiva turned.

'You should be ashamed to call Manobhu your uncle,' roared Kayna.

'Shut up, Kayna!' screamed all the other Pakratis.

But Kayna was beyond caring. His intense loathing for the Gunas had made him abandon his instinct for self-preservation. 'That coward!' he spat. 'Manobhu bleated like a goat as we shoved his intestines and his peace treaty down his throat!'

Shiva's eyes widened, as the rage bubbling under the surface broke through. Screaming at the top of his lungs, he drew his sword and charged. Without breaking a step, he swung viciously as he neared the Pakratis, beheading Kayna in one mighty blow. The severed head smashed into the Pakrati beside him, before ricocheting off to the distance.

'Shiva!' screamed Bhadra.

They needed the Pakratis alive if they were to find Yakhya. But Bhadra was too disciplined a tribesman to state the obvious. Besides, at that moment, Shiva didn't care. He swirled smoothly, swinging his sword again and again, decapitating the next Pakrati and the next. It was only a matter of moments before five beheaded Pakrati bodies lay in the mud, their hearts still pumping blood out of their gaping necks, making it pool around the bodies, almost as though they lay in a lake of blood.

Shiva breathed heavily, as he stared at the dead, his uncle's voice ringing loudly in his head.

'Anger is your enemy. Control it! Control it!'

— 𐊀 —

'I have been waiting for you, my friend,' said the teacher. He was smiling, his eyes moist. 'I'd told you, I would go anywhere for you. Even to *Patallok* if it would help you.'

How often had Shiva replayed these words uttered by the man who stood before him. But he had never fully understood the reference to *the land of the demons*. Now it all fell into place.

The beard had been shaved, replaced by a pencil-thin moustache. The broad shoulders and barrel chest were much better defined. The man must be getting regular exercise. The *janau, the holy thread of Brahmin identity,* was loosely slung over newly developed muscles. The head remained shaven, but the tuft of hair at the back appeared longer and neater. The deep-set eyes had the same serenity that had drawn Shiva to him earlier. It was his long-lost friend. His comrade in arms. His brother.

'Brahaspati!'

'It took you a very long time to find me.' Brahaspati stepped close and embraced Shiva. 'I have been waiting for you.'

Shiva hesitated for a moment before joyously embracing Brahaspati, allowing his emotions to take over. But no sooner had he regained his composure, than doubts started creeping into his mind.

Brahaspati created the illusion of his death. He allied with the Nagas. He destroyed his life's purpose, the great Mount Mandar. He was the Suryavanshi mole!

My brother lied to me!

Shiva stepped back silently. He felt Sati's hand on his shoulder, in silent commiseration.

Brahaspati turned to his students. 'Children, could you please excuse us?'

The students immediately rose and left. The only people left in the room were Shiva, Brahaspati, Sati, Ganesh and Kali.

Brahaspati stared at his friend, waiting for the questions. He could sense the hurt and anger in Shiva's eyes.

'Why?' he asked.

'I thought I would spare you the dreadful personal fate that is the inheritance of the Mahadevs. I tried to do your task. One cannot fight Evil and not have its claws leave terrible scars upon one's soul. I wanted to protect you.'

Shiva's eyes narrowed. 'Were you fighting Evil all by yourself? For more than five years?'

'Evil is never in a rush,' reasoned Brahaspati. 'It creeps up slowly. It doesn't hide, but confronts you in broad daylight. It gives decades of warnings, even centuries at times. Time is never the problem when you battle Evil. The problem is the will to fight it.'

'You say that you have been waiting for me. And yet you hid all traces of yourself. Why?'

'I always trusted you, Shiva,' said Brahaspati, 'but I could not trust all those who were around you. They would have prevented me from accomplishing my mission. I might even have been assassinated had they learnt about my plans. My mission, I admit, prevailed over my love for you. It was only when you parted ways with them, that I could meet you safely.'

'That's a lie. You wanted to meet me because you needed me for the success of your mission. Because you now know you cannot accomplish it by yourself.'

Brahaspati smiled wanly. 'It was never meant to be my mission, great Neelkanth. It was always yours.'

Shiva looked at Brahaspati, expressionless.

'You are partially right,' said Brahaspati. 'I wanted to meet you... No, I *needed* to meet you because I have failed. The coin of Good and Evil is flipping over and India needs the Neelkanth. It needs you, Shiva. Otherwise, Evil will destroy this beautiful land of ours.'

Shiva, while continuing to stare noncommittally at Brahaspati, asked, 'The coin is flipping over, you say?'

Brahaspati nodded.

Shiva remembered Lord Manu's words. *Good and Evil are two sides of the same coin.*

The Neelkanth's eyes widened. *The key question isn't 'What is Evil?' The key question is: 'When does Good become Evil? When does the coin flip?'*

Brahaspati continued to watch Shiva keenly. Lord Manu's rules were explicit; he could not suggest anything. The Mahadev had to discover and decide for himself.

Shiva took a deep breath and ran his hand over his blue throat. It still felt intolerably cold. It seemed as if the journey would have to end where it had begun.

What is the greatest Good; the Good that created this age? The answer was obvious. And therefore, the greatest Evil was exactly the same thing, once it began to disturb the balance.

Shiva looked at Brahaspati. 'Tell me why...'

Brahaspati remained silent, waiting... The question had to be more specific.

'Tell me why you think the Somras has tipped over from the greatest Good to the greatest Evil.'

Bits and pieces of the wreckage had been dutifully brought by the soldiers for examination by Parvateshwar and Bhagirath, who squatted at a distance.

Shiva had asked the Meluhan general and the Ayodhyan prince to investigate the wreckage. They had been tasked with determining the antecedents of the men who had attacked their convoy on the way to Panchavati. Parvateshwar and Bhagirath had stayed behind with a hundred soldiers while the rest of Shiva's convoy had carried on to Panchavati.

Parvateshwar glanced at Bhagirath and then turned back to the wooden planks. Slowly but surely, his worst fears were coming true.

He turned to look at the hundred Suryavanshi soldiers who stood at a respectable distance, as they had been instructed. He was relieved. It was best if they did not see what had been revealed. The rivets on the planks were clearly Meluhan.

'I hope Lord Ram has mercy on your soul, Emperor Daksha,' he shook his head and sighed.

Bhagirath turned towards Parvateshwar, frowning. 'What happened?'

Parvateshwar looked at Bhagirath, anger writ large on his face. 'Meluha has been let down. Its fair name has been tarnished forever; tarnished by the one sworn to protect it.'

Bhagirath kept quiet.

'These ships were sent by Emperor Daksha,' Parvateshwar said softly.

Bhagirath moved closer, his eyes showing disbelief. 'What? Why do you say that?'

'These rivets are clearly Meluhan. These ships were built in my land.'

Bhagirath narrowed his eyes. He had noticed something completely different and was stunned by the general's statement. 'Parvateshwar, look at the wood. Look at the casing around the edges.'

Parvateshwar frowned. He did not recognise the casing.

'It improves water-proofing in the joints,' said Bhagirath.

Parvateshwar looked at his brother-in-law, curious.

'This technology is from Ayodhya.'

'Lord Ram, be merciful!'

'Yes! It looks like Emperor Daksha and my weakling father have formed an alliance against the Neelkanth.'

— ⅄ⲰⲨ⇡⊛ —

Bhrigu, Daksha and Dilipa were in the Meluhan emperor's private chambers in Devagiri. Dilipa and Bhrigu had arrived the previous day.

'Do you think they have succeeded in their mission, My Lord?' asked Dilipa.

Daksha seemed remote and disinterested. He felt the intense pain of separation from his beloved daughter Sati. The terrible event at Kashi, more than a year ago, still haunted him. He'd lost his child and with it, all the love he ever felt in his heart.

A few months ago Bhrigu had hatched a plan to assassinate the Neelkanth, along with his entire convoy, en route to Panchavati. They had sent five ships up the Godavari River to first attack Shiva's convoy, and then move on to destroy Panchavati as well. There were to be no survivors who would bear witness to what actually took place. Attacking an unprepared enemy was not unethical. In one fell swoop, all those inimical to them would be destroyed. But it was possible only if Daksha and Dilipa joined hands, as they together had the means as well as the technology.

The people of India would be told that the ghastly Nagas had lured the simple and trusting Neelkanth to their city and assassinated him. Knowing the significance of simplicity in propaganda, Bhrigu had come up with a new title for Shiva: *Bholenath*, the *simple one*, the one who is easily misled. Laying the blame on the treachery of the Nagas and the simplicity of the Neelkanth would mean that Daksha and Dilipa would be spared the backlash. And the hatred for the Nagas would be strengthened manifold.

Bhrigu glanced at Daksha briefly and then turned his attention back to Dilipa. The *Saptrishi Uttradhikari* seemed to place his trust on Dilipa more than the Meluhan now. 'They should have succeeded. We'll soon receive reports from the commander.'

Dilipa's face twitched. He took a deep breath to calm his nerves. 'I hope it is never revealed that we did this. The wrath of my people would be terrible. Killing the Neelkanth with this subterfuge...'

Bhrigu interrupted Dilipa, his voice calm. 'He was not the Neelkanth. He was an imposter. The Vayuputra council did not create him. It did not even recognise him.'

Dilipa frowned. He had always heard rumours but had never really been sure as to whether the Vayuputras, the legendary tribe left behind by the previous Mahadev, Lord Rudra, actually existed.

'Then how did his throat turn blue?' asked Dilipa.

Bhrigu looked at Daksha and shook his head in exasperation. 'I don't know. It is a mystery. I knew the Vayuputra council had obviously not created a Neelkanth, for they are still debating whether Evil has risen. Therefore, I did not object to the Emperor of Meluha persisting with his search for the Neelkanth. I knew there was no possibility of a Neelkanth actually being discovered.'

Dilipa looked stunned.

'Imagine my surprise,' continued Bhrigu, 'when this endeavour actually led them to an apparent Neelkanth. But a blue throat did not mean that he was capable of being the saviour. He had not been trained. He had not been educated for his task. He had not been appointed for it by the Vayuputra council. But Emperor Daksha felt he could control this simple tribal from Tibet and achieve his ambitions for Meluha. I made a mistake in trusting His Highness.'

Dilipa looked at Daksha, who did not respond to the barb. The Swadweepan emperor turned back towards the great sage. 'In any case, Evil will be destroyed when the Nagas are destroyed.'

Bhrigu frowned. 'Who said the Nagas are evil?'

Dilipa looked at Bhrigu, nonplussed. 'Then, what are you saying, My Lord? That the Nagas can be our allies?'

Bhrigu smiled. 'The distance between Evil and Good is a vast expanse in which many can exist without being either, Your Highness.'

Dilipa nodded politely, not quite understanding Bhrigu's intellectual abstractions. Wisely though, he kept his counsel.

'But the Nagas are on the wrong side,' continued Bhrigu. 'Do you know why?'

Dilipa shook his head, thoroughly confused.

'Because they are against the great Good. They are against the finest invention of Lord Brahma; the one that is the source of our country's greatness. This invention must be protected at all costs.'

Dilipa nodded in affirmation. Once again, he didn't understand Bhrigu's words. But he knew better than to argue with the formidable maharishi. He needed the medicines that Bhrigu provided. They kept him healthy and alive.

'We will continue to fight for India,' said Bhrigu. 'I will not let anyone destroy the Good that is at the heart of our land's greatness.'

Chapter 2

What is Evil?

'That the Somras has been the greatest Good of our age is pretty obvious,' said Brahaspati. 'It has shaped our age. Hence, it is equally obvious that someday, it will become the greatest Evil. The key question is when would the transformation occur.'

Shiva, Sati, Kali and Ganesh were still in Brahaspati's classroom in Panchavati. Brahaspati had declared a holiday for the rest of the day so that their conversation could continue uninterrupted. The legendary 'five banyan trees', after which Panchavati had been named, were clearly visible from the classroom window.

'As far as I am concerned, the Somras was evil the moment it was invented!' spat out Kali.

Shiva frowned at Kali and turned to Brahaspati. 'Go on...'

'Any great invention has both positive and negative effects. As long as the positive outweighs the negative, one can safely continue to use it. The Somras created our way of life and has allowed us to live longer in healthy bodies. It has enabled great men to keep contributing towards the welfare of society, longer than was ever possible in the past. At first, the Somras was restricted to the Brahmins, who were expected to use the longer, healthier life – almost a second life – for the benefit of society at large.'

Shiva nodded. He had heard this story from Daksha many years ago.

'Later Lord Ram decreed that the benefits of the Somras should be available to all. Why should Brahmins have special privileges? Thereafter, the Somras was administered to the entire populace, resulting in huge progress in society as a whole.'

'I know all about this,' said Shiva. 'But when did the negative effects start becoming obvious?'

'The first sign was the Nagas,' said Brahaspati. 'There have always been Nagas in India. But they were usually Brahmins. For example, Ravan, Lord Ram's greatest foe, was a Naga and a Brahmin.'

'Ravan was a Brahmin?!' asked a shocked Sati.

'Yes, he was,' answered Kali, for every Naga knew his story. 'The son of the great sage Vishrava, he was a benevolent ruler, a brilliant scholar, a fierce warrior and a staunch devotee of Lord Rudra. He had some faults no doubt, but he wasn't Evil personified, as the people of the Sapt Sindhu would have us believe.'

'In that case, do you people think less of Lord Ram?' asked Sati.

'Of course not. Lord Ram was one of the greatest emperors ever. We worship him as the seventh Vishnu. His ideas, philosophies and laws are the foundation of the Naga way of life. His reign, *Ram Rajya*, will always be celebrated across India as the perfect way to run an empire. But you should know that it is believed by some that even Lord Ram did not see Ravan as pure evil. He respected his enemy. Sometimes there can be good people on both sides of a war.'

Shiva raised his hand to silence them, and turned

his attention back towards the Meluhan chief scientist. 'Brahaspati...'

'So the Nagas, though small in number initially, were usually Brahmins,' Brahaspati continued. 'But then, the Somras was used only by the Brahmins until then. Today, the connection seems obvious, but it didn't seem so at the time.'

'The Somras created the Nagas?' asked Shiva.

'Yes. This was discovered only a few centuries ago by the Nagas. I learnt it from them.'

'We didn't discover it,' said Kali. 'The Vayuputra council told us.'

'The Vayuputra council?' asked Shiva.

'Yes,' continued Kali. 'The previous Mahadev, Lord Rudra, left behind a tribe called the Vayuputras. They live beyond the western borders, in a land called *Pariha*, the *land of fairies*.'

'I know that,' said Shiva, recalling one of his conversations with a Vasudev Pandit. 'But I hadn't heard of the council.'

'Well, somebody needs to administer the tribe. And the Vayuputras are ruled by their council, which is headed by their chief, who is respected as a God. He is called Mithra. He is advised by the council of six wise people collectively called the Amartya Shpand. The council controls the twin mission of the Vayuputras. Firstly, to help the next Vishnu, whenever he appears. And secondly, have one of the Vayuputras trained and ready to become the next Mahadev, when the time comes.'

Shiva raised his eyebrows.

'You obviously broke that rule, Shiva,' said Kali. 'I'm sure the Vayuputra council must have been quite shocked when you appeared out of the blue. Because, quite clearly, they did not create you.'

'You mean this is a controlled process?'

'I don't know,' said Kali. 'But your friends will know a lot more.'

'The Vasudevs?'

'Yes.'

Shiva frowned, reached for Sati's hand, and then asked Kali, 'So how did you find out about the Somras creating the Nagas? Did the Vayuputras approach you or did you find them?'

'I did not find them. The Naga King Vasuki was approached by them a few centuries ago. They suddenly appeared out of nowhere, lugging huge hordes of gold, and offered to pay us an annual compensation. King Vasuki, very rightly, refused to accept the compensation without an explanation.'

'And?'

'And he was told that the Nagas were born with deformities as a result of the Somras. The Somras randomly has this impact on a few babies when in the womb, if the parents have been consuming it for a long period.'

'Not all babies?'

'No. A vast majority of babies are born without deformities. But a few unfortunate ones, like me, are born Naga.'

'Why?'

'I call it dumb luck,' said Kali. 'But King Vasuki believed that the deformities caused by the Somras were the Almighty's way of punishing those souls who had committed sins in their previous births. Therefore, he accepted the pathetic explanation of the Vayuputra council along with their compensation.'

'*Mausi* rejected the terms of the agreement with the Vayuputras the moment she ascended the throne,' said Ganesh, referring to his *aunt*, Kali.

'Why? I'm sure the gold could have been put to good use by your people,' exclaimed Shiva.

Kali laughed coldly. 'That gold was a mere palliative. Not for us, but for the Vayuputras. Its only purpose was to make them feel less guilty for the carnage being wrought upon us by the "great invention" that they protected.'

Shiva nodded, understanding her anger. He turned to Brahaspati. 'But how exactly is the Somras responsible for this?'

Brahaspati explained, 'We used to believe the Somras blessed one with a long life by removing poisonous oxidants from one's body. But that is not the only way it works.'

Shiva and Sati leaned closer.

'It also operates at a more fundamental level. Our body is made up of millions of tiny living units called cells. These are the building blocks of life.'

'Yes, I've heard of this from one of your scientists in Meluha,' said Shiva.

'Then you'd know that these cells are the tiniest living beings. They combine to form organs, limbs, and in fact, the entire body.'

'Right.'

'These cells have the ability to divide and grow. And each division is like a fresh birth; one old unhealthy cell magically transforms into two new healthy cells. As long as they keep dividing, they remain healthy. So your journey begins in your mother's womb as a single cell. That cell keeps dividing and growing till it eventually forms your entire body.'

'Yes,' said Sati, who had learnt all of this in the Meluha *gurukul*.

'Obviously,' said Brahaspati, 'this division and growth has to end sometime. Otherwise one's body would keep growing continuously with pretty disastrous consequences. So the Almighty put a limit on the number of times a cell can divide. After that, the cell simply stops dividing further and thus, in effect, becomes old and unhealthy.'

'And do these old cells make one's body age and thus eventually die?' asked Shiva.

'Yes, every cell reaches its limit on the number of divisions at some point or the other. As more and more cells in the body hit that limit, one grows old, and finally dies.'

'Does the Somras remove this limit on division?'

'Yes. Therefore, your cells keep dividing while remaining healthy. In most people, this continued division is regulated. But in a few, some cells lose control over their division process and keep growing at an exponential pace.'

'This is cancer, isn't it?' asked Sati.

'Yes,' said Brahaspati. 'This cancer can sometimes lead to a painful death. But there are times when these cells continue to grow and appear as deformities – like extra arms or a very long nose.'

'How polite and scientific!' said a livid Kali. 'But one cannot even begin to imagine the physical pain and torture that we undergo as children when these "outgrowths" occur.'

Sati stretched out and held her sister's hand.

'Nagas are born with small outgrowths, which don't seem like much initially, but are actually harbingers of years of torture,' continued Kali. 'It almost feels like a demon has taken over your body. And he's bursting out from within, slowly, over many years, causing soul-crushing pain that becomes your constant companion. Our bodies get twisted beyond recognition so that by adolescence, when further growth finally stops, we are stuck with what Brahaspati politely calls "deformities". I call it the wages of sins that we didn't even commit. We pay for the sins others commit by consuming the Somras.'

Shiva looked at the Naga queen with a sad smile. Kali's anger was justified.

'And the Nagas have suffered this for centuries?' asked Shiva.

'Yes,' said Brahaspati. 'As the number of people consuming the Somras grew, so did the number of Nagas. One will find that most of the Nagas are from Meluha. For that is where the Somras is used most extensively.'

'And what is the Vayuputra council's view on this?'

'I'm not sure. But from whatever little I know, the Vayuputra council apparently believes that the Somras continues to create good in most areas where it is used. The suffering of the Nagas is collateral damage and has to be tolerated for the larger good.'

'Bullshit!' snorted Kali.

Shiva could appreciate Kali's rage but he was also aware of the enormous benefits of Somras over several millennia. *On balance, was it still Good?*

He turned to Brahaspati. 'Are there any other reasons for believing that Somras is Evil?'

'Consider this: we Meluhans choose to believe that the Saraswati is dying because of some devious Chandravanshi conspiracy. This is not true. We are actually killing our mother river all by ourselves. We use massive amounts of Saraswati waters to manufacture the Somras. It helps stabilise the mixture during processing. It is also used to churn the crushed branches of the Sanjeevani tree. I have conducted many experiments to see if water from any other source can be used. But it just doesn't do the trick.'

'Does it really require that much water?'

'Yes, Shiva. When Somras was being made for just a few thousand, the amount of Saraswati water used didn't matter. But when we started mass producing Somras for eight million people, the dynamics changed. The waters started getting depleted slowly by the giant manufacturing facility at Mount Mandar. The Saraswati has already stopped reaching the Western Sea. It now ends its journey in an inland delta, south of Rajasthan. The desertification of the land to the south of this delta is already complete. It's a matter of time before the entire river is completely destroyed. Can you imagine the impact on Meluha? On India?'

'Saraswati is the mother of our entire *Sapt Sindhu* civilisation,' said Sati, speaking of *the land of the seven rivers.*

'Yes. Even our preeminent scripture, the Rig Veda, sings paeans to the Saraswati. It is not only the cradle, but also the lifeblood of our civilisation. What will happen to our future generations without this great river? The Vedic way of life itself is at risk. What we are doing is taking away the lifeblood of our future progeny so that our present generation can revel in the luxury of living for two hundred years or more. Would it be so terrible if we lived for only a hundred years instead?'

Shiva nodded. He could see the terrible side-effects and the ecological destruction caused by the Somras. But he still couldn't see it as Evil. An Evil which left only one option: a *Dharmayudh*, a *holy war,* to destroy it.

'What else?' asked Shiva.

'The destruction of the Saraswati seems a small price to pay when compared to another, even more insidious impact of the Somras.'

'Which is?'

'The plague of Branga.'

'The plague of Branga?' asked a surprised Shiva. 'What does that have to do with the Somras?'

Branga had been suffering continuous plagues for many years, which had killed innumerable people, especially children. The primary relief thus far had been the medicine procured from the Nagas. Or else exotic medicines extracted after killing the sacred peacock, leading to the Brangas being ostracised even in peace-loving cities like Kashi.

'Everything!' said Brahaspati. 'The Somras is not only difficult to manufacture, but it also generates large amounts of toxic waste. A problem we have never truly tackled. It cannot be disposed of on land, because it can poison entire districts through ground water contamination. It cannot be discharged into the sea. The Somras waste reacts with salt water to disintegrate in a dangerously rapid and explosive manner.'

A thought entered Shiva's mind. *Did Brahaspati accompany me to Karachapa the first time to pick up sea water? Was that used to destroy Mount Mandar?*

Brahaspati continued. 'What seemed to work was fresh river water. When used to wash the Somras waste, over a period of several years, fresh water appeared to reduce its toxic strength. This was proven with some experiments at Mount Mandar. It seemed to work especially well with cold water. Ice was even better. Obviously, we could not use the rivers of India to wash the Somras waste in large quantities. We could have ended up poisoning our own people. Therefore, many decades ago, a plan was hatched to use the high mountain rivers in Tibet. They flow through uninhabited lands and their waters are almost ice-cold. They would therefore work perfectly to clean out the Somras waste. There is a river high up in the Himalayas, called Tsangpo, where Meluha decided to set up a giant waste treatment facility.'

'Are you telling me that the Meluhans have come to my land before?'

'Yes. In secret.'

'But how can such large consignments be hidden?'

'You've seen the quantity of Somras powder required to feed an entire city for a year. Ten small pouches are all it takes. It is converted into the Somras drink at designated temples across Meluha when mixed with water and other ingredients.'

'So even the waste amount is not huge?'

'No, it isn't. It's a small quantity, making it easy to transport.

But even that small quantity packs in a huge amount of poison.'

'Hmmm... So this waste facility was set up in Tibet?'

'Yes, it was established in a completely desolate area along the Tsangpo. The river flowed east, so it would go to relatively unpopulated lands away from India. Therefore, our land would not suffer from the harmful effects of the Somras.'

Shiva frowned. 'But what about the lands farther ahead that the Tsangpo flowed into? The eastern lands that lie beyond Swadweep? What about the Tibetan land around Tsangpo itself? Wouldn't they have suffered due to the toxic waste?'

'They may have,' said Brahaspati. 'But that was considered acceptable collateral damage. The Meluhans kept track of the people living along the Tsangpo. There were no outbreaks of disease, no sudden deformities. The icy river waters seemed to be working at keeping the toxins inactive. The Vayuputra council was given these reports. Apparently, the council also sent scientists into the sparsely populated lands of Burma, which is to the east of Swadweep. It was believed the Tsangpo flowed into those lands and became the main Burmese river, the Irrawaddy. Once again, there was no evidence of a sudden rise in diseases. Hence it was concluded that we had found a way to rid ourselves of the Somras waste without harming anyone. When it was discovered that Tsangpo means "purifier" in the local Tibetan tongue, it was considered a sign, a divine message. A solution had been found. This came down to the scientists of Mount Mandar as received wisdom as well.'

'What does this have to do with the Brangas?'

'Well, you see, the upper regions of the Brahmaputra have never been mapped properly. It was simply assumed that the river comes from the east; because it flows west into Branga. The Nagas, with the help of Parshuram, finally mapped the upper course of the Brahmaputra. It falls at almost calamitous speeds from the giant heights of the Himalayas into the plains of Branga through gorges that are sheer walls almost two thousand metres high.'

'Two thousand metres!' gasped Shiva.

'You can well imagine that it is almost impossible to navigate a river course such as the Brahmaputra's. But Parshuram succeeded and led the Nagas along that path. Parshuram, of course, did not realise the significance of the discovery of the river's course. Queen Kali and Lord Ganesh did.'

'Did you go up the Brahmaputra as well?' asked Shiva. 'Where does the river come from? Is it connected to the Tsangpo in any way?'

Brahaspati smiled sadly. 'It *is* the Tsangpo.'

'What?'

'The Tsangpo flows east only for the duration of its course in Tibet. At the eastern extremities of the Himalayas, it takes a sharp turn, almost reversing its flow. It then starts moving south-west and crashes through massive gorges before emerging near Branga as the Brahmaputra.'

'By the Holy Lake,' said Shiva. 'The Brangas are being poisoned by the Somras waste.'

'Exactly. The cold waters of the Tsangpo dilute the poisonous impact to a degree. However, as the river enters India in the form of the Brahmaputra, the rising temperature reactivates the dormant toxin in the water. Though the Branga children also suffer from the same body-wracking pain as the Nagas, they are free from deformities. Sadly, Branga also has a high incidence of cancer. Being highly populous, the number of deaths is simply unacceptable.'

Shiva began to connect the dots. 'Divodas told me the Branga plague peaks during the summer every year. That is the time when ice melts faster in the Himalayas, making the poison flow out in larger quantities.'

'Yes,' said Brahaspati. 'That is exactly what happens.'

'Obviously, since both the Nagas and Brangas are being poisoned by the same malevolence, our medicines work on the Brangas as well,' Kali spoke up. 'So we send them our medicines to help ameliorate their suffering a little. Even though we told King Chandraketu how his kingdom was being poisoned, some Brangas prefer to believe that the plague strikes every year because of a curse that the Nagas have cast upon them. If only we were that powerful! But it appears that at least Chandraketu believes us. This is why he sends us men and gold regularly, to stealthily attack Somras manufacturing facilities, the root of all our problems.'

'Evil should never be fought with subterfuge, Kali,' said Shiva. 'It must be attacked openly.'

Kali was about to retort but Shiva had turned back to Brahaspati.

'Why didn't you say something? Raise the issue in Meluha or with the Vayuputras?'

'I did,' said Brahaspati. 'I took up the matter with Emperor Daksha. But he doesn't really understand scientific things or involve himself with technical details. He turned to the one intellectual he trusts, the venerable *royal priest*, *Raj guru* Bhrigu. Lord Bhrigu seemed genuinely interested and took me to the Vayuputra council so I could present my case before them, but they were not at all supportive. This was where the issue was effectively killed. Nobody was willing to believe me about the source of the Brahmaputra. They also laughed when they heard that I was ostensibly listening to the Nagas. According to them, the Nagas were now ruled by an extremist harridan whose frustration with her own karma made everyone else the object of her ire.'

'I'll take that as a compliment!' said Kali.

Shiva smiled at Kali before turning back to Brahaspati.

'But how did the Vayuputras rationalise what's happening in Branga?'

'According to them,' said Brahaspati, 'the Brangas were a rich but uncivilised lot, with strange eating habits and disgusting customs. So the plague could have been caused by their bad practices and karma rather than the Somras. Remember, there is little sympathy for the Brangas amongst the Vayuputras because it is well known that they drink the blood of peacocks, a bird that is held holy by any follower of Lord Rudra.'

'And you gave up?' retorted Shiva. 'Shouldn't you have pressed on? Emperor Daksha is weak and can be easily influenced. He could have brought about changes in Meluha. The Vayuputra council does not govern your country.'

'Well, there was a good reason for me to not persist with the argument.'

'What reason?'

'Tara, the woman I intended to marry, suddenly went missing,' continued Brahaspati. 'The last time I saw her, she was in Pariha. On returning to Meluha I received a letter from her telling me that she was disappointed with my tirades against the Somras. I asked Lord Bhrigu to check with his friends in Pariha. I was told that she had just disappeared.'

Shiva frowned.

'I know it sounds lame,' said Brahaspati. 'But somewhere deep within, I do believe Tara was taken hostage. It was a message for me. Keep quiet or else...'

'And you gave up?' Shiva repeated. 'Why would you do that if you believed you were right?'

'I didn't,' continued Brahaspati defensively. 'But by then I was losing credibility amongst the senior scientists of other realms. Had I made the issue any bigger within Meluha, I would have lost what little standing I have amongst the Suryavanshis as well. I would have lost my ability to do anything at all. Though I knew I had to do something, I also realised that the strategy of open lobbying and debate had become counter-productive. There were too many vested interests tied into the Somras. Only the Vayuputra council could have had the moral strength to stop it openly, through the institution of the Neelkanth. But they refused to believe that the Somras had turned evil.'

'What happened thereafter?' asked Shiva.

'I opted for silence,' said Brahaspati. 'At least on the surface. But I had to do something. Maharishi Bhrigu was convinced there was nothing to fear from the Somras waste. So the manufacturing of Somras continued at the same frantic pace. The Saraswati kept getting prodigiously consumed. Somras waste was being generated in huge quantities. Since the empire now believed that cold, fresh water had worked in disposing of the toxic waste, new plans were being drawn up to use other rivers. This time the idea was to use the upper reaches of either the Indus or the Ganga.'

'Lord Ram, be merciful,' whispered Shiva.

'Millions of lives would have been at risk. We were going to unleash toxic waste right through the heart of India. Almost as a message from the *Parmatma*, the *ultimate soul*, I was approached by Lord Ganesh around this time. He had formulated a plan, and I must admit his words made eminent sense. There could be only one possible solution. The destruction of Mount Mandar. Without Mount Mandar, there would be no Somras. And with the Somras gone, all these problems would disappear too.'

Shiva cast a quick look towards Sati.

'Whatever little doubts I may have had,' said Brahaspati, 'disappeared when I was confronted with a new scenario. When it happened, I knew in my heart that it was time for the destruction of Evil.'

'What new scenario?' asked Shiva.

'You appeared on the scene,' answered Brahaspati. 'Even without the Vayuputra council's permission, perhaps even without their knowledge... The Neelkanth appeared. It was the final sign for me: the time to destroy Evil was upon us.'

Vishwadyumna quickly gave hand signals to his Branga soldiers. The hunting party went down on their knees.

Kartik, who was right behind Vishwadyumna, whistled softly as his eyes lit up. 'Magnificent!'

Vishwadyumna turned towards Kartik. While most of Shiva's convoy was settling itself into the visitor's camp outside Panchavati, a few hunting parties had been sent out to gather meat for the large entourage. Kartik, having proved himself as an accomplished hunter throughout the journey to Panchavati, was the natural leader of one of the groups. Vishwadyumna had accompanied the son of the Neelkanth. He intensely admired the fierce warrior skills of Kartik.

'It's a rhinoceros, My Lord,' said Vishwadyumna softly.

The rhinoceros was a massive animal, nearly four metres in length. It had bumpy brownish skin that hung over its body in multiple layers, suggestive of tough armour. Its most distinctive feature was its nasal horn, which stuck out like a fearsome offensive weapon, to a height of nearly fifty centimetres.

'I know,' whispered Kartik. 'They live around Kashi as well. They're nearly as big as a small elephant. These beasts have terrible eyesight, but they have a fantastic sense of smell and hearing.'

Vishwadyumna nodded at Kartik, impressed. 'What do you propose, My Lord?'

The rhinoceros was a tricky beast to hunt. They were quiet animals who kept to themselves, but if threatened, they could charge wildly. Few could survive a direct blow from their massive body and terrifying horn.

Kartik reached over his shoulder and drew out the two swords sheathed on his back. In his left hand was a short twin-blade, like the one his elder brother Ganesh favoured. In his right was a heavier one with a curved blade which was certainly not appropriate for thrusting. This weapon was perfect for swinging and slashing – a style of fighting Kartik excelled at.

Kartik spoke softly, 'Fire arrows at its back. Make as much noise as you can. I want you to drive it forward.'

Vishwadyumna's eyes filled with terror. 'That is not wise, My Lord.'

'This animal is huge. Too many soldiers charging in will cramp us. All it would need to do is swing its mighty horn and it would cause several casualties.'

'But we can fire arrows to kill it from a distance.'

Kartik raised his eyebrows. 'Vishwadyumna, you should know better. Do you really think our arrows can actually penetrate deep enough to cause serious damage? It's not the arrows but the noise that you will create, which will make it charge.'

Vishwadyumna continued to stare, still unsure.

'Also, it is standing upwind and your positioning behind it would be perfect. Along with the noise, the stench of your soldiers will also drive the animal forward. It's a good thing they haven't bathed in two days,' said Kartik, without any hint of a smile at the joke.

Like all warriors, Vishwadyumna admired humour in the face of danger. But he checked his smile, not sure if Kartik was joking. 'What will you do, My Lord?'

Kartik whispered, 'I'll kill the beast.'

Saying this, Kartik slowly edged forward. Right on to the path that the bull would charge on, when attacked by Vishwadyumna's soldiers. The soldiers meanwhile, moved upwind, behind the rhinoceros. Having reached his position, Kartik whistled softly.

'NOW!' shouted Vishwadyumna.

A volley of arrows attacked the animal as the soldiers began to scream loudly. The rhinoceros raised its head, ears twitching as the arrows bounced harmlessly off its skin. As the soldiers drew closer, some of the missiles managed to penetrate enough to agitate the beast. The animal snorted mightily and stomped the dirt, radiating strength and power as light gleamed off its tiny black eyes. It lowered its head and charged, its feet thundering against the ground.

Kartik was in position. The beast only had side vision and could not see straight ahead. Therefore, it was no surprise that it crashed into an overhanging branch in its path, which made it change its direction slightly. At which point, it saw Kartik standing to its right. The furious rhinoceros bellowed loudly, changed course back to the original path and charged straight towards the diminutive son of Shiva.

Kartik remained stationary and calm, with his eyes focused on the beast. His breathing was regular and deep. He knew that the rhinoceros couldn't see him since he stood straight ahead. The animal was running, guided by the memory of where it had seen Kartik last.

Vishwadyumna fired arrows into the animal rapidly, hoping to slow it down. But the thick hide of the beast ensured that the arrows did not make too much of a difference. It was running straight towards Kartik. Yet Kartik didn't move or flinch. Vishwadyumna could see the boy warrior holding his swords lightly. That was completely wrong for a stabbing action, where the blade needs to be firmly held. The weapon would fall out of his hands the moment he'd thrust forward.

Just when it appeared that he was about to be trampled underfoot, Kartik bent low and, with lightning speed, rolled towards the left. As the rhinoceros continued running, he slashed out, his left sword first, pressing the lever on the hilt as he swung. One of the twin-blades extended out of the other, slicing through the front thigh of the beast, cutting through muscles and veins. As blood spurted rapidly, the animal's injured leg collapsed from under it and it grunted, confused, trying to put weight on the appendage, now flopping uselessly against its belly. Admirably, it still continued its charge, its three good legs heaving against its bulk as it struggled to turn and face its attacker. Kartik ran forward, following the movement of the animal, now circling in from behind the beast. He hacked brutally with his right hand, which held the killer curved sword. The blade sliced through the thigh of the hind leg, cutting down to the bone with its deep curvature and broad metal. With both its right legs incapacitated, the rhinoceros collapsed to the ground, rolling sideways as it tried to stand with only two good legs, writhing in pain. Its blood mixed with the dusty earth to make a dark red-brown mud that smeared across its body as it flailed against the ground, panting in fear.

Kartik stood quietly at a short distance, watching the animal in its final throes.

Vishwadyumna watched from behind, his mouth agape. He had never seen an animal brought down with such skill and speed.

Kartik approached the rhinoceros calmly. Even though immobilised, the beast reared its head menacingly at him, grunting and whining in a high-pitched squeal. Kartik maintained a safe distance as the other soldiers rapidly ran up to him.

The son of the Neelkanth bowed low to the animal. 'Forgive me, magnificent beast. I am only doing my duty. I will finish this soon.'

Suddenly, Kartik moved forward and stabbed hard, right through the folds of the rhinoceros' skin, plunging deep into the beast's heart, feeling the shudder go through its body, until at last it was still.

— ⚹ —

'My Lord, a bird courier has just arrived with a message for your eyes only,' said Kanakhala, the Meluhan prime minister. 'That's why I brought it personally.'

Daksha occupied his private chambers, a worried Veerini seated beside him. He took the letter from Kanakhala and dismissed her.

With a polite Namaste towards her Emperor and Empress, Kanakhala turned to leave. Glancing back, she glimpsed a rare intimate moment between them as they held each other's hands. The last few months had inured her to the strange goings-on in Meluha. Daksha's past betrayal of Sati during her first pregnancy had shocked her enormously. Kanakhala had lost all respect for her emperor. She continued with her job because she remained loyal to Meluha. She had even stopped questioning the strange orders from her lord; like the one he'd given the previous day about making arrangements for Bhrigu and Dilipa to travel to the ruins of Mount Mandar. She could understand Maharishi Bhrigu's interest in going there. But what earthly reason could there be for the Swadweepan emperor to go as well? Kanakhala saw Daksha letting go of Veerini's hand and breaking the seal of the letter as she shut the door quietly behind her.

Daksha began to cry. Veerini immediately reached over and snatched the letter from him.

As she read through it quickly, Veerini let out a deep sigh of relief as tears escaped from her eyes. 'She's safe. They're all safe...'

On the surface, the plan to assassinate the Neelkanth worked towards the unique interests of all the three main conspirators, Maharishi Bhrigu, Emperor Daksha and Emperor Dilipa. For Bhrigu, the greatest gain would be that the Somras would not be targeted by the Neelkanth. The faith of the people in the legend of the Neelkanth was strong. If the Neelkanth declared that the Somras was evil and decided to toe the Naga line, so would his followers. For Dilipa it meant the killing of two birds with a single stone. Not only would he continue to receive the elixir from Bhrigu, but he'd also do away with Bhagirath, his heir and greatest threat. Daksha would be rid of the troublesome Neelkanth and be able to blame all ills on the Nagas once again. The plan was perfect. Except that Daksha could not countenance the killing of his daughter. He was willing to put everything on the line to ensure that Sati was left unharmed. Bhrigu and Dilipa had hoped that with the rupture in relations between Daksha and his daughter, the Meluhan emperor would support this mission wholeheartedly. They were wrong. Daksha's love for Sati was deeper than his hatred for Shiva.

Upon Veerini's advice, Daksha had sent the Arishtanemi brigadier Mayashrenik, known for his blind loyalty to Meluha and deep devotion to the Neelkanth, on a secret mission. Mayashrenik was to accompany the five ships that had been sent to attack the Neelkanth's convoy. Veerini had covertly kept in touch with her daughter Kali through all these years of strife, and had made Daksha aware of the river warning and defence system of the Nagas. All that had to be done was to get the alarm triggered in time. Mayashrenik's mission was to ensure that the alarms went off. He was to escape and return to Meluha after that. The Arishtanemi brigadier and acting general of the Meluhan army had carried a homing pigeon with him to deliver the news of the subsequent battle to Daksha. The happy message for the Meluhan emperor was that the progeny Daksha cared for – Sati and Kartik – were alive and safe.

Veerini looked at her husband. 'If only you would listen to me a bit more.'

Daksha breathed deeply. 'If Lord Bhrigu ever finds out...'

'Would you rather your children were dead?'

Daksha sighed. He would do anything to ensure Sati's safety. He shook his head. 'No!'

'Then thank the *Parmatma* that our plan worked. And never breathe a word of this to anyone. Ever!'

Daksha nodded. He took the letter from Veerini and set it aflame, holding it by the edge for as long as possible, to ensure that every part of it had charred beyond recognition.

Chapter 3

The Kings Have Chosen

'Do you believe Brahaspati?' asked Shiva.

Night had fallen on the Panchavati guest colony just outside the main city. Injured and fatigued, Shiva's entourage had retired to their quarters for a well-deserved rest.

Sati and Shiva were in their chambers, having just returned from the city. They had not spoken to a soul about what they'd learnt at the Panchavati school. They had not even told the Suryavanshis that Brahaspati, their beloved chief scientist, was still alive. They were to meet him again the next day.

'Well, I don't think Brahaspati*ji* is lying,' said Sati. 'I do remember that more than two decades ago, Lord Bhrigu had spent many months in Devagiri, which was highly unusual for the *Raj guru*. He is a rare sight in Meluha, since he usually chooses to spend his time meditating in his Himalayan cave.'

'Aren't *Raj gurus* supposed to stay in the royal palace and guide the king?'

'Not someone like Lord Bhrigu. He helped my father get elected as emperor because he believed my father would be good for Meluha. Beyond that Lord Bhrigu has had no interest in the day-to-day governance of Meluha. He is a simple man, rarely seen in the so-called powerful circles.'

'So he spent a lot of time in Devagiri. That may have been unusual, but what about the other things that Brahaspati said?'

'Well, Lord Bhrigu, my father and Brahaspati*ji* were indeed away for many months. It had been announced as an important trade trip; but I can't imagine Lord Bhrigu or Brahaspati*ji* being interested in trade. Perhaps they were in Pariha at the time. And yes, the talented and lovely Tara*ji*, who worked at Mount Mandar and had been sent to Pariha for a project, did disappear suddenly. It was announced that she had taken *sanyas*. Renouncing public life is very common in Meluha. But what Brahaspati*ji* revealed today was something else altogether.'

'So you believe Brahaspati speaks the truth?'

'All I'm saying is that Brahaspati*ji* may believe this to be the truth. But is it actually so or is he mistaken? This decision of yours can change the course of history. What you do now will have repercussions for generations to come. It is a momentous occasion, a big battle. You have to be completely sure.'

'I must speak with the Vasudevs.'

'Yes, you must.'

'But that is not all you wanted to say to me, is it?'

'I think there is another aspect to be considered. What made Brahaspati*ji* disappear for over five years? What was he doing in Panchavati all this while? I feel this is an important question; perhaps linked to the back-up manufacturing facility for the Somras that father had told me about.'

'Yes, I didn't give it much importance then. But if the Somras is Evil, that facility is the key.'

'Actually, the Saraswati is the key. A manufacturing facility can always be rebuilt. But wherever it is built, it will always need the Saraswati waters. Kali told me at Icchawar that her people attacked Meluhan temples and Brahmins only if they were directly harming the Nagas. Maybe those temples were production centres that used the powder from Mount Mandar to manufacture the Somras drink for the locals. She also said that a final solution would emerge from the Saraswati. That the Nagas were working on it. I don't know what that cryptic statement meant. We need to find out.'

'You did not tell me about your conversation with Kali.'

'Shiva, this is the first honest conversation we are having about Kali and Ganesh since you met my son at Kashi.'

Shiva became quiet.

'I'm not blaming you,' continued Sati. 'I understood your anger. You thought that Ganesh had killed Brahaspati*ji*. Now that the truth has emerged, you are willing to listen.'

Shiva smiled and embraced Sati.

— ⁂ —

'Are you sure?' asked Shiva.

It was late the next morning, four hours into the second prahar. Shiva sat with Sati at his side in his private chambers. Parvateshwar and Bhagirath stood in front, holding a plank. The Meluhan general and the Ayodhyan prince had just returned after surveying the destroyed battleships.

'Yes, My Lord. The evidence is indisputable,' said Bhagirath.

'Show me.'

Bhagirath stepped forward. 'The rivets on these planks are clearly Meluhan. Lord Parvateshwar has identified them.'

Parvateshwar nodded in agreement.

'And the casing,' continued Bhagirath, 'that improves the water-proofing is clearly Ayodhyan.'

'Are you suggesting that Emperor Daksha and Emperor Dilipa have formed an alliance against us?' Shiva asked softly.

'They've used the best technologies available in both our

lands. These ships had navigated through a lot of sea water, judging by the molluscs on them. They needed the best to be able to make the journey quickly.'

Shiva breathed deeply, lost in thought.

'My Lord,' said Bhagirath. 'For all his faults, I cannot imagine my father would be capable of leading a conspiracy such as this. He simply does not have the capability. He is just a follower in this plot. You have to target him, of course. But don't make the mistake of thinking that he is the main conspirator. He is not.'

Sati leaned towards Shiva. 'Do you think my father can do this?'

Shiva shook his head. 'No. Emperor Daksha too is incapable of leading this conspiracy.'

Parvateshwar, still shame-faced at the dishonour brought upon his empire, said quietly, 'The Meluhan code enjoins upon us to follow the rules, My Lord. Our rules bid us to carry out our king's orders. In the hands of a lesser king, this can lead to a lot of wrong.'

'Emperor Daksha may have issued the orders, Parvateshwar,' said Shiva. 'But he didn't dream them up. There is a master who has brought the royalty of Meluha and Swadweep together. Someone who also managed to procure the feared *daivi astras*. Heaven alone knows if he has any more *divine weapons*. It was a brilliant plan. By Lord Ram's grace, we were saved by the skin of our teeth. It cannot be Emperor Daksha or Emperor Dilipa. This is someone of far greater importance, intelligence and resource. And, one who is clever enough to conceal his identity.'

— ⋆ —

'Return to Meluha?!' asked Veerbhadra.

Veerbhadra and Krittika were in Shiva's private chambers. Kali and Sati were also present.

'Yes, Bhadra,' said Shiva. 'It was the Meluhans and the Ayodhyans who attacked us together.'

'Are you sure Meluha is involved?' asked Veerbhadra.

'Parvateshwar has himself confirmed it.'

'And now you are worried about our people.'

'Yes,' said Shiva. 'I'm worried the Gunas will be arrested and held hostage as leverage over us. Before they do so, I want you to slip into Meluha quietly and take our people to Kashi. I will meet you there.'

'My scouts will guide Krittika and you through a secret route,' said Kali. 'Using our fastest horses and speediest boats, my people can get you close to Maika in two weeks. After that, you are on your own.'

'Meluha is a safe country to travel in,' said Krittika. 'We can hire fast horses up to the mouth of the Saraswati. After that we can travel on boats plying on the river. It's an easy route. With luck, we will reach Devagiri in another two weeks. The Gunas are in a small village not far from there.'

'Perfect,' said Shiva. 'Time is of the essence. Go now.'

'Yes Shiva,' said Veerbhadra as he turned to leave with his wife.

'And Bhadra...' said Shiva.

Veerbhadra and Krittika turned around.

'Don't try to be brave,' said Shiva. 'If the Gunas have been arrested already, leave Meluha quickly and wait for me at Kashi.'

Veerbhadra's mother was with the Gunas. Shiva knew Veerbhadra would not abandon her to her fate so easily.

'Shiva...' whispered Veerbhadra.

Shiva got up and held Veerbhadra's shoulder. 'Bhadra, promise me.'

Veerbhadra remained quiet.

'If you try to release them by yourself, you will be killed. You will be of no use to your mother if you are dead, Bhadra.'

Veerbhadra stayed silent.

'I promise you, nothing will happen to the Gunas. If you cannot get them out, I will. But do not do anything rash. Promise me.'

Veerbhadra placed his hand on Shiva's shoulder. 'There is something you aren't telling me. What have you discovered here? Why are you so afraid suddenly? Is there going to be a war? Is Meluha going to become our enemy?'

'I'm not sure, Bhadra. I haven't made up my mind as yet.'

'Then tell me what you do know.'

It was Shiva's turn to remain silent now.

'I'm going back to Meluha, Shiva. Had you asked me a month back, I would have said this would be the safest journey possible. A lot has changed since then. You have to tell me the truth. I deserve that.'

Shiva sat them down and revealed everything he had discovered during the course of the last few days.

— ⁂ —

'And you killed the rhino all by yourself?' asked an impressed Anandmayi, her face suffused with a broad smile.

'Yes, Your Highness,' said Kartik, stoic and expressionless as usual.

Anandmayi, Ayurvati and Kartik were settled comfortably on soft cushions in the dining room. Kshatriya in word and deed, Anandmayi and Kartik partook of the delicious rhinoceros meat. The Brahmin Ayurvati restricted herself to *roti*, *dal* and vegetables.

'Have you decided to stop smiling altogether?' asked

Anandmayi. 'Or is this just temporary?'

Kartik looked up at Anandmayi, a hint of a smile on his face. 'Smiling takes more effort than it's worth, Your Highness.'

Ayurvati shook her head. 'You are just a child, Kartik. Don't trouble yourself so much. You need to enjoy your childhood.'

Kartik turned to the Meluhan chief physician. 'My brother Ganesh is a great man, Ayurvati*ji*. He has so much to contribute to society, to the country. And yet, he was almost eaten alive by dumb beasts because he was trying to save me.'

Ayurvati reached across and patted Kartik.

'I will never be so helpless again,' swore Kartik. 'I will not be the cause of my family's misery.'

The door swung open. Parvateshwar and Bhagirath walked in.

Just by looking at them, Anandmayi could tell that they had discovered what she feared. 'Was it Meluha?'

Ayurvati winced. She could not imagine her great country's name being dragged into a vile conspiracy like the attack on the Neelkanth's convoy at the outskirts of Panchavati. And yet, after what she had discovered of Emperor Daksha's perfidy during Sati's pregnancy at Maika, she would not be surprised if Meluhan ships had carried out this dastardly act.

'It's worse,' sighed Bhagirath as he sat down.

Parvateshwar sat next to Anandmayi and held her hand. He looked at Ayurvati, his pained expression bearing witness to his stark misery. The general prized his country, his Meluha, as Lord Ram's ultimate legacy. It was the custodian of Ram Rajya. How could this great country's emperor have committed a dastardly act such as this?

'Even worse?' prompted Anandmayi.

'Yes. It seems Swadweep is in on the conspiracy as well.'

Anandmayi was stunned. 'What?!'

'It's either only Ayodhya or all of Swadweep. I cannot be sure if other kingdoms of Swadweep are following Ayodhya's lead. But Ayodhya is certainly involved.'

Anandmayi looked at Parvateshwar. He nodded, confirming Bhagirath's words.

'Lord Rudra, be merciful,' said Anandmayi. 'What is wrong with father?'

'I for one am not surprised,' said Bhagirath, barely able to conceal his contempt. 'He is weak and gets easily exploited. It doesn't take much for him to succumb.'

For once Anandmayi didn't rebuke her brother for denigrating their father. She looked at Parvateshwar. He seemed lost and unsure. Change was horrible for the Suryavanshis, for the people of the masculine, used as they were to unchanging rules and stark predictability. Anandmayi turned her husband's face towards herself and kissed him gently, reassuringly. She smiled warmly. He half-smiled back.

Kartik quietly put his plate down, washed his hands and walked out of the room.

— ⁂ —

It was early afternoon as Kartik and Ganesh's steps led them around the five banyan trees from whose existence Panchavati derived its name. Non-Nagas were not allowed inside the inner city. In truth, many of them, Brangas included, refused to enter due to a strong superstition about the misfortune that would befall those that did. But the Neelkanth's family did not believe in it. And anyway, nobody wanted to enforce an entry ban on them.

'Why have only Lord Ram's idols been depicted on these trees, *dada*?' Kartik asked his *elder brother*.

'You mean why have his wife, Lady Sita, and his brother,

Lord Lakshman, not been shown?'

'Not just them, even his great devotee, Lord Hanuman, is missing.'

Ganesh and Kartik were admiring the beautiful idols of Lord Ram sculpted into the main trunk of each of the five banyans. The five tree idols showed the ancient King, respected as the seventh Vishnu, in the five different roles of his life known to all: a son, a husband, a brother, a father and a Godly king. Each banyan trunk depicted him in a different form. In each form, in a manner that somehow appeared natural, the sculptors had made the idols look towards the temple of Lord Rudra and Lady Mohini at one corner of the square. Their idols, on the other hand, were placed in the front section of the temple as opposed to the back as in most temples, with the effect that the two deities appeared to be looking at all five tree idols as well. It seemed as if the architects intended to show the great Mahadev and the noble seventh Vishnu being respectful to each other.

'It's in keeping with Bhoomidevi's instructions,' answered Ganesh. 'I know his traditional depiction in the Sapt Sindhu is always along with his three favourite people in the world, Lady Sita, Lord Lakshman and Lord Hanuman. But it was an order of Bhoomidevi, our founding Goddess, that Lord Ram always be shown alone in Panchavati. Especially at the five banyans.'

'Why?'

'I don't know. Perhaps she wanted us to always remember that great leaders, like the Vishnus and the Mahadevs, may have millions following them. But at the end of the day, they carry the burden of their mission alone.'

'Like *baba*?' asked Kartik, referring to their *father*.

'Yes, like *baba*. He is the one who stands between Evil and India. If he fails, life in the subcontinent will be destroyed by Evil.'

'*Baba* will not fail.'

Ganesh smiled at Kartik's response.

'Do you know why?' asked Kartik.

Ganesh shook his head. 'No. Why?'

Kartik clasped Ganesh's right hand and held it to his chest, like the brother-warriors of yore. 'Because he is not alone.'

Ganesh smiled and embraced Kartik. They walked silently around the banyan trees, doing the holy *parikrama* of Lord Ram's idols.

'What is going on, *dada*?' asked Kartik, as they continued their circumambulation.

Ganesh frowned.

'Why have both the emperors allied against *baba*?'

Ganesh breathed deeply. He never lied to Kartik. He considered his brother an adult and treated him as such. 'Because *baba* threatens them, Kartik. They are the elite. They are addicted to the benefits they derive from Evil. *Baba's* mission is to fight for the oppressed; to be the voice of the voiceless. It is obvious that the elite will want to stop him.'

'What is the Evil that *baba* is fighting? How has it entrenched its claws so deeply?'

Ganesh took Kartik by the hand and made him sit at the foot of one of the banyans. 'This is for you alone, Kartik. You are not to tell anyone else. For it is *baba's* right to decide when and how others are to be informed.'

Kartik nodded in response.

Ganesh sat next to Kartik and explained to him about what Brahaspati and Shiva had discussed the previous day.

— ⁂ —

'What have you been doing these past five years, Brahaspati?'

asked Shiva.

Sati and Shiva had joined the chief scientist in the Naga queen's chambers. Brahaspati felt like he was being interrogated. But he could understand Shiva's need to get to the bottom of the issue.

'I was trying to find a permanent solution to the Somras problem,' answered Brahaspati.

'Permanent solution?'

'Destroying Mount Mandar is a temporary solution. We know it will get rebuilt. The Nagas tell me the reconstruction has been surprisingly slow. It shouldn't have taken five years. Not with Meluhan efficiency. But it's only a matter of time before it gets rebuilt.'

Shiva looked at Sati, but she didn't say anything.

'Once Mandar is back to full manufacturing capacity, the destruction of the Saraswati and the production of the toxic waste will begin in large measure once again. So we have to find a permanent solution. The best way to do that is to examine the Somras' ingredients. If we can somehow control that, we could possibly control the poisonous impact of the Somras waste. Many ingredients can be easily replaced. But two of them cannot. The first are the bark and branches of the Sanjeevani tree, and the second is the Saraswati water. We cannot control the availability of the Sanjeevani tree. Meluha has large plantations of it across its northern reaches. How many plantations can one destroy? Besides, trees can always be replanted. That brings us to the Saraswati. Can we somehow control its waters?'

Shiva remembered parts of a conversation with Daksha when he had first arrived in Devagiri. 'I was told by Emperor Daksha that the Chandravanshis did try to destroy the Saraswati more than a hundred years ago. By taking one of its main tributaries, the Yamuna, away from it and redirecting its flow towards the Ganga. It didn't really make much sense to me but the Meluhans seem to believe it.'

Brahaspati sniggered. 'The Chandravanshi ruling class cannot even build roads in their own empire. How can anyone think that they would have the ability to change the course of a river? What happened a hundred years ago was an earthquake that changed the course of the Yamuna. The Meluhans subsequently defeated the Chandravanshis and the resultant treaty mandated that the early course of the Yamuna would become no-man's land. And Meluhans do have the technology to change the course of rivers. They built giant embankments to block and change the course of the Yamuna to make it flow back into the Saraswati.'

'So what was your plan? Destroy the Yamuna embankments?'

'No. I had considered it, but that is impossible as well. They have many fail-safe options. It would take five brigades and months of open work to be able to destroy those embankments. We would obviously have had to work in secret with a small number of people.'

'So what was your plan?'

'An alternative. We cannot take the Saraswati away. But could we make the Saraswati much less potent in the production of the Somras? Is it possible to add something to the Yamuna waters, at its source, which would then flow into the Saraswati and control the amount of waste being produced? I thought that we had found one such ingredient.'

'What?'

'A bacterium which reacts with the Sanjeevani tree and makes it decay almost instantly.'

'I thought the Sanjeevani tree was already unstable and decayed rapidly. Ayurvati had told me the Naga medicine is created by mixing the crushed branches of another tree with the Sanjeevani bark to stabilise it. If the Sanjeevani is already unstable, why would it need bacteria to aid the decay? Wouldn't it just decay anyway?'

'The Sanjeevani bark becomes unstable once stripped off the branch. The entire branch, if used, is not. The bark is easier for small-scale manufacture, but for manufacturing the Somras in large quantities, we have to use crushed branches. This is what we did at Mount Mandar. But it is a method known only to my scientists.'

'So what you want to do is make the Sanjeevani branch also unstable.'

'Yes. And, I discovered that it was possible to do so with this bacterium. But it is only available in Mesopotamia.'

'Is this what you picked up from Karachapa when you accompanied me on my initial travels through Meluha? You had said you were expecting a shipment from Mesopotamia.'

'Yes,' said Brahaspati. 'And it would have worked perfectly. The Somras cannot be made without both the Sanjeevani tree and the Saraswati water. The presence of bacteria in the Saraswati water would render useless the Sanjeevani tree at the beginning of the process itself. And in any case, without the Saraswati water, the Somras cannot be made. Without the power of the Sanjeevani, the Somras would not be as potent. It will not triple or quadruple one's lifespan, but only increase it by twenty or thirty years. However, it would also mean that there would be practically no production of Somras waste. By sacrificing some of the powers of the Somras, we would take away all the poison of the Somras waste. Furthermore, these bacteria also mix with water and then multiply prodigiously. All we needed to do was release it in the Yamuna and the rest would follow.'

'Sounds perfect. Why didn't you?'

'There is no free lunch,' said Brahaspati. 'The bacteria came with its own problems. It is a mild toxin in itself. If we mix it in large quantities, as would be required in the Saraswati, we could create a new set of diseases for all living beings dependant not just on the Saraswati but also the Yamuna. We would have only replaced one problem with another.'

'So you were trying to see if the poisonous effect of the bacteria could be reduced or removed, without disturbing its ability to destroy the Sanjeevani tree?'

'Yes. Secrecy was required. If those who support the Somras knew about these bacteria, they would try to kill it at its source. Had they known I was working on an experiment such as this, they would have had me assassinated.'

'Aren't you afraid of being killed now?' asked Shiva. 'A lot of Meluhans will be angry with you when they discover you weren't the victim, but the perpetrator of the attack on Mount Mandar.'

Brahaspati breathed deeply. 'Earlier, it was important for me to remain alive since I alone could have done this research. But I have failed. And the solution to the Somras problem is not in my hands anymore. It's in your hands. It doesn't matter if I live any longer. Mount Mandar will be reconstructed. It's a matter of time. And Somras production will begin once again. You have to stop it, Shiva. For the sake of India, you have to stop the Somras.'

'The reconstruction is a charade, Brahaspati*ji*,' said Sati. 'It's to mislead enemies into thinking that it will take time to get Somras production back on track. To make them think that Meluha must be surviving on lower quantities of Somras.'

'What? Is there another facility?' asked Brahaspati, as he looked quickly at Kali. 'But that cannot be true.'

'It is,' answered Sati. 'I was told by father himself. Apparently, it was built years ago. As a back-up to Mount Mandar, just in case...'

'Where?' asked Kali.

'I don't know,' replied Sati.

'Damn!' exclaimed Kali, scowling darkly as she turned to Brahaspati. 'You had said that that was not possible. The churners needed materials from Egypt. They could not be built from Indian material. We have allies constantly watching those Egyptian mines. No material has gone to Meluha!'

Brahaspati's face turned white as the implications dawned on him. He held his head and muttered, 'Lord Ram, be merciful... How can they resort to this?'

'Resort to what?' asked Shiva.

'There's another way in which the Saraswati waters can be mixed with the crushed Sanjeevani branches. But it's considered wasteful and repugnant.'

'Why?'

'Firstly, it uses much larger quantities of the Saraswati water. Secondly, it needs animal or human skin cells.'

'Excuse me!' cried Shiva and Sati.

'It doesn't mean that one skins a live animal or human,' said Brahaspati, as though reassuring them. 'What is needed is old and dead skin cells that we shed every minute that we are alive. The cells help the Saraswati waters to grate the Sanjeevani branches at molecular levels. The waters mixed with dead skin cells are simply poured over crushed branches placed in a chamber. This process does not require any churning. But as you can imagine, it wastes a lot of water. Secondly, how would one find animals and humans who would come to a faraway facility and get into a pool of water above a chamber which contains crushed Sanjeevani branches? It is risky.'

'Why?'

'Dead skin cells of humans or animals are best shed while bathing. A human sheds between two to three kilograms every year. Bathing hastens the process.'

'But why is this risky?'

'Because Somras production is inherently unstable; the skin cell route even more so. One doesn't want large populations anywhere close to a Somras facility. If anything goes wrong, the resultant explosion can kill hundreds of thousands. Even in the usual, less risky churning process, we do not build Somras production centres close to cities. Can you imagine what would happen if the riskier skin cell process was being conducted close to a city with a large number of humans ritually bathing above a Somras production centre?'

Shiva's face suddenly turned white. 'Public baths in Meluhan cities...' he whispered.

'Exactly,' said Brahaspati. 'Build the facility within a city, below a public bath. One would have all the dead skin cells that one would need.'

'And if something goes wrong... If an explosion takes place...'

'Blame the *daivi astras* or the Nagas. Blame the Chandravanshis if you want,' fumed Brahaspati. 'Having created so many evil spectres, you can take your pick!'

— ⁂ —

'Something is wrong,' said Bhrigu.

He was surveying the destroyed remains of Mount Mandar with Dilipa. The Somras manufacturing facility looked nowhere near completion though reconstruction was on.

Dilipa turned towards the sage. 'I agree, Maharishi*ji*. It has been more than five years since the Nagas destroyed Mandar. It's ridiculous that the facility has still not been reconstructed.'

Bhrigu turned to Dilipa and waved his hand dismissively. 'Mount Mandar is not important anymore. It's only a symbol. I'm talking about the attack on Panchavati.'

Dilipa stared wide-eyed at the sage. *Mount Mandar is not*

important? This means that the rumours are true. Another Somras manufacturing facility does exist.

'I had given a whole kit of homing pigeons to the attackers,' continued Bhrigu, not bothering with Dilipa's incredulous look. 'All of them had been trained to return to this site. The last pigeon came in two weeks back.'

Dilipa frowned. 'You can trust my man, My Lord. He will not fail.'

Bhrigu had appointed an officer from Dilipa's army to lead the attack on Shiva's convoy at Panchavati. He did not trust Daksha's ability to detach himself from his love for his daughter. 'Of that I am sure. He has proven himself trustworthy, strictly complying with my instructions to send back a message every week. The fact that the updates have suddenly stopped means that he has either been captured or killed.'

'I'm sure a message is on its way. We needn't worry.'

Bhrigu turned sharply towards Dilipa. 'Is this how you govern your empire, great King? Is it any wonder that your son's claim to the throne appears legitimate?'

Dilipa's silence was telling.

Bhrigu sighed. 'When you prepare for war, you should always hope for the best, but be ready for the worst. The last despatch clearly stated that they were but six days' sail from Panchavati. Having received no word, I am compelled to assume the worst. The attack must have failed. Also, I should assume Shiva knows the identity of the attackers.'

Dilipa didn't speak, but kept staring at Bhrigu. He thought Bhrigu was over-reacting.

'I'm not over-reacting, Your Highness,' said Bhrigu.

Dilipa was stunned. He hadn't uttered a word.

'Do not underestimate the issue,' said Bhrigu. 'This is not about you or me. This is about the future of India. This is about protecting the greatest Good. We cannot afford to fail! It is our duty to Lord Brahma; our duty to this great land of ours.'

Dilipa remained silent. Though one thought kept reverberating in his mind. *I am way out of my depth here. I have entangled myself with powers that are beyond mere emperors.*

Chapter 4

A Frog Homily

The aroma of freshly-cooked food emerged from Shiva's chambers as his family assembled for their evening meal. Sati's culinary skill and effort were evident in the feast she had lined up for what was practically their first meal together as a family. Shiva, Ganesh and Kartik waited for her to take a seat before they began the meal.

In keeping with custom, the family of the Mahadev took some water from their glasses and sprinkled it around their plates, symbolically thanking Goddess Annapurna for her blessings in the form of food and nourishment. After this, they offered the first morsel of food to the Gods. Breaking with age-old tradition though, Shiva always offered his first morsel to his wife. For him, she was divine. Sati reciprocated by offering her first morsel to Shiva.

And thus the meal began.

'Ganesh has got some mangoes for you today,' said Sati, looking indulgently at Kartik.

Kartik grinned. 'Yummy! Thanks *dada*!'

Ganesh smiled and patted Kartik on his back.

'You should smile a little more, Kartik,' said Shiva. 'Life is not so grim.'

Kartik smiled at his father. 'I'll try, *baba*.'

Looking at his other progeny, Shiva inhaled sharply. 'Ganesh?'

'Yes... *baba*,' said Ganesh, unsure of the response to his calling Shiva *father*.

'My son,' whispered Shiva. 'I misjudged you.'

Ganesh's eyes moistened.

'Forgive me,' said Shiva.

'No, *baba*,' exclaimed Ganesh, embarrassed. 'How can you ask me for forgiveness? You are my father.'

Brahaspati had told Shiva that he had made Ganesh take an oath of secrecy; nobody was to know that the former Meluhan chief scientist was alive. Brahaspati did not trust anyone and wanted his experiments on the Mesopotamian bacteria to remain secret. Ganesh had kept his word even at the cost of almost losing his beloved mother and of grievously damaging his relationship with Shiva.

'You're a man of your word,' said Shiva. 'You honoured your promise to Brahaspati, without sparing a thought for the price you would be paying.'

Ganesh remained quiet.

'I'm proud of you my son,' said Shiva.

Ganesh smiled.

Sati looked at Shiva, Kartik and then at Ganesh. Her world had come full circle. Life was as perfect as it could possibly be. She did not need anything else. She could live her life in Panchavati till the end of her days. But she knew that this was not to be. A war was coming; a battle that would require major sacrifices. She knew she had to savour these moments for as long as they lasted.

'What now, *baba*?' asked Kartik seriously.

'We're going to eat!' laughed Shiva. 'And then, hopefully, we will go to sleep.'

'No, no,' smiled Kartik. 'You know what I mean. Are we going to proclaim the Somras as the ultimate Evil? Are we going to declare war against all those who continue to use or protect the Somras?'

Shiva looked at Kartik thoughtfully. 'There has already been a lot of fighting, Kartik. We will not rush into anything.' Shiva turned to Ganesh. 'I'm sorry, my son, but I need to know more. I have to know more.'

'I understand, *baba*. There are only two groups of people who know all there is to know about this.'

'The Vasudevs and the Vayuputras?'

'Yes.'

'I'm not sure if the Vayuputra council will help me. But I know the Vasudevs will.'

'I'll take you to Ujjain, *baba*. You can speak to their chief directly.'

'Where is Ujjain?'

'It's up north, beyond the Narmada.'

Shiva considered it for a bit. 'That would be along the shorter route to Swadweep and Meluha, right?'

With the security of Panchavati uppermost in her mind, Kali had led Shiva and his entourage from Kashi to Panchavati via an elaborate route which took a year to traverse. The party had first headed east through Swadweep then south from Branga. They then moved west from Kalinga through the dangerous Dandak forests before they reached the headwaters of the Godavari where Panchavati lay. Shiva realised that there must be a shorter northern route to Meluha and Swadweep, which was impossible to traverse without a Naga guide, because of the impregnable forests that impeded the path.

'Yes, *baba*. Though *mausi* is very secretive about this route, I know that she would be happy to share it with the three of you.'

'I understand,' said Sati. 'The Nagas have many powerful enemies.'

'Yes, *maa*,' said Ganesh, before turning to Shiva. 'But that is not the only reason. Let's be honest. Though the war has not yet begun, we already know that the most powerful emperors in the land are against us. Which side everyone takes, including those waiting in the Panchavati guesthouse colony, will become clear over the next few months. Panchavati is a safe haven. It's not wise to give away its secrets just as yet.'

Shiva nodded. 'Let me figure out what I should do with my convoy. There aren't too many kings in the Sapt Sindhu I can readily trust at this point of time. Once I've made up my mind, we can make plans to leave for Ujjain.'

Kartik turned to Ganesh. '*Dada*, there's one thing I simply don't understand. The Vayuputras are the tribe left behind by Lord Rudra. They helped the great seventh Vishnu, Lord Ram, complete his mission. So how is it that these good people do not see the Evil that the Somras has become today?'

Ganesh smiled. 'I have a theory.'

Shiva and Sati looked up at Ganesh, while continuing to eat.

'You've seen a frog, right?' asked Ganesh.

'Yes,' said Kartik. 'Interesting creatures; especially their tongues!'

Ganesh smiled. 'Apparently, an unknown Brahmin scientist had conducted some experiments on frogs a long time ago. He dropped a frog in a pot of boiling water. The frog immediately jumped out. He then placed a frog in a pot full of cold water; the frog settled down comfortably. The Brahmin then began raising the temperature of the water gradually, over many hours. The frog kept adapting to the increasingly warm and then hot water till it finally died, without making any attempt to escape.'

Shiva, Sati and Kartik listened in rapt attention.

'Naga students learn this story as a life lesson,' said Ganesh.

'Often, our immediate reaction to a sudden crisis helps us save ourselves. Our response to gradual crises that creep up upon us, on the other hand, may be so adaptive as to ultimately lead to self-destruction.'

'Are you suggesting that the Vayuputras keep adapting to the incremental ill-effects of the Somras?' asked Kartik. 'That the bad news is not emerging rapidly enough?'

'Perhaps,' said Ganesh. 'For I refuse to believe that the Vayuputras, the people of Lord Rudra, would consciously choose to let Evil live. The only explanation is that they genuinely believe the Somras is not evil.'

'Interesting,' said Shiva. 'And, perhaps you are right too.'

Sati chipped in with a smile, almost as if to lighten the atmosphere. 'But do you really believe the frog experiment?'

Ganesh smiled. 'It is such a popular story around here that I'd actually tried it, when I was a child.'

'Did you really boil a frog slowly to death? And it sat still all the while?'

Ganesh laughed. '*Maaaaa!* Frogs don't sit still no matter what you do! Boiling water, cold water or lukewarm water, a frog always leaps out!'

The family of the Mahadev laughed heartily.

— ⁂ —

Shiva and Sati were exiting the Panchavati Rajya Sabha, having just met with the Naga nobility. Many of the nobles were in agreement with Queen Kali, who wanted to attack Meluha right away and destroy the evil Somras. But some, like Vasuki and Astik, wanted to avoid war.

'Vasuki and Astik genuinely want peace. But for the wrong reasons,' said Shiva, shaking his head. 'They may be Naga nobility, but they believe that their own people deserve their cruel fate, because they are being punished for their past-life sins. This is nonsense!'

Sati, who believed in the concept of karma extending over many births, could not hold back her objection. 'Just because we don't understand something doesn't necessarily mean it is rubbish, Shiva.'

'Come on, Sati. There is only this life; this moment. That is the only thing we can be sure of. Everything else is only theory.'

'Then why were the Nagas born deformed? Why did I live as a Vikarma for so long? Surely it must be because in some sense we'd deserved it. We were paying for our past-life sins.'

'That's ridiculous! How can anyone be sure about past-life sins? The Vikarma system, like every system that governs human lives, was created by us. You fought the Vikarma system and freed yourself.'

'But I didn't free myself, Shiva. You did. It was your strength. And all the Vikarmas, including me, were set free because that was your karma.'

'So how does this work?' asked Shiva disbelievingly. 'That the compounded totality of sins committed by all the Vikarma over their individual previous lives was nullified at the stroke of a quill when I struck down this law? On that fateful day, in a flash, several lifetimes of sins sullying every Vikarma soul were washed away? A day of divine pardon, indeed!'

'Shiva, are you mocking me?'

'Would I ever do that, dear?' asked Shiva, but his smile gave him away. 'Don't you see how illogical this entire concept is? How can one believe that an innocent child is born with sin? It's clear as daylight: a new-born child has done no wrong. He has done no right either. He has just been born. He could not have done anything!'

'Perhaps not in this life, Shiva. But it's possible that the child committed a sin in a previous life. Perhaps the child's ancestors committed sins for which the child must be held accountable.'

Shiva was unconvinced. 'Don't you get it? It's a system designed to control people. It makes those who suffer or are oppressed, blame themselves for their misery. Because you believe you are paying for sins committed either in your own previous lives or those committed by your ancestors, or even community. Perhaps even the sins of the first man ever born! The system therefore propagates suffering as a form of atonement and at the same time does not allow one to question the wrongs done unto oneself.'

'Then why do some people suffer? Why do some get far *less* than what they deserve?'

'The same reason why there are others who get far *more* than what they deserve. It's completely random.'

Shiva gallantly reached out to help Sati mount her steed but she declined and gracefully slid onto the stallion. Her husband smiled. There was nothing he loved more than her intense sense of self-sufficiency and pride. Shiva leapt onto his own horse and with a quick spur matched Sati's pace.

'Really, Shiva,' said Sati, looking towards him. 'Do you believe that the *Parmatma* plays dice with the universe? That we are all handed our fate randomly?'

The Nagas on the road recognised Shiva and bowed low in respect. They didn't believe in the legend of the Neelkanth, but clearly, their queen respected the Mahadev. And that made most Nagas believe in Shiva as well. He politely acknowledged every person even as he replied to Sati without turning. 'I think the *Parmatma* does not interfere in our lives. He sets the rules by which the universe exists. Then, He does something very difficult.'

'What?'

'He leaves us alone. He lets things play out naturally. He lets His creations make decisions about their own lives. It's not easy being a witness when one has the power to rule. It takes a Supreme God to be able to do that. He knows this is our world, our *karmabhoomi*,' said Shiva, waving his hand all around as though pointing out the *land of their karma*.

'Don't you think this is difficult to accept? If people believe that their fate is completely random, it would leave them without any sense of understanding, purpose or motivation. Or why they are where they are.'

'On the contrary, this is an empowering thought. When you know that your fate is completely random, you have the freedom to commit yourself to any theory that will empower you. If you have been blessed with good fate, you can choose to believe it is God's kindness and ingrain humility within. But if you have been cursed with bad fate, you need to know that no Great Power is seeking to punish you. Your situation is, in fact, a result of completely random circumstances, an indiscriminate turn of the universe. Therefore, if you decide to challenge your destiny, your opponent would not be some judgemental Lord Almighty who is seeking to punish you; your opponent would only be the limitations of your own mind. This will empower you to fight your fate.'

Sati shook her head. 'Sometimes you are too revolutionary.'

Shiva's eyes crinkled. 'Maybe that is itself a result of my past-life sins!'

Laughing together, they cantered out of the city gates.

Seeing the Panchavati guest colony in the distance, Shiva whispered gravely, 'But one man will have to account to his friends for his karma in this life.'

'Brahaspati*ji*?'

Shiva nodded.

'What do you have in mind?'

'I had asked Brahaspati if he'd like to meet Parvateshwar and Ayurvati, to explain to them as to how he is still alive.'

'And?'

'He readily agreed.'

'I would have expected nothing less from him.'

— ⅄ⲰƱ⍋⊗ —

'Are you all right?' asked Anandmayi.

Parvateshwar and Anandmayi were in their private room in the Panchavati guesthouse colony.

'I'm thoroughly confused,' said Parvateshwar. 'The ruler of Meluha should represent the best there is in our way of life – truth, duty and honour. What does it say about us if our emperor is such a habitual law-breaker? He broke the law when Sati's child was born.'

'I know what Emperor Daksha did was patently wrong. But one could argue that he is just a father trying to protect his child, albeit in his own stupid manner.'

'The fact that he did what was wrong is enough, Anandmayi. He broke the law. And now, he has broken one of Lord Rudra's laws by using the *daivi astras*. How can Meluha, the finest land in the world, have an emperor like him? Isn't something wrong somewhere?'

Anandmayi held her husband's hand. 'Your emperor was never any good. I could have told you that many years ago. But you don't need to blame all of Meluha for his misdeeds.'

'That's not the way it works. A leader is not just a person who gives orders. He is also the one who symbolises the society he leads. If the leader is corrupt, then the society must be corrupt too.'

'Who feeds this nonsense to you, my love? A leader is just a human being, like anyone else. He doesn't symbolise anything.'

Parvateshwar shook his head. 'There are some truths that cannot be challenged. A leader's karma impacts his entire land. He is supposed to be his people's icon. That is a universal truth.'

Anandmayi bent towards him with a soft twinkle in her eyes. 'Parvateshwar, there is your truth and there is my truth. As for the universal truth? It does not exist.'

Parvateshwar smiled as he brushed a stray strand of hair away from her face. 'You Chandravanshis are very good with words.'

'Words can only be as good or as bad as the thoughts they convey.'

Parvateshwar's smile spread wider. 'So what is your thought on what I should do? My emperor's actions have put me in a situation where my God, the Neelkanth, may declare war on my country. What do I do then? How do I know which side to pick?'

'You should stick to your God,' said Anandmayi, without any hint of hesitation in her voice. 'But this is a hypothetical question. So don't worry too much about it.'

— ⅄ ◎ Ʊ ⍋ ⊛ —

'My Lord, you called,' said Ayurvati.

She had been as surprised as Parvateshwar when the both of them had been summoned to Shiva's chambers. Since their arrival in Panchavati, Shiva had spent most of his time with the Nagas. Ayurvati was convinced that the Nagas were somehow complicit in the attack on Shiva's convoy. She also believed the Neelkanth was perhaps investigating the roots of Naga treachery in Panchavati.

'Parvateshwar, Ayurvati, welcome,' said Shiva, 'I called you here because it is time now for you to know the secret of the Nagas.'

Parvateshwar looked up, surprised. 'But why only the two of us, My Lord?'

'Because the both of you are Meluhans. I have reason to suspect that the attack on us at the Godavari is linked to many things: the plague in Branga, the plight of the Nagas and the drying up of the Saraswati.'

Parvateshwar and Ayurvati were flummoxed.

'But I am certain about one thing,' said Shiva. 'The attack is connected to the destruction of Mount Mandar.'

'What?! How?'

'Only one man can explain it. One whom you believe is dead.'

Ayurvati and Parvateshwar spun around as they heard the door open.

Brahaspati walked in quietly.

— ⁂ —

'The Somras is Evil?' asked Anandmayi incredulously. 'Is that what the Lord Neelkanth thinks?'

Parvateshwar and Anandmayi were in their chambers at the Panchavati guest colony. Bhagirath had just joined them.

'I'm not sure about what he thinks,' said Parvateshwar. 'But Brahaspati seems to think so.'

'But Evil is supposed to be Evil for everybody,' said Bhagirath. 'Why should a Suryavanshi turncoat decide what Evil is? Why should we listen to him? Why should the Neelkanth listen to him?'

'Bhagirath, do you expect me to defend Brahaspati, the man who destroyed the soul of our empire?' asked Parvateshwar.

'Just a minute,' said Anandmayi, raising her hand. 'Think this through... If the plague in Branga is linked to the Somras, if the slow depletion of the river Saraswati is linked to the Somras, if the birth of the Nagas is linked to the Somras, then isn't it fair to think that maybe it is Evil?'

'So what is the Neelkanth planning to do? Does he want to ban the Somras?' asked Bhagirath.

'I don't know, Bhagirath!' snapped an irritated Parvateshwar, his world having turned upside down because of Daksha and now Brahaspati. 'You keep asking me questions, the answers to which I do not know!'

Anandmayi placed her hand on Parvateshwar's shoulders. 'Perhaps the Neelkanth is just as shocked as we are. He needs to think things over. He cannot afford to make hasty decisions.'

'Well, he has made one already,' said Parvateshwar.

Bhagirath and Anandmayi looked at Parvateshwar curiously.

'We are to leave for Swadweep once all have recovered from their injuries. The Lord has asked us to wait for him at Kashi till he decides his next move. He believes King Athithigva has not sold out to Ayodhya in the conspiracy to assassinate us on the Godavari.'

'But if we go to Kashi, my father will get to know that we are alive,' said Bhagirath. 'He will know his attack has failed.'

'We have to keep quiet about it. We have to pretend that nothing happened, that we were not attacked at all. That we made an uneventful journey to Panchavati and back.'

'Won't they wonder about their ships?'

'The Lord says that's all right. Many things can happen during long sea and river voyages. They may believe their ships met with an accident before they could attack us.'

Bhagirath raised his eyebrows. 'My father may be stupid enough to believe that story. But he is not the leader.

Whoever put together a conspiracy of this scale will certainly investigate what went wrong.'

'But investigations take time, allowing the Neelkanth to check whatever else it is that he needs to.'

'The Lord is not coming with us?' asked a surprised Anandmayi.

Parvateshwar shook his head. 'No. And the Lord has said we should let it be known that neither his family nor he is with us at Kashi. It should be publicised that he remains in Panchavati. The Lord believes that it will keep us safe as the attack was aimed at him.'

'That can mean only one thing,' said Bhagirath. 'He chooses to take Brahaspati at face value but wants to ascertain a few more things before he makes up his mind.'

Anandmayi looked at her husband with concern in her eyes. She knew that a war was approaching. Perhaps the biggest war that India had ever seen. And in all probability, Meluha and Shiva would be on opposite sides. Which side would her husband choose?

'Whatever happens,' said Anandmayi, holding Parvateshwar's face, 'we must have faith in the Neelkanth.'

Parvateshwar nodded silently.

Shiva, Parshuram and Nandi were sitting on the banks of the Godavari. Shiva took a deep drag from the chillum as he looked towards the river, lost in thought. He let out a sigh as he turned to his friends. 'Are you sure, Parshuram?'

'Yes, My Lord,' replied Parshuram. 'I can even take you to the uppermost point of the mighty Brahmaputra, where it is the Tsangpo. But I wouldn't recommend it, for fatalities can be high on that treacherous route.'

Shiva's silence provoked Parshuram to probe further, 'What is it about that river, My Lord?' He had been intrigued by the abnormal interest shown by the Nagas in the Brahmaputra's course as well. 'First the Nagas, now you; why is everyone so interested in it?'

'It may be the carrier of Evil, Parshuram.'

Nandi looked up in surprise. 'Doesn't the Tsangpo begin close to your own home in Tibet, My Lord?'

'Yes, Nandi,' said Shiva. 'It seems Evil has been closer than it initially appeared.'

Nandi remained quiet. He was one of the few who knew the ships that attacked Shiva's convoy were from Meluha. He knew what he had to do. If it came to a choice between Shiva and his country, he would choose Shiva. But it still hurt him immensely. He knew he might have to be a part of an army that would attack his beloved motherland, Meluha. He hated his fate for having put him in such a situation.

— ⁂ —

'I think I know how to find the mastermind, My Lord,' said Bhagirath.

He had sought an appointment with Shiva as soon as he had stepped out of Parvateshwar's chambers. He knew that his father had decided to oppose the Neelkanth. It made sense therefore for Bhagirath to immediately prove his loyalty to Shiva. He didn't expect Shiva to lose. Regardless of the opinion of the kings, the people would be with the Neelkanth.

'How?' asked Shiva.

'You'd agree that my father hardly has the wherewithal to draw up such an elaborate plan. I'd say his selfish needs have made him succumb to the evil designs of another.'

Shiva edged forward, intrigued. 'You think he has been bribed? Your father is in no need of money.'

'What can be a better bribe than life itself, My Lord? Had you seen my father a few years back, you would have thought he was but a small step away from the cremation pyre. A life of debauchery and drink had wreaked havoc within his body. But today, he looks younger than I have ever known.'

'The Somras?'

'I don't think so. I know he had tried the Somras in the past. It hadn't worked. Somebody is supplying him with superior medicines. Something that is otherwise unavailable to even a king.'

Shiva's eyes widened. *Who could be more powerful, more knowledgeable than a king?*

'Do you think a maharishi is helping him?'

Bhagirath shook his head. 'No, My Lord. I think a maharishi is *leading* him.'

'But who can that maharishi be?'

'I don't know. But when I go back to Ayodhya...'

'Ayodhya?'

'If we are to maintain that no ships attacked us on the Godavari, My Lord, then what reason can there be for my not going back to Ayodhya? It will arouse suspicion. More importantly, I can only uncover the true identity of the master when I'm in *Ayodhya*. Despite my father's best efforts, I still have eyes and ears in the *impregnable city*.'

Shiva considered this for a moment. He agreed with the train of thought. Moreover, now that Dilipa had chosen to align himself against Shiva, Bhagirath would be even more eager to prove his loyalty to him.

Shiva nodded. 'All right, go to Ayodhya.'

'But My Lord, when the time comes, I hope Ayodhya and Swadweep will be shown some kindness.'

'Kindness?'

'We have not used the Somras excessively, My Lord. Only a few Chandravanshi nobles use it, and that too, sparingly. It is the Meluhans who have abused its usage. That is what has made Evil rise. Therefore it is only fair that when the *Somras* is banned, this ban be imposed only on Meluha. Swadweep has not benefited from the *drink of the Gods*. I hope we will be allowed to use it.'

'You didn't *choose* to use less Somras, Bhagirath,' said Shiva. 'You just didn't have the opportunity to do so. If you had, the situation would have been very different. You know that just as much as I do.'

'But Meluha...'

'Yes, Meluha has used more. So naturally, they will suffer more. But let me make one thing clear. If I decide the Somras is Evil, then no one will use it. No one.'

Bhagirath kept silent.

'Is that clear?' asked Shiva.

'Of course, My Lord.'

Chapter 5

The Shorter Route

A caravan of five hundred people was moving up the northern path from Panchavati towards the Vasudev city of Ujjain. Shiva and his family were in the centre, surrounded by half a brigade of joint Naga and Branga soldiers in standard defensive formations. Kali did not want to reveal this route to anyone from Shiva's original convoy, so none of them were included. Nandi and Parshuram were the only exceptions. Brahaspati had been included for Shiva might need his advice in understanding what the Vasudevs had to say about the Somras.

Whereas Shiva persisted in his quest and questions with Brahaspati, the old brotherly love that they had shared was missing.

Parvateshwar, Ayurvati, Anandmayi and Bhagirath, along with the original convoy, had stayed back at Panchavati. They were to leave for Kashi in a few weeks, their eastern route going through the Dandak forest, onward through Branga. Vishwadyumna was to accompany them as a guide up to Branga.

'Ganesh, does Ujjain fall on the way from Panchavati to Meluha or do we take a detour?' asked Shiva, goading his horse forward over the path built through the forest. It was fenced by two protective hedges. The inner layer comprised the harmless Nagavalli creepers, while the outer one had poisonous vines to prevent wild animals from entering.

'Actually, *baba*, Ujjain is on the way to Swadweep. It's to the north-east. Meluha lies to the north-west.'

Sati tried to get her bearings of Meluha and Maika at the dried mouth of the Saraswati. The Meluhan city of births was not too far from the mouth of the Narmada. 'Does the Narmada serve as your waterway? One can sail west for Meluha and east for Ujjain and Swadweep.'

'Yes, *maa*,' answered Ganesh.

Shiva turned to his son. 'Have you ever been to Maika? How do abandoned Naga children get adopted?'

'Maika is the one place where there is no bias against the Nagas, *baba*. Perhaps the sight of helpless Naga babies, shrieking in pain as a cancerous growth bursts through their bodies, melts the hearts of the authorities. The Maika governor takes personal interest in attempting to save as many Naga babies as he can in the crucial first month after their birth. A Naga ship sails down the Narmada every month, docks at Maika late at night, and the babies born in that month are handed over to us by the Maika record-keeper. Some non-Naga parents choose to stay back and move to Panchavati for the sake of their children.'

'Don't the Maika authorities stop them?'

'Actually, the tenets of Meluhan law require parents to accompany their Naga children to Panchavati. In doing so, they are following their law. But others refuse to do so. They abandon their children and return to their comfortable life in Meluha. In such cases, only the child is handed over. The Maika governor pretends not to notice this breach of law.'

Sati shook her head. She had lived in Meluha for more than one hundred years, a few of which were in Maika as an infant.

She had never known any of this. It was almost like she was discovering her seemingly upright nation anew. Her father had not been the only one to break the law. It appeared as if many Meluhans valued the comforts of their land more than their duty towards their children or towards observing Lord Ram's laws.

Shiva looked ahead to see a large ship anchored in a massive lagoon. The waters were blocked on the far side by a dense grove. Having seen the grove of floating Sundari trees in Branga, Shiva assumed these trees must also have free-floating roots. The route ahead seemed obvious. 'I guess we have reached your secret lagoon. I assume the Narmada is beyond that grove.'

'There is a massive river beyond that grove, *baba*,' said Ganesh. 'But it is not the Narmada. It is the Tapi. We have to cross to the other side. After that it is a few more days' journey to the Narmada.'

Shiva smiled. 'The Lord Almighty has blessed this land with too many rivers. India can never run short of water!'

'Not if we abuse our rivers the way we are now abusing the Saraswati.'

Shiva nodded, silently agreeing with Ganesh.

— ⁂ —

Bhrigu tore open the letter. It was exactly what he had expected. The Vayuputras had excommunicated him.

Lord Bhrigu,

It has been brought to our attention that daivi astras *were loaded onto a fleet of ships in Karachapa. Investigations have led to the regrettable conclusion that you manufactured them, using materials that were given to you strictly for research. While we understand that you would never misuse the weapons expressly banned by our God, Lord*

Rudra, we cannot allow the unauthorised transport of these weapons to go unpunished. You are therefore prohibited from ever entering Pariha or interacting with a Vayuputra again. We do hope you will honour the greater promise that every friend of a Vayuputra makes to Lord Rudra: that of never using the daivi astras. *It is the expectation of the council that you will surrender the weapons at once to Vayuputra Security.*

What surprised Bhrigu was that the note had been signed by the Mithra, leader of the council. It was rare for the Mithra to sign orders personally. Usually, it was done by one of the Amartya Shpand, the six deputies on the council. The Vayuputras were clearly taking this very seriously.

But Bhrigu believed that he had not broken the law. He had already written to the Vayuputras that they were making the institution of the Neelkanth a mockery by not acting against this self-appointed imposter. But alas, the Vayuputras had done nothing. However, he could see how they would think he had misused their research material. Ironically, he had not. Even if he had got over his qualms about using that material, Bhrigu knew there was simply not enough to make the quantity of *daivi astras* that were needed. He had made his own stockpile of such weapons, using materials he himself had compiled over the years. Perhaps that was the reason why they did not have the destructive potency of the Vayuputra material. They had entire laboratories, whereas Bhrigu worked alone.

Bhrigu sighed. He had used all the weapons that he had manufactured. The only mystery was whether they had achieved their purpose; whether the Neelkanth had been assassinated. Talking to Daksha was an exercise in futility. He seemed to be in a state of shock since the rupture of his relations with his daughter. Bhrigu had sent off another ship, manned by men drawn from Dilipa's army, to the mouth of the Godavari to investigate the matter. But it would be months before he knew what had happened.

'Anything else, My Lord?' asked the attendant.

Bhrigu dismissed her with an absent-minded wave. Perhaps the job was done. Maybe the Neelkanth was no more. But it was also possible that Bhrigu's ships had failed. Even worse, the Neelkanth may have been persuaded by the Nagas and was plotting to turn the people against the Somras. Nothing was certain till he received news of the five ships he had sent earlier to attack Shiva's convoy. For now, much as he disliked living in Devagiri, he had no choice but to wait. He had to stay till he knew the Somras was safe. He believed India's future was at stake.

Bhrigu took a deep breath and went back into a meditative trance.

— ⁂ —

Shiva's convoy had covered ground quickly after crossing the Tapi and was waiting at the edge of another secret lagoon, while the Nagas prepared to set sail. Beyond the floating grove guarding this lagoon, flowed the mighty Narmada, mandated by Lord Manu as the southern border of the *Sapt Sindhu, the land of the seven rivers.*

'How much farther, *dada*?'

'Not too far, Kartik. Just a few more weeks,' answered Ganesh. 'We will sail east up the Narmada for a few days, then march on foot through the passes of the great Vindhya Mountains till we reach the Chambal River. We would then have to sail for only a few days down the Chambal to reach Ujjain.'

Sati watched the sailors pull the gangway plank towards the rudimentary dock, preparing the ship for loading. She wished that her sister Kali had accompanied them on this journey. But she also knew that being a queen, Kali had many responsibilities in Panchavati.

Her thoughts were interrupted by the ship's gangway plank landing on the dock with a loud thud.

— ⁂ —

Parvateshwar, Anandmayi, Bhagirath and Ayurvati were dining together in the late afternoon. They had just entered the first of five clearings on the *Dandakaranya* road from Panchavati. The road led to the hidden lagoon on the Madhumati in Branga. Accompanied by the convoy of sixteen hundred soldiers that had set out with Shiva more than a year ago, they were marching back to Kashi to await Shiva's return.

Bhagirath looked at the five paths in wonder. Only one of these was correct while the others were decoys that would lead trespassers to their doom. 'These Nagas are obsessive about security.'

Anandmayi looked up. 'Can we blame them? Do not forget that it was this attitude that saved our lives when those ships attacked us on the Godavari.'

'True,' said Bhagirath. 'The Nagas will no doubt prove to be good allies. Their loyalty to the Neelkanth isn't suspect, though the reasons might well be. When the moment of truth is upon us, all will have to answer a simple question: Will they fight the world for the Neelkanth? I know I will.'

Anandmayi's eyes flashed as she looked at Parvateshwar and then back at Bhagirath, chiding him. 'Get back to your food, little brother.'

Parvateshwar looked at Anandmayi with a tortured expression. 'I don't think the *Parmatma* will be so unkind to me. He could not have made me wait for more than a century to find my living God, only to force me to choose between my country and him. I'm sure the Almighty will find a way to ensure that Meluha and the Lord Neelkanth are not on opposite sides.'

Parvateshwar's sad smile told Anandmayi he himself did not believe that. She touched her husband's shoulder gently.

Bhagirath played with his *roti* absent-mindedly. He was beginning to believe they could not count on Parvateshwar. That would be a huge loss for the Neelkanth's army. Parvateshwar's strategic abilities had the capacity to turn the tide in any war.

Ayurvati looked at Parvateshwar with sympathy. She could identify with his inner conflict. In her case though, a decision had emerged that sat comfortably in her heart. Her emperor had committed heinous acts which dishonoured Meluha. This was no longer the country she had loved and admired all her life. She knew in her heart that Lord Ram would not have condoned the immorality that Meluha had descended into, under Daksha's watch. Her path was clear: in a fight between Meluha and Shiva, she would choose the Neelkanth. For he would set things right in Meluha as well.

— ⁂ —

The Naga ship was anchored close to the Chambal shore. Shiva, Sati, Ganesh and Kartik climbed down rope ladders to the large boat that had been tied to the ship's anchor line. Brahaspati, Nandi and Parshuram followed them, accompanied by ten Naga soldiers.

When everyone had disembarked, they began to row ashore. The Vasudevs being even more secretive than the Nagas, Shiva did not expect to find any sign of habitation close to the river.

Almost touching the river bank, a wall of dense foliage blocked the view beyond. Weeds had spread over the gentle Chambal waters, making rowing a back-breaking task. Ganesh navigated the boat towards a slender clearing between two immense palm trees. Shiva could sense something unnatural about the clearing, but couldn't put his finger on it. He turned towards Kartik, who was staring at the clearing as well.

'*Baba*, look at the trees behind the clearing,' said Kartik. 'You'll have to bend down to my level.'

As Shiva bent low the image became clear. The trees behind the clearing were organised unnaturally, given the dense, uncontrolled growth surrounding it. Placed equidistant, they seemed to grow in height as one looked farther away. This was because the ground itself sloped upwards in a gentle gradient. It was obviously not a natural hillock. A majority of the trees behind the clearing were the Gulmohur, their flaming orange flowers suggestive of fire. Shiva blinked at what appeared to be an optical illusion. He suddenly stood up, rocking the boat as Sati and Ganesh reached out to hold him steady. The Gulmohur trees had been placed in a specific pattern that was visible from a certain distance as one placed oneself directly in front of the small clearing between the twin palms. It was in the shape of a flame; a specific symbol that Shiva recognised.

'*Fravashi*,' whispered Shiva.

Surprised, Ganesh asked, 'How do you know that term, *baba*?'

Shiva looked at Ganesh and then back at the Gulmohur trees. The pattern had disappeared. Shiva sat down and turned towards Ganesh. 'How do *you* know that term?'

'It's a Vayuputra term. It represents the feminine spirit of Lord Rudra, which has the power to assist us in doing what is right. We are free to either accept it or reject it. But the spirit never refuses to help. Never.'

Shiva smiled as he began to understand his ancient memories.

'Who told you about *Fravashi*, *baba*?' asked Ganesh again.

'My uncle Manobhu,' said Shiva. 'It was among the many concepts and symbols that he made me learn. He said it would help me when the time came.'

'Who was he?'

'I thought I knew,' said Shiva. 'But I'm beginning to wonder if I knew him well enough.'

The conversation came to a halt as the boat hit the banks. Two Naga soldiers jumped out and pulled the boat farther up, onto dry land. Tugging hard on the line, they tied the craft to a conveniently placed tree stump. The landing party quickly disembarked. Kartik surveyed the palms that marked the clearing. He turned towards Ganesh, who was standing at the centre of the clearing.

'Can everyone stand behind me, please,' requested Ganesh. 'I do not want anybody between me and the palm trees.'

The others moved away as Ganesh closed his eyes to drown out the distractions surrounding him and find his concentration.

Ganesh breathed deeply and clapped hard repeatedly in an irregular beat. The claps were set in the Vasudev code and were being transmitted to the gatekeeper of Ujjain. *This is Ganesh, the Naga lord of the people, requesting permission to enter your great city with our entourage.*

Shiva heard the soft sounds of claps reverberating back. Ujjain's gatekeeper had answered. *Welcome, Lord Ganesh. This is an unexpected honour. Are you on your way to Swadweep?*

No. We have come to meet with Lord Gopal, the great chief Vasudev.

Was there something specific you needed to discuss, Lord Ganesh?

Clearly, the Vasudevs were still not comfortable with the Nagas, despite the fact that they had reached out to Ganesh for the Naga medicines to help with the birth of Kartik. The Ujjain gatekeeper was trying to parry off Ganesh's request while trying not to insult him.

Ganesh continued to clap rhythmically. *It is not I who seeks Lord Gopal, honoured gatekeeper. It is the Lord Neelkanth.*

Silence for a few moments. Then the sound of claps in quick succession. *Is the Lord Neelkanth at the palm clearing with you?*

He is standing with me. He can hear you.

Silence once again, before the gatekeeper responded. *Lord Ganesh, Lord Gopal himself is coming to the clearing. We will be honoured to host your convoy. It will take us a day to get there; please bear with us till then.*

Thank you.

Ganesh rubbed his palms together and looked at Shiva. 'It will take a day for them to get here, *baba*. We can wait in our ship till they arrive.'

'Have you ever been to Ujjain?' asked Shiva.

'No. I have met the Vasudevs just once at this very clearing.'

'All right, let's get back to our ship.'

— ⁂ —

'Are you telling me Lord Bhrigu visited Ayodhya eight times in the last year?' asked a surprised Surapadman.

The crown prince of Magadh maintained his own espionage network, independent of the notoriously inefficient Royal Magadh spy service. His man had just informed him of the goings-on in the Ayodhya royal household.

'Yes, Your Highness,' answered the spy. 'Furthermore, Emperor Dilipa himself has visited Meluha twice in the same period.'

'That, I am aware of,' said Surapadman. 'But the news you bring throws new light on it. Perhaps Dilipa was not going to meet that fool Daksha after all. Maybe he was going to meet Lord Bhrigu. But why would the great sage be interested in Dilipa?'

'That I do not know, Your Highness. But I'm sure you have heard of Emperor Dilipa's newly-acquired youthful appearance. Perhaps Lord Bhrigu has been giving him the Somras?'

Surapadman waved his hand dismissively. 'The Somras is easily available to Swadweepan royalty. Dilipa doesn't need to plead with a maharishi for it. I know Dilipa has been using the Somras for years. But when one has abused the body as much as he has, even the Somras would find it difficult to delay his ageing. I suspect Lord Bhrigu is giving him medicines that are even more potent than the Somras.'

'But why would Lord Bhrigu do that?'

'That's the mystery. Try to find out. Any news of the Neelkanth?'

'No, Your Highness. He remains in Naga territory.'

Surapadman rubbed his chin and looked out of the window of his palace chambers along the Ganga. His gaze seemed to stretch beyond the river into the jungle that extended to the south; the forests where his brother Ugrasen had been killed by the Nagas. He cursed Ugrasen silently. He knew the truth of his brother's murder. Addicted to bull-racing, Ugrasen had indulged in increasingly reckless bets. Desperate to get good child-riders for his bulls, he used to scour tribal forests, kidnapping children at will. On one such expedition he had been killed by a Naga, who was trying to protect a hapless mother and her young boy. What he could not understand though was why a Naga would risk his life to save a forest woman and her child.

But the death had narrowed Surapadman's choices. The Neelkanth would lead his followers against whoever he decided was Evil. A war was inevitable. There would be those who would oppose him. Surapadman did not care much about this war against Evil. All he wanted was to ensure that Magadh would fight on the side opposed to Ayodhya. He intended to use wartime chaos to establish Magadh as the overlord of Swadweep and himself as emperor. But Ugrasen's killing had deepened his father King Mahendra's distrust of the Nagas into unadulterated hatred. Surapadman knew Mahendra would force him to fight against whichever side the Nagas allied with. His only hope lay in the Nagas and the Emperor of Ayodhya choosing the same side.

— ⁂ —

Kanakhala waited patiently in the chambers of Maharishi Bhrigu at Daksha's palace. The maharishi was in deep meditation. Though his chamber was in a palace, it was as simple and severe as his real home in a Himalayan cave. Bhrigu sat on the only piece of furniture in the room, a stone bed. Kanakhala therefore had no choice but to stand. Icy water had been sprinkled on the floor and the walls. The resultant cold and clammy dampness made her shiver slightly. She looked at the bowl of fruit at the far corner of the room on a small stand. The maharishi seemed to have eaten just one fruit over the previous three days. Kanakhala made a mental note to order fresh fruit to be brought in. An idol of Lord Brahma had been installed in an indentation in the wall. Kanakhala stared fixedly at the idol as she repeated the soft chanting of Bhrigu.

Om Brahmaye Namah. Om Brahmaye Namah.

Bhrigu opened his eyes and gazed at Kanakhala contemplatively before speaking. 'Yes, my child?'

'My Lord, a sealed letter has been delivered for you by bird courier. It has been marked as strictly confidential. Therefore, I thought it fit to bring it to you personally.'

Bhrigu nodded politely and took the letter from Kanakhala without saying a word.

'As instructed, we have also kept the pigeon with us. It can return to where it came from. Of course, this would not be possible if the ship has moved. Please let me know if you'd like to send a message back with the pigeon.'

'Hmmm...'

'Will that be all, My Lord?' asked Kanakhala.

'Yes. Thank you.'

As Kanakhala shut the door behind her, Bhrigu broke the seal and opened the letter. Its contents were disappointing.

My Lord, we have found some wreckage of our ships at the mouth of the Godavari. They have obviously been blown up. It is difficult to judge whether they were destroyed as a result of sabotage or an accident owing to the goods they carried. It is also difficult to say if all the ships were destroyed or if there are any survivors. Await further instructions.

The words gave Bhrigu information without adding to his understanding of the situation. Not one of the five ships that he had sent to assassinate the Neelkanth and destroy Panchavati had returned or sent a message. The wreckage of at least some of the ships had been discovered, having drifted down the Godavari. Both the possible conclusions were disturbing: either the ships had been destroyed or some of them had been captured. Bhrigu could not afford to send another ship up the Godavari to try and dig deeper. He might end up gifting another well-built warship to the enemy just before the final war. Of course, there was also the possibility that the ships may have succeeded in their mission and had been destroyed subsequently. But Bhrigu simply could not be sure.

Bhrigu would have to wait. Maybe an angry Neelkanth would emerge from the jungles of Dandak. He could rally his followers and attack those allied against him. If that did not happen then the sage would assume that the Neelkanth threat had passed.

Bhrigu rang the bell, summoning the guard outside. He would send a message to the ship at the mouth of the Godavari with orders to return. He would also have to order Meluha and Ayodhya to prepare their armies for battle. Just in case.

Chapter 6

The City that Conquers Pride

It was a full moon night. Shiva stood at the anchored ship's balustrade as he looked into the dark expanse of forest on the Chambal's banks. Deep in the distance was what seemed to be a massive hill made of pure black stone. Shiva had been observing that hill all evening. It was too smooth to be natural. Even more unusually, it had an inverted bowl-like structure at the top that was distinctly a cupola. It was coloured a deeper hue of black as compared to the rest of the hill, which it was certainly not a part of.

'It's man-made, *baba*,' said Kartik.

Shiva, Ganesh and Brahaspati turned towards Kartik, who was crouching, looking at the bank of the river from a lower height. Shiva went down to the same level as Kartik. He observed the area behind the palm tree clearing; he could clearly see the pattern of the ancient Vayuputra image, *Fravashi*. As his eyes traced the path of the slope, he realised that had the incline continued, it would have ended at the very top of the black hill in the distance, at the cupola.

Brahaspati spoke up. 'The slope with the trees is probably the remnant of a very long ramp that was used to carry that stone cupola to the top of the hill.'

Shiva smiled at the precise engineering skills of the

Vasudevs. He had known his mysterious advisors for years. He looked forward to finally meeting their leader.

— ⅄ⓂƱ⇡⊗ —

Daksha gazed at the full moon reflected in the shimmering Saraswati waters. He was standing by the large window of his private palace chamber. He had increasingly isolated himself in the last few months, avoiding meeting people as far as possible. He was especially terrified of meeting Maharishi Bhrigu, convinced as he was, that the maharishi would read his mind and realise that it was Daksha who had foiled the attack on Panchavati in an attempt to save his beloved daughter.

But this period of isolation had done wonders for Daksha and Veerini's relationship. They were conversing, even confiding in each other once again, almost like the first few years of their marriage. Before Daksha had developed ambitions to become the ruler of Meluha.

Veerini walked up to her husband and placed her hand on his shoulder. 'What are you thinking?'

Daksha pulled back from his wife. Veerini frowned. Then she noticed Daksha's hands. He was holding an amulet that showed his chosen-tribe, the self-declared ranking within the caste hierarchy that is adopted by young men and women. It was a subordinate rank, a lowly goat. Many Kshatriyas felt that the goat chosen-tribe was so low that it did not entitle its members to be considered complete Kshatriyas. In Daksha's case it was his father Brahmanayak who had selected his chosen-tribe, clearly reflecting his contempt for his son.

'What's the matter, Daksha?'

'Why does she think I'm a monster? I got rid of her son for her own good. And we didn't abandon Ganesh. He was well taken care of in Panchavati. And how can she imagine that I would even think of getting her husband killed? It wasn't me.'

Veerini stayed silent. Now was not the time to confront her husband with the truth. Had he wanted to, he could have saved Chandandhwaj, Sati's first husband. Daksha may not have got the killing done through commission, but he was complicit by omission. However, weak people never admit that they are responsible for their own state. They always blame either circumstances or others.

'I'm saying once again, Daksha, let's forget everything,' said Veerini. 'You have achieved all you wanted to. You are the Emperor of India. We cannot live in Panchavati anymore. We lost that opportunity long ago. Kali and Ganesh despise us. And I don't blame them for it. Let us take *sanyas,* retreat to the Himalayas and live out the rest of our lives in peace and meditation. We will die with the name of the Lord on our lips.'

'I will not run away!'

'Daksha...'

'Everything is clear to me now. I needed the Neelkanth to conquer Swadweep. He has now served his purpose. Sati will be back once he's gone and we will be happy again.'

A horrified Veerini stared at her husband. 'Daksha, what in Lord Ram's name are you thinking?'

'I can set everything right by...'

'Trust me, the best thing to do is to leave all this alone. You should never even have tried to become emperor. You can still be happy if...'

'Never tried to become emperor? What nonsense! I am the emperor. Not just of Meluha, but of India. You think some barbarian with a blue throat can defeat me? That a chillum-smoking, uncouth ingrate is going to take my family away from me?'

Veerini held her head in despair.

'I made him,' said Daksha. 'And I will finish him.'

— ⅄ⓄƱ↑⊛ —

'My Lord,' exclaimed Parshuram. 'Look.'

Shiva turned to look towards the dense forests beyond the palm tree clearing.

In the distance, they saw a sudden flight of birds flying off into the sky, obviously disturbed by massive movement. The approaching mass was effortlessly pushing trees aside as it forged through the forest.

'They're here,' said Nandi.

Shiva turned around and spoke loudly. 'Ganesh, lower the boats.'

— ⅄ⓄƱ↑⊛ —

Having left a majority of the soldiers onboard, Shiva and his entourage of two hundred were already at the clearing when enormous elephants burst through the jungle. They wore intricately carved, ceremonial forehead gear made of gold. The *human handlers of the elephants,* or *mahouts,* sat just behind the beasts' heads and were secured into their position with ropes. They were covered from head to toe in cane armour, which protected them from the whiplash of the branches that the elephants effortlessly pushed aside. With the aid of gentle prodding with their feet as well as the *hand-held hooks* called *ankush*, the *mahouts* expertly guided the elephants into the clearing. Firmly secured on the backs of the elephants were large, strong wooden *howdahs* fashioned to extend horizontally from the sides of the animals. Completely covered from all sides, they afforded protection to the people inside. Angled slats allowed access to air and a side door to the *howdahs* facilitated entry.

Shiva's eyes were fixed on the first elephant in the line. As it halted, the side door flung open and a rope ladder was flung down. A tall and lanky Pandit clad in a saffron *dhoti* and *angvastram*, climbed down. As soon as the Pandit's feet touched the ground he turned towards Shiva, his hands folded in a respectful Namaste. He had a flowing white beard and a long silvery mane. His wizened face, calm eyes and gentle smile showed a deep understanding of true wisdom. The wisdom of *sat-chit-anand*, of *truth-consciousness-bliss*; the unrelenting bliss of having one's consciousness and mind drowned in truth.

'Namaste, Pandit*ji*,' said Shiva. 'It's an honour to finally meet the Chief Vasudev.'

'Namaste, great Mahadev,' said Gopal politely. 'Believe me, the honour is all mine. I have lived for this moment.'

Shiva stepped forward and embraced Gopal. The surprised Chief Vasudev responded tentatively at first, and then returned the embrace as the open-heartedness of the Neelkanth made him smile.

Shiva stepped back and looked at the large number of men and elephants waiting patiently. 'It's a little crowded, isn't it?'

Gopal smiled. 'This is a small clearing, great Mahadev. We don't really meet too many people.'

'Well, let's climb aboard your elephants and leave for Ujjain.'

'Certainly,' said Gopal as he gestured towards his men.

— ⁂ —

The *howdahs* were surprisingly spacious and could seat up to eight people in relative comfort. The carriage with Gopal and Shiva also carried Sati, Ganesh, Kartik, Brahaspati, Nandi and Parshuram.

'I hope your journey was comfortable,' said Gopal.

'Yes, it certainly was,' said Shiva, before pointing towards Ganesh. 'My son guided us well.'

'The Lord of the People has the reputation of a wise man,' agreed Gopal. 'And stories of the warrior spirit of your other son Kartik have already reached our ears.'

Kartik acknowledged the compliment with a slight nod and folded his hands into a respectful Namaste.

'Pandit*ji*, is it because of the distance that it takes us a day to reach Ujjain, or is it the density of the forest?' asked Shiva.

'A bit of both, great Neelkanth. We have not built any roads from the clearing on the Chambal into the city of Ujjain. We do not really meet a lot of people. But when we do need to travel, we have well-trained elephants that make it possible for us.'

— ⁂ —

The people sitting in the *howdahs* had got used to the sounds of foliage crashing and scraping against the outside of the closed carriage. It had been a long and steady ride, due to which their attention was immediately drawn when the sounds stopped.

Gopal spoke up before any of them could make enquiries. 'We're here.'

As he said this, Gopal pressed a lever to his left. Hydraulic action made three sides of the *howdah*, the left, right and rear, slowly collapse outwards. Support pillars on the sides remained strong and held the *howdah* roof up. Horizontal metal railings ensured no passenger fell out. But none were paying attention to the engineering behind the *howdah*. They were all transfixed by *Ujjain*, the *city that conquers pride*.

The entirely circular city had been laid out within a giant, perfect-square clearing in the dense forest. A sturdy ring of stones, almost ten feet in depth and thirty feet in height, ran around the city; a strong and effective fort wall. The Shipra River, a tributary of the Chambal, which flowed along Ujjain, had been channelled into a moat around the walls. The moat followed the dimensions of the forest clearing. Therefore, the circular city was enclosed within a square moat. The moat was infested with crocodiles. The elephants ambled slowly towards the moat, where much to everyone's surprise, there did not appear to be any bridge.

Shiva had seen many forts across India with retractable drawbridges across their moats. These moats provided effective defence against the siege engines that an enemy used to attack a city's fort walls. He expected the elephants to stop and wait till the drawbridge was lowered. But neither did the elephants stop nor was there any sign of a drawbridge being lowered. Instead, there were twenty armed men who stood on the raised embankments which ran around the moat. As the elephants neared, two men stepped back and pushed hard on what appeared like cobbled ground. A button, the size of a stone block, depressed into the embankment with a soft hiss. This in turn triggered a part of the ground, just before the embankment, to slide sideways, revealing broad, gentle steps descending deep into the earth. The steps led to a well-lit tunnel which the elephants entered. The Vasudev guards went down on their knees in obeisance to the Neelkanth.

Kartik looked at Ganesh, smiling. 'What a brilliant idea, *dada*!'

'Yes. Instead of building a bridge over the moat they have built a tunnel underneath it. And the door to the tunnel merges completely into the cobbled ground, thus being effectively camouflaged.'

'The entire ground around the moat is cobbled. This will

prevent animal tracks from appearing around the tunnel entries.'

'Unless an enemy knows exactly where the entrance is, he can never find a way to cross the moat and enter the city.'

Nandi looked at Gopal. 'Your tribe is brilliant, Pandit*ji*.'

Gopal smiled politely.

As the elephants moved towards the city gates, the passengers noticed large geometric patterns along the walls. They were a series of concentric circles boxed within a single perfect square that skirted the outermost circle. It seemed to symbolise the aerial layout of Ujjain. The circular fort wall of the city was not an accident but the culmination of what the Vasudevs believed was the perfect geometric design.

'We have built the entire city in the form of a *mandal*,' said Gopal.

'What is the *mandal*, Pandit*ji*?' asked Shiva.

'It's a symbolic representation of an approach to spirituality.'

'How so?'

'The square boundary of the moat symbolises *Prithvi*, the land we live on. It is represented by a square that is bound on four sides, just like our land which is also bound by the four directions. The space within the square represents *Prakriti* or *nature*, as the land that we live on is uncultured and a wild jungle. Within it, the path of consciousness is the path of the *Parmatma*, which is represented by the circle.'

'Why a circle?'

'The *Parmatma* is the supreme soul. It is infinite. And if you want to represent infinity through a geometric pattern, you cannot do better than with a circle. It has no beginning. It has no end. You cannot add another side to it. You cannot remove a side from it. It is perfect. It is infinity.'

Shiva smiled.

A bird's eye view of Ujjain would show that within the

circular fort wall, there were five tree-lined ring roads that had been laid out in concentric circles. The outermost road skirted the fort walls. The remaining four were arranged in concentric circles of decreasing diameter. The smallest ring road circled the massive Vishnu temple at the centre of the city. Twenty paved radial roads extended in straight lines from the outermost ring road to the innermost.

These roads effectively divided Ujjain into five zones. The outermost zone, between the fourth and the fifth ring road, had massive wooden stables for various domesticated animals such as cows and horses. The pride of place was occupied by the thousands of well-trained elephants. The next zone, between the third and the fourth ring road, was for the residences of the novices and trainees. It also housed their schools, markets and entertainment districts. The zone between the second and the third ring road housed the Kshatriyas, Vaishyas and Shudras amongst the Vasudevs. The one between the first and the second ring road housed the Brahmins, the community which administered the tribe of Vasudevs. And within the first ring road, in the heart of the city, was the holiest place in Ujjain, their central temple.

The temple was made of black bricks and was what had appeared as a 'hill' to Shiva from the Chambal. Entirely man-made, this temple was in the shape of a perfect, inverted cone, with its base in a circle, supported by a thousand pillars running along its circumference. The conical temple was completely hollow inside and rose in ever smaller circles to reach its peak at a height of a gigantic two hundred metres. A central pillar, made of hard granite, had been erected within the temple, to support the massive weight of the ceiling. A giant cupola, made of black limestone, had been placed at the apex of the temple. Weighing almost forty tonnes, the cupola had been rolled onto the top of the temple by using elephants to pull the stone over a twenty-kilometre long gradual incline. It was the remnants of this incline that Shiva had seen at the Chambal.

Of course, Shiva and his entourage were yet to see this grandeur. As the elephants emerged from the tunnel onto the outer ring road along the inner fort wall, all eyes fell upon the vision that was impossible to miss from any part of Ujjain: the Vishnu temple at the centre. The entire entourage stared in wonder at the awe-inspiring sight. Only Brahaspati voiced what everyone felt within.

'Wow!'

Chapter 7

An Eternal Partnership

Shiva's entourage had been housed in Ujjain's Brahmin zone, abutting the central Vishnu temple. After a comfortable night's rest, Shiva had just finished breakfast with his family when a Vasudev pandit came over and then escorted him to the Vishnu temple. Shiva had a meeting with Gopal in the morning.

The simple grandeur of the massive Vishnu temple became even more apparent as Shiva approached it. It was built on a circular platform, of polished granite stones that were fixed together using metal. Contiguous holes and channels were drilled into stones and then molten metal poured into them; as the metal solidified, it bound the stones together in an unbreakable grip. Although expensive, this technique ensured strength as compared to the stones being bound together by mortar. There were no carvings on the platform at all, in keeping with its simplicity. In fact, statues and carvings would have been an unnecessary distraction given the marvel of engineering that the structure itself was. Steps had been chiselled all along the sides of the circular platform so that visitors could approach the great seventh Vishnu, Lord Ram, from all directions.

A thousand cylindrical pillars made of granite stood atop the platform, their bases buried deep. Lathe machines powered by elephants had achieved perfect evenness and uniform solidity in the pillars, which allowed them to efficiently bear the weight of the conical spire on top. The massive black-stone spire looked as smooth from up close as from a distance. Each stone block was of the same dimension, fitted in perfectly and polished smooth. A giant cupola made of black limestone had been placed on top of the spire. The Vasudev pandit remained silent as he watched Shiva climb the steps of the temple in wonder.

As he entered the main temple, he noticed that the spire was completely hollow from the inside, giving a magnificent view of the giant conical ceiling that enveloped a cavernous hall. This temple, unlike the others that Shiva had seen in India, did not have a separate sanctum sanctorum. The inside of the temple was an open, communal place of worship. The ceiling was ablaze with paintings in bright colours depicting the life of Lord Ram: his birth, his education, his exile and eventual triumphant return. Large frescoes on a prominent wall were devoted to the Lord's life after ascending the throne of Ayodhya; his real enemies, the wars he waged against them, his intense relationship with his inspirational wife, Lady Sita, and his founding of Meluha.

A giant pillar made of white granite stood in the centre of the hall. It was almost two hundred metres high, extending all the way to the top of the conical spire. Shiva was aware that granite was amongst the hardest stones known to man and extremely difficult to carve; hence he was surprised to see the detailed carvings on the pillar. They were giant images of Lord Ram and Lady Sita. Dressed simply, with no royal ornaments or crowns, they wore plain hand-spun cotton, the clothes of the poorest of the poor. These were the garments worn by the divine couple during their fourteen-year exile, most of it in dense jungles. Even more intriguing was the absence of Lord Lakshman and Lord Hanuman, who were normally included in all depictions of the seventh Vishnu. Lady Sita held his right hand from below, as if in support.

'Why has the worst phase of their life been chosen for depiction?' asked Shiva. 'This was when they had been banished from Ayodhya, when Lady Sita was later kidnapped by the demonic King Ravan and Lord Ram fought a fierce battle to rescue her.'

The Vasudev pandit smiled. 'Lord Ram had said that even if his entire life was forgotten, this phase, the one that he had spent in exile along with his wife, his brother and his follower Hanuman, should be remembered by all. For he believed that this was the period that had made him who he was.'

Gopal stood close to the base of the central pillar. Next to him were two ceremonial chairs, one at the feet of the statue of Lady Sita and the other at the feet of Lord Ram. A small ritual fire burned between the two chairs. The presence of the purifying Lord Agni, the God of Fire, signified that no lies could pass between those who sat on either side. Many Vasudev pandits stood patiently behind Gopal.

Gopal bowed to Shiva and joined his hands in a respectful Namaste. 'A Vasudev exists to serve but two purposes. The next Vishnu must arise from amongst us and we must serve the Mahadev, whenever he should choose to come.'

Shiva bowed low to Gopal in reciprocation.

'Every single one of us present here is honoured,' continued Gopal, 'that one of our missions will be fulfilled within our lifetime. We are yours to command, Lord Neelkanth.'

'You are not my follower, Lord Gopal,' said Shiva. 'You are my friend. I have come here to seek your advice, for I'm unable to come to a decision.'

Gopal smiled and gestured towards the chairs.

Shiva and Gopal took their seats as the other Vasudev pandits sat around them on the floor, in neat rows.

— ⅄@Ʊ↑⊗ —

Ganesh, Kartik and Brahaspati had set off on a short tour of Ujjain, accompanied by a Vasudev Kshatriya. Ganesh was deeply interested in the animal enclosures in the outermost zone. Specifically, the elephant stables.

Pulling his horse close to Ganesh's mount, the Vasudev Kshatriya asked, 'Why are you so interested in the elephants, My Lord?'

'They are important for the impending war. They will play a big role if they are as well trained as I hope.'

The Vasudev smiled and prodded his horse forward, leading the way to the enclosures. He was happy to see the son of the Neelkanth interested in their war elephants. The Kshatriyas amongst the Vasudevs had revived the art of training them, much against the advice of the ruling Vasudev pandits. These magnificent beasts had once formed the dominant corps in Indian armies. However, counter tactics had been developed in recent times that offset their fearsome power; foremost among them was the use of specific drums, which disturbed the elephants and made them run amok, resulting in casualties within their own ranks. Most armies had stopped using them. But it was undeniable that well-trained elephants could be devastating on a battlefield. Ganesh had heard about the skilfully trained elephants in the Vasudev army. But their famous reticence made it difficult to believe whether this was true or in fact just rumours. Kartik leaned close to his brother. 'But *dada*, we've seen their elephants already when we rode them here from the Chambal. They are exceptionally well-trained and disciplined.'

'Yes they are, Kartik,' answered Ganesh. 'But those were female elephants that are not used in war. They are used for domestic work, like ferrying people or material. It is the male elephants that are required in times of war.'

'Is that because they're more aggressive?'

'Notwithstanding their otherwise calm temperament, elephants can be provoked, even trained, to be more aggressive. It is difficult to train a female elephant to be more aggressive though, for she will kill only with good reason, for example when her offspring is threatened. A male elephant, however, can be trained to be belligerent far more easily.'

'Why is that so?' asked Kartik. 'Are they less intelligent in comparison?'

'Well, I have heard that on average, the female of the species is smarter. But it's a little more complicated. Elephant herds are matriarchal and it's usually the oldest female who makes all the decisions in the wild: when they will move, where they will feed, who remains in the herd and who gets kicked out.'

'Kicked out?'

'Yes, male elephants are made to leave the herd when they reach adolescence. They either learn to fend for themselves or join nomadic male elephant herds.'

'That's unfair.'

'Nature is not concerned with fairness, Kartik. It's only interested in efficiency. The male elephant is not of much use to the herd. The females are quite capable of defending themselves and taking care of each other's calves. The male is only required when a female wants to have a child.'

'So how do they...'

'During the mating season, the female herd accepts a few nomadic male elephants for some time so that the females can get impregnated. Then the males are abandoned once again.'

Kartik shook his head. 'That's so cold.'

'Well, that is the way it is. The female wild elephants have well-defined social behaviour and group dynamics, enforced by the matriarch. The male elephant, on the other hand, is a nomad with no ties to anyone of his kind. Since he is usually a loner, he would have to be much more aggressive to survive. Therefore he is more difficult to break and one needs to catch him young. But once he is broken in, he is much easier to handle and remains loyal to the *mahout*, his rider. More importantly, unlike a female elephant, he will kill without sufficient reason, just because his *mahout* orders him to do so.'

'My Lords,' said the Vasudev Kshatriya, interrupting the conversation as he pointed forward, 'the elephant stables.'

— ⚹ —

'I guess you already know what I suspect is Evil,' said Shiva, looking at Gopal sitting across the small ritual fire.

'I wouldn't be much of a mind-reader if I didn't,' smiled Gopal. 'But I suppose you are more interested in knowing if I agree.'

'Yes. And if you do, what are your reasons?'

'Well, first things first. Of course we agree with you. Every single Vasudev agrees with you.'

'Why?'

'We are faithful followers of the institution of the Mahadev. We *have* to agree with you, once you have the right answer.'

Shiva caught on to something. 'Once I have the right answer?'

'Yes. Despite so many challenges, you have arrived at the right answer to the question posed to every Mahadev: What is Evil?'

'Does that mean you were already aware of the right answer?'

'Of course. What I did not know were the answers to the questions posed to me. The questions for the institution of the Vishnu are very different. The Mahadev's key question is: What is Evil? For the Vishnu, there are two key questions: What is the next great Good? And *when* does Good become Evil?'

'*When?*'

'Yes. While a Mahadev is an outsider, a Vishnu has to be an insider. His job is to use a great Good to create a new way of life and then lead men to that path. The great Good could be anything: a new technology like the *daivi astras* or a creation like the Somras; it could even be a philosophy. Most leaders just follow what has been ordained by a previous Vishnu. But once in a while a Vishnu emerges who uses a great Good to create a new way of life. Lord Ram used more than one, such as the idea that we can choose our own community rather than being stuck with the community that we are born into. He also allowed for the widespread use of the Somras so that not just the elite but everyone could benefit from its powers. But remember, great Good will, more often than not, lead to great Evil.'

'I understood that from the teachings of Lord Manu. I'd like to hear your reasons for why this is so.'

'We have a philosophical book in our community that answers this question beautifully. It contains the teachings of great philosophers who we have revered over the centuries, like Lord Hari and Lord Mohan. It also contains the teachings of the chiefs of the Vasudev tribe, beginning with our founder, Lord Vasudev. The book is called the "Song of our Lord".'

'*Song of our Lord?*'

'Yes. It is called the *Bhagavad Gita* in old Sanskrit. The Gita has a beautiful line that encapsulates what I want to convey:

Ati sarvatra varjayet. Excess should be avoided; excess of anything is bad. Some of us are attracted to Good. But the universe tries to maintain balance. So what is good for some may end up being bad for others. Agriculture is good for us humans as it gives us an assured supply of food, but it is bad for the animals that lose their forest and grazing land. Oxygen is good for us as it keeps us alive, but for anaerobic creatures that lived billions of years ago, it was toxic and it destroyed them. Therefore, if the universe is trying to maintain balance, we must aid this by ensuring that Good is not enjoyed excessively. Or else the universe will re-balance itself by creating Evil to counteract Good. That is the purpose of Evil: it balances the Good.'

'Why can't there be a Good that does not create Evil? Why can't we establish a way of life that does not imbalance the universe?'

'That is impossible. Our being alive itself creates imbalances. In order to live, we breathe. When we breathe, we take in oxygen and exhale carbon dioxide. Aren't we creating an imbalance by doing so? Isn't carbon dioxide evil for some? The only way we can stop creating evil is if we stop doing good as well; if we stop living completely. But if we have been born, then it is our duty to live. Let us look at it from the perspective of the universe. The only time the universe was in perfect balance was at the moment of its creation. And the moment before that was when it had just been destroyed; for that was when it was in perfect imbalance. Creation and destruction are the two ends of the same moment. And everything between creation and the next destruction is the journey of life. The universe's dharma is to be created, live out its life till its inevitable destruction and then be created once again. We are a downscaled version of the universe.'

'These are just theories, Pandit*ji*.'

'Yes they are. But they explain a lot of things that otherwise seem abstruse.'

'Even if I were to agree with you, how would it work at our level? We are minuscule compared to the universe.'

'Yes, that is true, but the universe lives within us in a minute model of itself. Good and Evil are a way of life for every living entity, including us. Our creation and destruction is through Good and Evil; through balance and imbalance. This is true for animals, plants, planets, stars, everything. What makes us humans special is that we can choose how to control Good and Evil. Most creatures are not given that opportunity. There were giant creatures that lived on Earth many millions of years ago. Climate change made them extinct. We have good reason to believe that they were not responsible for this but were victims of the "Evil" which suddenly reared its head. Humans, however, have been blessed with intelligence, the greatest gift of the Almighty. This allows us to make choices. We have the power to consciously choose Good and improve our lives. We also have the ability to stop Evil before it destroys us completely. Our relationship with nature is different from that of other living creatures. Others have nature's will forced upon them. We have the privilege, at times, of forcing our will upon nature. We can do this by creating and using Good, like we created agriculture. What is forgotten, however, is that many times the Good we create leads to the Evil that will destroy us.'

'Is that where the Mahadev comes in?'

'Yes. Good emerges from creative thinkers and scientists like Lord Brahma. But it needs a Vishnu to harness that Good and lead humanity on the path of progress. Paradoxically, imbalance in society is embedded in this very progress. At other times, a Vishnu arises and intervenes to move society away from the Evil which Good may be leading it to; he creates an alternative Good. By diluting the potency and hence the toxic effects of the Somras waste, Brahaspati was attempting just such an intervention. Had he succeeded, we Vasudevs would inevitably have helped him fulfil that mission. A new way of life based on a benign Somras would have been established. Alas, Brahaspati did not succeed and that path is closed. There exists only the path of the Mahadev now; to confront and then lead people away from the Good that has now become Evil.'

'So a Vishnu can make people move away from a Good that has turned Evil, by offering an alternate Good. But a Mahadev has to ask people to give up a Good without offering anything in return.'

'Yes. And that is not an easy thing to do. The Somras is still Good for a lot of people. It increases their lifespan dramatically and enables them to lead youthful, disease-free and productive lives. But it is evil for society as a whole. We are asking people to sacrifice their selfish interests for the sake of a greater good, while giving them nothing in return. This requires an outsider, a leader, who people will follow blindly. This requires a God who excites fervent devotion. This requires the Mahadev.'

'So you always knew the Somras was Evil?'

'We always knew it would eventually become Evil. What we didn't know is *when*. Remember, Good needs to run its course. If we remove a Good too early from society, we are obstructing the march of civilisation. However, if we remove it too late, we risk the complete destruction of society. So in the battle against Evil, the institution of the Vishnu has to wait for the institution of the Mahadev to decide if the time has come. In our case, a Mahadev emerged and his quest led him to the conclusion that the Somras is Evil. Therefore, we knew that it was time for Evil to be removed. The Somras had to be taken out of the equation.'

Ganesh, Kartik and Brahaspati stood at the entrance to the elephant stables. There were ten circular enclosures, built of massive stone-blocks. Each enclosure could house between eight hundred to one thousand animals. Five of the enclosures were for the female elephants and their calves. The remaining five were reserved for the male elephants that were regularly trained for war.

The female elephant enclosures had massive pools of water at their centre, allowing the beasts to submerge, have a mud bath, and spray themselves with water. The area around the pools was also a social meeting point for the animals. Piles of nutritious leaves around the central pool catered to the voluminous appetites of the animals. The female elephants were also taken to the jungle in small herds to feast on fresh vegetation. These outings also allowed the beasts to rub their skin against trees, which would scale off their dead skin. The resting areas in the female enclosure did not have partitions and they were allowed to mix freely. They usually grouped into herds, led by their specific matriarchs.

The enclosures for the male elephants though, were completely different. To begin with, the shelters were partitioned into separate sections for each elephant. The animal's individual *mahout* lived just above the elephant's enclosure, spending practically all his time with the beast under his control. This developed an attachment on the part of the elephant, for his *mahout*. The beasts were not expected to do any work. They did not rub their skin against rocks and trees to scrub the dead skin off; instead, the *mahouts* bathed them daily. They did not walk to a central area for their meals; instead, freshly-cut plants were supplied to them outside their own specific shelter. The male-elephants had only one task – train for war.

The central area of the male elephant enclosures had been

suitably prepared for that purpose. There was a pool of water in the central enclosure, just like in the female enclosure. But the pool was much deeper. Here the elephants were taught to put their inborn swimming skills to better use; they were taught to ram and sink boats. Around the pool were massive training grounds where the elephants were trained for specific tasks like mowing down opposing army lines. They were also toughened to survive the heat of battle. The Vasudevs were aware of the recent wide-spread use of drums with low frequency sounds to trouble elephants and drive them crazy. To combat this, the Vasudevs had developed an innovative ear plug for them. Furthermore, the elephants were also subjected to a daily bout of low frequency war drums, to help them get used to the sounds.

Ganesh, Kartik and Brahaspati were led into one of the male elephant enclosures. The Vasudev led them directly to one of the animals that he was personally proud of. As he reached the enclosure he called out to the *mahout*, instructing him to bring the elephant out of his shelter. The *mahout* immediately did so, sitting proudly on top of the beast, just behind its head. To Ganesh's surprise, the elephant's eyes had been covered by its head gear. The Vasudev Kshatriya clarified that the covers could be removed easily by the *mahout* from his position. It was used when they wanted the elephant to act solely on the *mahout's* instruction and not based on what it saw. A metallic cylindrical ball was tied to its trunk with a bronze chain. The Vasudev then proceeded to set up a round wooden board as a target. It was roughly three times the size of a human head.

'You may want to step back,' said the Vasudev to the assemblage.

As the visitors stepped back, the Vasudev looked towards the *mahout* and nodded. The man gently pressed his feet into the back of the elephant's ears, in a series of instructions.

The elephant stepped languidly up to the wooden target and shook his head, acknowledging the orders. Then all of a sudden, with the speed of lightning, it swung its mighty trunk, hitting the wooden board smack in the centre with the metallic ball, smashing the target to smithereens.

Kartik whistled softly in appreciation.

Ganesh looked towards the Vasudev. 'Can we make the target a little more interesting?'

The Vasudev was so confident of his elephant that he immediately agreed. Another wooden target was brought in, but placed on a board with wheels at the bottom, as Ganesh had instructed. He painted a smaller circle on the wooden board as a target; it was the size of a human head. In addition, Ganesh asked for the metallic ball tied to the elephant's trunk to be painted a bright red; thus they'd know exactly where the ball would hit the target. The *mahout* was tasked with ensuring that the elephant struck the smaller circle with his metallic ball, even as two other soldiers moved the board around with long ropes. The target simulated a man trying to avoid the elephant's blow. If the elephant could be used to kill a specific man rather than for mass butchery, then one could target the leader of an opposing army, rendering it headless.

Everyone stepped back. The *mahout* kept his eyes pinned to the board as he issued instructions through his feet, making the elephant move slowly towards the target. The soldiers with the ropes were alternately pulling and releasing their lines, keeping the target in constant motion. Suddenly, the *mahout* dug in deep with his right foot and the elephant swung his mighty trunk. The metallic ball hit the centre of the wooden board. It was a killer blow.

Ganesh smiled and swore in the name of the legendary *Lord of the Animals*. 'By the great *Pashupatinath* himself, what an elephant!'

Chapter 8

Who is Shiva?

'What if I had arrived at a different answer?' asked Shiva.

'Then we would have known that it is not yet time for Evil to have risen,' answered Gopal. 'That the Somras is still a force for Good.'

'Isn't that rather simplistic? Did you really believe that a random, untested foreigner would arrive at the right answer to the most important question of this age? Is this the way the system works?'

Gopal smiled. 'In truth, no. The system is very different. If I'm not mistaken, one of the Vasudev pandits has told you about the Vayuputras. Just like we are the tribe left behind by the previous Vishnu, the Vayuputras are the tribe left behind by the previous Mahadev, Lord Rudra. The institutions of the Vishnu and the Mahadev work in partnership with each other. The Vasudevs interact closely with the Vayuputras. We defer to them for the question that has been reserved by Lord Manu for them: What is Evil? And they defer to us for the question that has been reserved for us: What is the next great Good? The Vayuputras control the institution of the Neelkanth. They train possible candidates for the role of the Neelkanth and if they believe that Evil has risen, they allow the identification of a Neelkanth.'

'Kali did tell me about this. But how do the Vayuputras engineer a man's throat turning blue at a time of their choosing?'

'I have heard that they administer some medicine to the candidate as he enters adolescence. The effect of this medicine remains dormant in his throat for years till it manifests itself on his drinking the Somras at a specific age. I believe the Somras reacts with the traces of the medicine already present in the man's throat to make his neck appear blue. All of these activities have to be done at specific time periods in the man's life if this is to happen the way it has been conceptualised. For example, if a man drinks the Somras more than fifteen years after adolescence, his throat will not turn blue even if he had taken the Vayuputra medicine as a child.'

Shiva's eyes opened wide. 'This is seriously complicated!'

'It's a means by which the system could be controlled. As you can imagine, it is only the Vayuputras who could control the process such that a man's throat would turn blue at the appointed hour. People's blind faith in the legend would ensure that they would follow the Neelkanth and Evil would be taken out of the equation. I must mention that for some time now we had begun to believe that the Somras was turning evil. But we do not control the institution of the Neelkanth. The Vayuputras do. And they believed that the Somras was still Good. Therefore, they refused to release their Neelkanth nominee. Even though we were convinced that it was time for the Neelkanth to appear, it did not happen.'

'Did you present your case to the Vayuputras?'

'We did. But they did not agree. The only alternative available to us was to try and find a solution by the Vishnu method, of creating another Good. That is what we were deeply engaged with when an event occurred that stunned everyone, including the Vayuputras.'

Shiva pointed at himself. 'I suddenly emerged out of nowhere.'

'Yes. Nobody really understood what had happened. We knew you were not a Vayuputra-authorised candidate. Many Vayuputras in fact believed that you were a fraud who would be exposed soon enough. Some even wanted you assassinated in the interests of the institution of the Neelkanth. But the leader of the Vayuputras, the Mithra, prevailed upon them and decreed that you be allowed to live out your karma.'

'Why would the Mithra do that?'

'I don't know. That is a mystery. There was a lot of debate amongst us as well. Some of us believed that your emergence proved us right and we should use you to take the Somras out of the equation. There were others who thought that you were an unknown entity who could use the Neelkanth legend to create chaos; therefore we should have nothing to do with you. But there were also those amongst us who believed it is not our job to determine the fate of Evil. That is the sole preserve of the Neelkanth. Still others debated against us that you were after all, with due apologies, a mere barbarian, and chances were you'd arrive at an incorrect conclusion as to what constituted Evil. But the view that finally prevailed was that if the *Parmatma* has chosen to make you the Neelkanth, he will also lead you to the right answer. And we should, with all humility, accept that.'

'And I arrived at the Somras.'

'Doesn't it make the decision obvious then? You were not marked for this task. Yet somehow, you were given the Vayuputra medicine at the right age. Furthermore, you also arrived in Meluha at the appropriate time and were administered the Somras that made your throat turn blue. You were not trained for the role of a Neelkanth. Nobody gave you the answer to the key question. We consciously refused to say anything that would create a bias in your mind. We were very careful in our communications with you regarding your task. And yet, you arrived at the right answer. Isn't this ample proof that you have been chosen by the *Parmatma,* and that you are, truly, the Mahadev? Doesn't it make my decision easy then; that in following you, we are following the *Parmatma* Himself?'

Shiva leaned back on his chair, rubbing his forehead. His brow felt uncomfortable.

— ⅄ⵀⴲ𐊠✡ —

On returning from their short tour of Ujjain, Brahaspati, Ganesh and Kartik joined Sati, Nandi and Parshuram at the guesthouse.

'How is the city, Brahaspati*ji*?' asked Sati.

'Beautiful and well-organised,' answered Brahaspati. 'This city is a better rendition of Lord Ram's principles than even Meluha and Panchavati.'

Sati turned to Ganesh and Kartik. 'My sons, did you like the city?'

Ganesh's tactical mind reflected in his opinion. 'Though Ujjain is nice, what fascinated me were the elephant stables. We watched the *mahouts* tend to these beasts of war, each one of the five thousand of them equivalent to a thousand foot soldiers. I dare say our strength has increased manifold, given that the Vasudevs follow the Neelkanth. With these elephants on our side, we are not as precariously placed as we were earlier.'

'Precariously placed?' asked Parshuram. 'Lord Ganesh, forgive me for disagreeing with you. But how can you say that? We have the Neelkanth with us. That means a vast majority of Indians will be with us. I would say that the odds overwhelmingly favour us.'

'Parshuram, I have always admired your bravery and your utter devotion to the Neelkanth. But hope alone does not win battles. Only an honest evaluation of one's weaknesses, followed by their mitigation, can win the day.'

'What weaknesses can we have? We are led by the Neelkanth. The people will follow him.'

'The people will follow the Neelkanth, but their kings won't. And remember, the people do not control the army, kings do. Emperor Daksha is already against us. So is Emperor Dilipa. Together they have the technological wizardry of Meluha and the sheer numbers of Swadweep. That makes a very strong army.'

'But *dada*,' argued Kartik, 'even the most capable army is of little use if it is led by incapable leaders. Do you see any good generals on their side? I see none.'

Ganesh shook his head and looked at Brahaspati and Nandi before turning back to Kartik. 'They have the best. They have Lord Parvateshwar.'

Sati burst in angrily. 'Ganesh, I have warned you to desist from insulting *Pitratulya*.'

'I know he is *like a father* to you, *maa*,' said Ganesh politely. 'But the truth is Lord Parvateshwar will fight for Meluha.'

'No, he will not. Your father trusts him completely. How can you believe he will escape and join those who tried to kill the Neelkanth?'

'*Maa*, Parvateshwar*ji* has too much honour to escape. He will leave openly, once he has revealed his intentions to *baba*. And trust me, *baba* will let him go. He will not even try to stop him. For they are both honourable men who'd rather bring harm upon themselves than forsake their honour.'

'Indeed, he's an honourable man, Ganesh. Will that sense of duty not bind him to the path of the Neelkanth?'

'No. Parvateshwar*ji* is with *baba* because he is inspired

by him, not because he is honour-bound to follow him. He is supremely committed to one value alone, as in fact all Meluhans are: the protection of Meluha. You can ask any of the Meluhans here.'

Nandi's eyes flashed with anger as the normally affable man stared at Shiva's son, his eyes unblinking. 'Lord Ganesh, I have already made my choice. I live for the Neelkanth. And I will die for the Neelkanth. If that means I have to oppose my country, so be it. I will face my karma for having betrayed my country. But I will not have you questioning my loyalty again.'

Ganesh immediately reached out to Nandi. 'I was not questioning your loyalty, brave Nandi. I was wondering how you think General Parvateshwar will react.'

'I don't know what the General thinks. I only know what I think,' Nandi bristled.

'Well, I know how Parvateshwar thinks,' said Brahaspati. 'I realise this will hurt you Sati, but Ganesh is right. Parvateshwar will not abandon Meluha. In fact, he will battle those who seek to hurt Meluha. And if Shiva, as I hope, decides that the Somras is Evil, then Meluha will be our primary enemy. The battle lines are drawn, my child.'

Wordlessly, Sati looked out of the window at the Vishnu temple and sighed.

— ⁂ —

Shiva rubbed his throbbing brow as he pondered over the mysteries of his childhood.

Gopal bent forward. 'What is it, great Neelkanth?'

'It is not the hand of fate, Pandit*ji*,' said Shiva. 'Neither is it the grand plan of the *Parmatma* that I emerged as the Neelkanth. I suspect it was my uncle's doing. Though how he did all this is a mystery to me.'

'What do you mean?'

'I remember being administered some medicine in my childhood by my uncle. I used to suffer severe burning between my brows from when I was very young. My uncle's medicine helped me calm the burning sensation. The throbbing persists to this day but it is not as bad as it used to be. I still recall his words as he readied the medicine: "We will always remain faithful to your command, Lord Rudra, this is the blood oath of a Vayuputra". Then he'd pricked his index finger and let the blood drop into the potion. It was this mix that he gave to me, and bade me rub it into the back of my throat.'

Gopal's eyes had been pinned on Shiva, fascinated. He briefly looked at the Vasudev pandit from the Ayodhya temple, who was sitting in the first row.

The Ayodhya Vasudev spoke up. 'Great Neelkanth, what was the name of your uncle?'

'Manobhu,' said Shiva.

The stunned Ayodhya Vasudev turned to Gopal. 'In the great name of Lord Ram!'

'What is it?' asked a surprised Shiva.

'Lord Manobhu was your uncle?' asked Gopal.

'*Lord* Manobhu?'

'He was a Vayuputra Lord, one of the Amartya Shpand, a member of the council of six wise men and women who rule the Vayuputras under the leadership of the Mithra.'

'He was a Vayuputra Lord?!!'

'Yes, he was. Many years ago, when we were still trying to convince the Vayuputras about the Somras having turned evil, he was the only one amongst the Amartya Shpand who had agreed with us. Unfortunately, he got no support from the others in the council. The Mithra had also overruled Lord Manobhu.'

'What happened thereafter?'

'I remember that conversation as if it happened yesterday,' said Gopal. 'Lord Manobhu and I had spoken for hours about the Somras. It was obvious that we would not be able to convince the council. He had promised that he would ensure a Neelkanth arose. When I asked him how he would do it, he had said that Lord Rudra would help him. He made me promise that when the Neelkanth did rise, the Vasudevs and I would support him wholeheartedly. I had assured him that this was our duty in any case.'

'And then what happened?'

'Lord Manobhu disappeared. Nobody knew what happened to him. Some believed that he had gone back to his homeland of Tibet since he had been isolated in the Vayuputra council. Some thought he had been killed. I tended to believe the latter for only death could have stopped a man like him from fulfilling his promise. But he did not fail. He created you. Where is he now? How did he contrive to get you invited to Meluha and receive the Somras?'

'He didn't. He died many years ago, at a peace conference, in a cowardly ambush mounted on him by the Pakratis, our local enemies in Tibet.'

'Then how were you invited into Meluha within that specific period? As I've told you, your throat could turn blue only if you drank the Somras within fifteen years of entering adolescence.'

'I don't know,' answered Shiva. 'Nandi just happened to come to Mansarovar at that time, asking for immigrants.'

Gopal looked up at the central pillar of the temple, towards the idols of Lord Ram and Lady Sita. 'It is obvious then. It was the will of the Almighty that events unfolded the way they did.'

Shiva looked at Gopal, his eyes revealing his scepticism that his life was somehow all part of a divine plan.

Gopal tactfully changed the topic. 'My friend, you said that your brow has throbbed from a very young age. Did it happen after a specific incident? Did your uncle give you something which started the burning sensation?'

Shiva frowned. 'No, I've had it for as long as I can remember. I think from when I was born. Whenever I'd get upset, my brow would start throbbing.'

'Would this happen when your heart rate went up dramatically?'

Shiva thought about it for a second. 'Yes. Whenever I am angry or upset, my heart does beat dramatically. Or when I think of Sati, but that is a happy heartbeat.'

Gopal smiled. 'Which means your third eye has been active from the time of your birth, and that is very rare. It convinces me that you are the one chosen by the *Parmatma*.'

'Third eye?'

'It is the region between one's brows. It is believed that there are seven chakras or vortices within the human body which allow the reception and transmission of energy. The sixth chakra is called the *ajna chakra*, the vortex of the third eye. These chakras are activated by yogis after years of practice. Of course, they can also be activated by medicines. The Vayuputras use medicines to activate the third eye of those amongst their young who are potential candidates. But in all my one hundred and forty years, I have yet to hear of a child born with his third eye active.'

'So what is so special about that? It just causes me trouble. It burns dreadfully.'

Gopal smiled. 'That is just a small side-effect. I believe that your active third eye could be one of the reasons why your uncle thought you may have been the chosen one. For it set your body up to easily accept the Vayuputra medicine.'

'How so?'

'The Parihan system of medicine believes that the pineal gland, which exists deep within our brain, is the third eye. It is a peculiar gland. The cortical brain is divided into two equal hemispheres within which most components exist in pairs. The singular pineal gland, however, is present between the two hemispheres. It is a little like an eye and is impacted by light; darkness activates it and light inhibits it. A hyperactive pineal gland is regenerative. This is probably what made your body such that the Somras did not only lengthen your life but also repaired your injuries. Furthermore, the pineal gland is not covered by the blood barrier system.'

'Blood barrier system?'

'Yes. One's blood flows freely throughout the body. But there is a barrier when it approaches the brain. Perhaps this is so as to prevent germs and infections from affecting the brain, the seat of one's soul. However, the pineal gland, despite being lodged between the two hemispheres, is not covered by the blood barrier system. It is obvious why your third eye throbs when you are upset; this is the result of blood gushing through your hyperactive pineal gland.'

Shiva nodded slowly. 'Does this happen to others?'

'Yes, it does. But only amongst those who practice decades of yoga to train their third eye. Or it is active amongst those who are given medicines to stimulate it. What is unnatural about your case is that you were born with an active third eye. This is unheard of.'

Shiva shifted uneasily in his chair. 'So a congenital event just set me up for this role? My uncle could have got it all wrong. I could still be an erroneous choice and maybe I will not achieve the purpose set out for me.'

'But I am sure your uncle did not give you the medicine merely because of your active third eye. He would have judged your character and found you worthy. He must have trained you for this.'

'I was trained by him, no doubt. He taught me ethics, warfare, psychology, arts. But he did not say anything to me about my purported task. '

'You must concede he did an excellent job, though. For you have done well as the Neelkanth.'

'Just luck,' said Shiva wryly.

'Great Neelkanth, a non-believer will credit luck for one's achievements. But a believer in the *Parmatma*, like me, will know that the Neelkanth has achieved all that he has because the *Parmatma* willed it. And that means that the Neelkanth will complete his journey and eventually succeed in taking Evil out of the equation.'

Shiva smiled. 'Sometimes, faith can lean towards over-simplicity.'

Gopal smiled in return. 'Maybe simplicity is what this world needs right now.'

Shiva laughed softly and looked at the audience of Vasudev pandits, listening to the two of them with rapt attention. 'Well, many of my doubts have been cleared. The Somras is the greatest Good and will therefore, one day, certainly emerge as the greatest Evil. But how do we know that the moment has arrived? How can we be sure?'

One of the Vasudev pandits answered. 'We can never be completely sure, great Neelkanth. But if you allow me to express an opinion, we have had a Good which has had a glorious journey for thousands of years and humanity has grown tremendously with its munificence. However, we also know that it is close to becoming Evil now. It is possible that the Somras is taken out of the equation a trifle early, and the world will lose out on a few hundred years of additional good that it could do. But that pales in comparison to the enormous contribution it has already made for thousands of years. On the other hand, there is the risk that the Somras is getting closer to Evil and is likely to lead to chaos and destruction. It is already causing it in substantial measure; I'm not merely referring to the plague of Branga or the deformities of the Nagas. It is believed that the Somras is also responsible for the drastic fall in the birth rate of the Meluhans.'

'Really?'

'Yes,' answered Gopal. 'Perhaps in refusing to embrace death, they pay the price of not seeing their own genes propagate.'

Shiva acknowledged that he'd understood with a gentle nod. The massive images of Lord Ram and Lady Sita that formed the carved central pillar seemed to smile at him. Accepting their blessings, his eyes were drawn farther, towards a grand painting depicting Lord Ram at the feet of Lord Rudra in the backdrop of holy Rameshwaram. Shiva smiled at the giant circle of life. He joined his hands together in a respectful Namaste, closed his eyes and prayed. *Jai Maa Sita. Jai Shri Ram.*

Shiva was resolute as he opened his eyes and beheld Gopal. 'I have made my decision. We will strive to avoid war and needless bloodshed. But should our efforts prove futile, we shall fight to the last man. We will end the reign of the Somras.'

Chapter 9

The Love-struck Barbarian

'Your uncle was a Vayuputra Lord?' asked an amazed Sati.

Sati and Shiva were in their private chambers. Shiva had just related his entire conversation with the Vasudevs and the decision that he had arrived at.

'Not just an ordinary Lord!' smiled Shiva. 'An Amartya Shpand.'

Sati raised her arms and rested them on Shiva's muscular shoulders, her eyes teasing. 'I always knew there was something special about you; that you couldn't have been just another rough tribal. And now I have proof. You have pedigree!'

Shiva laughed loudly, holding Sati close. 'Rubbish! You thought I was an uncouth barbarian when you first laid your eyes on me!'

Sati edged up on her toes and kissed Shiva warmly on his lips. 'Oh, you are still an uncouth barbarian...'

Shiva raised his eyebrows.

'But you are *my* uncouth barbarian...'

Shiva's face lit up with the crooked smile he reserved for Sati; the smile that made her weak in the knees. He held her tight and lifted her up, close to his lips. Her feet dangling in the air, they kissed languidly; warm and deep.

'You are my life,' whispered Shiva.

'You are the sum of all my lives,' said Sati.

Shiva continued to hold her up in the air, embracing her tight, resting his head on her shoulders. Sati had her arms around her husband, her fingers running circles in his hair.

'So, are you going to let me down sometime?' asked Sati.

Shiva just shook his head in answer. He was in no hurry.

Sati smiled and rested her head on his shoulders, content to let her feet dangle in mid-air, playing with Shiva's hair.

— ⁂ —

'Here you go,' said Sati.

Shiva took the glass of milk from her. He liked his milk raw: no boiling, no jaggery, no cardamom, nothing but plain milk. Shiva drained the glass in large gulps, handed it to Sati and sank back on his chair with his feet up on the table. Sati put the glass down and sat next to him. Shiva looked across the balcony, towards the Vishnu temple. He took a deep breath and turned to Sati. 'You're right. Much as I respect Ganesh's tactical thinking, this time he is wrong. Parvateshwar will not leave me.'

Sati nodded emphatically in agreement. 'Without an inspirational leader like him, the armies of Meluha and Swadweep, though strong, will lack motivation as well as sound battle tactics.'

'That is true. But let us hope that the people themselves will rise up in rebellion and there will be no need for war.'

'How can we ensure that, though? If you send the proclamation banning the Somras to the kings, they will make sure that the general public will not know.'

'That's exactly what the Vasudevs and I discussed. My proclamation should not only reach the royalty but every citizen of India directly. The best way to ensure this is to display the proclamation in all the temples. All Indians visit temples regularly, and when they do, they will read my order.'

'And I'm sure the people will be with you. Let's hope that the kings listen to the will of their people.'

'Yes, I cannot think of another way to avoid war. I expect unflinching support from only the royalty of Kashi, Panchavati and Branga. Every other king will make his choice based on selfish interests alone.'

Sati held Shiva's hand and smiled. 'But we have the King of Kings, the *Parmatma* himself with us. We will not lose.'

'We cannot afford to lose,' said Shiva. 'The fate of the nation is at stake.'

— ⁂ —

'Are you sure you can do this, Kartik?' asked Ganesh.

Kartik looked up at his brother with eyes like still waters. 'Of course, I can. I'm your brother.'

Ganesh smiled and stepped away from the elephant mounting platform. Kartik and another diminutive Vasudev soldier were sitting on a *howdah* atop one of the largest bull elephants in the Ujjain stables. The *howdah* had been altered from its standard structure; the roof had been removed and the side walls cut by half. This reduced the protection to the riders, but dramatically improved their ability to fire weapons. Kartik had come up with an innovative idea that used the elephant as more than just a battering ram for enemy lines; instead, it could be used as a high platform from which to fire weapons in all directions.

This strategy envisioned a deliberate and co-ordinated movement of war elephants as opposed to a wild charge.

The issue of the choice of weapons, however, remained. Arrows discharged from elephant-back could never be so numerous as to cause serious damage. The Vasudev military engineers were ready with a solution – an innovative flame-thrower which used a refined version of the liquid black fuel imported from Mesopotamia. This devastating weapon spewed a continuous stream of fire, burning all that stood in its path. The fuel tanks occupied a substantial part of the *howdah,* leaving just enough room for two such weapons and infantrymen. The flame-throwers were not just heavy but released intense heat while operational. Therefore, they required strong operators. But constraints of space in the *howdah* also meant that the operators be, perforce, of short stature. Kartik, along with such a soldier, had volunteered to man this potential inferno.

Ganesh stood at a distance along with Parshuram, Nandi and Brahaspati. He shouted out to his brother. 'Are you ready, Kartik?'

Kartik shouted back, 'I was born ready, *dada*.'

Ganesh smiled as he turned towards the Vasudev commander. 'Let's begin, brave Vasudev.'

The commander nodded and waved a red flag.

Kartik and the Vasudev soldier immediately struck a flame and lit the weapons. Two devilishly long streams of fire burst out and reached almost thirty metres, on both sides of the elephant. A protective covering around the elephant's sides ensured it did not feel the heat. Kartik and the Vasudev had been tasked with reducing some thirty mud statues to ashes. The 'enemy' mud soldiers had been spread out, to test the range and accuracy of the weapon. Though heavy, the fire-weapons were surprisingly manoeuvrable. The *mahout* concentrated on following Kartik's orders and the mud-soldiers were reduced to ashes in no time.

Parshuram turned towards Ganesh. 'These can be devastating in war, Lord Ganesh. What do you think?'

Ganesh smiled as he borrowed a phrase from his father. 'Hell yes!'

'We have transcribed your proclamation, Lord Neelkanth,' said Gopal.

Gopal and Shiva were in the Vishnu temple, near the central pillar. Shiva read the papyrus scroll.

To all of you who consider yourselves the children of Manu and followers of the Sanatan Dharma, this is a message from me, Shiva, your Neelkanth.

I have travelled across our great land, through all the kingdoms we are divided into, met with all the tribes that populate our fair realm. I have done this in search of the ultimate Evil, for that is my task. Father Manu had told us Evil is not a distant demon. It works its destruction close to us, with us, within us. He was right. He told us Evil does not come from down below and devour us. Instead, we help Evil destroy our lives. He was right. He told us Good and Evil are two sides of the same coin. That one day, the greatest Good will transform into the greatest Evil. He was right. Our greed in extracting more and more from Good turns it into Evil. This is the universe's way of restoring balance. It is the Parmatma's *way to control our excesses.*

I have come to the conclusion that the Somras is now the greatest Evil of our age. All the Good that could be wrung out of the Somras has been wrung. It is time now to stop its use, before the power of its Evil destroys us all. It has already caused tremendous damage, from the killing of the Saraswati River *to birth deformities to the diseases that plague some of our kingdoms. For the sake of our descendants, for the sake of our world, we cannot use the Somras anymore.*

Therefore, by my order, the use of the Somras is banned forthwith.

To all those who believe in the legend of the Neelkanth: Follow me. Stop the Somras.

To all those who refuse to stop using the Somras: Know this. You will become my enemy. And I will not stop till the use of the Somras is stopped. This is the word of your Neelkanth.

Shiva looked up and nodded.

'This will be distributed to all the pandits in all the Vasudev temples across the Sapt Sindhu,' said Gopal. 'Our Vasudev Kshatriyas will also travel to other temples across the land. They will carry your proclamation carved on stone tablets and fix them on the walls of temples. All of them will be put up on the same night, one year from now. The kings will have no way to control it since it will be released simultaneously all over. Your word will reach the people.'

This is exactly what Shiva wanted. 'Perfect, Pandit*ji*. This will give us one year to prepare for war. I would like to be in Kashi when this proclamation is released.'

'Yes, my friend. Until then, we need to prepare for war.'

'I also need to use this one year to uncover the identity of my true enemy.'

Gopal frowned. 'What do you mean, great Neelkanth?'

'I don't believe that either Emperor Daksha or Emperor Dilipa is capable of mounting a conspiracy of this scale. They are obviously being led by someone. That person is my real enemy. I need to find him.'

'I thought you know who your real enemy is.'

'Do you know his identity?'

'Yes, I do. And you are right. He is truly dangerous.'

'Is he so capable, Pandit*ji*?'

'A lot of people are capable, Neelkanth. What makes a capable person truly dangerous is his conviction. If we believe that we're fighting on the side of Evil, there is moral weakness in our mind. Somewhere deep within, the heart knows that we're wrong. But what happens if we actually believe in the righteousness of our cause? What if your enemy genuinely believes that he is the one fighting for Good and that you, the Neelkanth, are fighting for Evil?'

Shiva raised his eyebrows. 'Such a person will never stop fighting. Just like I won't.'

'Exactly.'

'Who is this man?'

'He is a maharishi, in fact most people in India revere him as a *Saptrishi Uttradhikari*,' said Gopal, using the Indian term for the *successors of the seven great sages of yore*. 'His scientific knowledge and devotion to the *Parmatma* are second to none in the modern age. His immense spiritual power makes emperors quake in his presence. He leads a selfless, frugal life in Himalayan caves. He comes down to the plains only when he feels that India's interests are threatened. And he has spent the whole of last year in either Meluha or Ayodhya.'

'Does he genuinely believe that the Somras is Good?'

'Yes. And he believes that you are a fraud. He knows that the Vayuputras did not select you. In fact, we believe that the Vayuputras are on his side. For who else could have given him the *daivi astras* that were used in the attack at Panchavati?'

'Is there a possibility that he could have made the *daivi astras* himself? That is what I assumed must have happened.'

'Trust me, that is not possible. Only the Vayuputras have the know-how to make the *daivi astras*. Nobody else does; not even us.'

Shiva stared at Gopal, stunned. 'I didn't expect the Vayuputras to support me; I am not one of them. But I thought that they would at least be neutral.'

'No, my friend. We must assume that the Vayuputras are on the side of your enemy. They may even be in agreement with him about the Somras still being Good.'

Shiva breathed deeply. This man sounded formidable. 'Who is he? '

'Maharishi Bhrigu.'

— ⅄ⵙꓵ⇞⊗ —

Bhrigu's eyes scanned the distance, observing the Meluhan soldiers practising their art. Daksha stood next to him with his eyes pinned to the ground. Mayashrenik, the stand-in general of the Meluhan army in the absence of Parvateshwar, was a few metres ahead.

Bhrigu said softly, without turning towards Daksha, 'Your soldiers are exceptional, Your Highness.'

Daksha did not answer as he continued to study the ground.

Bhrigu shook his head. 'Your Highness, I said that your soldiers are well trained.'

Daksha turned his attention towards Bhrigu. 'Of course, My Lord. I'd already mentioned this to you. There is no need to worry. To begin with, a war is unlikely. But even the possibility of war leaves little to fear for I have the combined Ayodhyan and Meluhan armies at my command which...'

'We have much to fear,' said Bhrigu, interrupting Daksha. 'Your soldiers are well trained. But they are not well led.'

'But Mayashrenik...'

'Mayashrenik is not a leader. He is a great second-in-command. He will follow orders unquestioningly and implement them effectively. But he cannot lead.'

'But...'

'We need someone who can think; someone who can strategise; someone who is willing to suffer for the sake of the greater good. We need a leader.'

'But I am their leader.'

Bhrigu looked contemptuously at Daksha. 'You are not a

leader, Your Highness. Parvateshwar is a leader. But you sent him off with that fraud Neelkanth. I don't know if he is alive, or even worse, if he has switched loyalties to that barbarian from Tibet.'

Daksha took offence at Bhrigu's criticism. 'Parvateshwar is not the only great warrior in Meluha, My Lord. We can use Vidyunmali. He's a capable strategist and would make a great general.'

'I don't trust Vidyunmali. And I'd like to suggest that Your Highness is hardly the best judge of people.'

Daksha promptly went back to studying the ground that had held his fascination a few moments back.

Bhrigu took a deep breath. This discussion was pointless. 'Your Highness, I'm going to Ayodhya. Please make the arrangements.'

'Yes, Maharishi*ji*,' said Daksha.

— ⁂ —

Bhagirath and Anandmayi were in the last clearing of the forests of Dandak. It would take a few more months to reach Branga and from there on, Kashi. But the remaining journey was the last thing on Bhagirath's mind.

'What have they been talking about for so long?' asked Bhagirath.

Anandmayi turned in the direction of Bhagirath's gaze. Ayurvati and Parvateshwar were gesticulating wildly. But the tone of their voices, true to Meluhan character, remained soft and polite. They seemed to be in the middle of an intense debate.

Anandmayi shook her head. 'I don't have supernatural abilities. I can't hear what they're saying.'

'But I can take a good guess,' said Bhagirath. 'I hope that Ayurvati succeeds.'

Anandmayi turned towards Bhagirath, frowning.

'Ayurvati has already made her decision. She is with us. She is with the Mahadev. And now, I think, she is trying to convince Parvateshwar.'

Anandmayi knew that her brother was probably right, but love was forcing her to hope. 'Bhagirath, Parvateshwar has not made his decision as yet. He is devoted to the Mahadev. Don't assume...'

'Trust me, if it comes down to a war and he has to choose between Lord Shiva and his precious Meluha, your husband will choose Meluha.'

'Bhagirath, shut up!'

Bhagirath turned towards Anandmayi, irritated. 'I am only speaking the truth.'

'That is a matter of opinion.'

'I am the crown prince of Ayodhya. Many will say my opinion is the truth.'

Anandmayi tapped her brother on his head. 'And I, as the crown prince's elder sister, have the right to shut him up any time I choose!'

— ⁂ —

'Parvateshwar, you have not thought this through,' said Ayurvati.

Parvateshwar smiled sadly. 'I have not been thinking of much else in the last few months. I know the path that I must take.'

'But will you be able to act against the living God you worship?'

'Since there is no other choice, I must.'

'But Lord Ram had said that we must protect our faith. The Mahadevs and the Vishnus are our living Gods. How do we protect our religion if we do not fight alongside our living Gods?'

'You are confusing faith and religion. They are two completely different things.'

'No, they are not.'

'Yes, they are. The Sanatan Dharma is my religion. But it is not my faith. My faith is my country. My faith is Meluha. Only Meluha.'

Ayurvati sighed and looked up at the sky. She shook her head and turned back towards Parvateshwar. 'I know how devoted you are to the Neelkanth. Can you go to war against the Lord; do you have it in your heart to even harm him?'

Parvateshwar breathed deeply, his eyes moist. 'I will fight all who seek to harm Meluha. If Meluha must be conquered, it will be over my dead body.'

'Parvateshwar, do you really think that the Somras is not Evil? That it should not be banned?'

'No. I know it should be banned. I have already stopped using the Somras. I stopped using it the day Brahaspati told us about all the evil that it has been responsible for.'

'Then why are you willing to fight to defend this *halahal*?' asked Ayurvati, using an old Sanskrit term for *the most potent poison in the universe.*

'But I am not defending the Somras,' said Parvateshwar. 'I'm defending Meluha.'

'But the both of them are on the same side,' said Ayurvati.

'That is my misfortune. But defending Meluha is my life's purpose; this is what I was born to do.'

'Parvateshwar, Meluha is not what it used to be. You're well aware of the fact that Emperor Daksha is no Lord Ram. You are fighting for an ideal that does not exist anymore. You are fighting for a country whose greatness lives on only in memory. You are fighting for a faith that has been corrupted beyond repair.'

'That may be so, Ayurvati. But this is my purpose; to fight and die for Meluha.'

Ayurvati shook her head in irritation, but her voice was unfailingly polite. 'Parvateshwar, you are making a mistake. You are pitting yourself against your living God. You are defending the Somras, which even you believe has turned evil. And you are doing all this to serve some "purpose". Does the purpose of defending Meluha justify all the mistakes that you know you are making?'

Parvateshwar spoke softly, '*Shreyaan sva dharmo vigunaha para dharmaat svanushthitat.*'

Ayurvati smiled ruefully as she recalled the old Sanskrit *shloka*, a *couplet* attributed to Lord Hari, after whom the city of Hariyupa had been named. It meant that it was better to commit mistakes on the path that one's soul is meant to walk on, than to live a perfect life on a path that is not meant for one's soul. Discharge one's own *swadharma, personal law*, even if tinged with faults, rather than attempt to live a life meant for another.

Ayurvati shook her head. 'How can you be sure that this is your duty? Should you just be true to the role the world has foisted upon you? Aren't you blindly obeying what society is forcing you to do?'

'Lord Hari also said that those who allow others to dictate their own duties are not living their own life. They are, in fact, living someone else's life.'

'But that is exactly what you are doing. You are allowing others to dictate your duties. You are allowing Meluha to dictate the purpose of your soul.'

'No, I am not.'

'Yes, you are. Your heart is with Lord Shiva. Can you deny that?'

'No, I can't. My heart is with the Neelkanth.'

'Then how do you know that protecting Meluha is your duty?'

'Because I know,' said Parvateshwar firmly. 'I just know that this is my duty. Isn't that what Lord Hari had said? Nobody in the world, not even God, can tell us what our duty is. Only our soul can. All we have to do is surrender to the language of silence and listen to the whisper of our soul. My soul's whisper is very clear. Meluha is my faith; protecting my motherland is my duty.'

Ayurvati ran her hand over her bald pate, touching her *choti*, the knot of hair signifying Brahmin antecedents. She turned to look at Anandmayi and Bhagirath in the distance. She knew that there was nothing more to be said.

'You will be on the losing side, Parvateshwar,' said Ayurvati.

'I know.'

'And you will be killed.'

'I know. But if that is my purpose, then so be it.'

Ayurvati shook her head and touched Parvateshwar's shoulder compassionately.

Parvateshwar smiled wanly. 'It will be a glorious death. I shall die at the hands of the Neelkanth.'

Chapter 10

His Name Alone Strikes Fear

Reclining in an easy chair, his legs outstretched on a low table, Shiva, along with Sati, contemplated the Ujjain temple from their chamber balcony. Ganesh leaned against the doorway, while Kartik had balanced himself on the railing. Shiva had just related to his family his entire conversation with the Vasudevs, including the identity of their real enemy.

The Neelkanth looked up at the evening sky before turning towards Sati. 'Say something.'

'What can I say?' asked Sati. 'Lord Bhrigu... Lord Ram, be merciful...'

'He can't be all that powerful.'

Sati looked up at Shiva. 'He is one of the *Saptrishi Uttradhikaris*. His spiritual and scientific powers are legendary. But it is not the fear of his powers which has shaken me. It is the fact that a man of his strength of character has chosen to oppose us.'

'Why would you say that?'

'He is singularly unselfish and a man of unimpeachable moral integrity.'

'And yet, he sent five ships to eliminate us.'

'Yes. He must truly believe that the Somras is Good, and we are Evil to try to stop its usage. If he is convinced of it, could it be possible that we are wrong?'

Kartik was about to interject when Shiva raised his hand.

'No,' said Shiva. 'I am sure. The Somras is Evil and it has to be stopped There is no turning back.'

'But Lord Bhrigu...' said Sati.

'Sati, why would a man of such immense moral character use the *daivi astras*, which we all know have been banned by Lord Rudra himself?'

Sati looked at Shiva silently.

'Lord Bhrigu's attachment to the Somras has made him do this,' said Shiva. 'He thinks he is doing it for the greater good. But, in truth, he has become attached to the Somras. It is attachment that makes people forget not only their moral duties but even who they really are.'

Kartik finally spoke up. '*Baba* is right. And if this is what the Somras can do to a man of Lord Bhrigu's stature, then it surely must be Evil.'

Shiva nodded before turning back to Sati. 'What we are doing is right. The Somras must be stopped.'

Sati didn't say anything.

'We need to concentrate our minds on the impending war,' said Shiva. 'They admittedly have a leader of the calibre of Lord Bhrigu, along with the armies of Meluha and Ayodhya. The odds are stacked against us. How do we remedy this?'

'Divide their capabilities,' said Kartik.

'Go on.'

Kartik went into his bedchamber and returned with a map. '*Baba*, would you please...'

As Shiva lifted his feet off the table, Kartik laid out the map and looked at Ganesh before speaking. '*Dada* and I agreed that their strength lies in the technological wizardry of Meluha coupled with the sheer numbers of Ayodhya. If we can divide that, it would even out the odds.'

'By ensuring that Meluha and Ayodhya joined hands and

conspired to assassinate us at Panchavati, Lord Bhrigu has played his cards well. When they realise that I'm alive, they will be compelled to treat me as a common foe and hence ally with each other. After all, an enemy's enemy is a friend.'

Kartik smiled. 'I wasn't talking about breaking their alliance, *baba,* but dividing their capabilities.'

Sati, who had been studying the map all this while, was struck by the obvious. 'Magadh!'

'Exactly,' said Kartik as he tapped on the location of Magadh. 'The roads in Swadweep are either pathetic or non-existent. That is why the armies, especially the big ones, use rivers to mobilise. The Ayodhyan army will not come to Meluha's aid by cutting through dense forests. They will sail down the Sarayu in ships, then up the Ganga to the newly built pathway to Devagiri that Meluha has constructed.'

Shiva nodded. 'The Ayodhyan ships would have to pass Magadh, at the confluence of the Sarayu and Ganga rivers. If Magadh blockades that river, the ships will not be able to pass through. We can hold back their massive army with only a small naval force from Magadh.'

'Right,' said Kartik.

A smiling Shiva patted Kartik on his shoulder, 'I'm impressed, my boy.'

Kartik smiled at his father.

Sati looked at Shiva. 'We must first rally Prince Surapadman to our side. Bhagirath had told me it's the Magadhan prince who makes all the decisions and not his father King Mahendra.'

Shiva concurred before turning towards Ganesh.

Ganesh remained silent. He seemed a little unsettled by this new development.

— ⁂ —

'That is a good idea,' said Gopal.

Shiva, Sati, Ganesh and Kartik were with Gopal at the Vishnu temple.

'It should be relatively easy to bring Magadh to our side,' continued Gopal. 'King Mahendra is old and indecisive but his son, Surapadman, is a fearsome warrior and a brilliant tactician. And most importantly, he is a calculating and ambitious man.'

'His ambition should make him smell the opportunities in the coming war,' said Shiva. 'He can use it to bolster his position and declare independence from Ayodhya.'

'Exactly,' said Sati. 'Whatever may be the reason behind his choosing to back us, an alliance with him will help us win the war.'

Gopal suddenly noticed a pensive Ganesh. 'Lord Ganesh?'

Ganesh reacted with a start.

'Does something about this plan trouble you?' asked Gopal.

Ganesh shook his head. 'Nothing that needs to be mentioned at this point of time, Pandit*ji*.'

Ganesh was worried that he had inadvertently ruined any likelihood of an alliance with Magadh, for he had killed the elder Magadhan prince, Ugrasen. He had done so while trying to save an innocent mother and her son from Ugrasen. He hoped Surapadman was not aware of his identity.

'*Dada* and I have discussed this,' said Kartik. 'And we believe we should not assume Magadh will come to our side. We should also be prepared to conquer Magadh, if need be.'

'Well, hopefully that situation will not arise,' said Shiva, turning towards Ganesh. 'But yes, we should make contingent plans to fight Magadh. It could be one of our opening gambits in the war.'

'Then I shall start making plans for our departure to Magadh,' said Gopal.

'Are you going to come with us, Pandit*ji*?' asked a surprised Shiva. 'That would reveal your allegiance openly.'

'There was a time to remain hidden, my friend,' said Gopal. 'But now we need to come out in the open, for the battle with Evil is upon us. We have to pick our side openly. There are no bystanders in a holy war.'

— ⅄ⓄƱ⇡⊛ —

Parvateshwar and Anandmayi rode their favourite steeds, whispering to each other. He had leaned a bit to his right, holding Anandmayi's hand. He had just told her that if it came to a war, he would have no choice but to fight on the side of Meluha. Anandmayi, in turn, had told Parvateshwar that she would have no choice but to oppose Meluha.

'Aren't you even going to ask me why?' asked Anandmayi.

Parvateshwar shook his head. 'I don't need to. I know how you think.'

Anandmayi looked at her husband, her eyes moist.

'And I guess you know how I think,' said Parvateshwar. 'For you didn't ask me either.'

Anandmayi smiled sadly at Parvateshwar, squeezing his hand.

'What do we do now?' asked Parvateshwar.

Anandmayi took a deep breath. 'Keep riding together.'

Parvateshwar stared at his wife.

'Till our paths allow us...'

— ⅄ⓄƱ⇡⊛ —

Shiva leaned against the balustrade of the ship as it sailed gently down the Chambal. Beyond the banks, he could see dense forests. There was no sign of human habitation for miles in any direction. He looked back at the five ships following them, a small part of the fifty-ship Vasudev fleet. It had taken the Vasudevs a mere two months to mobilise for departure.

'What are you thinking, my friend?' asked Gopal.

Shiva turned to the chief Vasudev. 'I was thinking that the primary source of Evil is human greed. It's our greed to extract more and more from Good that turns it into Evil. Wouldn't it be better if this was controlled at the source itself? Can we really expect humans to not be greedy? How many of us would be willing to control our desire to live for two hundred years? The dominance of the Somras over many thousands of years has admittedly done both Good and Evil, but it will soon perish for all practical purposes. Isn't it fair to say then that it has served no purpose in the larger scheme of things? Perhaps it would have been better had the Somras not been invented. Why embark on a journey when you know that the destination takes you back to exactly where you began?'

'Are there any journeys which do not take you back to where you began?'

Shiva frowned. 'Of course there are.'

Gopal shook his head. 'If you aren't back to where you began, all it means is that the journey isn't over. Maybe it will take one lifetime. Maybe many. But you will end your journey exactly where you began. That is the nature of life. Even the universe will end its journey exactly where it began – in an infinitesimal black hole of absolute death. And on the other side of that death, life will begin once again in a massive big bang. And so it will continue in a never-ending cycle.'

'So what's the point of it all?'

'But that is the biggest folly, great Neelkanth; to think that we are on this path in order to get somewhere.'

'Aren't we?'

'No. The purpose is not the destination but the journey itself. Only those who understand this simple truth can experience true happiness.'

'So are you saying that the destination, even purpose, does not matter? That the Somras had to just experience all this; to create so much Good for millennia and then to descend into creating Evil in equal measure. And then to have a Neelkanth rise who would end its journey. If one believes this, then in the larger scheme of things, the Somras has achieved nothing.'

'Let me try to put it another way. I'm sure you're aware of how it rains in India, right?'

'Of course I am. One of your scientists had explained it to me. I believe the sun heats the waters of the sea, making it rise in the form of gas. Large masses of this water vapour coalesce into clouds, which are then blown over land by monsoon winds. These clouds rise when they hit the mountains, thus precipitating as rain.'

'Perfect. But you have only covered half the journey. What happens after the water has rained upon us?'

Shiva's knowing smile suggested that he was beginning to follow.

Gopal continued. 'The water finds its way into streams and then rivers. And finally, the river flows back into the sea. Some of the water that comes as rain is used by humans, animals, plants – anything that needs to stay alive. But ultimately, even the water used by us escapes into the rivers and then back into the sea. The journey always ends exactly where it began. Now, can we say that the journey of the water serves no purpose? What would happen to us if the sea felt that there is no point to this journey since it ends exactly where it begins?'

'We would all die.'

'Exactly. Now, one may be tempted to think that this

journey of water results in only Good, right? Whereas the Somras has caused both Good and Evil.'

'But of course,' Shiva smiled wryly, 'you would disabuse me of any such notion!'

Gopal's smile was equally dry. 'What about the floods caused by rains? What about the spread of disease that comes with the rains? If we were to ask those who have suffered from floods and disease, they may hold that rain is evil.'

'Excessive rains are evil,' corrected Shiva.

Gopal smiled and conceded. 'True. So the journey of water from the sea back into the sea serves a purpose as it makes the journey of life possible on land. Similarly, the journey of the Somras served a purpose for many, including you. For your purpose is to end the journey of the Somras. What would you do if the Somras hadn't existed?'

'I can think of so many things! Lazing around with Sati for example. Or whiling away my time immersed in dance and music. That would be a good life...'

Gopal laughed softly. 'But seriously, hasn't the Somras given purpose to your life?'

Shiva smiled. 'Yes it has.'

'And your journey has given purpose to my life. For what is the point of being a chief Vasudev if I can't help the next Mahadev?'

Shiva smiled and patted Gopal on his back.

'Rather than the destination it is the journey that lends meaning to our lives, great Neelkanth. Being faithful to our path will lead to consequences, both good as well as evil. For that is the way of the universe.'

'For instance, my journey may have a positive effect on the future of India. But it will certainly be negative for those who are addicted to the Somras. Perhaps that is my purpose.'

'Exactly. Lord Vasudev had held we should be under no

illusion that we are in control of our own breathing. We should realise the simple truth that we are "being breathed"; we are being kept alive because our journey serves a purpose. When our purpose is served, our breathing will stop and the universe will change our form to something else, so that we may serve another purpose.'

Shiva smiled.

Chapter 11

The Branga Alliance

Parvateshwar's entourage had sailed up the Madhumati to the point where it broke off from the mighty Branga River. There they had dropped anchor as they waited for Bhagirath's return. Bhagirath's ship had turned east and sailed down the main distributary of the Branga, the massive Padma. A week later his ship docked at the port of Brangaridai, the capital city of the Branga kingdom.

King Chandraketu had been informed of Bhagirath's arrival. The King of Branga had ensured that the Prince of Ayodhya was escorted with due honour to his palace. As Bhagirath was led into the private palace rather than the formal court, he acknowledged that Chandraketu was not treating him as the crown prince of Swadweep, but as a friend.

Bhagirath found Chandraketu waiting at the palace door along with his wife and daughter. The King of Branga folded his hands in a formal Namaste. 'How are you doing, brave Prince of Ayodhya?'

Bhagirath smiled and bowed his head as he returned the Namaste. 'I'm doing well, Your Highness.'

Chandraketu looked at his consort with a fond smile. 'Prince Bhagirath, this is my wife Queen Sneha.'

Bhagirath bowed towards Sneha. 'Greetings, Your Highness.'

A chivalrous Bhagirath then went down on one knee to face the six-year-old girl who looked at him with twinkling eyes. 'And who might this lovely lady be?'

Chandraketu smiled. 'That is my daughter, Princess Navya.'

'Namaste, young lady,' said Bhagirath.

Navya slid behind her mother, hiding her face.

Bhagirath smiled broadly. 'I am a friend of your father, my child. You don't have to be afraid of me.'

'You smell funny...' whispered Navya, sticking her face out.

A startled Bhagirath burst into laughter.

Chandraketu folded his hands together. 'My apologies, Prince Bhagirath. She can be a little direct sometimes.'

Bhagirath controlled his mirth. 'No. No. She's speaking the truth.' He turned to Navya. 'But young lady, I was always taught to be polite to strangers. Don't you think that's important as well?'

'Politeness does not mean lying,' said Navya. 'Lord Ram had said we should always speak the truth. Always.'

Bhagirath raised his eyebrows in surprise before turning to Chandraketu. 'Wow. Quoting Lord Ram at this age? She's smart.'

'Well, she is very intelligent,' said an obviously proud Chandraketu.

Bhagirath turned fondly towards Navya. 'Of course you're right, my child. I carry the odour of a long and rigorous voyage. I will make sure I bathe before I meet you next. You will not find my smell offensive the next time, I wager.'

Chandraketu laughed. 'Be warned, great Prince, little Navya has never lost a bet.'

Navya smiled at her mother. 'He does not seem all that bad, *maa*. I guess not all Ayodhyan royals are bad...'

Bhagirath laughed once again. 'King Chandraketu, I think we should retire to your chambers before any more assaults are made upon my dignity.'

A smiling Chandraketu nodded to his wife and then turned to Bhagirath. 'Come with me, Prince Bhagirath.'

— ⁂ —

'*Baba*...' whispered Ganesh.

Ganesh had just entered Shiva's chambers in the central ship of the joint Vasudev-Naga convoy.

Shiva looked up as he put the palm-leaf book aside. 'What is it, my son?'

A nervous Ganesh whispered, 'I need to speak with you.'

Shiva pointed to the chair next to him as he lifted his feet off the table.

Ganesh took a deep breath. '*Baba*, there may be some complications with Magadh.'

Shiva smiled. 'I was wondering when you were going to bring that up.'

Ganesh frowned. 'You knew?'

'I know Ugrasen was killed by a Naga. I understand that complicates things.'

Ganesh kept silent.

'Well? Do you know who killed him? If it was a criminal act then we should support Surapadman. Not only would justice be served but it would also help pull Magadh to our side.'

Ganesh didn't say anything.

Shiva frowned. 'Ganesh?'

'It was me,' confessed Ganesh.

Shiva's eyes widened. 'Well... this certainly complicates things...'

Ganesh stayed mute.

'Did you have a good reason?'

'Yes I did, *baba*.'

'What was it?'

'The Chandravanshi nobility has always patronised the tradition of bull racing. In the quest for the lightest riders, the sport has degenerated to the extent that innocent young boys are being kidnapped and forced to ride the charging bulls. This cruel sport has left innumerable children maimed and some have even died painful deaths.'

Shiva looked at Ganesh in horror. 'What kind of barbaric men would do that to children?'

'Men like Ugrasen. I found him trying to kidnap a young boy. The boy's mother was refusing to let him go, so Ugrasen and his men were on the verge of killing her. I had no choice...'

Shiva recalled something that Kali had mentioned. 'Is that the time when you were seriously injured?'

'Yes, *baba*.'

Shiva breathed deeply. Ganesh had once again shown tremendous character, fighting injustice even at risk to his own life. Shiva was proud of his son. 'You did the right thing.'

'I'm sorry if I have complicated the issue.'

Shiva smiled and shook his head.

'What happened, *baba*?'

'The ways of the world are really strange,' said Shiva. 'You protected an innocent child and his mother from an immoral prince. The Magadhans though, did not hesitate to spread a lie that Ugrasen died defending Magadh from a Naga terrorist attack. And people chose to believe that lie.'

Ganesh shrugged his shoulders. 'The Nagas have always been treated this way. The lies never stop.'

Shiva looked up at the ceiling of his cabin.

'What do we do now?' asked Ganesh.

'Nothing different. We'll stick to the plan. Let us hope

that Surapadman is ambitious enough to realise where the interests of Magadh lie.'

Ganesh nodded.

'And you stay in Kashi,' continued Shiva. 'Don't come with us to Magadh.'

'Yes, *baba*.'

— ⅄ⵔⵡⵠⴲ —

Fists clenched, Chandraketu tried hard to suppress the anger welling up within him. Bhagirath had just told him about the Somras waste being responsible for the plague that had been devastating Branga for generations.

'By all the fury of Lord Rudra,' growled Chandraketu, 'my people have been dying for decades, our children have suffered from horrific diseases and our aged have endured agonising pain, all so that privileged Meluhans can live for two hundred years!'

Bhagirath stayed silent, allowing Chandraketu to vent his righteous anger.

'What does the Lord Neelkanth have to say? When do we attack?'

'I will send word to you, Your Highness,' said Bhagirath. 'But it will be soon, perhaps in a few months. You must mobilise your army and be ready.'

'We will not only mobilise our army, but every single Branga who can fight. This is not just a war for us. This is vengeance.'

'My sailors are unloading some gifts from the Nagas and from Parshuram at the Brangaridai docks. As promised by the Neelkanth, all the materials required to make the Naga medicine are being delivered to you. A Naga scientist is also going to stay here and teach you how to make the medicine yourselves. These materials, combined with the herbs you already have in your kingdom, should keep you supplied with the Naga medicine for three years.'

Chandraketu smiled slightly. 'The Lord Neelkanth has honoured his word. He is a worthy successor to Lord Rudra.'

'That he is.'

'But I don't think we will need this much medicine. The combined might of Ayodhya and Branga will ensure the defeat of Meluha well within three years. We will stop the manufacturing of the Somras and destroy their waste facility in the Himalayas. Once the waste stops poisoning the Brahmaputra, there will be no plague and no further need for any medicine.'

Bhagirath narrowed his eyes, hesitating.

'What is it, Prince Bhagirath?'

'Your Highness, Ayodhya is probably not going to be with us in this war.'

'What? Are you saying Ayodhya may side with Meluha?'

'Yes. In fact, they have already thrown in their lot with Meluha.'

'Then why...'

Bhagirath completed the question. 'Why do I act against my own father and kingdom?'

'Yes. Why do you?'

'I am a follower of my Lord, the great Neelkanth. His path is true. And I will walk on it, even if it entails fighting my own kinsmen.'

Chandraketu rose and bowed to Bhagirath. 'It requires a special form of greatness to fight one's own for the ideal of justice. As far as I am concerned, you are fighting for justice for the Brangas. I shall remember this gesture, Prince Bhagirath.'

Bhagirath smiled, happy with the way the conversation had

progressed. He had accomplished the task that Shiva had given him, but in such a manner as to win the personal allegiance of the fabulously wealthy King of Branga. This alliance would prove useful when he made his move for the throne of Ayodhya. Having heard of Chandraketu's sentimental nature, Bhagirath thought it wise to seal the alliance in blood.

He pulled out his knife, slit his palm and held it up to the king. 'May my blood flow in your veins, my brother.'

A moist-eyed Chandraketu immediately pulled out his own knife, slit his palm and held it against Bhagirath's bloodied hand. 'And may my blood flow in yours.'

— ⁂ —

Sitting aft on the deck of the lead ship of the Vasudev-Naga fleet, Brahaspati, Nandi and Parshuram could make out the outlines of Ganesh and Kartik practising their swordsmanship in the vessel behind them. Farther back, Shiva sat with Sati on a higher deck.

Brahaspati's emotions were tinged with bitter regret. 'My mission has gained a leader but I have lost a friend.'

Nandi turned towards Brahaspati. 'Of course not, Brahaspati*ji*, the Lord Neelkanth continues to love you.'

Brahaspati raised his eyebrows and smiled. 'Nandi, lying does not behove you.'

Nandi laughed softly. 'If it makes you feel better, I can tell you that Lord Shiva missed you dearly when he believed that you were dead. You were always on his mind.'

'I wouldn't have expected any less,' said Brahaspati. 'But I don't think he understands why I did what I did.'

'To be honest,' said Nandi, 'neither do I. It was important to fake your death, I concede. But you probably should have revealed the truth to Lord Shiva.'

'I couldn't have,' said Brahaspati. 'Shiva is the son-in-law of Emperor Daksha, my prime enemy. Had Daksha known that I was alive, he would have sent assassins after me. I wouldn't have lived long enough to conduct the experiments I needed to. And I had no way of knowing whether Shiva would have enough faith in me to not reveal anything to Daksha.'

Parshuram tried to console Brahaspati. 'He has forgiven you. Trust me, he has.'

'He may have forgiven me, but I don't think he has understood me as yet,' said Brahaspati. 'I hope there comes a time when I will get my friend back.'

'It will happen,' said Parshuram. 'Once the Somras is destroyed, we will all go with the Lord to Mount Kailash and live happily ever after.'

Nandi smiled. 'Mount Kailash is far less hospitable than you imagine, Parshuram. I should know for I have been there. It is no luxurious paradise.'

'Any place would be paradise so long as we sit at the feet of Lord Shiva.'

— ⁂ —

'Have you worn *kajal* in your eyes?' asked a surprised Shiva.

Reclining in an easy chair on the raised private deck, Shiva had been gazing fondly at his children as they sparred with each other, swords at the ready. Sati seated herself and leaned close against him, briefly lost in the moment.

Shiva had rarely seen Sati use make-up. He believed her beauty was so ethereal that it did not need any embellishment.

Sati looked up at Shiva with a shy smile. Her pronounced Suryavanshi personality had been subtly influenced by Chandravanshi women, particularly Anandmayi. She was discovering the pleasures of beauty, especially when experienced through the appreciative eyes of the man she loved. 'Yes. I thought you hadn't noticed.'

The kohl accentuated Sati's large almond-shaped eyes and her bashful smile made her dimples spring to life.

Shiva was mesmerised, as always. 'Wow... It looks nice...'

Sati laughed softly as she edged up to Shiva's face, and kissed him lightly.

Ganesh and Kartik were engaged in a furious duel on the fore deck. As had become a tradition with them, they fought with real weapons instead of wooden swords. They believed that the risk of serious injury would focus their minds and improve their practice. They would halt just before a killer strike and demonstrate to the other that an opening had been found.

Converting his smaller size to his advantage, Kartik pressed close to Ganesh, cramping him and making it difficult for his taller opponent to strike freely. Ganesh stepped back and swung his shield down in a seemingly defensive motion, but halted the movement inches from Kartik's shoulder.

'Kartik, my shield has a knife,' said Ganesh, as he pressed a lever to release it. 'This is a strike on my account. I've said this to you before: fighting with two swords is too aggressive. You should use a shield. You ended up leaving an opening for me.'

Kartik smiled. 'No, *dada*. The strike is mine. Look down.'

Ganesh's eyes fell on his chest as he felt a light touch of metal. Kartik was holding his left sword the other way round, with a small blade sticking out of the hilt end. He had managed to turn the sword around, release the knife and bring it in close, all the while giving the feint of an open right flank to Ganesh. Shiva's elder son had assumed that Kartik had pulled his left sword out of combat.

Ganesh stood with his eyes wide open, seriously impressed

with his brother. 'How in Lady Bhoomidevi's name did you manage that?'

Shiva, who had seen the entire manoeuvre from his upper deck, was equally impressed with Kartik. He pulled back from Sati and shouted out, 'Bravo Kartik!'

Sensing angry eyes boring into him, Shiva immediately turned towards Sati. She was glaring at her husband, holding her breath irritably, her lips still puckered.

'I'm so sorry. I'm so sorry,' said Shiva, trying to draw close and kiss Sati again.

Sati pushed Shiva's face away with mock irritation. 'The moment's passed...'

'I'm so sorry. It's just that what Kartik did was...'

'Of course,' whispered Sati, shaking her head and smiling.

'It'll not happen again...'

'It better not...'

'I'm sorry...'

Sati shook her head and rested it on Shiva's chest. Shiva pulled her close. 'I love the *kajal*. I didn't think it was possible for you to look even more beautiful.'

Sati looked up at Shiva and rolled her eyes. She slapped him lightly on his chest. 'Too little, too late.'

Chapter 12

Troubled Waters

'How was it?' asked Anandmayi.

Bhagirath had sailed up the Padma and reached Parvateshwar's vessel which was anchored at the point where the river broke away from the Branga River. The captain was preparing to raise anchor and start sailing onward. Parvateshwar, Anandmayi and Ayurvati had been waiting for Bhagirath at the aft deck, eager for the news from Branga.

Bhagirath looked briefly at Parvateshwar and Ayurvati, before turning to Anandmayi. 'What do you think?'

'Did you tell him everything?' asked Ayurvati.

'That is exactly what the Lord Neelkanth had asked me to do,' answered Bhagirath.

Parvateshwar took a deep breath and walked away.

Anandmayi looked at her husband before turning back. 'So what did Branga say, Bhagirath?'

'King Chandraketu is livid that his people have been suffering from a murderous plague so that the Meluhans can live extra-long lives.'

'But I hope you told him that most Meluhans did not know this,' said Ayurvati. 'Had we known that the Somras was causing this evil in Branga, we would not have used it.'

Bhagirath looked disbelievingly at Ayurvati and sarcastically remarked, 'I did tell him that most Meluhans did not know about the devastation their addiction had caused. Strangely, it did not seem to lessen King Chandraketu's anger.'

Ayurvati remained silent.

Anandmayi spoke irritably, 'Can you stop being judgemental for a moment and just tell me what is going to happen in Branga now?'

'For now King Chandraketu is going to concentrate on manufacturing the medicines that his people need,' said Bhagirath. 'But at the same time, he has already started mobilising for war. He will be ready and waiting in three months for the Lord Neelkanth's orders.'

Ayurvati's eyes welled up with tears as she wistfully looked at Parvateshwar in the distance. She felt the anguish in his noble heart. For hers was just as heavy.

— ⁂ —

'My Lord,' said Siamantak, the Ayodhyan prime minister, as he entered Emperor Dilipa's chambers, 'I've just received word that Maharishi Bhrigu is on his way.'

'Lord Bhrigu?' asked a surprised Dilipa. 'Here?'

'The advance boat has just come in, Your Highness,' said Siamantak. 'Lord Bhrigu should be here by tomorrow.'

'Why wasn't I informed earlier?'

'I did not know either, Your Highness.'

'Meluha should not have done this. They should have informed us in advance before sending Lord Bhrigu here.'

'What can I say about Meluha, My Lord? Typically disdainful.'

A nervous Dilipa ran his hands across his face. 'Is there any news from the shipyard? Are our ships close to completion?'

Siamantak swallowed anxiously. 'No, Your Highness. You'd asked me to pay attention to the pavement dweller issue and...'

'I KNOW WHAT I'D ASKED YOU TO DO! JUST ANSWER MY QUESTION WITH A SIMPLE YES OR NO!'

'I'm sorry, Your Highness. No, the ships are nowhere near completion.'

'By when will the job be done?'

'If we stop doing everything else then I guess we should be ready in another six to nine months.'

Dilipa seemed to breathe easier. 'That's not so bad. Nothing's going to happen in the next nine months.'

'Yes, Your Highness.'

Emperor Dilipa was with Maharishi Bhrigu at the Ayodhya shipyard. The Meluhan brigadier, Prasanjit, stood at a distance.

Declining the hospitality which awaited him on landing, Bhrigu had headed directly for the shipyard. A flustered Dilipa had perforce followed him, courtiers and all. He gestured for Siamantak and all his courtiers to maintain a distance. He knew that Bhrigu was angry and expected an earful.

'Your Highness,' said Bhrigu slowly, keeping his temper on a tight leash, 'you had promised me that your ships would be ready.'

'I know, My Lord,' said Dilipa softly. 'But honestly, a few months' delay is not going to hurt us. It has been many months since our attack on Panchavati. There has been absolutely no news of the Neelkanth. I'm sure we have succeeded. We don't really need to be nervous. I honestly think that the likelihood of a war is substantially reduced.'

Bhrigu turned to Dilipa. 'Your Highness, may I request that you leave the thinking to me?'

Dilipa immediately fell silent.

'Was it not your suggestion to commandeer your trade ships and refit them for war?'

'Yes it was, My Lord,' said Dilipa.

'I had suggested that we are not likely to fight naval battles on the Ganga. I had told you that we will only need transport ships, for which your trade ships were good enough.'

'Yes, you had, My Lord.'

'Yet you had insisted that in the likelihood of there being river battles, it would be a good idea to have battleships.'

'Yes, My Lord.'

'And I agreed on one condition alone – that the battleships would be ready in six months. Correct?'

'Yes, My Lord.'

'It has been seven months now. You have stripped down the trade ships but have still not refitted them. So now, seven months later, not only do we not have any battleships, but we also don't have any trade-transport ships.'

'I know it looks very bad, My Lord,' said Dilipa, wiping his brow with his fingers. 'But the pavement-dwellers here had gone on a hunger strike.'

A confused Bhrigu raised his hands in exasperation. 'What does that have to do with the ships?'

'My Lord,' explained Dilipa patiently, 'in my benevolence, I had decreed that no Ayodhyan shall be roofless. Of course, this onerous task was assigned to the Royal Committee of Internal Affairs, which looks after both housing as well as the royal shipyard. The committee has been seriously debating the execution of this grand scheme over the last three years. Following our last conversation though, I thought it fit to direct the committee to focus on building ships. The resultant neglect of the free housing scheme angered the pavement-dwellers to the point of mass agitation. Public order being paramount, I redirected the committee to concentrate on the housing scheme. I am glad to say that the seventh version of the housing report, which judiciously takes into account the views of all the citizens, should be ready soon. Once accepted, obviously the committee can then give its undiluted attention to the matter of building ships.'

Bhrigu was staring wide-eyed at Dilipa, stunned.

'So you see, My Lord,' said Dilipa, 'I know this is not looking good, but things will be set right very soon. In fact, I expect the committee to start debating the shipyard issue within the next seven days.'

Bhrigu spoke softly, but his rage was at boiling point, 'Your Highness, the future of India is at stake and your committee is *debating*?!'

'But My Lord, debates are important. They help incorporate all points of view. Or else we may make decisions that are not...'

'In the name of Lord Ram, you are the king! Fate has placed you here so you can make decisions for your people!'

Dilipa fell silent.

Bhrigu maintained silence for a few seconds, trying to control his anger, then spoke in a low voice. 'Your Highness, what you do within your own kingdom is your problem. But I want the refitting of these ships to begin today. Understand?'

'Yes, Maharishi*ji*.'

'How soon can the ships be ready?'

'In six months, if my people work every day.'

'Make those imbeciles work day and night and have them ready in three. Am I clear?

'Yes, My Lord.'

'Also, please have your cartographers map the jungle route from Ayodhya to the upper Ganga.'

'Umm, but why should...'

Bhrigu sighed in exasperation. 'Your Highness, I expect Meluha to be the real battleground. Your Ayodhya is not likely to be at risk. These ships were needed to get your army to Meluha quickly, if necessary. Since they are not going to be ready now, we need an alternative plan if war is declared within the next few months. I would need your army to cut through the jungles in a north-westerly direction and reach the upper Ganga, close to Dharmakhet. Farther on, you can use the new road built by the Meluhans to reach Devagiri. Obviously, since you will be cutting through jungles, this route will be slow and could take many months, but it's better than reinforcements not getting to Meluha at all. And to ensure that your army does not get lost in the jungles, it would be good to have clear maps. I'm sure your commanders would want to reach Meluha in time to help your allies.'

Dilipa nodded.

'Also, I will be surprised if Ayodhya is attacked directly.'

'Of course. Why should anyone attack Ayodhya directly?' asked Dilipa. 'We have not harmed anyone.'

In truth, Bhrigu was not sure that Ayodhya would not be attacked. But he did not care. His only concern was the Somras. Meluha had to be protected in order to protect the Somras. Had it been possible to convince Dilipa to order the Ayodhyan army to leave for Devagiri right away, Bhrigu would not have hesitated to do so.

'I will order the cartographers to map the route through the jungles, My Lord,' said Dilipa.

'Thank you, Your Highness,' smiled Bhrigu. 'By the way, I notice that even your wrinkles are disappearing. Has the blood in your cough reduced?'

'Disappeared, My Lord. Your medicines are miraculous.'

'A medicine is only as good as the patient's responsiveness. All the credit is due only to you, Your Highness.'

'You are being too kind. What you have done to my body is magical. But My Lord, my knee continues to trouble me. It still hurts when I...'

'We'll take care of that as well. Don't worry.'

'Thank you.'

Bhrigu gestured behind him. 'Also, I have brought the Meluhan brigadier Prasanjit here. He will train your army on modern warfare.'

'Ummm, but...'

'Please ensure that your soldiers listen to him, Your Highness.'

'Yes, My Lord.'

— ⁂ —

The two ships carrying Parvateshwar and his team had just docked at the river port of Vaishali, the immediate neighbour of Branga. Shiva had asked Parvateshwar to speak to the King of Vaishali, Maatali, and get his support for the Neelkanth. However, keeping in mind his decision to oppose the Mahadev and protect Meluha, Parvateshwar was of the opinion that it would be unethical of him to approach the king. Therefore, he had requested Anandmayi to carry out the mission.

Bhagirath, Anandmayi and Ayurvati were standing aft while they waited for the gangplank to be lowered on to the Vaishali port. Parvateshwar, having opted to stay back, had decided to practise his sword skills with Uttanka on the lead ship. The waiting party gazed at the exquisite Vishnu temple dedicated to Lord Matsya, built very close to the river harbour. They bowed low towards the first Lord Vishnu.

'You will have to excuse me,' said Bhagirath, turning towards Anandmayi.

'Are you planning on leaving for Ayodhya right away?' asked Anandmayi.

'Yes. Why delay it? I intend to take the second ship and sail up the Sarayu to Ayodhya. The Vaishali King's allegiance is a given. He is blindly loyal to the Neelkanth. Your meeting him is a mere formality. I may as well concentrate on the other task that the Lord Neelkanth has given me.'

'All right,' said Anandmayi.

'Go with Lord Ram's blessings, Bhagirath,' said Ayurvati.

'You too,' said Bhagirath.

While the lead ships of Shiva's convoy berthed at the main Assi Ghat of Kashi, the others docked at the Brahma Ghat nearby. Along with a large retinue, King Athithigva waited in attendance for the ceremonial reception. On cue, drummers beat a steady rhythm and conches blared as Shiva stepped onto the gangplank. Ceremonial *aartis* and a cheering populace added to the festive air. Their living God had returned.

King Athithigva bowed low and touched Shiva's feet as soon as he stepped onto the Assi Ghat.

'*Ayushman bhav*, Your Highness,' said Shiva, blessing King Athithigva with *a long life*.

Athithigva smiled, his hands folded in a respectful Namaste. 'A long life is not of much use if we are not graced with your presence here in Kashi, My Lord.'

Shiva, always uncomfortable with such deference, quickly changed the subject. 'How have things been, Your Highness?'

'Very well. Trade has been good. But rumours have been going around that the Neelkanth is to make a big announcement soon. Is that so, My Lord?'

'Let us wait till we get to your palace, Your Highness.'

'Of course,' said Athithigva. 'I should also tell you that I have received word through a fast sailboat that Queen Kali is on her way to Kashi. She is just a few days' journey behind you. She should be here soon.'

With raised eyebrows, Shiva instinctively looked upriver from where Kali's ship would inevitably sail. 'Well, it will be good to have her here as well. We have a lot to plan for.'

Chapter 13

Escape of the Gunas

A delighted Shiva embraced Veerbhadra as Sati hugged Krittika. The duo had just entered Shiva's private chamber in the Kashi palace.

Veerbhadra and Krittika had had an uneventful journey through Meluha. Their reception at the village where the Gunas had been housed had taken them by surprise. There were no soldiers, no alarm, nothing out of the ordinary. Clearly, the Gunas were not being targeted as leverage against the Neelkanth. The system-driven Meluhans had achieved what their system had conceived – everybody being treated in accordance with the law with no special provisions for any particular people.

'Didn't you face any trouble?' asked Shiva.

'None,' said Veerbhadra. 'The tribe lived just like everyone else, in comfortable egalitarianism. We quickly bundled them into a caravan and quietly escaped. We arrived in Kashi a few months later.'

'That means they're not aware as yet of my escape at the Godavari,' said Shiva. 'Or else they would have arrested the Gunas.'

'That is the logical conclusion.'

'But it also means that if any Meluhan happens to check

the Guna village and finds them missing, they will assume that I'm alive and am planning a confrontation.'

'That is also a logical conclusion. But there's nothing we can do about that, can we?'

'No, there isn't,' agreed Shiva.

— ⁂ —

'*Didi*!' smiled Kali as she embraced her sister.

'How are you doing, Kali?' asked Sati.

'I'm tired. My ship had to race down the Chambal and Ganga to catch up with you!'

'Nice to meet you after so many months, Kali,' said Shiva.

'Likewise,' said Kali. 'How was Ujjain?'

'A city that is worthy of Lord Ram,' said Shiva.

'Is it true that some of the Vasudevs have accompanied you here?'

'Yes, including the chief Vasudev himself, Lord Gopal.'

Kali whistled softly. 'I was not even aware of the chief Vasudev's name till just the other day and now it looks like I will be meeting him soon. The scenario must be really grim for him to emerge from his seclusion like this.'

'Change doesn't happen easily,' said Shiva. 'I don't expect the supporters of the Somras to fade into the sunset. The Vasudevs in fact believe the war has already begun, regardless of whether it has been declared or not. That it's just a matter of time before actual hostilities break out. I agree.'

'Is that why my ship was dragged into the Assi River?' asked Kali. 'I was worried that it might not make it into the harbour. This river is so small that it should actually be called a culvert!'

'That is for the ship's protection, Kali,' said Shiva. 'It was Lord Athithigva's idea. The Kashi harbour, just like the city, is not protected by any walls. Our enemies may hesitate to attack the city itself due to their faith in Lord Rudra's protective spirit over Kashi. But any ships anchored on the Ganga would be fair game.'

'Hence the decision to move the ships into the Assi, which as you know, flows into the Ganga,' said Sati. 'The channel at the mouth of the river is narrow, thus not more than one enemy ship can come through at a time. Our ships therefore can be easily defended. Also, the Assi flows through the city of Kashi. Most Chandravanshis would not want to venture within, believing that the spirit of Lord Rudra would curse them for harming Kashi, even by mistake.'

Kali raised her eyebrows. 'Using an enemy's own superstition against him? I like it!'

'Sometimes good tactics can work better than a sword edge,' said Shiva, grinning.

'Aah,' said Kali, smiling. 'You're only saying that because you haven't encountered my sword!'

Shiva and Sati laughed convivially.

— ⁂ —

Shiva and his core group were in the main hall of the grand Kashi Vishwanath temple. Athithigva had stepped into the inner sanctum, along with the main pandit of the temple, to offer *prasad* to the idols of Lord Rudra and Lady Mohini. He returned thereafter with the *ritual offerings made to the Gods.*

'May Lord Rudra and Lady Mohini bless our enterprise,' said Athithigva, offering the *prasad* to Shiva.

Shiva took the *prasad* with both hands, swallowed it whole and ran his right hand over his head, thus offering his thanks to the Lord and Lady for their blessings. Meanwhile, the temple pandit distributed the *prasad* to everybody else. The ceremonies over, Athithigva sat down with the group to discuss the strategy for the war ahead. The pandit was led out of the temple by Kashi policemen and the entrance sealed. No one was to be allowed into the premises for the duration of the meeting.

'My Lord, my people are forbidden any acts of violence except if it is in self-defence,' said Athithigva. 'So we cannot join the campaign actively with you. But all the resources of my kingdom are at your command.'

Shiva smiled. The peace-loving Kashi people would, in any case, not really make good soldiers. He had no intention of leading them into battles. 'I know, King Athithigva. I would not ask anything of your people that they would be honour-bound to refuse. But you must be able to defend Kashi if attacked, for we intend to house many of our war resources here.'

'We will defend it to our last breath, My Lord,' said Athithigva.

Shiva nodded. He did not really expect the Chandravanshis to attack Kashi. He turned towards Gopal. 'Pandit*ji*, there are many things that we need to discuss. To begin with, how do we keep the Chandravanshis out of the war theatre in Meluha? Secondly, what strategy should we adopt with Meluha?'

'I think what Lord Ganesh and Kartik suggested is an excellent idea,' said Gopal. 'Let us hope we can rope in Magadh to our side.'

'Easier said than done,' said Kali. 'Surapadman would be compelled by his father to seek vengeance for his stupid brother Ugrasen. And I don't propose handing over Ganesh for what was, in fact, a just execution.'

'So what are you suggesting, Kali?' asked Sati.

'Well, I'm suggesting that we either fight Magadh right

away or we tell them that we will investigate and hand over the Naga culprit as soon as we lay our hands on him.'

Sati instinctively held Ganesh's hand protectively.

Kali laughed softly. '*Didi*, all I'm suggesting is that we make Surapadman *think* that we are going to hand him over. That way, we can buy some time and attack Ayodhya.'

'Are you saying that we lie to the Magadhans, Your Highness?' asked Gopal.

Kali frowned at Gopal. 'All I'm saying is we be economical with the truth, great Vasudev. The future of India is at stake. There are many who are counting on us. If we have to taint our souls with a sin for the sake of greater good, then so be it.'

'I will not lie,' said Shiva. 'This is a war against Evil. We are on the side of Good. Our fight must reflect that.'

'*Baba*,' said Ganesh. 'You know I would agree with you under normal circumstances. But do you think the other side has maintained the standards you are espousing? Wasn't the attack on us at Panchavati an act of pure deception and subterfuge?'

'I don't believe it is wrong to attack an unprepared enemy. Yes, their using *daivi astras* can be considered questionable. Even so, two wrongs don't make a right. I will not lie to win this war. We will win it the right way.'

Kartik remained silent. Whereas he agreed with the pragmatism of Ganesh's words, he was inspired by the moral clarity in Shiva's.

Gopal smiled at Shiva. '*Satyam vada. Asatyam mavada.*'

'What?' asked Shiva.

Kali spoke up. 'It's old Sanskrit. "Speak the truth, never speak the untruth".'

Sati smiled. 'I agree.'

'Well, I know some old Sanskrit too,' said Kali. '*Satyam bruyat priyam bruyat, na bruyat satyam apriyam.*'

Shiva raised his hands in dismay, 'Can we cut out the old Sanskrit one-upmanship? I don't follow what you people are saying.'

Gopal translated for Shiva. 'What Queen Kali said means "Speak the truth in a pleasing manner, but never speak that truth which is unpleasant to others".'

'It's not my line,' said Kali, turning to Shiva. 'It can be attributed to a sage of yore, I'm sure. But I think it makes sense. We don't have to reveal to Surapadman that we know who his brother's killer is. All we need to motivate him to do, is to wait till after we have attacked Ayodhya before choosing his friends and his enemies. His ambition will guide him in the direction that we desire.'

'The walls of Ayodhya are impregnable,' warned Gopal, drawing attention to another factor. 'We might be able to bog them down, but we won't be able to destroy the city.'

'I know,' said Ganesh. 'But our aim is not to destroy Ayodhya. It is to ensure that their navy is unable to sail their forces over to Meluha. Our main battle will be in Meluha.'

'But what if Surapadman attacks from the rear after we have laid siege on Ayodhya?' asked Gopal. 'Caught between Ayodhya in front of us and Surapadman behind us, we could get destroyed.'

'Actually, no,' said Ganesh. 'Surapadman attacking us from behind would make things easier for us. It's when he moves out of Magadh that we'll make our move.'

Shiva, Kartik and Sati smiled; they understood the plan.

'Brilliant,' exclaimed Parshuram.

The rest turned to Parshuram for a whispered explanation on the side.

'You don't have to lie,' continued Kali to Shiva. 'Refrain from telling Surapadman the entire truth, except for those portions which will make him pause. Let his ambition play out the rest. We require him to allow our ships to pass through the confluence of the Sarayu and Ganga, towards Ayodhya. Once that is done we will achieve our objective one way or the other; either by holding Ayodhya back or by destroying the Magadhan army.'

Shiva's brief nod acknowledged his assent. 'But what about Meluha? Should we launch a frontal attack with all our might? Or, should we adopt diversionary tactics to distract their armies while a small group searches for the secret Somras facility and destroys it?'

'Our Branga and Vaishali forces will battle in Magadh and Ayodhya, leaving the Vasudevs and the Naga armies for the Meluhan campaign,' said Sati. 'So we will have much smaller forces in Meluha. Of course, they will be exceptionally well-trained and will have superb technological skills, like the fire-spewing elephant corps that the Vasudevs have developed recently. But we have to respect the Meluhan forces; they're equally well-trained and technologically adept.'

'So are you suggesting that we avoid a direct attack?' asked Shiva.

'Yes,' said Sati. 'Our main aim has to be to destroy the Somras manufacturing facility. It will take them years to rebuild it. That much time is more than enough for your word to prevail amongst the people. The average Meluhan is devoted to the legend of the Neelkanth. The Somras will die a natural death. But if we attack directly, the war with Meluha will drag on for a long time. The more it drags on, the more innocent people will die. Also, the Meluhans will begin to look upon the war as an attack on their beloved country, and not the Somras. I'm sure there will be large numbers of Meluhans who would be willing to turn against the Somras, but if we challenge their patriotism, then we have no chance of winning.'

Kali was smiling.

'What?' asked Sati.

'I noticed that you said "they" instead of "we" when you referred to the Meluhans,' said Kali.

Sati seemed perplexed. She still believed Meluha was her own land. 'Umm, that's unimportant... It's still my country...'

'Sure it is,' smiled Kali.

Gopal cut in. 'Just for the sake of argument, let us imagine what would happen if there is a direct all-out war.'

'That is something we will have to avoid,' said Shiva. 'I see sense in what Sati is saying.'

'Nevertheless, let us consider what Lord Bhrigu and Daksha might think,' said Gopal. 'I agree, it is in our interest to not have a direct war. But it is in their interest to have one, and a destructive one at that. They will want tensions to escalate so that they can confuse the people. They will then say that the Neelkanth has betrayed Meluha. Like Lady Sati just pointed out, the patriotism of the Meluhans could drown out their faith in the Neelkanth.'

'I agree that Lord Bhrigu may want to escalate the situation,' said Shiva. 'What I do not understand is how he will manage it once it has. I have seen the Meluhan army from up close. It's a centralised, well-drilled unit. But the problem with such armies is their utter dependence on a good commander. Their general, Parvateshwar, is with us. Trust me, they do not have another man like him. If Lord Bhrigu is as intelligent as you say he is, he would know that too.'

Ganesh and Kartik sighed at the same time.

Shiva glared at his sons.

'*Baba*...' said Kartik.

'Dammit!' screamed Shiva. 'You will not doubt his loyalty! Am I clear?'

Ganesh and Kartik bowed their heads, their mouths pursed mutinously.

'Am I clear?' asked Shiva once again.

Kali frowned at Shiva before looking at Ganesh and Kartik, but remained silent.

Shiva turned back to Gopal. 'We have to avoid provocation. Our military formations have to be solidly defensive, so as to deter them from staging an open confrontation. The main task for our army is to keep them distracted, so that a smaller unit can search the towns on the Saraswati for signs of the Somras manufacturing facility. Once we succeed in destroying that facility, we will win the war.'

'Nandi,' said Sati, turning to the Meluhan major.

Nandi immediately laid out a map of Meluha. Everyone peered at it.

'Look,' said Sati. 'The Saraswati ends in an inland delta. The Meluhans will not be able to get their massive fleet from Karachapa into the Saraswati. Their defence doctrine covers just two possible threats – a naval attack via the Indus or a land-based army attack from the east. That is why they don't have a massive fleet on the Saraswati.'

Shiva grasped what Sati was alluding to. 'They're unprepared for a naval attack on the Saraswati...'

'You have to understand that this is with good reason. They assumed that no enemy ships could enter the Saraswati. No enemy-controlled rivers flow into it and the Saraswati does not open to the sea.'

'But isn't that just the problem?' asked a confused Athithigva. 'How will we get ships into the Saraswati?'

'We won't,' said Shiva. 'We will capture the Meluhan ships stationed in the Saraswati instead.'

Kali nodded. 'That is the last thing they would expect, which is the reason why it will work.'

'Yes,' said Sati. 'All we have to do is capture Mrittikavati, which is where most of the Saraswati command of the

Meluhan navy is stationed. Once we're in possession of those ships, we will control the Saraswati. We can quickly sail up, unchallenged, even as we continue our search for the Somras manufacturing facility.'

'That's correct,' said Brahaspati. 'The manufacturing facility can only be on the banks of the Saraswati. It cannot possibly be anywhere else.'

'This sounds like a good plan,' said Gopal. 'But how do we capture their ships? Where do we enter their territory from? Mrittikavati is not a border town. We will have to march in with an army. And we will obviously face resistance from the border town that falls on the way – Lothal.'

'Lothal?' asked Kartik.

'Lothal is the port of Maika,' said Gopal. 'They are practically twin cities. Maika is where all the Meluhan children are born and raised, while Lothal is the local army base.'

'Don't worry about Maika or Lothal,' said Kali. 'They will be on our side.'

Gopal, Shiva and Sati seemed genuinely surprised.

'If there are any Meluhans who will have sympathy for us, it will be the people of Maika,' continued Kali. 'They have seen the Naga children suffer. They have tried to help us on many occasions, even breaking their own laws in the process. The present Governor of Maika, Chenardhwaj, is also the administrator of Lothal. He was transferred from Kashmir a few years back. He is loyal to the institution of the Neelkanth. Furthermore, I have saved his life once. Trust me, both Maika and Lothal will be with us when hostilities break out.'

'I remember Chenardhwaj,' said Shiva. 'All right then, we will utilise the support of Lothal to conquer Mrittikavati. Then we'll use their ships to search the towns on the Saraswati. But remember, we must try and avoid a direct clash.'

Chapter 14

The Reader of Minds

'Do you believe we can convince him?' asked Shiva.

The Vasudev chief, Gopal, had just walked into Shiva's chamber. Sati and the Neelkanth were preparing to leave for Magadh with him. Ganesh and Kartik had come to say goodbye to their parents.

'I would have been worried had we been meeting Lord Bhrigu,' said Gopal. 'But it's only Surapadman.'

'What is so special about Lord Bhrigu?' asked Shiva. 'He is only human. Why are all of you so wary of him?'

'He is a maharishi, Shiva,' said Sati. 'In fact, like Gopal*ji* had mentioned, Lord Bhrigu is believed by many to be beyond a maharishi; he's a *Saptrishi Uttradhikari*.'

'You should respect a man, not his position,' said Shiva, before turning to Gopal. 'Once again I ask, my friend, why are you so nervous about him?'

'Well, for starters, he can read minds,' said Gopal.

'So?' asked Shiva. 'You and I can do that too. Every Vasudev pandit can, in fact.'

'True, but we can only do so while we're in one of our temples. Lord Bhrigu can read the mind of anyone around him, regardless of where he is.'

Ganesh looked genuinely surprised. 'How?'

'Well,' said Gopal, 'our brains transmit radio waves when we think. These thoughts can be detected by a trained person, provided he is within the range of a powerful transmitter. But it is believed that maharishis can go a step further. They do not need to wait till our thoughts are converted into radio waves, to be able to detect them. They can read our thoughts even as we formulate them.'

'But how?'

'Thoughts are nothing but electrical impulses in our brain,' said Gopal. 'These impulses make the pupils of our eyes move minutely. A trained person, like a maharishi, can decipher this movement in our pupils and read our thoughts.'

'Lord Ram, be merciful,' whispered a stunned Kartik.

'I still do not understand how this is possible,' remarked a sceptical Shiva. 'Are you saying all our thoughts are exposed by the movement of our pupils? What language would that communication be in? This makes no sense.'

'My friend,' said Gopal, 'you are confusing the language of communication with the internal language of the brain. Sanskrit, for example, is a language of communication. You use it to communicate with others. You also use it to communicate with your own brain, so that your conscious mind can understand your inner thoughts. But the brain itself uses only one language for its own working. This is a universal language across all brains of all known species. And the alphabet of this language has two letters, or signals.'

'Two signals?' asked Sati

'Yes,' said Gopal, 'only two – electricity on and electricity off. Our brain has millions of thoughts and instructions running simultaneously within. But at any one point of time, only one of these thoughts can capture our conscious attention. This particular thought gets reflected in our eyes through the language of the brain. A maharishi can read this conscious thought. So one has to be very careful about what one consciously thinks in the presence of a maharishi.'

'So the eye is indeed the window to one's soul,' said Ganesh.

Gopal smiled. 'It appears that it is.'

Shiva grinned, his brows raised. 'Well, I'll make sure that I keep mine shut when I meet Lord Bhrigu.'

Gopal and Sati laughed softly.

'Nevertheless, we will win,' said Gopal.

'Yes,' said Ganesh. 'We're on the side of Good.'

'That is true, without doubt. But that is not the reason, Lord Ganesh. We will win because of your father,' said Gopal.

'No,' said Shiva. 'It cannot be only me. We will win because we're all in this together.'

'It is you who brings us together, great Neelkanth,' said Gopal. 'Lord Bhrigu may be as intelligent as you are, maybe more. But he is not a leader like you. He uses, rather misuses his brilliance to cow down his followers. They don't idolise him; they are scared of him. You, on the other hand, are able to draw out the best in your followers, my friend. Don't think I did not understand what you did a few days back. You had decided upon your course of action already. But that did not stop you from having a discussion, allowing us to be a part of the decision. Somehow, you guided us all into saying what you wanted to hear. And yet, you made each one of us feel as if it was our own decision. That is leadership. Lord Bhrigu may have a bigger army than ours, but he fights alone. In our case, our entire army will fight as one. That, great Neelkanth, is a supreme tribute to your leadership.'

Shiva, embarrassed as always when complimented, quickly changed the topic. 'You are being too kind, Gopal*ji*. In any case, I think we should leave. Magadh awaits us.'

— ⁂ —

'Bhagirath is here?'

Siamantak nodded at his stunned emperor. 'Yes, My Lord.'

'But how did he...'

'Prime Minister Siamantak,' said Bhrigu, interrupting Dilipa. 'I would be delighted to meet him. Have Princess Anandmayi and her husband accompanied him?'

'No, My Lord,' said Siamantak. 'He has come alone.'

'That is most unfortunate,' said Bhrigu. 'Please show him in with complete honour into our presence.'

'As you wish, My Lord,' said Siamantak, as he bowed to Bhrigu and Dilipa before leaving the room.

As soon as he had left, Bhrigu turned towards Dilipa. 'Your Highness, you must learn to control yourself. Siamantak is unaware of the attack at the Godavari.'

'I'm sorry, My Lord,' said Dilipa. 'It's just that I'm shocked.'

'I'm not.'

Dilipa frowned. 'Why, My Lord! Did you expect this?'

'I can't say that I expected this specifically. But I had strong suspicions that our attack had failed. The only question was how they would be confirmed.'

'I don't understand, My Lord. Our ships could have got destroyed in so many ways.'

'It wasn't only the destruction of our ships. There is something else. I had asked Kanakhala to try and locate the Gunas.'

'Who are the Gunas?'

'They are the tribe of that fraud Neelkanth. The Gunas were immigrants in Meluha. There are standard policies in Meluha for immigrants, one of them being that their records are kept strictly secret. This system ensures that they are not targeted or oppressed, and are in fact, treated well. But the upshot was that the royal record-keeper was refusing to tell his own Prime Minister where the Gunas were settled.'

'How can the record-keeper do that? The Prime Minister's word would be the order of the Emperor. And his word is law!'

'Well,' smiled Bhrigu. 'Meluha is not like your empire, Lord Dilipa. They have this irritating habit of sticking to rules.'

Bhrigu's sarcasm was lost on Dilipa.

'So what happened, My Lord? Did you find the Gunas?'

'At first, Kanakhala seemed quite sure that the Gunas were in Devagiri itself. When that initial search yielded nothing, she had no choice but to approach Emperor Daksha. He passed an order through the Rajya Sabha that would force the Meluhan record-keeper to reveal the location of the Gunas. By the time we reached their village, they were gone.'

'Gone where?'

'I don't know. I was told this happens quite often. Many immigrants are not able to adapt to the civilised but regimented life in Meluha and choose to return to their homelands. So I was asked to believe that the Gunas must have gone back to the Himalayas.'

'And did you believe that?'

'Of course I didn't. I suspected the fraud Neelkanth must have spirited his tribe away before declaring war. But what could I do? I didn't know where the Gunas were.'

'But why is Bhagirath here? Why would the Neelkanth reveal his hand?'

'*Fraud* Neelkanth, Your Highness,' said Bhrigu, correcting Dilipa.

'I'm sorry, My Lord,' said Dilipa.

Bhrigu looked up at the ceiling. 'Yes, why has Shiva sent him here?'

'My God!' whispered Dilipa. 'Could he have been sent here to assassinate me?'

Bhrigu shook his head. 'That is unlikely. I don't think killing you, Your Highness, would serve any larger purpose.'

Dilipa opened his mouth to say something but decided instead to remain silent.

'Yes,' continued Bhrigu, narrowing his eyes, 'we do need to know why Prince Bhagirath is here. I look forward to meeting him.'

— ⅄ⵀ Ʊ ⍏ ⊗ —

'Father,' said Bhagirath as he walked confidently into Dilipa's chamber.

Dilipa smiled as best he could. He didn't really like his son. 'How are you, Bhagirath?'

'I'm all right, father.'

'How was your trip to Panchavati?'

Bhagirath glanced at Bhrigu, wondering who the old Brahmin was, before turning back to his father. 'It was an uneventful trip, father. Perhaps the Nagas are not as bad as we think. Some of us have returned early. The Lord Neelkanth will join us later.'

Dilipa frowned, as if surprised, and turned towards Bhrigu.

Bhagirath arched his eyebrow before turning towards Bhrigu as well with a Namaste and quick bow of his head. 'Please accept my apologies for my bad manners, Brahmin. I was overwhelmed with emotions on seeing my father.'

Bhrigu looked deep into Bhagirath's eyes.

Bhagirath is consumed with curiosity about who I am. I better put this to rest so that his conscious mind can move on to more useful thoughts.

'Perhaps it is I who should apologise,' said Bhrigu. 'I have not introduced myself. I'm a simple sage who lives in the Himalayas and goes by the name of Bhrigu.'

Bhagirath straightened up in surprise. Of course he knew who Bhrigu was, although he hadn't met him. Bhagirath stepped forward and bent low, touching the sage's feet.

'Maharishi Bhrigu, it is my life's honour to meet you. I'm fortunate to have the opportunity to seek your blessings.'

'*Ayushman bhav*,' said Bhrigu, blessing Bhagirath with *a long life*.

Bhrigu then placed his hands on Bhagirath's shoulders and pulled him up, while once again looking directly into his eyes.

Bhagirath has realised that his imbecile father is not the true leader. I am. And he's scared. Good. Now all I have to do is make him think some more.

'I trust the Neelkanth is well?' asked Bhrigu. 'I have still not had the pleasure of meeting the man who commoners believe is the saviour of our times.'

'He is well, My Lord,' said Bhagirath. 'And is worthy of the title he carries. In fact, there are those of us who believe that he even deserves the title of the Mahadev.'

So, Bhagirath volunteered to uncover the identity of the true leader. Interesting. That Tibetan barbarian understands that this fool Dilipa could not have been the one. He has more intelligence than I thought.

'Allow posterity to prevail upon the present in deciding the honour and title bestowed upon man, my dear Prince of Ayodhya,' said Bhrigu. 'Duty must be performed for its own sake, not for the power and pelf it might bring. I am sure that even your Neelkanth is familiar with Lord Vasudev's nugget of wisdom which encapsulates this thought: *Karmanye vaadhikaa raste maa phaleshu kadachana*.'

'Oh, the Neelkanth is the embodiment of that thought, Maharishi*ji*,' said Bhagirath. 'He never calls himself the Mahadev. It is we who address him as such.'

Bhrigu smiled. 'Your Neelkanth must be truly great to inspire such loyalty, brave Prince. By the way, how was Panchavati? I have never had the pleasure of visiting that land.'

'It is a beautiful city, Maharishi*ji*.'

They were attacked at the outskirts of Panchavati... So our ships did make it through. And their devil boats got us. Well, at least our information about the location of Panchavati is correct.

'With Lord Ram's blessings,' said Bhrigu, 'I will visit Panchavati someday.'

'I'm sure that the Queen of the Nagas would be honoured, My Lord,' said Bhagirath.

Bhrigu smiled. *Kali would kill me if she had half a chance. Her temper is even more volatile than Lord Rudra's legendary anger.*

'But Prince Bhagirath,' said Bhrigu, 'I must complain about an iniquity that you have committed.'

An astonished Bhagirath folded his hands together in an apologetic Namaste. 'I apologise profusely if I have offended you in any way, My Lord. Please tell me how I can set it right.'

'It's very simple,' said Bhrigu. 'I was really looking forward to meeting the Emperor's daughter and her new husband. But you have not brought Princess Anandmayi along with you.'

'Apologies for my oversight, My Lord,' said Bhagirath. 'I overlooked this only because I rushed here to pay obeisance to my respected father, whom I have not met for a long time. And Princess Anandmayi has dutifully accompanied her husband General Parvateshwar to Kashi.'

Bhrigu suddenly held his breath as he read Bhagirath's thoughts. *Parvateshwar wants to defect? He wants to return to Meluha?*

'I guess I will only have the pleasure of meeting Princess Anandmayi and General Parvateshwar when the Almighty wills it,' said Bhrigu.

The smile on Bhrigu's face left Bhagirath with a sense of unease.

'Hopefully that will be soon enough, My Lord,' said Bhagirath. 'If I may now be excused, I'd like to meet up with some people and then head to Kashi for some unfinished tasks.'

Dilipa was about to say something when Bhrigu raised his hand and placed it on Bhagirath's head. 'Of course, brave Prince. Go with Lord Ram.'

'Why did you let him go, My Lord?' said Dilipa, as soon as Bhagirath had left. 'We could have arrested him. The interrogation would have surely revealed what happened in Panchavati.'

'I'm already aware of what happened,' said Bhrigu. 'Our ships did reach Panchavati and even managed to kill a large number from amongst their convoy. But they did not kill the main leaders. Shiva is still alive. And our ships were destroyed in the battle.'

'Even so, we should not allow Bhagirath to leave. Why are we letting one of their main leaders go back unharmed?'

'I have blessed him with a long life, Your Highness. I'm sure you don't want me to be proven a liar.'

'Of course not, My Lord.'

Bhrigu looked at Dilipa and smiled. 'I know what you are thinking, Your Highness. Trust me, in chess as in war, one sometimes sacrifices a minor piece for the strategic advantage of capturing a more important piece several moves later.'

Dilipa frowned.

'Let me make myself very clear, Your Highness,' said Bhrigu. 'Prince Bhagirath must not be harmed in Ayodhya. I imagine he will leave your city within a day. He should leave safe and sound. I want them to think that we are none the wiser from Bhagirath's brief visit.'

'Yes, My Lord.'

'Provision and ready a fast sailboat. I must leave for Kashi immediately.'

'Yes, My Lord.'

'Please have the manifest of my ship state that I am going to Prayag. Bhagirath still has friends in Ayodhya. I don't want him to know that I'm leaving for Kashi. Is that clear?'

'Of course, My Lord. I will have Siamantak take care of this immediately.'

Chapter 15

The Magadhan Issue

Shiva, Sati and Gopal had just been led into the guest chambers of Surapadman's royal palace by Andhak, the Magadhan minister for ports.

Gopal waited for him to leave and then remarked, 'It's interesting that we are being housed in Surapadman's private residence and not King Mahendra's palace.'

'Surapadman wants to serve as the exclusive channel of information between us and his father,' said Sati. 'Being the sole intermediary also allows him the discretion of passing on things selectively. It actually makes me more hopeful of success.'

'I am far less hopeful,' countered Shiva. 'No doubt it is actually Surapadman's writ that runs large in Magadh. Besides being the prince, he is also the keeper of the king's seal. But even he would be wary of his father's reaction following the killing of Prince Ugrasen. Perhaps that is why he wants to talk to us in private here.'

'Perhaps,' said Gopal. 'Maybe that's the reason why we were received in Magadh by Andhak and not King Mahendra's prime minister.'

'Yes,' said Shiva. 'I believe Andhak is loyal to Surapadman.'

'Let's hope for the best,' said Sati.

As Shiva, Sati and Gopal entered the prince's court, Surapadman rose from his ceremonial chair. He walked up to the Neelkanth and then went down on his knees. Surapadman placed his head on Shiva's feet. 'Bless me, great Neelkanth.'

'*Sukhinah bhav*,' said Shiva, placing his hand on Surapadman's head, *blessing him with happiness*.

Surapadman looked up at Shiva. 'I hope by the time this conversation ends, My Lord, you will find it in your heart to bless me with victory along with happiness.'

Shiva smiled and placed his hands on Surapadman's shoulders as he rose. 'Please allow me to introduce my companions, Prince Surapadman. This is my wife, Sati.'

Surapadman bowed low towards Sati. She politely returned Surapadman's greeting.

'And this is my close friend and the chief of the Vasudevs, Gopal,' said Shiva.

Surapadman's hands came together in a respectful Namaste as his eyes widened with surprise. 'Lord Ram, be merciful!'

'Pray to him,' said Gopal, 'and he will be.'

Surapadman smiled. 'My apologies, Gopal*ji*. My informants have always assured me that the legendary Vasudevs are for real. But I believed they would not interfere with worldly affairs unless an existential crisis was upon us.'

'Such a time is upon us, Surapadman,' said Gopal. 'And all the true followers of Lord Ram must align themselves with the Neelkanth.'

Surapadman remained silent.

'Let us make ourselves comfortable, brave Prince of Magadh,' said Shiva.

Surapadman led them to the centre of the court where ceremonial chairs had been placed in a circle. Gopal noticed there was no official from the royal Magadhan court except for Andhak. Rumours suggesting that Andhak would soon be taking over the command of the Magadhan army were perhaps true. It could also be deduced that the rest of the Magadhan court was not really aligned with the Neelkanth. Considering Magadh's traditional rivalry with Ayodhya, one would have imagined that they would choose to align with the Neelkanth. But Ugrasen's murder seemed to have effectively queered the pitch.

'What can I do for you, My Lord?' asked Surapadman.

'I will come straight to the point, Prince Surapadman,' said Shiva. 'Your elite intelligence officials would have already briefed you that a war is likely.'

Surapadman nodded silently.

'Perhaps you would also be aware that Ayodhya has not chosen wisely,' said Gopal.

'Yes, I'm aware of that,' said Surapadman, allowing himself a hint of a smile. 'But given Ayodhya's penchant for indecision and confusion, few can be sure about which side they will eventually find themselves on!'

Sati smiled. 'And what do you intend to do, brave Prince?'

'My Lady,' said Surapadman, 'I am a believer in the legend of the Neelkanth. And the Lord has shown that he is a worthy inheritor of the title of the Mahadev.'

Shiva shifted in his seat awkwardly, still not comfortable with being compared to the great Lord Rudra.

'Furthermore, Ayodhya is a terrible overlord,' continued Surapadman. 'It needs to be challenged in the interests of Swadweep. And only Magadh has the ability to do that.'

'I can see that only mighty Magadh has the strength to confront Ayodhya,' said Sati.

'There you have it,' said Surapadman, 'I have given you two good reasons why I should choose to stand with the army of the Neelkanth.'

Shiva, Gopal and Sati remained silent, waiting for the inevitable 'but'.

'And yet,' said Surapadman, 'circumstances have made my situation a little more complex.'

Turning towards Shiva, Surapadman continued, 'My Lord, you must already be aware of my dilemma. My brother, Ugrasen, was killed in a Naga terrorist attack and my father is hell-bent on seeking vengeance.'

Keeping the sensitivity of the issue in mind, Shiva spoke softly, 'Surapadman, I think the incident...'

'My Lord,' said Surapadman, 'please forgive me for interrupting you, but I know the truth.'

'I'm not sure you do, Prince Surapadman. Or else your reaction would have been different.'

Surapadman smiled, looked briefly at Andhak and continued. 'My Lord, Andhak and I have investigated the case personally. We've visited the spot where my brother and his men were killed. We're aware of the incident.'

Sati couldn't help inquiring, 'Then why...'

'What can I do, My Lady?' asked Surapadman. 'My father is a grieving old man who has convinced himself that his favourite son was a noble and valiant Kshatriya, who died while defending his kingdom from a cowardly Naga attack. How can I tell him the truth? How do I tell him that Ugrasen was in fact a compulsive gambler who was trying to kidnap a hapless boy-rider so that he could win some money? Should I tell my father that my great brother tried to murder a mother who was protecting her own child? That the apparently wicked Nagas were actually heroes who saved a subject of his own kingdom from his son's villainy? Do you think he will even listen to me?'

'There is nobility in truth,' said Sati, 'even if it hurts.'

Surapadman laughed softly. 'This is not Meluha, My

Lady. Meluhans' devotion to "the truth" is seen by many here as nothing but rigidity of thought. Chandravanshis prefer to choose from several alternative truths which may simultaneously co-exist.'

Sati remained silent.

Surapadman turned to Shiva. 'My Lord, my father thinks that I am an ambitious warmonger who's impatient to ascend the throne. He preferred my elder brother, who was more attuned to my father's views. I think he suspects that I engineered the death of Ugrasen, in pursuit of my goals.'

'I'm sure that's not true,' said Shiva. 'You are his capable son.'

'It takes a very self-assured man to appreciate the talents of another, My Lord,' said Surapadman. 'Even when it comes to one's own progeny. Ironically, the Nagas have in fact helped me, for my path to the throne is clear. All I have to do is wait for my father to pass on. And desist from doing anything that will make him disinherit me and offer the throne to some relative. Given this, if I were to tell my father that his favourite son's murder by the "evil" Nagas was absolutely justified, I would probably go down in history as the stupidest royal ever.'

Gopal smiled slightly. 'It appears that we are at an impasse, Prince Surapadman. What do we do?'

Surapadman narrowed his eyes. 'Just give me a Naga.'

'I can't,' said Shiva.

'I'm not asking for the one who actually killed Ugrasen, My Lord,' said Surapadman. 'I guess he is someone important. All I'm asking for is a random Naga. I will present him to my father as Ugrasen's killer and we'll have him executed forthwith. My father will then happily retire and go into *sanyas* to pray for my brother's soul. And I, along with all the resources of Magadh, will stand beside you. I know the Brangas are with you. Victory is assured if Magadh and

Branga are on the same side. You will win the war, My Lord, and Evil will be destroyed. All you need to do is sacrifice an insignificant Naga, who is suffering for the sins of his past lives in any case. We will actually be giving him an opportunity to earn good karma. What do you say?'

Shiva did not hesitate even for a second. 'I cannot do that.'

'My Lord...'

'I will not do that.'

'But...'

'No.'

Surapadman leaned back in his chair. 'We indeed seem to be at an impasse, great Vasudev. My father will not allow me to fight in an army that includes the Nagas unless we can assuage his thirst for vengeance.'

Shiva spoke up before Gopal could respond. 'What if you do not pick any side at all?'

Surapadman frowned, intrigued.

'Convince your father to remain neutral,' continued Shiva. 'Allow my ships to proceed to battle with Ayodhya. If we are able to beat them, then your primary enemies are weakened. If they beat us, our army, including the Nagas, would be in retreat. Your imagination can fill in the rest. You win both ways.'

Surapadman smiled. 'That does have an attractive ring to it.'

— ⚹ —

Parvateshwar and Anandmayi were housed in a separate wing of the massive Kashi palace, having arrived in the city recently. Anandmayi and Ayurvati had gone to meet Veerbhadra and the Gunas.

The Meluhan general was sitting in his chamber balcony, looking out towards the Ganga flowing in the distance.

'My Lord,' called out the doorman.

Parvateshwar turned. 'Yes?'

'A messenger has just delivered a note for you.'

'Hand it to me.'

'Yes, My Lord.'

As the doorman came in, Parvateshwar asked, 'Who brought the message?'

'The main palace door-keeper, My Lord.'

Parvateshwar raised his brows. 'An outsider would not be allowed in, would he? What I wanted to know was who gave the message to the palace door-keeper?'

The doorman looked lost. 'How would I know, My Lord?'

Parvateshwar sighed. These Swadweepans had no sense of systems and procedures. It's a wonder that an enemy didn't just stroll into their key installations. He took the neatly sealed papyrus scroll from the doorman and dismissed him. Parvateshwar couldn't recognise the symbol on the seal. It appeared to be a star, the kind used in ancient astrological charts. He shrugged and broke it open. The script surprised him; it was one of the standard Meluhan military codes. This one was used exclusively by senior Suryavanshi military officers. It was meant for top secret messages during times of war. For all others, the words in the scroll would have been absolute gibberish.

Lord Parvateshwar, it's time to prove your loyalty to Meluha. Meet me in the garden behind the Sankat Mochan temple at the end of the third prahar. Come alone.

Parvateshwar caught his breath. He instinctively looked towards the door. He was alone. He tucked the scroll into the pouch tied to his waistband.

He knew what he had to do.

— ⁂ —

The sound of bells, drums and prayer chants rent the morning air, day after day, at the Sankat Mochan temple. Having thus awoken Lord Hanuman, the devotees then sing *bhajans,* as Lord Hanuman would do, to gently wake his master, Lord Ram. At the end of this elaborate *puja*, the great seventh Vishnu proceeds to grant *darshan*, the divine pleasure of *beholding him*. The silence at dusk, however, belied the exuberance of the dawn. This was the time when Parvateshwar strode into the great temple.

Parvateshwar looked back to ensure that nobody was following him. Then he walked swiftly towards the garden behind the temple. It was quiet. Parvateshwar approached a tree at the far end of the garden and sat leaning against it.

'How are you, General?' asked a soft, polite voice.

Parvateshwar looked up. 'I'll do a lot better when I see you.'

'Are you alone?'

'I wouldn't have come had I not been alone.'

There was silence for some time.

Parvateshwar got up to leave. 'If you are a true Meluhan, you would know that Meluhans don't lie.'

'Wait, General,' said Bhrigu, as he emerged from the shadows.

Parvateshwar was stunned. He recognised the *Saptrishi Uttradhikari*. He knew that despite wielding tremendous influence, Bhrigu had never interfered in the workings of Meluha. He found it hard to believe that Bhrigu could involve himself in mundane matters of the material world.

'I am taking a huge risk in meeting you face-to-face,' smiled Bhrigu. 'I had to be sure that you were alone.'

'What are you doing here, *Maharishiji*?' asked Parvateshwar, bowing to the *great sage*.

'I'm doing my duty. As you are doing yours.'

'But you have never interfered in earthly matters.'

'I have,' said Bhrigu. 'But only on rare occasion. And this is one such.'

Parvateshwar remained silent. *So Bhrigu is the true leader. He was the one who had sent the joint Meluha-Ayodhya fleet to attack Lord Shiva's convoy by stealth outside Panchavati.* Parvateshwar's respect for Bhrigu went down a notch. The great sage was human after all.

'You already know what you have to do,' said Bhrigu. 'I know that you will not support the fraud Neelkanth in attacking your beloved motherland.'

Parvateshwar bristled with anger. 'Lord Shiva is not a fraud! He's the finest man to have walked the earth since Lord Ram!'

Bhrigu stepped back, astonished. 'Perhaps I was wrong. Perhaps you do not love Meluha as much as I thought you did.'

'Lord Bhrigu, I would die for Meluha,' said Parvateshwar. 'For it is my duty to do so. But please don't make the mistake of thinking that I despise the Lord Neelkanth. He is my living God.'

Bhrigu frowned, even more surprised. He looked into Parvateshwar's eyes. The normally restrained sage's mouth fell open ever so slightly. He realised that he was looking at a rare man who spoke exactly what he thought. Bhrigu's tenor changed and became respectful. 'My apologies, great General. I can see that your reputation does you justice. I misunderstood you. Sometimes the hypocritical nature of the world makes us immune to a rare sincere man.'

Parvateshwar remained silent.

'Will you fight for Meluha?' asked Bhrigu.

'To my last breath,' whispered Parvateshwar. 'But I will fight according to Lord Ram's laws.'

'Of course.'

'We will not break the rules of war.'

Bhrigu nodded silently.

'I suggest, Maharishi*ji*,' said Parvateshwar, 'that you return to Meluha. I will follow in a few weeks.'

'It would not be wise to remain here, General,' said Bhrigu. 'If anything were to happen to you, the consequences for Meluha would be disastrous. Your army needs a good leader.'

'I cannot leave without taking my Lord's permission.'

Bhrigu thought he hadn't heard right. 'Excuse me? Did you say that you wanted to take permission from the Neelkanth before leaving?'

He was careful not to say 'fraud Neelkanth'.

'Yes,' answered Parvateshwar.

'But why would he allow you to leave?'

'I don't know if he will. But I know I cannot leave without his permission.'

Bhrigu spoke carefully. 'Uhhh, Lord Parvateshwar, I don't think that you realise the gravity of the situation. If you tell the Neelkanth that you are going to lead his enemies, he will kill you.'

'No, he won't. But, if he chooses to do so, then that will be my fate.'

'My apologies for sounding rude, but this is foolhardy.'

'No, it's not. This is what a devotee does if he chooses to leave his Lord.'

'But...'

'Lord Bhrigu, this sounds peculiar to you because you haven't met Lord Shiva. His companions don't follow him out of fear. They do so because he is the most inspiring presence in their lives. My fate has put me in a position where I am being forced to oppose him. It's breaking my heart. I need his blessings and his permission to give me the strength to do what I have to do.'

Bhrigu's slow nod revealed a glimpse of grudging respect. 'The Neelkanth must be a special man to inspire such loyalty.'

'He is not just a special man, Maharishi*ji*. He is a living God.'

Chapter 16

Secrets Revealed

'I think we've achieved what we came here for,' said Sati.

Gopal, Sati and Shiva had retired to their chambers in Surapadman's palace. As a mark of goodwill, Surapadman had persuaded them to stay on for a few days and allow him to ready a few weapons for Shiva's army.

'Yes, I agree,' said Gopal. 'Surapadman's offer of weapons, though token in nature, is symbolic of his having allied with us.'

'Not one other person from the Magadhan court has visited us though,' said Shiva. 'I hope that King Mahendra doesn't prevail upon Surapadman to do something unwise.'

'Do you think he may prevent our ships from passing through to Ayodhya?' asked Gopal.

'I can't be sure,' said Shiva. 'It's most likely he will cooperate, but it depends on how his father reacts.'

'Let's hope for the best,' said Sati.

'What about my proclamation, Pandit*ji*?'

'It will be ready and distributed in a few weeks from now,' said Gopal. 'Vasudev pandits from across the country will give us constant updates as to the reaction of the people as well as the nobility.'

'But what if the Vasudev pandits are discovered?'

'No, they won't. The royals may know that the Vasudev tribe has allied with the Neelkanth, but they will never know the identity of the Vasudevs within their kingdoms.'

Shiva let out a long-drawn breath. 'And so it shall begin.'

— ⅄ⵀⵡⴰⵣ —

Bhagirath arrived in Kashi late in the evening and proceeded directly to the palace. On reaching there, he was informed that Shiva had gone to Magadh to explore an alliance with Surapadman. Bhagirath, therefore, met Ganesh and Kartik to share his news with them.

'The Ayodhyans seem to have a back-up plan,' said Bhagirath. 'They expect Magadh to block their ships from carrying their soldiers onwards up the Ganga and towards Meluha. Hence, they intend to cut through the forests and have their army move north-west, right up to Dharmakhet. From there, they can cross the Ganga and then use the newly-built road to march to Meluha.'

'That's logical,' said Ganesh. 'But it will be slow. It will be many months before they can cut through the dense forests and reach Meluha. The war may actually be over by that time.'

Bhagirath agreed. 'True.'

Ganesh leaned forward. 'But I can see that there is more.'

Bhagirath could hardly contain himself. 'I know the identity of the one who leads our enemies.'

'Maharishi Bhrigu?' suggested Kartik.

Bhagirath was amazed. 'How did you know?'

'*Baba's* friends, the Vasudevs, told us,' answered Ganesh.

Bhagirath had heard stories about the legendary Vasudevs. 'Do the Vasudevs really exist?'

'Yes they do, brave Prince,' said Kartik.

Bhagirath smiled. 'With friends like them, Lord Shiva doesn't need followers like me!'

Ganesh laughed. 'He could not have known when he agreed to your suggestion, that the Vasudevs would reveal the identity of the main conspirator.'

'Of course,' said Bhagirath. 'But at least we now know about their back-up plan of marching through the impenetrable forests to the north-west of Ayodhya.'

'Yes, that is useful information, Bhagirath,' said Ganesh.

Kartik suddenly sat up. 'Prince Bhagirath, did you meet Maharishi Bhrigu personally?'

'Yes.'

Kartik looked at Ganesh with concern.

'What's the matter?' asked Bhagirath.

'Did he look into your eyes while speaking with you, Bhagirath?' asked Ganesh.

'Where else would he be looking if he was talking to me?'

Kartik looked up at the ceiling. 'Lord Ram, be merciful.'

'What happened?' asked a confused Bhagirath.

'We've been told that Lord Bhrigu can read your mind by looking into your eyes,' said Kartik.

'What? That's impossible!'

'He's a *Saptrishi Uttradhikari*, Bhagirath,' said Ganesh. 'Very few things are impossible for him. If he was distinctly looking into your eyes, chances are he has read your conscious thoughts. So he may have some very sensitive information about our plans.'

'Good Lord!' whispered Bhagirath.

'I want you to carefully recall what you were thinking about while speaking with Lord Bhrigu,' said Ganesh.

'I spoke about...'

Kartik interrupted Bhagirath. 'It doesn't matter what you spoke. What matters is what you thought.'

Bhagirath closed his eyes and tried to remember. 'I thought that my imbecile father could not have been the true leader of the conspiracy.'

'That's no secret,' said Ganesh. 'What else did you think about?'

'I remember a feeling of dread when I realised that Lord Bhrigu is the true leader.'

'I would have ideally not let him know your fears,' said Kartik. 'But this too cannot harm us.'

'I recall thinking that Lord Shiva had sent me to Ayodhya to discover the identity of the true leader.'

'Again,' said Ganesh, 'this is not very harmful information for an enemy to have.'

Bhagirath continued. 'I thought about being attacked by the joint Meluha-Ayodhya ships at Panchavati and how we repelled the attack.'

Ganesh cursed under his breath.

Bhagirath looked at Ganesh apologetically. 'So Maharishi Bhrigu knows about the Panchavati defences... I'm so sorry, Ganesh.'

Kartik patted Bhagirath reassuringly on his arm. 'You did not intend this to happen, Prince Bhagirath. Was there anything else?'

'Oh, Lord Rudra!' whispered Bhagirath.

Ganesh's eyes narrowed. 'What?'

'I thought about Parvateshwar wanting to defect to Meluha,' said Bhagirath.

Ganesh stopped breathing while Kartik held his head. 'What now, *dada*?'

'Get *mausi* here, Kartik,' said Ganesh, asking his brother to fetch the Queen of the Nagas, Kali. 'We know what we have to do, but *baba's* wrath will be terrible. *Mausi* can stand up to him. We need to know if she agrees with us.'

Kartik immediately left the room.

A shocked Bhagirath stared at Ganesh. 'I hope you are not thinking what I fear.'

'Do we have a choice, Bhagirath? Maharishi Bhrigu will try and contact Parvateshwar at the first opportunity and whisk him away.'

'Ganesh, Parvateshwar is my sister's husband. We cannot kill him!'

Ganesh raised his hands in exasperation. 'Kill him? What are you talking about, Bhagirath?'

Bhagirath remained silent.

'I only want to arrest General Parvateshwar so that he cannot escape.'

Bhagirath was about to say something when Ganesh interrupted him.

'We have no choice. If Parvateshwar goes over to their side, it would be disastrous for us. He is a brilliant strategist.'

Bhagirath sighed. 'I am not contradicting you. What needs to be done has got to be done. But we cannot kill him. I will not be responsible for making my sister a widow.'

'I wouldn't dream of killing a man like Parvateshwar. But we've got to arrest him. For all we know, Maharishi Bhrigu may already be attempting to make contact with him.'

A moonless night hung over an eerily quiet *Assi Ghat* in Kashi. The normally busy *Port of Eighty* did receive a small number of ships at night, but the darkness had kept away even the few brave captains who attempted night dockings.

A silent and pensive Parvateshwar was walking back from the ghat. He had just dropped a shrouded Bhrigu to a waiting rowboat which would take him to a ship anchored in the middle of the river. Bhrigu intended to stop at Prayag for a short while and then proceed to Meluha.

'General Parvateshwar!'

Parvateshwar looked up to see Kali. The flickering light from the torches revealed that she was accompanied by Ganesh, Kartik and about fifty soldiers. Parvateshwar smiled.

'You've brought fifty soldiers to down one man?' asked Parvateshwar, his hand resting on his sword hilt. 'You think too highly of me, Queen Kali.'

'Were you planning to escape, General?' asked Kali.

The soldiers rapidly surrounded Parvateshwar, making escape impossible.

Parvateshwar was about to answer when he saw a familiar figure next to Kartik.

'Bhagirath?'

'Yes,' answered Bhagirath. 'This is a sad day for me.'

'I'm sure it is,' said Parvateshwar sarcastically, before turning to Kali. 'So what do you plan on doing, Queen Kali? Kill me straight away or wait till the Lord Neelkanth returns?'

'So you admit that you are a traitor,' said Kali.

'I admit to nothing since you haven't asked anything.'

'I did ask you if you were attempting an escape.'

'If that were the case, I wouldn't be walking *away* from the Assi Ghat, Your Highness.'

'Have you met Maharishi Bhrigu?' asked Ganesh.

Parvateshwar never lied. 'Yes.'

Kali sucked in a sharp breath, reaching for her sword.

'*Mausi*,' said Ganesh, pleading with the Naga queen to keep her temper in check. 'Where is the Maharishi, General?'

'He's back on a boat,' said Parvateshwar, 'probably on his way to Meluha.'

'You know what comes next, don't you?' asked Kali.

'Do I get a soldier's death?' asked Parvateshwar. 'Will you

all attack me one by one so I have the pleasure of killing a few of you? Or will you just pounce on me like a pack of cowardly hyenas?'

'Nobody is getting killed, General,' said Ganesh. 'We Nagas have a justice system. Your treachery will be proven in court and then you will be punished.'

'No Naga is going to judge me,' said Parvateshwar. 'I recognise only two courts: the one sanctioned by the laws of Meluha and the other of the Lord Neelkanth.'

'Then you shall receive justice from the Neelkanth when he returns,' said Kali, before turning towards the soldiers. 'Arrest the General.'

Parvateshwar didn't argue. He stretched out his hands as he looked at the crestfallen face of the man handcuffing him. It was Nandi.

— ⚹ —

Shiva, Sati and Gopal were dining in the Neelkanth's chamber at Magadh.

'The captain of the ship met me in the evening,' said Sati. 'All the weapons have been loaded. We can sail for Kashi tomorrow morning.'

'Good,' said Shiva. 'We can begin our campaign within a few weeks.'

Gopal had anticipated this. 'I have already sent a message to the pandit of the Narsimha temple in Magadh. He will relay it to King Chandraketu, who will then set sail with an armada and await further instructions at the port of Vaishali.'

'Bhagirath, Ganesh and Kartik will travel with them to Ayodhya,' said Shiva. 'Ganesh will lead the Eastern Command.'

'A wise choice,' said Gopal.

'The Western Army, comprising the Vasudevs, the Nagas

and those Brangas who have been assigned to the Nagas, will attack Meluha under my command. We will set sail along with Kali and Parvateshwar within a week of reaching Kashi.'

'I have already sent a message to Ujjain,' said Gopal. 'The army has marched out with dismantled sections of our ships which will be reassembled on the Narmada. We will sail together to the Western Sea and farther up the coast, to Lothal.'

'What about your war elephants, Pandit*ji*?' asked Sati. 'How will they reach Meluha?'

'Our elephant corps will set out from Ujjain through the jungles, and meet us at Lothal,' answered Gopal.

'Gopal*ji*, can the Narsimha temple pandit send out a message to Suparna in Panchavati as well?' asked Shiva. 'Kali has appointed her the commander of the Naga army in her absence. They should join us at the Narmada.'

'I shall do that, Neelkanth,' said Gopal.

Chapter 17

Honour Imprisoned

An underground chamber beneath the royal palace had been converted into a temporary prison for General Parvateshwar. Though the public prisons of peaceful Kashi were humane, it would have been a slight to a man of Parvateshwar's stature to be imprisoned along with common criminals. The spacious chamber, though luxuriously appointed, was windowless. Not taking any chances, Parvateshwar's hands and legs had been securely shackled. While a platoon of crack Naga troops guarded the sole exit, two senior officers watched over Parvateshwar at all times. Nandi and Parshuram kept first watch.

'My apologies, General,' said Parshuram.

Parvateshwar smiled. 'You don't need to apologise, Parshuram. You are following orders. That is your duty.'

Nandi sat opposite Parvateshwar, but kept his face averted.

'Are you angry with me, Major Nandi?' asked Parvateshwar.

'What right do I have to be angry with you, General?'

'If there's something about me that's troubling you, then you have every right to be angry. Lord Ram had asked us to "always be true to ourselves".'

Nandi remained silent.

Parvateshwar smiled ruefully and then looked away.

Nandi gathered the courage to speak. 'Are you being true to yourself, General?'

'Yes, I am.'

'Forgive me, but you are not. You're betraying your living God.'

With visible effort, Parvateshwar kept his temper in check. 'It is only the very unfortunate who must choose between their God and their *swadharma*.'

'Are you saying that your *personal dharma* is leading you away from Good?'

'I'm saying no such thing, Major Nandi. But my duty towards Meluha is most important to me.'

'Rebelling against your God is treason.'

'Some may hold that rebelling against your country is a greater treason.'

'I disagree. Of course, Meluha is important to me, I would readily die for it. But I wouldn't fight my living God for the sake of Meluha. That would be completely wrong.'

'I'm not saying that you're wrong, Major Nandi.'

'Then you admit to being wrong yourself.'

'I didn't say that either.'

'How can that be, General?' asked Nandi. 'We're talking about polar opposites. One of us has got to be wrong.'

Parvateshwar smiled. 'It is such a staunch Suryavanshi belief: the opposite of truth has to be untruth.'

Nandi remained silent.

'But Anandmayi has taught me something profound,' said Parvateshwar. 'There is your truth and there is my truth. As for the universal truth, it does not exist.'

'The universal truth does exist, though it has always been an enigma to human beings,' smiled Parshuram. 'And it will continue to remain an enigma for as long as we are bound to this mortal body.'

— ⁂ —

Anandmayi stormed into Bhagirath's chambers in the Kashi palace, brushing the guard aside.

'What the hell have you done?' she shouted.

Bhagirath immediately rose and walked towards his sister. 'Anandmayi, we had no choice...'

'Dammit! He is my husband! How dare you?'

'Anandmayi, it is very likely he will share our plans with...'

'Don't you know Parvateshwar? Do you think he will ever do anything unethical? He used to walk away whenever you spoke about the Lord Neelkanth's directives. He's not aware of any of your "confidential" military plans!'

'You're right. I'm sorry.'

'Then why is he under arrest?'

'Anandmayi, it wasn't my decision...'

'That's rubbish! Why is he under arrest?'

'He might escape if...'

'Do you think he couldn't have escaped had he wanted to? He is waiting to meet the Lord Neelkanth. Only then will he leave for Meluha.'

'That's what he said but...'

'But? What the hell do you mean "but"? Do you think Parvateshwar can lie? Do you think he is even capable of lying?'

'No.'

'If he has said that he will not leave till Lord Shiva returns, then believe me he's not going anywhere!'

Bhagirath remained silent.

Anandmayi stepped up to her brother. 'Are you planning to assassinate him?'

'No, Anandmayi!' cried a shocked Bhagirath. 'How can you even think I would do such a thing?'

'Don't pull this injured act on me, Bhagirath. If anything were to happen to my husband, even an accident, you know that the Lord Neelkanth's anger will be terrible. You and your allies may discount me, but you are scared of him. Remember his rage before you do something stupid.'

'Anandmayi, we are not...'

'The Lord Neelkanth will be back in a week. Until then, I'm going to keep a constant vigil outside the chamber where you have imprisoned him. If anyone wants to harm him, he will have to contend with me first.'

'Anandmayi, nobody is going to...'

She turned and strode away stiffly, causing Bhagirath to trail off mid-sentence. She pushed aside the diminutive Kashi soldier standing in her path and slammed the door behind her even as the soldier fell.

— ⁂ —

Ayurvati placed a hand on Anandmayi's shoulders. The Ayodhyan princess was sitting outside the chamber where Parvateshwar had been imprisoned. She had refused to move for the last few days.

'Why don't you go to your room and sleep,' said Ayurvati. 'I'll sit here.'

A determined Anandmayi shook her head. Wild horses couldn't drag her away.

'Anandmayi...'

'They aren't even letting me meet him, Ayurvati,' sobbed Anandmayi.

Ayurvati sat down next to Anandmayi. 'I know...'

Anandmayi turned towards the Naga soldiers standing guard at the door. 'MY HUSBAND IS NO CRIMINAL!'

Ayurvati took Anandmayi's hand in hers. 'Calm down... These soldiers are only following orders...'

'He's no criminal... He's a good man...'

'I know...'

Anandmayi rested her head on Ayurvati's shoulders and began to cry.

'Calm down,' said Ayurvati soothingly.

Anandmayi raised her head and looked at Ayurvati. 'I don't care if the entire world turns against him. I don't even care if the Neelkanth turns against him. I will stand by my husband. He is a good man... a good man!'

'Have faith in the Neelkanth. Have faith in his justice. Speak to him the moment he arrives in Kashi.'

— ⅄ⓞ∪Ϯ⊛ —

The sun was directly overhead as Shiva's ship prepared to dock at Assi Ghat. Shiva, Sati and Gopal were at the balustrade.

'I do not understand why King Athithigva has to organise a grand reception every time I come here,' said Shiva as he looked at the giant canopy and vast throngs of people waiting.

Gopal smiled. 'I don't think Lord Athithigva orders his people to assemble, my friend. The people gather of their own accord to welcome their Neelkanth.'

'Yes, but it is so unnecessary,' said Shiva. 'They shouldn't be taking a break from their work to welcome me. If they really do want to honour me, they should work even harder at their jobs.'

Gopal laughed. 'People have a tendency to do what they want to do rather than what they should be doing.'

The ship was now close enough for them to see the expressions of the people on the dock, even the nobility standing farther away on higher ground.

'Something is not right,' said Sati.

'Why is everyone looking troubled?' asked Gopal.

Shiva studied the crowds carefully. 'You're right. Something's wrong.'

'King Athithigva seems disturbed,' said Sati.

'Kali, Ganesh, Kartik and Bhagirath are in a heated discussion,' said Shiva. 'What's troubling them so much?'

Sati tapped Shiva lightly. 'Look at Anandmayi.'

'Where?' asked Shiva, not finding her in the area cordoned off for the nobility.

'She's in the crowd,' said Sati, gesturing with her eyes. 'Right where the ship's gangplank will land.'

'Perhaps she wants to talk to you the moment you step off, my friend,' said Gopal.

'She looks deeply agitated, Shiva,' said Sati.

Shiva scanned the entire port area. And he softly asked, 'Where's Parvateshwar?'

— ⁂ —

The guards stepped aside as the Neelkanth stormed into the temporary prison. Sati, Gopal, Anandmayi and Kali could hardly keep pace.

He encountered Veerbhadra, Parshuram and Nandi in deep conversation with a fettered Parvateshwar.

'What the hell is the meaning of this?' shouted a livid Shiva.

'My Lord,' said Parvateshwar as he rose, the chains clinking.

Nandi, Veerbhadra and Parshuram rose too.

'Remove his chains!'

'Shiva,' said Kali softly, 'I don't think that is wise...'

'Remove his chains now!'

Nandi and Parshuram immediately set to work. The chains were removed with great haste. Parvateshwar rubbed his wrists, helping the blood flow freely.

'Leave me alone with Parvateshwar.'

'Shiva...' said Veerbhadra.

'Have I not made myself clear, Bhadra? Everybody leave right now!'

Kali shook her head disapprovingly, but obeyed. The others stepped out without any sign of protest.

Shiva turned to Parvateshwar, his eyes blazing with fury.

Parvateshwar was the first to speak. 'My Lord...'

Shiva raised his hand, signalling for him to keep quiet. Parvateshwar obeyed immediately. Shiva looked away as he walked back and forth, breathing deeply to calm his mind. He remembered his uncle Manobhu's words.

Anger is your enemy. Control it. Control it.

Much as he tried, Shiva could feel the fury welling up within him like a coiled snake waiting to strike. But his mind also told him that the issue at hand was far too important to allow anger to cloud his judgement.

Once he had breathed some calm into his mind and heart, Shiva turned to Parvateshwar. 'Tell me this is not true. Just say it and I will believe you, regardless of what anyone else says.'

'My Lord, this is the most difficult decision I have ever had to make in my life.'

'Do you intend to fight me, Parvateshwar?'

'No, My Lord. But I'm duty-bound to protect Meluha. I hope some miracle ensures that you and Meluha are not on opposite sides.'

'Miracle? Miracle? Are you a child, Parvateshwar? Do you think it is possible for me to compromise with Meluha where the Somras is concerned?'

'No, My Lord.'

'Do you think that the Somras is not evil?'

'No, My Lord. The Somras is evil. I have stopped using it from the moment you said that it was evil.'

'Then why would you fight to protect the Somras?'

'I will only fight to protect Meluha.'

'But they are on the same side!'

'That is my misfortune, My Lord.'

'You stubborn...'

Shiva checked himself in time. Parvateshwar remained silent. He knew the Neelkanth's anger was justified.

'Is Bhrigu forcing you to do this? Has he captured somebody who is important to you? We can take care of that. No one important to you will get hurt as long as I am alive.'

'Maharishi Bhrigu is not forcing me in any way, My Lord.'

'Then who in Lord Rudra's name is making you do this?'

'My soul. I have no choice. This is what I must do.'

'That does not make any sense, Parvateshwar. Do you actually believe that your soul is forcing you to fight for Evil?'

'My soul is only making me fight for my motherland, My Lord. This is a call that I cannot refuse. It is my purpose.'

'Your soul is taking you down a dangerous path, Parvateshwar.'

'Then so be it. No danger should distract one from walking one's path.'

'What nonsense is this? Do you think Bhrigu cares about you? All he cares for is the Somras. Trust me, once your purpose is served, you will be killed.'

'All of us will die when we have served our purpose. That is the way of the universe.'

Shiva covered his face with his hands in sheer frustration.

'I know you are angry, My Lord,' said Parvateshwar. 'But your purpose is to fight Evil. And you must do all that you can to accomplish it.'

Shiva continued to stare at Parvateshwar silently.

'All I am asking is for you to understand that just like you have to serve your purpose, I must serve mine. Your soul will not allow you to rest till you have destroyed Evil. My soul will not allow me to rest till I have done all that I can to protect Meluha.'

Shiva ran his hands over his face, trying desperately to maintain his calm. 'Do you think I am wrong, Parvateshwar?'

'Please, My Lord. How can I ever think that? You would never do anything that is wrong.'

'Then can you please explain the strange workings of your mind? You will not walk with me, although you admit that my path is right. Instead, you insist on walking on a path which leads to your death. In the name of Lord Rudra, why?'

'*Svadharma nidhanam shreyaha para dharmo bhayaavahah*,' said Parvateshwar. 'Death in the course of performing one's own duty is better than engaging in another's path, for that is truly dangerous.'

Shiva stared hard at Parvateshwar for what seemed like an eternity, then turned around and bellowed.

'Nandi! Bhadra! Parshuram!'

They rushed in.

'General Parvateshwar will continue to remain our prisoner,' said Shiva.

'As you command, My Lord,' said Nandi, saluting Shiva.

'And Nandi, the General will not be chained.'

Chapter 18

Honour or Victory?

'I say that we have no choice,' said Kali. 'I agree we cannot kill him, but he must remain our prisoner here till the end of the war.'

Shiva and his family, along with Gopal, were assembled in the Neelkanth's private chambers at the Kashi palace.

Ganesh glanced at a seething Sati and decided to hold his counsel.

Kartik, however, had no such compunctions. 'I agree with *mausi*.'

Shiva looked at Kartik.

'I know that it is a difficult decision,' continued Kartik. 'Parvateshwar*ji* has behaved with absolute honour. He was not privy to any of our strategy discussions. He could have escaped on multiple occasions, but did not. He waited till you returned so he could take your permission to leave. But you're the Neelkanth, *baba*. You have the responsibility for India on your shoulders. Sometimes, for the sake of the larger good, one has to do things that may not appear right at the time. Perhaps, a laudable end can justify some questionable means.'

Sati glared at her younger son. 'Kartik, how can you think that a great end justifies questionable means?'

'*Maa*, can we accept a world where the Somras continues to thrive?'

'Of course we can't,' said Sati. 'But do you think that this struggle is only about the Somras?'

Ganesh finally spoke up. 'Of course it is, *maa*.'

'No, it is not,' said Sati. 'It is also about the legacy that we will leave behind, of how Shiva will be remembered. People from across the world will analyse every aspect of his life and draw lessons. They will aspire to be like him. Didn't we all criticise Lord Bhrigu for using the *daivi astras* in the attack on Panchavati? The Maharishi must have justified what he did with arguments similar to what you're advocating. If we behave in the same way then what will differentiate us from him?'

'People only remember victors, *didi*,' said Kali. 'For history is written by victors. They can write it however they want. The losers are always remembered the way the victors portray them. What is important right now is for us to ensure our victory.'

'Please allow me to disagree, Your Highness,' said Gopal. 'It is not true that only victors determine history.'

'Of course, it is,' said Kali. 'There is a Deva version of events and an Asura version of events. Which version do we remember?'

'If you talk about the present-day India, then yes, the Deva version is remembered,' said Gopal. 'But even today, the Asura version is well known outside of India.'

'But we live here,' said Kali. 'Why should we bother about the beliefs that prevail elsewhere?'

'Perhaps I have been unable to make myself clear, Your Highness,' said Gopal. 'It's not just about the place, but also about the time. Will the Deva version of history always be remembered the way it is? Or is it possible that different versions will emerge? Remember, if there's a victor's version of events, then there's a victim's narrative that survives equally. For as long as the victors remain in command, their version holds ground. But if history has taught us one thing, it is that communities rise and fall in eminence just as surely as the tides ebb and flow. There comes a time when victors do not remain as powerful, when the victims of old become the elite of the day. Then, one will find that narratives change just as dramatically. This new version becomes the popular version in time.'

'I disagree,' dismissed Kali. 'Unless the victims escape to another land, like the Asuras, they will always remain powerless, their experiences dismissed as myths.'

'Not quite,' said Gopal. 'Let me talk about something that is close to your heart. In the times that we live, the Nagas are feared and cursed as demons. Many millennia ago, they were respected. After winning this war they will become respectable and powerful once again as loyal allies of the Neelkanth. Your version of history will then begin to gain currency once again, won't it?'

An unconvinced Kali chose to remain silent.

'An interesting factor is the conduct of the erstwhile victims in the new era,' said Gopal. 'Armed with fresh empowerment, will they seek vengeance on the surviving old elite?'

'Obviously the victims will nurse hatred in their hearts. Would you expect them to be filled with the milk of human kindness?' asked Kali, sarcastically.

'You hate the Meluhans, don't you?'

'Yes, I do.'

'But how do you feel about the founding father of Meluha, Lord Ram?'

Kali was quiet. She held Lord Ram in deep reverence.

'Why do you revere Lord Ram, but reject the people he left behind?' asked Gopal.

Sati spoke up on her sister's behalf. 'That is because Lord Ram treated even his enemies honourably, quite unlike the present-day Meluhans.'

Shiva observed Sati with quiet satisfaction.

'A man becomes God when his vision moves beyond the bounds of victors and losers,' said Sati. 'Shiva's message has to live on forever. And that can only happen if both the victors and the losers find validation in him. That he must win is a given. But equally critical is his winning the right way.'

Gopal was quick to support Sati. 'Honour must beget honour. That is the only way.'

Shiva walked to the balcony and gazed at the massive Kashi Vishwanath temple on the Sacred Avenue, and beyond it at the holy Ganga.

Everyone was poised for his decision.

He turned and whispered, 'I need some time to think. We will meet again tomorrow.'

— ⅄ⵀⵡ —

Sati looked down. The clear waters of the lake lay below her. The fish swam rapidly, keeping pace with her as she flew over the water, towards the banks in the distance.

She looked up towards a massive black mountain, different in hue from all the surrounding mountains, topped by a white cap of snow. As she drew close, her vision fell upon a yogi on the banks of the lake. He wore a tiger-skin skirt. His long, matted hair had been tied up in a bun. His muscular body was covered by numerous battle scars. A small halo, almost like the sun, shone behind his head. A crescent moon was lodged in his hair while a snake slithered around his neck. A massive trident stood sentinel beside him, half-buried in the ground. The face of the yogi was blurred, though. And then the mists cleared.

'Shiva!' said Sati.

Shiva smiled at her.

'Is this your home? Kailash?'

Shiva nodded, never once taking his eyes off her.

'We shall come here one day, my love. When it's all over, we shall live together in your beautiful land.'

Shiva's smile broadened.

'Where are Ganesh and Kartik?'

Shiva didn't answer.

'Shiva, where are our sons?'

Suddenly, Shiva started ageing. His handsome face was rapidly overrun by wrinkles. His matted hair turned white almost instantaneously. His massive shoulders began to droop, his taut muscles dissolving before Sati's very eyes.

Sati smiled. 'Will we grow old together?'

Shiva's eyes flew wide open. Like he was looking at something that did not make sense.

Sati looked down at her reflection in the waters. She frowned in surprise. She hadn't aged a day. She still looked as young as always. She turned back towards her husband. 'But I've stopped using the Somras. What does this mean?'

Shiva was horror-struck. Tears were flowing fiercely down his wrinkled cheeks as his face was twisted in agony. He reached out with his hand, screaming loudly. 'SATI!'

Sati looked down. Her body was on fire.

'SATI!' he screamed once again, getting up and running towards the lake. 'DON'T LEAVE ME!'

Still facing Shiva, Sati began to fly backwards, faster and faster, the wind fanning the flames on her body. But even through the blaze she could see her husband running desperately towards her.

'SATI!'

Sati woke up with a start. The beautifully carved Kashi palace ceiling looked ethereal in the flickering torch-light.

The only sound was that of the water trickling down the porous walls, cooling the hot dry breeze as it flowed in. Sati instinctively reached out to her left. Shiva wasn't there.

Alarmed, she was up in a flash. 'Shiva?'

She heard him call out from the balcony. 'I'm here, Sati.'

Walking across, she could make out Shiva's silhouette in the darkness as he leaned back in an easy chair, focussed on the Vishwanath temple in the distance. Nestling comfortably against him on the armrest, she reached out her hand and ran it lovingly through her husband's locks.

It wasn't a full moon night, but there was enough light for Shiva to clearly see his wife's expression.

'What's the matter?' asked Shiva.

Sati shook her head. 'Nothing.'

'Something's wrong. You look disturbed.'

'I had a strange dream.'

'Hmmm?'

'I dreamt that we were separated.'

Shiva smiled and pulled Sati close to him, embracing her. 'You can dream all you want, but you're never getting away from me.'

Sati laughed. 'I don't intend to.'

Shiva held his wife close, turning his gaze back to the Vishwanath temple.

'What are you thinking?' asked Sati.

'I'm just thinking that marrying you was the best thing I ever did.'

Sati smiled. 'I'm not going to disagree with that. But what specifically brought that up at this time?'

Shiva ran his hand along Sati's face. 'Because I know that for as long as you're with me, you will always keep me centred on the right path.'

'So, you've decided to do the right thing with...'

'Yes, I have.'

Sati nodded in satisfaction. 'We will win, Shiva.'

'Yes, we will. But it has to be the right way.'

'Absolutely,' said Sati, and quoted Lord Ram. 'There is no wrong way to do the right thing.'

— ⅄ⓄⅡ⇑⊗ —

A select assembly awaited the arrival of Parvateshwar, who was to be produced in the court of Kashi during the second prahar. The Kashi nobility was represented by Athithigva alone. Shiva sat impassively, his closest advisors around him in a semi-circle: Gopal, Sati, Kali, Ganesh and Kartik. Bhagirath and Ayurvati stood at a distance. Anandmayi was missing.

Shiva nodded towards Athithigva.

Athithigva called out loudly. 'Bring the General in.'

Parshuram, Veerbhadra and Nandi escorted Parvateshwar into the hall. The Meluhan general was unchained, keeping in mind Shiva's explicit orders. He glanced briefly at Sati before turning to look at Shiva. The Neelkanth's rigid face was inscrutable. Parvateshwar expected to be put to death. He knew Shiva would not have wanted to do it, but the others would have convinced him of the necessity of getting rid of the general.

Parvateshwar also knew that regardless of what happened to him, he would treat the Neelkanth with the honour that the Lord deserved. The general clicked his heels together and brought his balled right fist up to his chest. And then, completing the Meluhan military salute, he bowed low towards the Neelkanth. He did not bother with anyone else.

'Parvateshwar,' said Shiva.

Parvateshwar immediately looked up.

'I do not want to drag this on for too long,' said Shiva. 'Your rebellion has shocked me. But it has also reinforced my conviction that we are fighting Evil and it'll not make things easy for us. It can lead even the best amongst us astray, if not through inducements then through dubious calls of honour.'

Parvateshwar continued to stare at Shiva, waiting for the sentence.

'But when one fights against Evil, one has to fight with Good,' said Shiva. 'Not just on the side of Good, but with Good in one's heart. Therefore, I have decided to allow you to leave.'

Parvateshwar couldn't believe his ears.

'Go now,' said Shiva.

Parvateshwar was only half listening. This magnificent gesture from the Neelkanth had brought tears to his eyes.

'But let me assure you,' continued Shiva coldly, 'the next time we meet, it will be on a battlefield. And that will be the day I will kill you.'

Parvateshwar bowed his head once again, his eyes clouded with tears. 'That will also be the day of my liberation, My Lord.'

Shiva stayed stoic.

Parvateshwar looked up at Shiva. 'But for as long as I live, My Lord, I shall fight to protect Meluha.'

'Go!' said Shiva.

Parvateshwar smiled at Sati. She brought her hands together in a polite but expressionless Namaste. Parvateshwar mouthed the word *'Vijayibhav'* silently, blessing his God-daughter with *victory*.

As he turned around to leave, he saw Ayurvati and Bhagirath standing by the door. He walked up to them.

'My apologies, Parvateshwar,' said Bhagirath.

'I understand,' replied Parvateshwar, impassively.

Parvateshwar looked at Ayurvati.

Ayurvati just shook her head. 'Do you realise that you are leaving one of the most magnificent men ever born?'

'I do,' said Parvateshwar. 'But I will have the good fortune of dying at his hands.'

Ayurvati breathed deeply and patted Parvateshwar on his shoulder. 'I will miss you, my friend.'

'I will miss you too.'

Parvateshwar scanned the room quickly. 'Where's Anandmayi?'

'She's waiting for you at the port,' said Bhagirath, 'beside the ship that will take you away.'

Parvateshwar nodded. He looked back one last time at Shiva and then walked out.

The harbour master came up to him just as Parvateshwar reached the Assi Ghat. 'General, your ship is berthed in that direction.'

He began walking in the direction indicated. Parvateshwar saw Anandmayi by the gangplank of a small vessel, obviously a merchant ship.

'Did you know that I would be allowed to leave honourably?' asked a smiling Parvateshwar as soon he reached her.

'When they told me this morning to arrange a ship to sail up the Ganga,' said Anandmayi, 'I could surmise it was not to carry your corpse all the way to Meluha and display it to the Suryavanshis.'

Parvateshwar laughed.

'Also, I never lost faith in the Neelkanth,' said Anandmayi.

'Yes,' said Parvateshwar. 'He's the finest man born since Lord Ram.'

Anandmayi looked at the ship. 'It's not much, I admit. It will not be comfortable, but it's quick.'

Parvateshwar suddenly stepped forward and embraced Anandmayi. It took a surprised Anandmayi a moment to respond. Parvateshwar was not a man given to public displays of affection. She knew that it was deeply uncomfortable for him so she never tried to embrace him in public.

Anandmayi smiled warmly and caressed his back. 'It's all over now.'

Parvateshwar pulled back a little, but kept his arms around his wife. 'I will miss you.'

'Miss me?' asked Anandmayi.

'You have been the best thing that ever happened to me,' said an emotional Parvateshwar, tears in his eyes.

Anandmayi raised her eyebrows and laughed. 'And I will continue to happen to you. Let's go.'

'Let's go?'

'Yes.'

'Where?'

'Meluha.'

'You're coming to Meluha?'

'Yes.'

Parvateshwar stepped back. 'Anandmayi, the path ahead is dangerous. I honestly don't think that Meluha can win.'

'So?'

'I cannot permit you to put your life in danger.'

'Did I seek your permission?'

'Anandmayi, you cannot...'

Parvateshwar stopped speaking as Anandmayi held his hand, turned around and started walking up the gangplank. Parvateshwar followed quietly with a smile on his face and tears in his eyes.

Chapter 19

Proclamation of the Blue Lord

'I have a brilliant plan,' said Daksha.

Daksha and Veerini were dining at the royal palace in Devagiri. A wary Veerini put the morsel of roti and vegetables back on her plate. She stole a quick glance towards the attendants standing guard at the door.

'What plan?' asked Veerini.

'Believe me,' said an excited Daksha. 'If we can implement it, the war will be over even before it has begun.'

'But, Lord Bhrigu...'

'Even Lord Bhrigu would be impressed. We will be rid of the Neelkanth problem once and for all.'

'Wasn't it the Neelkanth *opportunity* some years ago?' asked a sarcastic Veerini.

'Don't you understand what is happening?' asked an irritated Daksha. 'Do I have to explain everything to you? War is about to break out. Our soldiers are training continuously.'

'Yes, I'm aware of that. But I think we should keep out of this and leave the matter entirely to Lord Bhrigu.'

'Why? Lord Bhrigu is not the Emperor of India. I am.'

'Have you told Lord Bhrigu that?'

'Don't irritate me, Veerini. If you're not interested in what I have to say, just say so.'

'I'm sorry. But I think it's better to leave all the decision-making to Lord Bhrigu. All we should be concerned about is our family.'

'There you go again!' said Daksha, raising his voice. 'Family! Family! Family! Don't you care about how the world will see me? How history will judge me?'

'Even the greatest of men cannot dictate how posterity will judge them.'

Daksha pushed his plate away, shouting, 'You are the source of all my problems! It is because of you that I haven't been able to achieve all that I could have!'

Veerini looked at the attendants and turned back towards her husband. 'Keep your voice down, Daksha. Don't make a mockery of our marriage.'

'Ha! This marriage has been a mockery from the very beginning! Had I a more supportive wife, I would have conquered the world by now!'

Daksha got up angrily and stormed out.

— ⁂ —

'This is a huge mistake,' said Kali. 'In his obsession for the right way, your father may end up losing the war.'

Ganesh and Kartik were in her chamber in the Kashi palace.

'I disagree, *mausi*,' said Kartik. 'I think *baba* did the right thing. We have to win, but we must do it the right way.'

'I thought you were in agreement with us,' said a frowning Kali.

'I was. But *maa's* words convinced me otherwise.'

'In any case, *mausi*,' said Ganesh. 'It has happened. Let us not fret over it. We should focus on the war instead.'

'Do we have a choice?' asked Kali.

'*Baba* told me that I will lead the war effort in Ayodhya,' said Ganesh. 'Kartik, you will be with me.'

'We'll destroy them, *dada*,' said Kartik, raising his clenched right fist.

'That we will,' said Ganesh. '*Mausi*, are you sure about Lothal and Maika?'

'I've already asked Suparna to send ambassadors to Governor Chenardhwaj,' said Kali. 'Trust me, he is a friend.'

— ⁂ —

Kartik bent and touched his mother's feet.

'*Vijayibhav*, my child,' said Sati, as she applied the red *tilak* on Kartik's forehead for good luck and victory.

Sati, Ganesh and Kartik were in the Neelkanth's chamber. Ganesh, whose forehead already wore the *tilak*, looked at his brother with pride. Kartik was still a child, but was already universally respected as a fearsome warrior. The two sons of Shiva were to set sail down the Ganga and meet their allies in Vaishali. From there, they were to turn back, sail up the Sarayu and attack Ayodhya. Ganesh turned towards his father and touched his feet.

Shiva smiled as he pulled Ganesh up into an embrace. 'My blessings are not as potent as those that emerge from your mother's heart. But I know that you will make me proud.'

'I'll try my best, *baba*,' smiled Ganesh.

Kartik turned and touched Shiva's feet.

Shiva embraced his younger son. 'Give them hell, Kartik!'

Kartik grinned. 'I will, *baba*!'

'You should smile more often, Kartik,' said Sati. 'You look more handsome when you do.'

Kartik smiled broadly. 'The next time we meet, I will certainly be grinning from ear to ear. For our army would have defeated Ayodhya by then!'

Shiva patted Kartik on his back before turning to Ganesh. 'If Ayodhya is willing to break ranks with Meluha after my proclamation is made public, then I would rather we don't attack them.'

'I understand, *baba*,' said Ganesh. 'This is why I'm taking Bhagirath along with me. His father may hate the Ayodhyan prince, but Bhagirath still has access to many members of the nobility. I'm hoping he'll be able to convince them.'

'When will the proclamation come out, *baba*?' asked Kartik.

'Next week,' answered Shiva. 'Stay in touch with the Vaishali Vasudev pandit for the reactions from across different kingdoms in Swadweep. You will know then what to expect in Ayodhya also.'

'Yes, *baba*,' said Kartik.

Shiva turned to Ganesh. 'I've been told that you have recruited Divodas and the Branga soldiers into the army.'

'Yes,' said Ganesh. 'We'll leave on board five ships and meet the combined Branga-Vaishali army at Vaishali. I'm told they have two hundred ships. Fifty of them have been deputed to the Western Army under your command and are on their way to Kashi. The remaining hundred and fifty ships will be with me. We will attack Ayodhya with a hundred and fifty thousand men.'

'That won't be enough to conquer them,' said Sati. 'But we should be able to tie them down.'

'Yes,' answered Ganesh.

'We'll hold them back, *baba*,' said Kartik. 'I promise you.'

Shiva smiled.

'How is she now?' asked Kali.

Kali was at the river gate of the eastern palace of the

Kashi king Athithigva. The palace had been built on the eastern banks of the Ganga, which was considered inauspicious for any permanent construction. The kings of Kashi had bought this land to ensure that no Kashi citizen lived on that side. It was in this palace that Athithigva had housed his Naga sister, Maya. Ganesh and Kali's open presence had given Athithigva the courage to let his sister come out of hiding.

'Your medicines have helped, Your Highness,' said Athithigva. 'At least she's not in terrible pain anymore. The *Parmatma* has sent you as an angel to help my sister.'

Kali smiled sadly. She knew it was a matter of time before Maya, a singular name for conjoined twins who were fused into one body from the chest down, would die. It was a miracle that Maya had lived for so long. On discovering her presence, Kali had immediately supplied Naga medicines to lessen her suffering. Since she was to leave with the Western Army the next day, she had come over to leave the rest of her medicines with Maya.

'I'm no angel,' said Kali. 'If the *Parmatma* had any sense of justice, he wouldn't make an innocent person like Maya suffer so much. I'm doing all I can to set right his injustices.'

Athithigva shrugged in resignation but was too pious to curse God.

Kali's gaze turned towards the Ganga where the fifty ships of the Branga armada had dropped anchor just the previous day. The mighty fleet covered the width of the river, stretching to the opposite bank. A nervous excitement was palpable throughout Kashi. The smell of war was in the air.

The flotilla's initial progress would be slow for they would first sail west against the current and then southwards up the Chambal. After disembarking, the soldiers would then march towards the Narmada. The second voyage would take them along the course of the Narmada out to the Western Sea and then north towards Meluha.

'Let's go in,' said Kali. 'I'd like to see Maya before I leave.'

'Your Highness!' said Kanakhala, running into Daksha's private office.

Daksha looked up at his prime minister as he slipped the papyrus he was reading back into the drawer of his desk. 'Where's the fire, Kanakhala?'

'Your Highness,' said a frantic Kanakhala, obviously carrying something within the folds of her *angvastram*, 'you need to see this.'

Kanakhala placed a thin stone tablet on her emperor's desk.

'What's this?' asked Daksha.

'You need to read it, Your Highness.'

Daksha bent over to read.

To all of you who consider yourselves the children of Manu and followers of the Sanatan Dharma, this is a message from me, Shiva, your Neelkanth.

I have travelled across our great land, through all the kingdoms we are divided into, met with all the tribes that populate our fair realm. I have done this in search of the ultimate Evil, for that is my task. Father Manu had told us Evil is not a distant demon. It works its destruction close to us, with us, within us. He was right. He told us Evil does not come from down below and devour us. Instead, we help Evil destroy our lives. He was right. He told us Good and Evil are two sides of the same coin. That one day, the greatest Good will transform into the greatest Evil. He was right. Our greed in extracting more and more from Good turns it into Evil. This is the universe's way of restoring balance. It is the Parmatma's *way to control our excesses.*

I have come to the conclusion that the Somras is now the greatest

Evil of our age. All the Good that could be wrung out of the Somras has been wrung. It is time now to stop its use, before the power of its Evil destroys us all. It has already caused tremendous damage, from the killing of the Saraswati River to birth deformities to the diseases that plague some of our kingdoms. For the sake of our descendants, for the sake of our world, we cannot use the Somras anymore.

Therefore, by my order, the use of the Somras is banned forthwith.

To all those who believe in the legend of the Neelkanth: Follow me. Stop the Somras.

To all those who refuse to stop using the Somras: Know this. You will become my enemy. And I will not stop till the use of the Somras is stopped. This is the word of your Neelkanth.

Daksha looked completely stunned. 'What the hell?!'

'I do not understand what this means, Your Highness,' said Kanakhala. 'Do we stop using the Somras?'

'Where did you find this?'

'I didn't, Your Highness,' said Kanakhala. 'It was hung on the outer wall of the temple of Lord Indra near the public bath. Half the citizens have seen this already and they would be talking to the other half by now.'

'Where is Maharishi Bhrigu?'

'My Lord, what about the Somras? Should I...'

'Where is Maharishi Bhrigu?'

'But if the Neelkanth has issued this order, we have no choice...'

'Dammit, Kanakhala!' screamed Daksha. 'Where is Maharishi Bhrigu?'

Kanakhala was silent for an instant. She did not like the way her Emperor had spoken to her. 'Maharishi Bhrigu had left Prayag a little more than a month back. That was the last I heard of him, Your Highness. It will take him at least two more months to reach Devagiri.'

'Then we will wait for him before deciding on a course of action,' said Daksha.

'But how can we oppose a proclamation from the Neelkanth, Your Highness?'

'Who is the Emperor, Kanakhala?'

'You are, Your Highness.'

'And have I taken a decision?'

'Yes, Your Highness.'

'Then that is the decision of Meluha.'

'But the people have already read this...'

'I want you to put up a notice stating that this proclamation is fraudulent. It cannot have been made by the true Neelkanth, for he would never go against the greatest invention of Lord Brahma, the Somras.'

'But is that true, Your Highness?'

Daksha's eyes narrowed, his temper barely in check. 'Kanakhala, just do what I tell you to do. Or I will appoint someone else as prime minister.'

Kanakhala brought her hands together in a formal but icy Namaste, and turned to leave. She couldn't resist a final parting shot, though. 'What if there are other notices like this?'

Daksha looked up. 'Send bird couriers across the empire. If they see such a notice anywhere, it must be pulled down and replaced with what I have asked you to put up instead. This notice is bogus, do you understand?'

'Yes, Your Highness,' said Kanakhala.

As she closed the door behind her, Daksha angrily flung the tablet on the floor. 'Mine is the only practical way to stop this. Maharishi Bhrigu *has* to listen to me.'

Chapter 20

The Fire Song

Gopal was shown into Shiva's private chamber the moment he arrived. He joined Shiva and Sati in the balcony and seated himself in an empty chair beside them.

'What news do you have, Pandit*ji*?' asked Shiva.

It had been a week since Shiva's proclamation banning the Somras had been released simultaneously across Meluha and Swadweep. He was hoping that the people would follow his edict.

'My pandits across the country have sent in their reports.'

'And?'

'The reactions in Meluha are very different from those in Swadweep.'

'I expected that.'

'It appears that the Swadweepan public has embraced the proclamation. It feeds into their bias against Meluha. It is seen as yet another instance of the Meluhans unfairly conspiring to stay ahead of the rest. And remember, none of them use the Somras anyway. So it's no real sacrifice for them.'

'But how have the kings reacted?' asked Sati. 'They are the ones in control of the armies.'

'It's too early to say, Sati*ji*,' said Gopal. 'But I do know that all the kings across Swadweep are in intense consultations with their advisors even as we speak.'

'But,' said Shiva, 'the Meluhans have rejected my proclamation, haven't they?'

Gopal took a deep breath. 'It's not so simple. My pandits tell me that the Meluhan public seemed genuinely disturbed by your proclamation initially. There were serious discussions in city squares and a lot of them believed that they needed to follow their Neelkanth's words.'

'Then what happened?'

'The Meluhan state is supremely efficient, my friend. The notices were taken down within the first three days, at least in all the major cities. They were replaced by a Meluhan royal order stating that they had been put up by a fraud Neelkanth.'

'And the people believed it?'

'The Meluhans have learnt to trust their government completely over many generations, Shiva,' said Sati. 'They will always believe everything that their government tells them.'

'Also,' said Gopal, 'you have been missing from Meluha for many years, my friend. There are some who are genuinely beginning to wonder if the Neelkanth has forgotten Meluha.'

Shiva shook his head. 'It looks like a war is inevitable.'

'Daksha, and more importantly Lord Bhrigu, will ensure that,' said Gopal. 'But at least our message has reached most Meluhans. Hopefully some of them will start asking questions.'

Shiva looked at the ships of the Brangas, Vasudevs and the Nagas anchored on the Ganga. 'We set sail in two days.'

— ⁂ —

'No, no!' Shiva shook his head in dismay. 'You've got it all wrong!'

Light and shadows from the bonfire danced on the faces of Brahaspati, Veerbhadra, Nandi and Parshuram as they looked at Shiva, suitably chastened. It was a moonless night and a cold wind swept in from the river. The Ganga's waters shimmered in the reflected light of the torches from the Branga fleet.

In keeping with ancient tradition, the Gunas sang paeans to the five holy elements ahead of major war campaigns, to invoke their protection and as a mark of manhood in the face of danger. The friends of the great Guna, Shiva, had gathered to honour this custom. For they would set sail at the crack of dawn tomorrow.

Shiva passed his chillum to Parshuram and decided to teach his friends the fine art of singing.

'The real trick is in here,' said Shiva, pointing towards his diaphragm.

'I thought it was in here,' said Veerbhadra playfully, pointing to his throat.

Shiva shook his head. '*Bhadra!* The vocal chords are basically a wind instrument. Your skill depends on the control over your breath, which means, essentially, the lungs. And lungs can be regulated through the diaphragm. Try to sing from here and you will find that you can project and modulate your voice with much greater ease.'

Nandi sang a note and then asked, 'Am I doing it right, My Lord?'

'Yes,' said Shiva, looking at Nandi's immense stomach. 'If you can feel the pressure of your diaphragm on your stomach, then you're doing it right. The other thing is to know when to take a breath. If you time it right, you will not have to struggle towards the end of the line. And if you don't struggle, then you will be able to finish your tune without having to rush through the last few notes at the end.'

Brahaspati, Parshuram and Nandi listened with rapt attention.

Veerbhadra however, was sarcastically nodding, his eyes mirthful. He didn't much care for tuneful singing. 'Shiva, you're taking it too seriously! It's the thought that counts. So long as I sing it with my heart, I don't think anybody should object even if I murder the song!'

Parshuram waved his hand at Veerbhadra before turning to Shiva. 'My Lord, why don't you sing and show us how it's done?'

As everyone pinned their eyes upon him, Shiva looked up at the sky, rubbed his cold neck and cleared his throat.

'Enough of the theatrics,' said Veerbhadra. 'Start singing now.'

Shiva slapped Veerbhadra playfully on his arm.

'All right now,' said Shiva with a genial grin. 'Silence!'

Veerbhadra light-heartedly put his finger on his lips as Brahaspati glared at him. Veerbhadra reached out, took the chillum from Parshuram, and inhaled deeply.

Shiva closed his eyes and went within himself. A sonorous hum emerged from within his very being, as he hit the perfect note right away. A lilting melody of words followed and the enraptured audience understood their significance. It was the prayer of a warrior to *agni* or *fire*, imploring it for a blessing. The warrior would repay this honour by feeding his enemies in combat to the hungry flames of a cremation pyre. The listeners intrinsically understood that Shiva's *prakriti* was closest to fire rather than the other four elements, each of which had Guna war songs dedicated to them.

It was a short song but the audience was spellbound. Shiva ended his performance to a robust round of applause.

'You still have it in you,' smiled Veerbhadra. 'That cold throat hasn't thrown your voice off.'

Shiva smiled and took the chillum from Veerbhadra. He

was about to take a drag when he heard someone cough softly near the entrance of the terrace. All the friends turned to find Sati standing there.

Shiva put the chillum down as he smiled. 'Did we wake you?'

Sati laughed as she walked up to Shiva. 'You were loud enough to awaken the entire city! But the song was so beautiful that I didn't mind being woken up.'

Sati took a seat next to Shiva as everyone laughed.

Shiva smiled. 'It's a song from back home. It steels a warrior's heart for battle.'

'I think the singing was more beautiful than the song,' said Sati.

'Yeah, right!' said Shiva.

'Why don't you try to sing it, My Lady?' asked Nandi.

'No, no,' said Sati. 'Of course not.'

'Why not?' asked Veerbhadra.

'I would love to hear you sing, my child,' said Brahaspati.

'Come on,' pleaded Shiva.

'All right,' said a smiling Sati. 'I'll try.'

Shiva picked up the chillum and offered it to Sati. She shook her head.

Sati had been playing close attention to Shiva's singing. The song, its melody and lyrics, had already been committed to memory. Sati closed her eyes, drew in a deep breath and entrusted herself to the music. The song began on a very low octave. She reproduced his earlier performance precisely, allowing the words to flow out in a flood when needed and letting them hang delicately when required. She quickened her breathing as she approached the end and took the notes higher and higher into a crescendo where the song finished in a flourish. Even the bonfire seemed to respond to the call of the elemental fire song from Sati.

'Wow!' exclaimed Shiva, embracing her as she finished. 'I didn't know you could sing so beautifully.'

Sati blushed. 'Was it really that good?'

'My Lady!' said a stunned Veerbhadra. 'It was fantastic. I always thought that Shiva was the best singer in the universe. But you are even better than him.'

'Of course not,' said Sati.

'Of course, yes,' said Shiva. 'It almost seemed like you had pulled all the surrounding fire into yourself.'

'And I shall keep it within me,' said Sati. 'We're going to be fighting the war of our lives. We need all the fire that we can get!'

— ⋆ —

Ganesh and Kartik had been housed in the private chambers of King Maatali of Vaishali. They were accompanied by the Ayodhyan prince Bhagirath and the Branga king Chandraketu. Their information was that Magadh was not preparing a blockade to stop their ships from sailing to Ayodhya. But the Magadhan army had been put on alert and training sessions had been doubled. Either this was a precautionary step taken by Surapadman or the Magadhans planned on attacking them once they had exhausted themselves against the Ayodhyans.

'We cannot afford to lose either men or ships as we pass Magadh,' said Ganesh. 'We've got to be prepared for the worst.'

'The way I see it,' said Bhagirath, pointing to the river map on the table, 'their primary catapults will be in the main fort on the west bank of the Sarayu. They have a small battlement on the east side as well, from where they can load catapults and throw fire barrels at us, but considering the size of this battlement, I don't think that the range will be long. So my suggestion is that we sail our ships closer to the eastern bank of the Sarayu.'

'But not too close though!' said Chandraketu.

'Of course,' said Bhagirath. 'We don't want to be the casualties of the smaller catapults from the east either.'

'Also, we can make sure that we don't just depend on our sails but also have our oarsmen in position to row the ships rapidly,' said the Vaishali king, Maatali.

'But no matter which side of the river we sail and how quickly we row, we will still lose people if they decide to attack,' said Ganesh. 'Remember, we are on ships, so we cannot get our men to disembark fast enough to retaliate.'

'Why don't we increase their risks?' asked Kartik.

'How?' asked Ganesh.

'Have half the soldiers from every ship go ashore before Magadh. We could get them to march on the eastern banks alongside our ships. The reduced load will make our ships move faster. Also, the Magadhan battlement on the eastern bank would know there is a massive contingent of enemy soldiers marching just outside their walls. They would have to think twice before doing anything stupid.'

'I like the idea,' said Bhagirath.

'I've thought of something even simpler,' said Chandraketu.

Ganesh looked at the Branga king.

'The Magadh royalty is amongst the poorest in Swadweep,' said Chandraketu. 'It's a powerful kingdom but King Mahendra has lost a considerable part of his fortune owing to both his son Ugrasen's as well as his own gambling addiction.'

'Do you want to bribe them?' asked Bhagirath.

'Why not?'

'For one, we would need massive amounts of money. A few thousand gold coins will not suffice. We won't be negotiating with some army officers but the royalty itself.'

'Will one million gold coins be enough?'

Bhagirath was stunned. 'One million?'

'Yes.'

'Just to make it through unharmed?'

'Yes.'

'Lord Rudra, be praised. That will be nearly six months of tax collections for the Magadhan royalty.'

'Exactly. I'll dispatch Divodas to Magadh with half the amount in the first ship. The other half can be handed over once our last ship has passed by safely.'

'But they could use this wealth to buy weapons,' said Kartik.

'They will not be able to do that quickly enough,' said Chandraketu. 'And what they do with the money after the war is over is not my concern.'

'Can you really afford to give away so much gold, Your Highness?' asked Ganesh.

Chandraketu smiled. 'We have more than enough, Lord Ganesh. But it means nothing to us. I would give away all the gold that we have to stop the Somras.'

'All right,' said Ganesh. 'I see no reason why it won't work.'

Chapter 21

Siege of Ayodhya

The cool northerly wind was a welcome relief for Shiva as he sat on the deck of the lead ship with Gopal, Sati and Kali clustered around him. As the fifty-six vessel armada made steady progress upriver, he knew that in just a few weeks they would reach close to the headwaters of the Chambal from where the soldiers would disembark and march to the Narmada.

'Pandit*ji*, do your ships that wait for us at the Narmada have the additional capacity to carry the fifty-five thousand soldiers who accompany us?' asked Kali.

'Yes, Your Highness,' said Gopal. 'Our ships have been specially designed to handle this additional load since we knew that we would not be able to use the ships we're currently on.'

'Judging by the maps we've seen,' said Sati, 'we should reach Lothal in three months, right Pandit*ji*?'

'Yes, Sati*ji*,' said Gopal. 'If the winds favour us, we may even make it earlier.'

'Have you received word from the Lothal governor, Kali?' asked Shiva.

'My ambassador will be waiting with the information at the Narmada,' answered Kali. 'Trust me, we will gain easy entry into Lothal. But don't expect a huge addition of troops into our army. Lothal doesn't have more than two or three thousand soldiers.'

'We don't really need their soldiers,' said Shiva. 'We have enough troops of our own. Along with the Vasudev army that waits for us at the Narmada, your own Naga army and this Branga force, we have more than a hundred thousand men. That's equal to the strength of the Meluhan army.'

'We can easily defeat them,' said Kali.

'I do not intend to attack,' said Shiva.

'I think you should.'

'All we need to do is destroy the Somras manufacturing facility, Kali.'

'But you have the Nagas with you. You shouldn't be afraid of a direct confrontation.'

'I'm not afraid. I just don't see the sense in it. It will distract us from our main purpose – the destruction of the Somras. We do not want to destroy Meluha. Don't forget that.'

'I'll count on you to remind me of that every time I forget,' said Kali.

Shiva smiled and shook his head.

The voyage up the Sarayu had been surprisingly uneventful. The Magadhans did not attack Ganesh's ships. The massive convoy was so long that the guards on the Magadhan towers spent an entire day watching ships go by.

A little over a week later, Ganesh ordered his ships to drop anchor. Kartik, Bhagirath, Chandraketu and Ganesh got into a small boat and rowed ashore. The forest had been cleared up to a fair distance. Divodas, the leader of the Branga immigrants in Kashi, waited there along with twenty men.

Ganesh jumped off as soon as the boat beached, and

waded through the shallow water to the river bank. The others followed. He touched his head to the ground as he reached the shore. He looked deep into the forest, remembering a time long ago when he had hidden behind the trees and observed his mother. 'Kartik, this is the Bal-Atibal Kund. This is where *Saptrishi* Vishwamitra taught Lord Ram his legendary skills.'

Kartik's eyes were wide open in awe. He bent down and touched the ground with his hand and whispered, 'Jai Shri Ram.'

The others around him repeated it. 'Jai Shri Ram.'

'Kartik,' said Ganesh, 'this ground was blessed by *Saptrishi* Vishwamitra and Lord Ram. But its greatness has been forgotten by many. We may have to redeem the honour of this land with blood.'

Kartik took a moment to understand. 'Do you think Surapadman might chase us?'

Ganesh smiled. 'He *will* chase us. Trust me. I see the siege of Ayodhya as a bait to draw Surapadman out of Magadh. Once he is out, we will destroy his army and capture his city. We'll be able to stop Ayodhyan ships easily with Magadh blockading the Ganga. And the battle to decide the fate of Magadh should be fought here. For this is where I would like *you* to attack him.'

'I would have thought that Surapadman would prevail on his father.'

'He is a clever man, Kartik. From what I have understood, his instinct was to support us but in the face of so much opposition, he will do what is now in his best interest. And he does have much to gain. He will win the favour of his father and his countrymen by taking revenge for his brother's death. He will come as the saviour for Ayodhya, albeit a little late so that Ayodhya is weakened. And who knows, he may even capture the sons of the Neelkanth...

Wouldn't that make him a strong ally of Bhrigu?' asked Ganesh with an ironic smile. 'Yes, brother, he will attack and he will learn that clever men should always listen to their instincts.'

Kartik took a deep breath and looked up at the sky before turning back to Ganesh with resolve writ large in his eyes. 'We will turn the river red with blood, *dada*.'

Bhagirath looked at Kartik with a familiar sensation of fascination and fear.

'Why this ground, Lord Ganesh?' asked Chandraketu.

'Your Highness,' answered Ganesh, 'as you can see, this stretch is long and narrow. That will lure Surapadman into anchoring his ships along the banks, thus stretching his army thin. The forest is not too far from the shore. Which means our main army can remain hidden behind the trees. We will leave only a small contingent on the beach.'

Bhagirath smiled. 'That will be a very juicy bait. Surapadman will probably imagine that this is a small brigade that has deserted the siege of Ayodhya. He'll want to kill them to give his soldiers a taste of victory.'

'Right,' said Ganesh. 'But the main battle will not be on land. We just have to pin him down here, which will, in all honesty, take a lot of courage, since he will have a large force. That is why I want Kartik here. But Surapadman will be defeated in the river itself.'

'How?' asked Chandraketu.

'I'll move back from Ayodhya and ram his ships from the front,' said Ganesh. 'I've also asked King Maatali to wait in the Sharda River along with thirty ships. The Sharda meets the Sarayu downriver. The Vaishali fleet will sail up the Sarayu once Surapadman's ships have passed, placing them behind the Magadhans. My contingent will attack from in front while the Vaishali forces will hit them from behind. Kartik has to hold Surapadman in position for long enough to make his fleet of ships immobile.'

'He will be sandwiched between King Maatali's ships and yours,' said Chandraketu. 'He won't stand a chance.'

'Exactly.'

'Sounds like a good plan,' said Bhagirath.

'The success of the battle hinges on two points,' said Ganesh. 'Firstly, Kartik has to entice Surapadman to anchor his ships and attack our soldiers on shore. In the absence of that he will keep moving, and his larger boats will ram through my smaller ships and possibly turn the tide in his favour. Our ships are light, manoeuvrable and built for speed. The Magadhan ships are bigger and have been built for strength. If Kartik fails to lure Surapadman ashore, my side of our fleet may face heavy casualties. I must be in command to take care of that possibility.'

'And the second point?' asked Bhagirath.

'King Maatali must be positioned to block Surapadman's escape back to Magadh. That will close the pincer trap.'

Chandraketu doubted neither Kartik's courage nor his strategic mind. His words to the young warrior bespoke respect. 'You're on your own, Kartik. It's all up to you now.'

Kartik narrowed his eyes, his hand on his sword hilt. 'I'll draw him in, King Chandraketu. And once I do, I assure you I'll obliterate his entire army myself. Our ships won't even be required to join the battle.'

Ganesh smiled at his brother.

Ganesh reached for another document from the stack on the desk and began to read, then paused to rub his tired eyes. He was seated in his private cabin, surrounded by messages from his informants about the progress of the assault. There were dozens of missives telling him every aspect from the mood of the Ayodhyan populace to the progress of the armourers in meeting the archers' demand for arrows. He had hardly slept in the weeks since the battle had begun and his body ached for rest, but these reports could not wait. It appeared that Ayodhya stood poised on the brink of surrender, and any misstep now could spell disaster. Kartik and Chandraketu sat patiently by his side, assisting Ganesh with the endless stream of messages. The three sat together in silence as they awaited Bhagirath's return, to hear news of his mission.

The siege of Ayodhya had begun over a month ago. Ganesh's navy had assaulted the city in the classical manner of the ancient war manuals. A large part of the fleet had been anchored along the west banks of the Sarayu in a double line, out of the range of the catapults on the fort walls of the eastern banks. The lined ships had extended up to the north of Ayodhya, just shy of the sheer cliff upriver where the Sarayu descended in a waterfall. Small lifeboats had been tied to the right of the ships in Ganesh's convoy, with guards present round the clock. This was to prevent devil boats from attempting to set fire to the vessels from the Ayodhya end. A section of the army had camped to the left of the ships, on the shore itself, to thwart guerrilla attacks from the Ayodhyans.

Farther to the south, Ganesh had anchored his ships and tied them together, across the river in rows of ten. Another line-up was just behind the first level of the blockade ships. Behind these, five fast-moving cutters would patrol the river farther downstream to attack any Ayodhyans who attempted to escape. Thus, any Ayodhyan ship attempting to run the river blockade had to battle through a thick line of twenty enemy ships and five quick cutters.

The forest around Ayodhya had been cleared by the defending army to give it a clear line of sight in case of an attack. Prasanjit, the Meluhan brigadier who had been left behind by Bhrigu, had tried hard to convince the Ayodhyans to extend the clearing area farther, but he had been unsuccessful. Ganesh had got his troops to cut a second line of trees beyond the clearing, as a precautionary fire line. Once the outer fire line had been established, Ganesh had ordered that the trees within the two clearings be set aflame. The intense heat generated would have resulted in the collapse of any tunnels around Ayodhya that could have served as passages for food to be smuggled into the city. The fire had burned for four continuous days and had had a demoralising effect on the citizens of 'the impenetrable city', establishing the steely resolve of their blockaders.

A cataract on a sheer cliff to the north of Ayodhya served as a natural barrier, which prevented ships from navigating farther north on the Sarayu. The Ayodhyans had built a channel into their walled shipyard just short of the cataract. The singular narrow channel of entry had been designed to be easily defendable. While this channel, passing through a gated wall, protected the Ayodhyan shipyard, it also allowed the enemy to block the exit route of their ships. Ganesh had used the leftover logs from the forest clearing to block this channel, effectively extending the siege of the city to the shipyard as well. All he had wanted was to box them in, and blocking the channel had ensured that he did not have to divert too many ships to blockade the shipyard.

Ganesh had known that the Meluhans had set up a bird courier system for the Ayodhyans. He had hit upon a very simple strategy to destroy this. He had placed six hundred archers on various treetops outside Ayodhya and along the Sarayu. These archers worked in eight-hour shifts, changing three times a day, maintaining a continuous twenty-four hour vigil. The orders had been very simple: shoot any and every bird that they saw in the sky. Most of these dead birds were retrieved by trackers. In doing so, not only did they retrieve messages exchanged between Meluha and Ayodhya, but the dead pigeons and other game birds were also a source of fresh meat for the soldiers.

Ayodhya drew fresh drinking water from the Sarayu through channels that extended from the river to within the city walls. The channels were fed by ingeniously designed giant water wheels constructed along the Sarayu. These wheels used the flow of the river to rotate. A series of buckets tied around the diameter would fill up with water and disgorge into the channels as they reached the top. Tall walls had been built around the wheels to protect them from any attack. However, there was a breach in the wall just below the water surface, from where the buckets filled up with water. This opening was fortified with bronze bars that were wide enough to allow water to run through, but not so wide as to allow a man to swim in between. But that hadn't stopped Ganesh.

Ganesh had deployed soldiers to swim across the Sarayu at night pulling small, floating wooden barrels. Within these barrels were smaller iron cans filled with oil. Water in the space between the wooden barrel and the iron can, and a slow fuse made of hemp, completed the device. Once lit, the fuse would ignite the oil, bringing the water to a boil. The consequent pressure of escaping steam would cause an explosion with the iron and wood themselves serving as shrapnel. The task of the skilled swimmers had been to strategically place the devices within the buckets of the water wheels, thus destroying them. The existing wells of Ayodhya could never quench the thirst of its innumerable residents.

Ganesh had allowed a small number of non-combatant

women and priests to come out of the city every day, to draw small amounts of water for personal use. He had also ordered that this number be progressively reduced every day until the Ayodhyans surrendered. It was a slow squeeze designed to ultimately make the people rise against their leaders. Ganesh's soldiers had added to the psychological warfare by berating the emerging Ayodhyans for going against the wishes of their Neelkanth and siding with Meluha. They had been informed that the only reason why Ganesh had refrained from shooting missiles into Ayodhya was so as not to harm innocent citizens who had had nothing to do with the decision of their emperor, Dilipa.

The daily two-way traffic of some Ayodhyans had also served another important purpose. It had enabled the hidden Vasudev pandit of the Ramjanmabhoomi temple to send an emissary to Ganesh with information collected from all the Vasudev pandits from across the temples of India.

After a couple of weeks, Ganesh had offered to send Bhagirath to meet with the nobles of his father's kingdom to reach a mutually acceptable compromise. The opportunity had been instantly grabbed by the Ayodhyans.

Ganesh stretched his tired muscles and glanced at Kartik and Chandraketu seated beside him in the cabin. They also had hardly slept but masked their exhaustion and continued to peruse the documents. Ganesh smiled to himself. When this is done, he thought, we're all going to lock ourselves in our cabins and sleep for a week!

There was the sound of footsteps and a brief knock at the cabin door before it was pushed open. Bhagirath bowed slightly to Ganesh, his hair slightly ruffled from the wind, before entering to take a seat with the three men.

'What news, Bhagirath?' asked Ganesh, pushing the pile of messages to one side.

'I'm afraid it's not good.'

'Really?' asked Chandraketu. 'I thought the Ayodhyan army must be deeply divided. I cannot think of another reason why we were able to lay siege on the city so easily. No skirmishes, no guerrilla attacks, nothing. It could only mean that the army doesn't intend to fight.'

Bhagirath shook his head. 'You don't know Ayodhya, King Chandraketu. It was not the cowardice of their army but the indecisiveness of their nobility which worked in our favour. They have not been able to agree on the best way to attack us. Furthermore, Maharishi Bhrigu had brought in a Meluhan brigadier, Prasanjit, to oversee the Ayodhyan war preparations. All it achieved was further divisions within the city. By the time they agreed upon a strategy, we were already in control of the river. There was not much that they could do after that.'

'So?' asked Ganesh. 'Haven't their troubles opened the eyes of some at least?'

'No,' said Bhagirath. 'There is tremendous confusion within the city. Many Ayodhyans are fanatical devotees of Lord Shiva and are certain that the Neelkanth will not harm them. They refuse to believe that he has ordered this attack. This blind devotion seems to be working against us.'

'So who do they think has ordered this attack?' asked Chandraketu.

'Seeing the number of Brangas in the army, they think that it is you,' said Bhagirath.

Chandraketu raised his hands. 'Why would I attack Ayodhya?'

'They believe that Branga wants to be the overlord of Swadweep,' said Bhagirath. 'In the absence of Lord Shiva, there is nothing we can do to convince them otherwise. There are a few who do believe in the proclamation that was put up, but they are in a minority. They are outshouted by a very simple logic: "We have never used the Somras, so why would the Neelkanth attack us? He should attack Meluha." Of course, a few members of the nobility do use the Somras, but the people do not know that.'

'It is the opinion of the nobility that is more important right now,' said Kartik. 'The people do not control the army. So what do the nobles think?'

'The nobility is sharply divided. Some of them actually want us to succeed, which would give them a plausible reason to refuse to help Meluha. Others believe surrendering will mean terrible loss of face. These people want the army to gallantly strike out and sail to Meluha if only to prove to the rest of Swadweep that Ayodhya has the strength to do what it chooses to do.'

'How do we assist those who do not want to come to the aid of Meluha?' asked Ganesh.

'It's difficult,' said Bhagirath. 'My father made a brilliant move last week. He promised all of them a lifetime supply of the Somras.'

'What?'

'Yes. He told them that Lord Bhrigu has promised to supply the Somras powder to Ayodhya in massive quantities.'

'But how can Maharishi Bhrigu promise that?' asked Kartik. 'Where will it come from? Is the manufacturing facility capable of producing so much more?'

'It clearly must be,' said Bhagirath. 'In any case, this offer is open only to the nobility. So the numbers will be small.'

'Damn!' said Ganesh.

'My thoughts precisely,' said Bhagirath. 'This will allow them to remain alive for a hundred more years. No amount of gold can compete with that.'

'What do we do now?' asked Chandraketu.

'Prepare for war,' said Ganesh. 'They will make earnest attempts to break the siege.'

Chapter 22

Magadh Mobilises

Shiva, along with Sati, Gopal and Kali, watched the massive army board the Vasudev and Naga ships on the banks of the Narmada. The Vasudevs had tied some logs together to create floating platforms for the army to reach the anchored ships. A viewing platform had been built on a banyan tree near the banks. The leaves had been shorn off, to afford a panoramic view of the boarding operations. The line of ships stretched as far as the eye could see. Over one hundred thousand soldiers, comprising the Brangas, Vasudevs and Nagas, were boarding the vessels in an orderly manner. The voyage would be uncomfortable with two thousand men on every ship, but fortunately, the journey to Lothal would be short.

'We should be ready to sail out by tomorrow, Shiva,' said Kali.

'Has Suparna boarded?' asked Shiva.

Suparna, a fearsome warrior, was the leader of the Garuda Nagas.

'Not yet,' said Kali.

'May I meet her? I'd like to exchange some thoughts on the Nagas under her command.'

Kali raised her eyebrows. She had expected to lead the Nagas into the war.

'I'd like you to be with me, Kali,' said Shiva, mollifying her. 'I trust you. I'm going to be leading the search party into Meluhan cities to try and locate the Somras manufacturing facility. We'll have to work quietly and anonymously, while our army outside the city keeps the Meluhans busy.'

'You are very tactful, Shiva.'

Shiva frowned.

'You know how to get your way without making one feel that one has been cut down to size,' said Kali.

Shiva smiled, once again silent.

'But I understand that the search for the Somras facility is crucial,' said Kali. 'So it will be my honour to accompany you.'

'Excellent,' said Shiva, turning to Gopal. 'Any news from the Vasudevs, Pandit*ji*?'

'The siege of Ayodhya has been surprisingly easy,' said Gopal. 'The Ayodhyans have not fought back. Ganesh has a stranglehold over the city.'

'But has King Dilipa changed his stance?'

'Not yet. And Ganesh is, very wisely, not resorting to violence since that may rally the citizens around their king. We will have to be patient.'

'As long as the Ayodhyan army doesn't come to Meluha's aid, I'm happy. What about Magadh?'

'His ships are ready,' said Gopal. 'But Surapadman's army has not been mobilised as yet.'

Shiva raised his brows, clearly surprised. 'I didn't think Surapadman would let go of an opportunity like this. I would also imagine that his father, King Mahendra, would pressure him to attack us.'

'Let us see,' said Sati. 'Maybe Surapadman wants Ayodhya and our army to battle first. He would then be attacking a weakened enemy.'

Shiva nodded. 'Perhaps.'

— ⅄ⲰƱ⇞⊛ —

'Look, Bhagirath,' said Ganesh.

The prince had just entered Ganesh's cabin. One of the soldiers had left a note from Meluha that was recovered from an injured bird. It was coded. But Bhagirath knew the encryption codes of Meluha-Ayodhya communication and had already trained Ganesh's soldiers on how to decrypt the messages.

Bhagirath read aloud. 'Prime Minister Siamantak, has Lord Bhrigu returned to Ayodhya? It has been months since he left Prayag but has still not reached Meluha. Should you have the knowledge, we would like to be informed about the location of Lord Shiva and General Parvateshwar.'

Ganesh didn't say anything, waiting for Bhagirath's reaction.

'It's been signed by Prime Minister Kanakhala,' said Bhagirath. 'Interesting.'

'Interesting indeed,' said Ganesh. 'Where is Lord Bhrigu? And why is the Meluhan Prime Minister enquiring about General Parvateshwar? Has he not reached as yet? Do they not know he has defected to their side?'

'Where do you think they are?' asked Bhagirath.

'They're certainly not in Meluha,' said Ganesh. 'That makes things easier for my father.'

'Do you think Lord Shiva has reached Meluha by now?'

'I think he's still a few weeks away.'

'And the Ayodhya army has not been able to leave,' said Bhagirath. 'The news just keeps getting better.'

Kartik suddenly rushed in. *'Dada!'*

'What's the matter, Kartik?'

'Magadh is mobilising.'

'Who told you? The Vasudev pandit?' asked Bhagirath.

'Yes,' said Kartik, turning back to Ganesh. 'I believe armaments are being loaded on to the ships. Soldiers have been asked to be on stand-by.'

Ganesh smiled. 'How many soldiers?'

'Seventy-five thousand.'

'Seventy-five thousand?' asked a surprised Bhagirath. 'Is Surapadman committing everything? Magadh will be left defenceless.'

'When are they expected to set sail?' asked Ganesh.

'Probably in two weeks' time,' said Kartik. 'At least that's what the Vasudev pandit surmised.'

'You should leave in the next few days,' said Ganesh. 'Take one hundred thousand men.'

'Why so many, *dada*?' asked Kartik. 'Don't you need some men here, with you?'

'I just need enough to be able to sail ships and shoot fire-arrows,' said Ganesh. 'If you do not succeed in holding Surapadman off at the Bal-Atibal Kund, he will just ram into us with his larger ships and drown us all. Our soldiers will be put to better use at your end, not mine.'

'I'll prepare to leave right away,' said Kartik.

— ⁂ —

A hundred thousand well-motivated soldiers reached the forests near the Bal-Atibal Kund in the early afternoon. The Ayodhyan prince had accompanied the army as the chief advisor to Kartik. King Chandraketu had stayed back with Ganesh to ensure that the Branga soldiers in Kartik's army would not be confused about the chain of command.

Immediately upon arrival, Kartik ordered the construction of water-proofed coracles which would serve as devil boats to set the Magadh fleet on fire. A thousand soldiers constructed them and then hid them on the eastern banks on the opposite side of the kund. They would destroy the enemy ships from the other side, even as the battle ensued in the area around the kund.

Hidden platforms had been constructed atop the trees to facilitate the relay of information back and forth between the two sides. A simple communication tool had been manufactured for these soldiers: small metallic pipes fitted on top of earthen pots containing anthracite, which burns with a short, but more importantly smokeless flame. The caps on these metallic pipes could be easily lifted open and then shut, allowing light out in a controlled manner. The apertures were small enough to give the impression of a collection of fire flies. For Kartik's soldiers though, the light signals would carry coded messages from both sides of the river.

Kartik wanted the area around the Bal-Atibal Kund to be left undisturbed. The army was to stay strictly within the forested area.

'I don't understand, Kartik. We do want our men on the beach if they're to serve as bait, don't we? At least, that is what Ganesh had in mind.'

'I would hesitate to underestimate Surapadman, Prince Bhagirath. And I daresay, he will not underestimate us either. If he sees a small number of our soldiers casually stationed in an area visible from the river, he may smell a trap. After all, if we were deserting our army, we wouldn't be stupid enough to camp where we could be seen, would we?'

'Fair enough. So what do you suggest?'

'We are on the west bank. Magadh is farther to our south, also on the west bank of the Sarayu. If we were to march along the river, where the forest is not too dense, Magadh would not be more than two or three weeks from here.'

Bhagirath smiled. 'You want Surapadman to guess our

actual strategy, that the Ayodhya siege was a feint to try to draw him out. He will realise that by conquering Magadh, we will have much more effective control over Ayodhyan ships sailing by, as compared to besieging Ayodhya itself.'

'Exactly. And if he is smart enough to suspect that, as I'm sure he is, he will have scouts looking out towards the forests running along the river. And when he gets reports of our massive army, he will draw the obvious conclusion: that we have marched out to conquer Magadh, while he is wasting his time sailing to Ayodhya.'

'Leave your home defenceless to conquer another land and you may find your own home getting conquered instead.'

'You got it,' said Kartik. 'Also, it will have credibility in Surapadman's eyes, for that's what he would expect a smart enemy to do. I do not see him underestimating us.'

'But what would stop him from just turning around and sailing back to Magadh?'

'Turning a large fleet of ships around in a river is easier said than done, especially if one is short of time. But even if Surapadman manages to do so, and speeds down the river to reach Magadh before us, he would know that our army could simply stop marching and not appear at the gates of his city. His own Magadhans may then believe that Surapadman ran away from the battle at Ayodhya using the false pretext of Magadh itself being in danger. A crown prince cannot afford to be perceived as a coward. So he would have no choice but to attack us here itself. What do you think?'

'I like the plan,' said Bhagirath. 'It should work with a good general like Surapadman, for he will have scouts riding along the river banks to keep him informed of what's going on. We have to be sure to attack those scouts but allow some of them to escape with information about the size of our army. Also, our camp in the forest stretches up to two kilometres.

When their ships pass our position, we should have soldiers disturb the birds on top of the trees at the beginning of our camp. Also, we could have some fires left "carelessly" aflame towards the end of our camp. Judging the vast distance between these two signals, Surapadman would assume that there is a massive enemy army marching south along the river bank. He would be forced to attack.'

'Right.'

'Let's have some devil boats on the western bank as well.'

'But the battle will be fought here on the west bank,' said Kartik, frowning. 'Their men would engage in battle here and our fire coracles would be clearly visible. Devil boats can set fire to ships only when they have an element of surprise. If they are visible then they can be easily sunk. That's why I have set up the devil boats on the eastern banks.'

'The fighting would happen on our side,' said Bhagirath. 'But Surapadman would be forced to land his men on the sands of the Bal-Atibal Kund, and nowhere else on the western side. It's almost impossible to land men in large numbers in the dense forest which runs along the river farther north. So if we keep our coracles up north, they would remain hidden from enemy eyes. As soon as his ships anchor to investigate our position, we'll attack them at the north end of his convoy.'

'Good point. I'll issue those orders.'

— ⅄⦾Ʊ⍏⊗ —

Kartik's army was ready and poised for action as they heard the sounds of a massive navy rowing up the Sarayu. Judging by the dull drum-beats of the timekeepers and the faint sound of the oars negotiating the waters, it was fair to assume that the Magadhan ships would reach the Bal-Atibal Kund within the next hour or two.

Soldiers were immediately ordered to take battle positions. Weapons were checked, defences were tested.

Kartik walked up to the edge of the forest and surveyed the sands of the Bal-Atibal Kund as well as the river beyond. A crescent moon had failed to lift the darkness of the late hour of the night, which suited his strategy. A light seasonal fog had begun to spread along the river. Perfect! With a practiced eye he checked whether the communication pots were still visible in the fog and was pleased with what he saw.

Kartik turned to Bhagirath, and then looked farther ahead towards Divodas and the other commanders of the Branga army.

'My friends,' said Kartik. 'Unlike my father, I'm not good with words. So I will keep this short. The Magadhans will be fighting only for conquest and glory. Those are weak motivations. You are fighting for vengeance and retribution. For your families and for the soul of your nation. You are fighting to stop the Somras that has killed your children and crippled your people. You are fighting to stop the scourge of this Evil. You have to fight to the end; until they are finished. I don't want prisoners. I want them dead. If anyone takes the side of Evil, they forfeit the right to live. Remember! Remember the pain of your children!'

The Branga commanders roared together. 'Death to the Magadhans!'

'This land that we stand upon,' continued Kartik, 'has been blessed by the feet of Lord Ram. We shall honour him today with blood. Jai Shri Ram!'

'Jai Shri Ram!'

'To your positions!' ordered Kartik.

The Branga commanders hurried away. As soon as the men were out of earshot, Bhagirath spoke, 'Kartik, why do you want them all dead?'

'Prince Bhagirath, if there are too many Magadhan prisoners, we will have to leave behind a large force to keep watch over them. Our eventual purpose is to get as many soldiers as possible to Meluha. If the Magadhan army is decimated, we will not need to keep too many of our own soldiers in Magadh. Just a few thousand of them would be enough to control the city. Also, the killing of all the Magadhans would send a message to Ayodhya. It might make them reconsider their alliance with Meluha.'

Bhagirath was forced to accept Kartik's brutal but effective line of thought.

Chapter 23

Battle of Bal-Atibal Kund

The lead ship of the Magadhan navy passed the Bal-Atibal Kund. Kartik's army had heard the low monotonous sounds of rowing and the drumbeats of the timekeepers long before they had sighted the Magadhan ships.

Kartik motioned for a signal to be relayed by hand over a line of men who had been positioned for this purpose, till the message reached the southern end of the camp, more than a kilometre away. A group of soldiers pulled a rope quietly, releasing a net that had been tightly cast over a flock of birds. The birds took off suddenly, startled by their unexpected freedom. Kartik detected some movement in the Magadhan ships. They had clearly heard the birds.

Kartik strained his eyes. The Magadhan soldiers had their eyes pinned towards the top of the main masts.

'Shit!' whispered Bhagirath, as he realised the implications.

A small wry smile of appreciation for a worthy enemy flickered on Kartik's face. He turned to Divodas who stood right behind him. 'Divodas, send messages to our tree-top soldiers that the Magadhans have lookouts stationed on their crow's nests. Our soldiers should remain low to avoid detection.'

A crow's nest is built on top of the main masthead of the ship, where sailors would be stationed as lookouts to survey far and wide so as to report to the captain below on deck. This was a common practice on sea-faring ships, but was rarely used in river ships. Surapadman was obviously a cautious man for he had built crow's nests on his ships. Divodas left quietly to carry out Kartik's orders.

'The ships are pulling back their oars,' said Bhagirath, pointing forward.

As they were sailing against the natural flow of the river current, the Magadhan ships slowed down quickly. The sails were re-adjusted to bring the ships to a halt. Their earlier speed was such though, that at least ten ships passed the area where Kartik stood before Surapadman's fleet came to a standstill. The soldiers on the ships stared hard into the dense forests on the western banks.

'Now we wait,' said Kartik.

Bhagirath leaned over to Kartik. 'Their scout is a short distance behind us, close to the water's edge.'

Kartik stretched his arms in an exaggerated manner and then spoke to Divodas, loud enough for the Magadhan scout to hear. 'Check if their ships have started moving up ahead.'

Divodas moved towards the river, making the scout fall back silently. He returned almost instantaneously. 'Lord Kartik, their scout is swimming back to the ship.'

Kartik immediately rose and crept to the edge of the forest. He could see the Magadhan scout swimming noiselessly away.

'I expect the attack soon,' said Bhagirath. 'We should fall back to our positions.'

'Let's wait a few moments,' said Kartik. 'I want to see which ship he boards. It'll tell us where Surapadman is.'

'It's been almost half an hour,' said Bhagirath. 'What is he waiting for?'

Kartik and his army remained behind the forest line. They wanted to give Surapadman the impression that the Brangas did not wish to engage in a battle. They hoped he would be lulled into believing that he could launch a surprise attack.

Kartik suddenly exclaimed, 'Son of a bitch!'

'Lord Kartik?' asked Divodas.

'Send a message to our lookouts,' said Kartik. 'Tell them to communicate with those on the other side. I want to know what is happening there.'

Bhagirath slapped his forehead. 'Oh my God! We'd asked our lookouts to stay low!'

Divodas rushed off and messages were soon relayed across the Sarayu using light signals. He was back in no time with worrying news. 'They're mobilising on the other side, hidden by their massive vessels. Row boats are being lowered quietly into the river and soldiers are boarding it even as we speak. It looks like they're preparing to row downriver.'

'That cunning son of a flea-bitten dog!' said Bhagirath. 'He intends to row downriver, hidden by his own ships, and attack us from the south.'

'What do we do, Lord Kartik?' asked Divodas.

'Ask our lookouts if the Magadhans are disembarking from their tenth ship. That is where Surapadman is.' Turning to Bhagirath, Kartik continued. 'Prince Bhagirath, I suspect he will launch a two-pronged attack. There will be one at Bal-Atibal Kund. Surapadman would want to keep us busy here. In the meantime, another contingent of Magadhans would row down south, flank our southern side and aim to enter our camp from behind. We would be sandwiched between two sections of his army.'

'Which means we need to break up,' said Bhagirath. 'One

of us will stay here at the Bal-Atibal Kund, and the other will ride out to meet their southern force.'

'Exactly,' said Kartik.

Meanwhile, Divodas returned. 'Lord Kartik, they are disembarking from Surapadman's ship.'

'Prince Bhagirath,' said Kartik, 'You will lead our main force here. We have to ensure the Magadhans don't get past Bal-Atibal. I want this to be a death trap for them.'

'It'll be so, Kartik, I assure you. But do not leave too many from our forces with me. You will need a large number of soldiers to battle Surapadman in the south.'

'No I won't,' said Kartik. 'He's rowing downriver. He will not have any horses. I will.'

Bhagirath understood immediately. A single mounted cavalry warrior was equal to ten foot soldiers. He had the advantage of height as well as his horse's fearsome kicks. 'All right.'

Kartik snapped orders to Divodas even as he rose. 'Ride down south. Inform our forces to expect a Magadhan charge soon. You will be leading them. I'm going to ride out with two thousand cavalrymen in a giant arc from the west. I intend to attack Surapadman's forces from behind. Between my horses and your troops, we will crush them.'

Divodas smiled. 'That we will!'

'You bet!' said Kartik. 'Har Har Mahadev!'

'Har Har Mahadev!' said Divodas.

Divodas ran to his horse, swung onto the saddle and rode away.

Kartik appeared to be running over the instructions in his mind, not wanting to miss out a single detail.

'I have fought many battles, Kartik,' said Bhagirath with an amused look. 'Go fight yours. Let me take care of mine.'

Kartik smiled. 'We'll gift my father a famous victory.'

'That we shall,' said Bhagirath.

Kartik walked up to his horse, stretched up to put his left foot into the stirrup, for he was still quite short, and swung his right leg over to the other side, mounting his horse. Bhagirath, who had followed Kartik, saw the same steely look in thc boy's eyes that he had seen many times during the animal hunts. A familiar sense of fear and fascination entered Bhagirath's heart. He smiled nervously and whispered, 'God have mercy on Surapadman...'

Kartik heard the remark and chuckled softly. 'He will have to be the one, for I won't.'

The son of the Neelkanth turned his horse and galloped away into the dark.

The slender moon was now cloaked in clouds, its faint light hidden in the mist. Bhagirath could barely make out the lines of men in the wood beside him. He sensed them now by the sound of their breath rasping in the darkness. The metallic smell of sweat hung heavy in the air. Bhagirath could feel the perspiration beading on his upper lip, trickling into the corner of his mouth. Whispers came floating back to his ears from up and down the line – 'Har Har Mahadev... Har Har Mahadev...' – like a prayer as the men braced to face Surapadman's army.

Suddenly the moon burst through the clouds and Bhagirath could see men running up and down the length of the enemy ships carrying fire torches. They were lighting the arrows for the archers.

'Shields up!' screamed Bhagirath.

Bhagirath's soldiers, primarily Brangas, immediately prepared for the volley of arrows that would soon descend upon them. The sky lit up as the archers shot their fire arrows.

They flew out in a great arc before descending into the jungle. Bhagirath had kept his men strictly within the forest line, so the trees worked as their first line of defence. The few that got through were easily blocked by the raised shields.

The Magadhans had hoped that their fire arrows would set the forest aflame, causing chaos and confusion amongst the Brangas. But mist and the cold of the night had ensured dew formation on the leaves. The trees simply did not catch fire.

As the arrows stopped, Bhagirath roared loudly. 'Har Har Mahadev!'

His soldiers followed him as their cry rent the air, 'Har Har Mahadev!'

The Magadhans quickly lit another line of arrows and shot. Once again, the trees and the Branga shields ensured that Bhagirath's soldiers suffered no casualties.

The Brangas put their shields aside and let out their war cry, taunting their enemies. 'Har Har Mahadev!'

Bhagirath could see the rowboats being lowered from the ships. The attack was about to begin. The fire arrows were just a cover. As he watched the arrows being loaded again, he turned to his men. 'Shields!'

The Brangas effortlessly defended themselves against another volley of fire arrows.

'Send a message to our men on the other side to launch their fire coracles! Now!'

As his aide rushed away, Bhagirath saw his enemies rowing out towards the kund. And yet another shower of arrows was fired.

'Don't move!' shouted Bhagirath, keeping his men in check. 'Let them land first.'

In order to inflict maximum casualties Bhagirath would allow a large contingent of enemy soldiers to land ashore before launching a three-pronged attack from the adjoining forest. An impregnable phalanx of his infantry, standing shoulder to shoulder, shields in front, would advance and push at the frontline Magadhan soldiers with unstoppable force. The enemy soldiers bringing up the rear would inevitably be forced into the water. Weighed down by their weapons and armour, they would drown. The frontline, hopelessly outnumbered, would then be decimated.

'Shields!' ordered Bhagirath once again as he saw the arrows being lit.

His gut feel was that this would be the last volley. Enemy soldiers were jumping off their boats onto the sands of Bal-Atibal. Brutal hand-to-hand combat was moments away. Bhagirath could feel the adrenaline rushing through his veins. He could almost smell the blood that was about to be shed.

'Charge!' bellowed Bhagirath.

— ⁂ —

Kartik rode furiously with his two-thousand strong cavalry. Even through the dense foliage, he could see fire arrows being shot from Magadhan ships. They had commenced battle, which meant that the southern contingent of the Magadhan army was in position.

'Faster!' roared Kartik to his horsemen.

They could see that the ships at the centre of the fleet had already caught fire. The devil boats had struck. Bhagirath was obviously hurting the Magadhan navy. What was surprising though, was that the southern end was also aflame. The Vaishali forces must have arrived and were attacking the Magadhan navy from behind.

Kartik was distracted by the din up ahead; it was the sound of a fierce battle between the southern contingent of the Magadhans and Divodas' Brangas.

'Ride harder!'

Surapadman's men had probably shot fire arrows here as well, for parts of the camp were on fire. But this served as a beacon for Kartik's horsemen. They kicked their horses hard, spurring them on. The Brangas at the southern end were hard at work, holding almost twenty thousand soldiers at bay. The Magadhans, who had expected to decimate an unprepared enemy, were shocked by the fierce resistance they were facing. Things would get a lot worse though, for the Magadhans did not expect danger from the back as well.

'Har Har Mahadev!' yelled Kartik as he drew his long sword.

'Har Har Mahadev!' roared the Branga horsemen as they charged.

The last rows of the Magadhan foot soldiers, completely unprepared for a cavalry charge from the rear, were ruthlessly butchered within minutes. Kartik and his cavalry cut a wide swathe through the Magadhan units, their horses trampling hapless soldiers, their swords slicing all those who stood in their path.

Initially, the rear attack of the Branga cavalry went unnoticed due to the massive size of the rival armies and the brutal din and clamour of a battle well joined. Quickly overcoming their surprise, many brave Magadhan soldiers leapt at the horsemen, stabbing at the beasts and even fearlessly holding on to the stirrups, hoping to bring them down. Sensing that he led the cavalry charge, a clutch of infantrymen tripped Kartik's steed bringing them both down in a crash. They would soon wish that they hadn't.

With cat-like reflexes, Kartik sprang to his feet, viciously drawing his second sword as well, and cutting at the first of the soldiers pressing on to him. The Magadhan crumpled in midstep and fell silently to the ground, his windpipe severed, a gush of air bursting from his slit throat, splattering blood on those around him. A second soldier charged, and was cut down before he'd taken two steps, a single stroke of Kartik's blade slicing through his torso, almost to his spine.

The remaining soldiers paused, cautious now of this boy who could kill with such ease. They spread out in a circle around him, swords at the ready. Kartik knew they would charge together from all sides, and waited for them to make their move.

The charge came, two from the front, one from the back and a fourth from the left. Kartik crouched, and with near-inhuman speed sidestepped to the left and swung fiercely. Generating fearful blade speed through his swinging strikes, he brutally sliced limb, sinew, head and trunk all around him. Blood and entrails were splattered all over.

He paused, panting, the swords in his hands dripping red with blood. He looked around him, selected an opponent and charged again. As the *Bhagavad Gita* would say, Kartik had become Death, the destroyer of worlds.

The fighting raged for half an hour as the tide of the battle tipped more and more against the Magadhans. But they fought on as no quarter was given either by Kartik or his army.

Slowly the screams of the dying lessened, and then were silenced as Surapadman's army perished. Soldiers stopped their slaughter and stood quietly on the battlefield, leaning exhausted on their swords and panting. But Kartik did not slacken, pressing attack after attack on all those that remained standing.

Divodas tried to run as he approached Kartik, but his legs were weak and trembling, and he could scarcely manage more than a stumbling trot. He was covered in blood from a dozen small cuts, and a deep gash on his shoulder left his right arm dangling limply to his side. 'My Lord,' he called out, breathless and hoarse, 'My Lord!'

Kartik swung viciously, the speed of his movement building formidable power in his curved blade. Divodas took the blow on his shield as his hand reverberated with the shock of blocking the brutal blow, numbing his left arm to the shoulder.

'My Lord!' he pleaded in desperation. 'It is I, Divodas!'

Kartik suddenly stopped, his long sword held high in his right hand, his curved blade held low to his left, his breathing sharp and heavy, his eyes bulging with bloodlust.

'My Lord!' shrieked Divodas, his fear palpable. 'You have killed them all! Please stop!'

As Kartik's breathing slowed, he allowed his gaze to take in the scene of destruction all around him. Hacked bodies littered the battlefield. A once proud Magadhan army completely decimated. Divodas' frontal attack combined with the rear cavalry charge had achieved Kartik's plan.

Kartik could still feel the adrenalin coursing furiously through his veins.

Divodas, still afraid of Kartik, whispered. 'You have won, My Lord.'

Kartik raised his long sword high and shouted, 'Har Har Mahadev!'

The Brangas roared after him, 'Har Har Mahadev!'

Kartik bent down and flipped a Magadhan's decapitated head with his sword, then turned to Divodas. 'Find Surapadman. If there's life left in him, I want him brought to me alive.'

'Yes, My Lord,' said Divodas and rushed to obey.

Kartik wiped both his swords on the clothing of a fallen Magadhan soldier and carefully caged the blades in the scabbards tied across his back. The Branga soldiers maintained a respectful distance from him, terrified of the brutal violence they had just witnessed. He walked slowly towards the river, bent down, scooped some water in his palms and splashed it on his face. The river had turned red due to the massive bloodletting that had just occurred. He was covered with blood and gore. But his eyes were clean. Still. The bloodlust had left him.

Later in the day, when the dead were counted, it would emerge that seventy thousand of the Magadhan army from amongst seventy-five thousand had been slaughtered, burned or drowned. Kartik, on the other hand, had lost only five thousand of his one hundred thousand men. This was not a battle. It had been a massacre.

Kartik looked up at the sky. The first rays of the sun were breaking on the horizon, heralding a new day. And on this day, a legend had been born. The legend of Kartik, the Lord of War!

Chapter 24

The Age of Violence

The golden orb of a rising sun peeked from the mainland to the right as a strong southerly wind filled their sails, racing them towards the port of Lothal. Shiva, with Sati at his side, stood poised on the foredeck, eyes transfixed northwards, wishing their ship all speed.

'I wonder how the war has progressed in Swadweep,' said Sati.

Shiva turned to her with a smile. 'We do not know if there has been a war at all, Sati. Maybe Ganesh's tactics have worked.'

'I hope so.'

Shiva held Sati's hand. 'Our sons are warriors. They are doing what they are supposed to. You don't need to worry about them.'

'I'm not worried about Ganesh. I know that if he can avoid bloodshed, he will. Not that he's a coward, but he understands the futility of war. But Kartik... He loves the art of war. I fear he will go out of his way to court danger.'

'You're probably right,' said Shiva. 'But you cannot change his essential character. And in any case, isn't that what being a warrior is all about?'

'But every other warrior goes into battle reluctantly. He

fights because he has to. Kartik is not like that. He's enthused by warfare. It seems that his *swadharma* is war. That worries me,' said Sati, expressing her anxieties about what she felt was Kartik's *personal dharma.*

Shiva drew Sati into his arms and kissed her on her lips, reassuringly. 'Everything will be all right.'

Sati smiled and rested her head on Shiva's chest. 'I must admit that helped a bit...'

Shiva laughed softly. 'Let me help you some more then.'

Shiva raised Sati's face and kissed her again.

'Ahem!'

Shiva and Sati turned around to find Veerbhadra and Krittika approaching them.

'This is an open deck,' said a smiling Veerbhadra, teasing his friend. 'Find a room!'

Krittika hit Veerbhadra lightly on his stomach, embarrassed. 'Shut up!'

Shiva smiled. 'How're you, Krittika?'

'Very well, My Lord.'

'Krittika,' said Shiva. 'How many times do I have to tell you? You are my friend's wife. Call me Shiva.'

Krittika smiled. 'I'm sorry.'

Shiva rested his hand on Veerbhadra's shoulder. 'What did the captain say, Bhadra? How far are we?'

'At the rate we're sailing, just a few more days. The winds have been kind.'

'Hmmm... have you ever been to Lothal or Maika, Krittika?'

Krittika shook her head. 'It's difficult for me to get pregnant, Shiva. And that is the only way that an outsider can enter Maika.'

Shiva winced. He had touched a raw nerve. Veerbhadra did not care that Krittika couldn't conceive, but it still distressed her.

'I'm sorry,' said Shiva.

'No, no,' smiled Krittika. 'Veerbhadra has convinced me that we are good enough for each other. We don't need a child to complete us.'

Shiva patted Veerbhadra's back. 'Sometimes we barbarians can surprise even ourselves with our good sense.'

Krittika laughed softly. 'But I have visited the older Lothal.'

'Older Lothal?'

'Didn't I tell you?' asked Sati. 'The seaport of Lothal is actually a new city. The older Lothal was a river port on the Saraswati. But when the Saraswati stopped reaching the sea, there was no water around the old city, ending its vibrancy. The locals decided to recreate their hometown next to the sea. The new Lothal is exactly like the old city, except that it's a sea port.'

'Interesting,' said Shiva. 'So what happened to old Lothal?'

'It's practically abandoned, but a few people continue to live there.'

'So why didn't they give the new city a different name? Why call it Lothal?'

'The old citizens were very attached to their city. It was one of the greatest cities of the empire. They didn't want the name to disappear in the sands of time. They also assumed most people would forget old Lothal.'

Shiva looked towards the sea. 'New Lothal, here we come!'

— ⋆ —

The sun had risen high over Bal-Atibal Kund. It was the third hour of the second prahar. The bodies of the fallen Maghadans and Brangas were being removed to a cleared area in the forest where, to the drone of ritual chanting, their mortal remains were being cremated. Considering the massive number of Magadhan dead, this was back-breaking work. But Kartik had been insistent. Valour begot respect, whether in life or in the aftermath of death.

'Has Surapadman not been found yet?' asked Bhagirath, his eyes scanning the sands of the kund. Yesterday they were pristine white. Today they were a pale shade of pink, discoloured by massive quantities of blood.

'Not as yet,' said Kartik. 'Initially I thought he was fighting on the southern front. We were unable to find him there so I assumed he would be here.'

Maatali, the Vaishali king, had proved his naval acumen by destroying the rearguard of the Magadhan fleet. Having heard of Kartik's valour and ferocity, he now viewed him with newfound respect. Gone were the last traces of indulgence for the son of the Neelkanth.

'How far is my brother's fleet, King Maatali?' asked Kartik.

'I've sent some of my rowboats upriver. It is clogged with the debris of the Magadhan ships. Our boats are trying to clear up the mess, but it will take time. And Lord Ganesh is moving carefully so the ships don't sustain any damage. So he will take some time to get here.'

Kartik nodded.

'But he has been informed about your great victory, Lord Kartik,' said Maatali. 'He is very proud of you.'

Kartik frowned. 'It's not *my* victory, Your Highness. It's *our* victory. And it would not have been possible without my elder brother, who destroyed the northern end of the Magadhan navy.'

'That he did,' said Maatali.

'My Lord!' hailed Divodas, crossing over from the dense forest to the sands of the Bal-Atibal Kund. Still weak from injuries and bandaged across his shoulder, he was being assisted by five men as they together dragged something with ropes.

It took Kartik a moment to recognise what they were dragging. 'Divodas! Treat him with respect!'

Divodas stopped at once. Kartik ran towards them, followed by Bhagirath and Maatali. The corpse they had been dragging was that of a tall, well-built, swarthy man. His clothes and armour were soaked dark with blood, and his body was covered with wounds, some dried and black, others still fresh, red and wet. His skull had been split open near his temple, showing how he had died. His injuries were too numerous to be counted, clearly indicating the valour of this combatant. All the wounds were in the front, not one on the back. It had been an honourable death.

'Surapadman...' whispered Bhagirath.

'He was on the southern front, My Lord,' said Divodas.

Kartik pulled out his knife, bent down to cut the ropes tied around Surapadman's shoulders, and then gently lowered the fallen prince back onto the ground. He noticed Surapadman's right hand, still tightly gripping his sword. He touched the sword, its blade caked with dried blood. Divodas tried to pry open Surapadman's fingers.

'Stop,' commanded Kartik. 'Surapadman will carry his sword into the other world.'

Divodas immediately withdrew his hand and fell back.

Surapadman's mouth was half open. The ancient Vedic hymns on death claim that the soul leaves the body along with the last breath. Therefore, the mouth is open at the point of death. But there is a superstition that the mouth should be closed quickly after death, lest an evil spirit enters the soulless body.

Kartik closed Surapadman's mouth gently.

'Find the chief Brahmin,' said Kartik. 'Prepare Surapadman's body. He shall be cremated like the prince that he was.'

Divodas nodded.

Kartik turned to Bhagirath. 'We shall wait till my brother returns. Surapadman will then be cremated with full state honours.'

Ganesh stood at the ramparts of the Magadhan fort, watching the great Sarayu merge into the mighty Ganga. The setting sun had tinged the waters a brilliant orange. King Mahendra and the citizens of Magadh, stunned by the complete annihilation of their army and the death of their Prince Surapadman, had surrendered meekly when Ganesh's forces had entered the city. He did not expect any rebellion, since there were practically no soldiers left in Magadh. Ganesh planned to leave a small force of ten thousand soldiers to man the fort and blockade any Ayodhya ships. He would sail out with his other soldiers to meet with his father's army in Meluha. They were to leave the next day.

The war in Swadweep had worked perfectly for Ganesh. He was now able to block the movements of the Ayodhyan army with far less soldiers than would have been required if he was besieging Ayodhya itself.

'What are you thinking, *dada*?' asked Kartik.

Ganesh smiled at his brother as he pointed at the *confluence*. 'Look at the *sangam*, where the Sarayu meets the Ganga.'

Even before he turned his gaze, Kartik could hear the swirling waters of the *sangam*. What he saw was a young, impetuous Sarayu crashing into the mature, tranquil Ganga, jostling for space within her banks. Though she sometimes relented, the Ganga would often push aside the waters of the Sarayu with surprising ease, creating eddies and currents in its wake. This jostling continued till Ganga, the eternal mother, eventually drew the ebullient tributary into her bosom till they could be distinguished no more in the calm flow.

'There is always unity at the end,' said Ganesh, 'and it brings a new tranquillity. But the meeting of two worlds causes a lot of temporary chaos.'

Kartik smiled, bemused.

'This could not have been avoided,' said Ganesh. 'But the stricken visage of King Mahendra was heartbreaking. Every single house in Magadh has lost a son or a daughter in the Battle of Bal-Atibal.'

'But King Mahendra was the one who had forced Prince Surapadman to attack. He can only blame himself,' said Kartik. 'I've heard reports that Prince Surapadman had really wanted to remain neutral.'

'That may be true, Kartik. But that still doesn't take away from the fact that we have killed half the adult population of Magadh.'

'We had no choice, *dada*,' said Kartik.

'I know that,' said Ganesh, turning back to look at the sangam of the Ganga and the Sarayu. 'The rivers fight with each other with the only currency that they know: water. We humans fight with the only currency that we know in this age: violence.'

'But how else does one establish one's standpoint, *dada*?' asked Kartik. 'There are times when reason does not work, and peaceful efforts prove inadequate. Violence is ultimately the last resort. This is the way it has always been. The world will, perhaps, never be any different.'

Ganesh shook his head. 'It will be, one day. We live in the age of the Kshatriya. That's why we think that the only currency to bring about change is violence.'

'Age of the Kshatriya? I've never heard of that.'

'You would have heard of the four *yugs, cyclical eras* that time traverses repeatedly through a never-ending loop: the *Sat yug, Treta yug, Dwapar yug* and *Kali yug*.'

'Yes.'

'Within each of these yugs there are smaller cycles dominated by different caste-professions. There is the age of the Brahmin, of the Kshatriya, of the Vaishya and of the Shudra.'

'Age of the Brahmin, *dada*? I haven't heard of that either.'

'Sure you have. All of us have been told stories of the Prajapati; of a time of magic.'

Kartik smiled. 'Of course! Knowledge seems like magic to the ignorant.'

'Yes. The main currency of the age of the Brahmin was knowledge. And in our age, it is violence. Some philosophers believe that after our epoch will be the age of the Vaishya.'

'And the people in that age will not use violence to establish their writ?'

'Violence will never die, Kartik. Neither will knowledge. But they will not be the determining factors, since it will be an age dominated by the way of the Vaishya, which is profit. They will use money.'

'I can't imagine a world like that, *dada*.'

'It will come. I pray that it doesn't take too long. Not that I'm afraid of violence, but it leaves too many grieving hearts in its wake.'

'*Dada*, even if I do believe that such a time will come, are you saying that money will cause less devastation than violence? Will there not be winners and losers even then? Will sadness disappear?'

Ganesh raised his eyebrows, surprised. He smiled and patted his brother on his back. 'You are right. There will always be winners and losers. For that is the way of the world.'

Kartik put his arm around his brother's waist as Ganesh

put his around Kartik's shoulders. 'But that still doesn't take away from the grief of knowing that we have caused suffering to others.'

— ⅄ⵀⵡⵠⵙ —

'This may sound strange to you,' said Shiva, reclining in the comfort of the Lothal governor's residence. 'But I feel as if I've come home. Meluha is where my journey began.'

Just as Kali had expected, the Lothal governor, Chenardhwaj, had broken ranks with the Meluhan nobility and opened the doors of his city for Shiva's army, pledging loyalty to the Neelkanth.

'And this is where it'll end,' said Sati. 'Then we can all go and live in Kailash.'

Shiva smiled. 'Kailash is not as idyllic as you imagine. It's a difficult, barren land.'

'But you will be there. That'll make it heaven for me.'

Shiva laughed, bent forward and kissed his wife lovingly, holding her close.

'But first, we need to deal with those who defend the evil Somras,' said Sati.

'That has already begun with the defeat of the Magadhans.'

'Hmmm... that's true, we can easily blockade the Ayodhyan navy, now that Magadh is firmly in our control. When will Ganesh and Kartik leave for Meluha?'

'They have left already.'

'And when do we leave for Mrittikavati?'

'In a few days.'

Sati had learnt to recognise the resolute expression Shiva now wore and couldn't help feeling a twinge of anxiety for her homeland. 'For their own sake, I hope they surrender.'

'I hope so too.'

Chapter 25

God or Country?

'By the great Lord Brahma!' growled Bhrigu.

Bhrigu had finally reached Devagiri. He had been delayed on the recently-built road between Dharmakhet in Swadweep and Meluha, by the floodwaters of an overflowing Yamuna, which had submerged the pathway. While he was stuck in this no-man's land between the Chandravanshi and Suryavanshi empires, Bhrigu availed of the facilities of the traveller's guesthouse, built by the Meluhans alongside the road. Not that its comforts calmed him though, for he needed to be in Devagiri. What did alleviate his stress was the arrival of Parvateshwar, along with Anandmayi. They travelled together from there onwards, and Bhrigu used this opportunity to discuss battle strategy with him. The flooding of the Yamuna had transformed what should have been a quick journey of a few weeks, into many months.

Bhrigu, Daksha, Parvateshwar and Kanakhala conferred in the private royal office of Devagiri, examining the ramifications of the Neelkanth's proclamation.

'May I see the notice, Maharishi*ji*?' asked Parvateshwar.

Bhrigu handed over the stone tablet and then turned to Daksha and Kanakhala. 'When were they put up?'

'A few months ago, My Lord,' said Daksha.

'At all major temples in practically every city within the Empire,' added Kanakhala.

'And was this a simultaneous event, orchestrated on the same day?' asked Parvateshwar, obviously impressed by the logistical feat.

'Yes,' said Kanakhala. 'Only the Neelkanth could have organised this. But why would he do it? He loves Meluha and we worship him. We therefore assumed that it had to be someone else who was trying to slander the reputation of our Lord. Sadly, we still haven't made any headway in our investigation and do not know who the real perpetrators are.'

'Do you have traitors in your administration, Your Highness?' asked Bhrigu.

Daksha bristled, but did not dare make his anger apparent. 'Certainly not, My Lord. You can trust the Meluhans like you trust me.'

Bhrigu's ironic smile did not leave much to the imagination. 'What do you make of it, Lord Parvateshwar?'

'I would have expected nothing less from the Neelkanth,' said Parvateshwar.

Kanakhala was stunned by this revelation, but prudently chose silence.

'But I must tell you that we responded well, My Lord,' said Daksha to Bhrigu. 'They were removed within a few days and were replaced with official notices stating that the earlier ones had been put up by a fraud and should not be believed.'

Kanakhala reeled from shock. She had inadvertently sinned when she put up the new notices that Daksha had asked her to, and become party to a lie. She considered resigning from her position. However, it was obvious that a war was imminent. And her war-time duties were clear: complete and unquestioning loyalty to the king and country. She had never faced a situation where her duties stood in direct conflict with her dharma. The confusion was bewildering.

'So you see, My Lord, this particular problem has been handled,' said Daksha. 'We need to now focus on how to repel Shiva's forces.'

Bhrigu gestured towards Daksha. 'Not now, Your Highness. Let me first confer with General Parvateshwar in private.'

Kanakhala was still lost in the turmoil within her conscience, and did not notice the exchange.

— ⸻ —

'The proclamation was made by the Lord Neelkanth. How can we go against his word? This is wrong. If the Lord says that the Somras is not to be used, then I don't see how we can go against this diktat.'

Parvateshwar had accompanied Kanakhala to her office after the meeting. He could tell that she was very disturbed by the events of the morning.

'I've already stopped using the Somras, Kanakhala.'

'As will I, from this instant. But that is not what troubles me. The Neelkanth wants the whole of Meluha to stop using the Somras. And the consequences of ignoring his decision are very clear from his message: if we don't, then we become his enemies.'

'I'm aware of that. For all practical purposes, war has already been declared. His army is mobilising even as we speak.'

'Meluha must stop using the Somras.'

'Does the law allow either you or me to pass an order banning the Somras?'

'No, only the Emperor can do that.'

'And he hasn't, has he? Also, the Emperor's orders are unquestionable in times of war.'

'Can't we avoid a war in some way? Why don't you speak to Maharishi Bhrigu? He respects you.'

'The Maharishi is not convinced that the Somras has turned evil.'

'Then we should approach the people directly.'

'Kanakhala, you know better than that. It would mean breaking your oath as prime minister, since you would be directly going against the order of your Emperor.'

'But why should I follow his orders? He made me lie to our own people!'

'I assure you that nothing like that will happen again for as long as I'm alive and in Meluha.'

Kanakhala looked away as she struggled to get a grip over her raging emotions.

'Kanakhala, let's say we do approach the Meluhans directly,' said Parvateshwar. 'We will have to convince our countrymen to voluntarily choose to end their life much before it normally would have. And we will have nothing to give them in return. Convincing people to do this is not an easy task, even with those as duty-bound and honourable as the Meluhans. It will take time. The Neelkanth, however, is not patient when it comes to the Somras. He wants its use to end right now. The only way he can do that is to attack the epicentre.'

'Which is Meluha...'

'Exactly. Right now our task is to protect our country. You know Lord Ram's laws state very clearly that our primary duty is towards our country. He had said that even if it comes to choosing between Lord Ram and Meluha, we should choose Meluha.'

'Who would have imagined that it would *actually* come down to such a choice, Parvateshwar? That we would need to choose between our God and our country?'

Parvateshwar smiled sadly. 'My duty to my country is above all others, Kanakhala.'

Kanakhala ran her hand over her bald pate and touched the knotted tuft of hair at the back of her head, trying to draw strength from it. 'What kind of challenge is fate throwing at us?'

— ⅄ⵀⵡⵠ⊛ —

'It's a stupid idea, Your Highness,' said Bhrigu. 'Your problem is that you do not look beyond the next three months when you dream up your strategies.'

Daksha had been sitting expectantly at the maharishi's feet, eagerly awaiting his response. For he had just unfolded to Bhrigu his 'brilliant' scheme to avoid the war altogether.

An unmoved Bhrigu then leaned towards him from his stone bed. 'We're not fighting with the Neelkanth, but the devotion that he inspires in your people. Making him a martyr will turn your people against you, and inevitably, the Somras.'

Daksha expressed acknowledgement. 'You're right, My Lord. Had we succeeded in killing him in Panchavati, the people would have blamed the Nagas. That failure was most unfortunate.'

'Also, Your Highness, while it is not unethical to attack an unprepared enemy, there are some codes that just cannot be broken, even in times of war, like killing a peace ambassador or even a messenger.'

'Of course, My Lord,' said a distracted Daksha. His mind, in fact, was already working on refining his plan.

'Are you listening, Your Highness?' asked an irritated Bhrigu.

A chastened Daksha looked up immediately. 'Of course I am, My Lord.'

Bhrigu sighed and waved his hand, dismissing him from his chamber.

— ⅄ⓞƱ↟⊛ —

Parvateshwar strode into his house and nodded towards the attendant even as he ran up the steps that skirted the central courtyard. As he approached the first floor, he seemed to remember something and stepped back towards the landing overlooking the central courtyard.

'Rati!'

'Yes, My Lord?' answered the attendant.

'Isn't it the day of the week when Lady Anandmayi bathes in milk and rose petals?' asked Parvateshwar.

'Yes, My Lord. Warm water on all days of the week except the day of the Sun, when she bathes in milk and rose petals.'

Parvateshwar smiled. 'So, is it ready?'

Rati smiled indulgently. She had served Parvateshwar her entire life, but had never seen her master smile as much as he had in the last few days, since he had returned with the new mistress. 'It'll be ready any moment now, My Lord.'

'Be sure to inform the lady as soon as it's ready.'

'Yes, My Lord.'

Parvateshwar turned and ran up the remaining two flights of stairs, before reaching his private chamber on top. He found Anandmayi relaxing in the balcony on a comfortable chair, as she observed the goings-on in the street below. A cloth canopy screened out the evening sun. She turned around as she heard Parvateshwar rush in.

'What's the hurry?' asked a smiling Anandmayi.

Parvateshwar stopped, smiling broadly. 'I just wanted to know how you're doing.'

Anandmayi smiled and beckoned Parvateshwar. The

Meluhan general walked over and sat down beside her on the armrest. Anandmayi rested her head on his arm as she continued to study the street below. The markets were still open, but unlike the loud and garrulous Chandravanshis, the citizens of Devagiri were achingly polite. The road, the houses, the people, everything reflected the prized Suryavanshi values of sobriety, dignity and uniformity.

'What do you think of our capital?' asked Parvateshwar. 'Isn't it astonishingly well-planned and orderly?'

Anandmayi looked at Parvateshwar with an indulgent smile playing on her lips. 'It's heartbreakingly lacklustre and colourless.'

Parvateshwar laughed. 'You're more than enough to add colour to this city!'

Anandmayi placed her hand on Parvateshwar's as she remarked, 'So, this is the land where I will die...'

Parvateshwar turned his hand around and held hers, in reply.

'Any news?' asked Anandmayi. 'Has the Lord entered the territory of Meluha?'

'No reports as yet,' said Parvateshwar. 'But what is truly worrying is the absence of bird couriers from Ayodhya.'

Anandmayi's visage transformed as she straightened up with concern. 'Has Ayodhya been conquered?'

'I don't know, darling. But I don't think the Lord has enough men to conquer Ayodhya. The city has seven concentric walls, albeit badly designed. That is formidable defence, even if the soldiers are ill-trained.'

Anandmayi narrowed her eyes in irritation. 'They are poorly led, Parvateshwar, but the soldiers are brave men. My country's generals may be idiots, but the commoners will fight hard for their homeland.'

'This reinforces my argument that the Lord Neelkanth

couldn't have conquered Ayodhya with just the one hundred and fifty thousand soldiers of Branga and Vaishali.'

'So what do you think has happened?'

'Clearly, Meluhan interests are not being served in Ayodhya. One possibility is that your father, King Dilipa, has aligned with the Neelkanth.'

'Impossible. My father is too much in love with himself. He's getting medicines from Lord Bhrigu which is keeping him alive. He will not risk that for anything.'

'The people of Ayodhya may have rebelled against their King and thrown in their lot with the Neelkanth.'

'Hmmm... That's possible. My people are certainly more devoted to the Neelkanth than to my father.'

'And if the Neelkanth has Ayodhya under control, he will quickly turn his attention to his main objective: Meluha.'

'He aims to destroy the Somras, Parva. He will not indulge in wanton destruction. Why would he do that? It would turn your people against him. He will only go for the Somras.'

Parvateshwar's eyes flashed open. 'Of course! He will target the secret Somras manufacturing facility and its scientists. That would end the supply of the Somras. People will have no choice but to learn to live without it.'

'There you are. That's his target. Where *is* this secret Somras manufacturing facility?'

'I don't know. But I will find out.'

'Yes, you should.'

'In any case,' said Parvateshwar. 'I've told Kanakhala not to send any more messages to Ayodhya. We could just be passing on information to the enemy.'

'If Ayodhya is already in their control, and they leave now, they could be in Meluha quite soon.'

'Yes, it could be as early as six months. Also, along with Ayodhya, the Lord would have a massive army.'

'Redouble your preparations.'

'Hmmm... I'll also order Vidyunmali to leave for Lothal with twenty thousand soldiers.'

'Lothal? Just because they didn't send you their monthly report? Isn't that a bit of an over-reaction?'

'I don't have a good feeling about them,' said Parvateshwar, slowly shaking his head. 'They didn't respond to my bird courier.'

'Can you afford to send twenty thousand soldiers away based on a mere hunch?'

'Lothal is not too far away. Also, it's a border town. It is the closest Meluhan city from Panchavati. It may not be such a bad idea to reinforce it.'

Chapter 26

Battle of Mrittikavati

The exhausted scout stumbled into the military tent, barely able to conceal his anxiety. Shiva jerked his head up from the map he'd been poring over, as the soldier managed a hasty salute. 'What?'

Shot like an arrow, Shiva's voice made Kali, Sati, Gopal and Chenardhwaj look up too, worry creasing their faces. Shiva's army had marched in quickly from Lothal and was just a day away from Mrittikavati.

'My Lord, I have bad news.'

'Give me the facts. Don't jump to conclusions.'

'Mrittikavati is much better defended now than it had been earlier. Brigadier Vidyunmali sailed into the city a few days back. Apparently, he was on his way to Lothal to strengthen Meluha's defences at the border. Clearly, Emperor Daksha has no idea as yet that Lothal has pledged loyalty to you, My Lord.'

'How many men does Vidyunmali have?' asked Chenardhwaj.

'Around twenty thousand, My Lord. Added to which are the five thousand soldiers already stationed at Mrittikavati.'

'We're still at a substantial advantage in terms of numbers, My Lord,' said Chenardhwaj. 'But Mrittikavati's defences can make even twenty-five thousand men seem like a lot.'

Shiva shook his head. 'I don't think that should be a problem. It doesn't matter how many soldiers they have. We just want to commandeer their ships, not conquer their city. If Vidyunmali has sailed with twenty thousand soldiers, his transport ships would also be in the Mrittikavati port, right? So there are even more ships for us to capture.'

Kali smiled. 'That's true!'

'Prepare to march to Mrittikavati,' said Shiva. 'We attack in two days.'

Shiva could see the panic-stricken people rush back into the city as the warning conches were blown repeatedly from the ramparts of Mrittikavati. The unexpected appearance of a massive enemy force had shocked the Meluhans.

Atop his horse at a vantage point on the hill, Shiva could clearly see the city of Mrittikavati and its port. Like most Meluhan cities, it had also been built on a massive platform a kilometre away from the Saraswati, as a protection against floods. But it was the port, obviously built on the banks of the great river, which fascinated Shiva.

The circular harbour was massive, with the waters of the Saraswati going into it through a narrow opening. A semi-circular dock was separated by a pool of water from the outer ring of the port. A dome-covered inner dock protected the various repair yards. Ships were anchored along the outer side of the inner dock and the inner side of the outer pier. This ingenious design could hold nearly fifty ships in a relatively small space. The expanse of water between the two parallel circles of ships allowed for free movement of the vessels. The ships could move fairly quickly within the harbour in a single file. Being relatively small, the harbour gate afforded the entry or exit of only one ship at a time. But considering that ships could tail each other in the circular channel within the port, the narrow gate did not affect the speed at which the ships could enter or leave the port. However, it did allow for effective defence against enemy ships. The gate was shut and Shiva could see the numerous points across the harbour walls from where a defence could be mounted.

Shiva smiled. *Typically foolproof Meluhan planning.*

Kali leaned across to Shiva. 'The fortified pathway between the city and the port may be a weakness.'

'Yes,' said Sati. 'Let's attack from there. If we succeed in making them feel vulnerable, they will be forced to shut the gates of the city that lead to this pathway, and pull their soldiers within. The city and the port are not next to each other, which means they will have to sacrifice one or the other if the pathway walls are breached. I would imagine they would compromise and give up the port.'

Shiva looked at Sati. 'Vidyunmali is aggressive. He doesn't like to make compromises. Once he realises that we are after their ships and not the city itself, he may take a gamble. He may choose to step out of the city and mount a rearguard assault on our attacking forces. That may appear like a sensible choice to him. He may think that he can rout us on the pathway, thus saving both the port and the city. I hope he makes that mistake.'

— ⁂ —

Shiva rode up and down the line of his all-inclusive army, consisting of Brangas, Vasudevs, Nagas and some Suryavanshis from Lothal. Sati and Kali were on horseback, leading their sections of the army. The soldiers were ready but knew that the Meluhans were well fortified.

'Soldiers!' roared Shiva. 'Mahadevs! Hear me!'

Silence descended on the men.

'We're told a great man walked this earth a thousand years ago. Lord Ram, *Maryada Purushottam*, the most celebrated amongst the kings. But we know the truth! He was more than a man! He was a God!'

The soldiers listened in pin-drop silence.

'These people,' said Shiva, pointing to the Meluhans stationed on the fort walls of Mrittikavati, 'only remember his name. They don't remember his words. But I remember the words of Lord Ram. I remember he had said: "If you have to choose between my people and dharma, choose dharma! If you have to choose between my family and dharma, choose dharma! Even if you have to choose between me and dharma, always choose dharma!"'

'Dharma!' bellowed the army in one voice.

'The Meluhans have chosen Evil,' bellowed Shiva. 'We choose dharma!'

'Dharma!'

'They have chosen death! We choose victory!'

'Victory!'

'They have chosen the Somras!' roared Shiva. 'We choose Lord Ram!'

'Jai Shri Ram!' shouted Sati.

'Jai Shri Ram!' Kali joined the war cry.

'Jai Shri Ram!' shouted all the soldiers.

'Jai Shri Ram!'

'Jai Shri Ram!'

The familiar cry from the Neelkanth's army reverberated within the walls of Mrittikavati; it was a cry that usually charged the Meluhans. But this time it infused fear.

Shiva turned to Kali, surrounded by the roars of his warriors, and nodded at her. A small cold smile curved Kali's lips and she nodded in return, her eyes glittering, and swung her sword so it flashed in the sun. Then she raised a single hand to the soldiers behind her, and a wave of silence rolled out across the army until all that could be heard was the wind snapping at the banners flying above their heads. She signalled again and the men tensed and readied their weapons. Then she raised one sword, pointed towards the sky, and with a blood-curdling scream, brought her blade forward to unleash a roaring tide of men at the walls.

Shiva keenly observed the battle raging in a narrow section of the fortified pathway. Kali was engaged in making repeated assaults with the Vasudev elephants and makeshift catapults, concentrating all resources on breaching one small section. A small number of exceptionally brave Naga soldiers fought against daunting odds as the Meluhans shot arrows and poured boiling oil from the battlements that lined the pathway. Famed for their superhuman courage, the Nagas were ideal for this battle of attrition. Small breaches began opening up on the pathway walls; Shiva's soldiers would soon be able to block the city's access to its port. This triggered the reaction that Shiva expected from Vidyunmali. The main gates of Mrittikavati were thrown open and the Meluhans marched out, arranged in a formation that they had learnt from Shiva himself.

The Meluhan soldiers had formed themselves into squares of twenty by twenty men. Each soldier covered the left half of his body with his shield and the right half of the soldier to the left of him. The soldier behind used his shield as a lid to cover himself and the soldier in front. Each warrior used the space between his own shield and the one next to him to hold out his long spear. This formation provided the defence of a tortoise but could also be used as a devastatingly offensive battering ram with long spears bearing in on the enemy.

However, the tortoise had one weakness that was known to the creator of the formation himself: Shiva. This chink in the armour was at its rear; if attacked from behind, there was little that the soldiers could do. They were weighed down with heavy spears which pointed ahead. It was difficult to turn around quickly. Furthermore, there was no shield protection at the back of the formation. So if an enemy were to get behind, he could attack the soldiers and rout them completely.

Shiva turned towards Sati with a smile. 'Vidyunmali is so predictable.'

Sati nodded. 'To formation?'

'To formation,' agreed Shiva.

Sati immediately turned her horse and rode out to the right, quickly extending the line of the army under her command towards the pathway wall. She steadily put herself between the Meluhan tortoises emerging from the city gates, and Kali's brave Nagas who were attacking the fortified pathway behind her. Her task was to first fight hard and then begin retreating slowly, giving the Meluhans a false sense of imminent victory, keeping them marching forward. It would be a tough battle which would lead to heavy casualties, as she would be right in front of the unstoppable tortoise formations. As the Meluhans moved ahead, space would open up behind them, allowing Shiva to ride out with his cavalry and attack them from the rear.

Shiva, meanwhile, rode towards the elephant corps and the cavalry on the left.

'Steady!' Shiva ordered the Vasudev brigadier in command of the elephant corps.

Shiva had to move quickly. But he also had to move at the right time. If he charged too early, Vidyunmali would smell the trap.

As Veerbhadra saw the Meluhan tortoise charge into Sati's army, he turned to Shiva, worried. 'The task is too difficult for Sati. We should…'

'Stay focused, Bhadra,' said Shiva. 'She knows what she is doing.'

The tortoise formations were bearing down hard on Sati and her soldiers. In the best traditions of Suryavanshi warfare, Sati led from the front. She could see the wall of shields moving steadily towards her at a slow, jostling run, a forest of spears bristling out of every crevice. The sun bounced off the polished metal with every thudding step they took. She breathed out slowly and urged her horse forward into a smooth canter, then a gallop as she held herself just out of the saddle, poised and still, waiting for her moment.

Closer and closer she came to the formation, eyes searching for a gap. For a moment a shield shifted slightly out of alignment as they ran, exposing the neck of a soldier. Without shifting in her seat, Sati drew a knife from her sheath and flung it with deadly accuracy, striking home and felling the soldier in midstep.

The tortoise was almost upon her. She pulled hard on the reins, her horse rearing up as she tried to turn backwards. She felt a sharp pain in her shoulder and heard her horse neigh desperately as it faltered beneath her. Gasping in pain from the spear thrust, she tried to kick free from her dying mount as it came to its knees. She looked up to see which soldier had stabbed her, but could not make out which pair of eyes, peering over their shields, held the spear that was buried in her shoulder. The spear was thrust deeper, and she cried out, half in pain and half in anger, her eyes watering. She swung her sword violently, hacking the spear in two, as she rolled off the horse and onto her feet.

A few arrows sped past Sati's shoulders, striking more soldiers in the tortoise through the gap she had just created. For a moment, the Meluhan charge slowed and faltered, the shield line crumbling in slightly as replacement soldiers struggled to come forward and seal the breach. Admirably though, the Meluhans were back in formation quickly and resumed their charge. Sati stepped back a pace and in the same movement, almost like they were in lock-step, her army stepped back as well, imperceptibly, as they fought on bravely. They kept withdrawing gradually, as though being mowed down by the unstoppable tortoise corps. Just a few more minutes of steady retreat by Sati's men and the Meluhans would have marched forward far enough for Shiva to ride out behind them and destroy their formations.

Shiva observed the battle raging in the distance. His eyes fell on the Meluhan chariots on the side of the tortoise formations, providing protection to their flanks. Each chariot had a charioteer to steer the horses and a warrior to engage in combat. The two-man team allowed for frightening speed and brutal force. These chariots could stall the impending charge of Shiva's cavalry.

'I want your elephants to take out those chariots. Now,' he ordered the Vasudev brigadier.

The Vasudev brigadier turned to his *mahouts*, quickly relaying the orders.

The elephants raced out at a fearsome pace, making the ground rumble with their charge. The Meluhan warriors on the chariots confidently observed the elephants approach. They immediately relieved their charioteers of the reins of their horses, who in turn pulled out drums stored for just such an occasion. The Meluhans still remembered the battles against Chandravanshi elephants. Loud noises from drums always disturbed the giant animals, making them run amuck, often crushing their own army. But these beasts had been trained by the Vasudevs to tolerate sudden loud sounds. Much to the shock of the Meluhan charioteers, the elephants continued their charge.

Seeing their tactic fail, they immediately abandoned the drums and took up the reins of their horses. The warriors pulled out their spears and readied themselves for battle. The Meluhan chariots moved quickly as the Vasudev elephants drew near, weaving around the pachyderms as they charged, throwing their spears at the giant beasts, hoping to injure or at least slow them down. But the elephants were prepared. There were massive metallic balls tied to their trunks. The elephants swung their trunks expertly, smashing the metallic balls into the bodies of the horses and the charioteers. Some of the Meluhans were fortunate enough to die instantly, but others had the balls smash through their bones, leaving them alive to suffer in agony. And as if this wasn't bad enough, a second surprise was in store for the Meluhan charioteers. All of a sudden, fire spewed out of the elephant *howdahs*!

The Vasudevs had fitted their elephants with machines designed by their engineers. Two Vasudev soldiers kept pushing the levers, shooting out an almost continuous stream of flames which burned all in its path. The few unfortunate Meluhan chariots that did not get burned were stamped out of existence under massive elephant feet. The chariot corps of the Meluhans was no match for the Vasudev elephants.

Shiva drew his sword and held it high. He turned to his cavalry, and shouted over the din, 'Ride hard into the rear of those formations! Charge into them! Destroy them!'

Even as Shiva's cavalry thundered out, Sati was playing her part perfectly. Her soldiers had been progressively stepping back, drawing the Meluhans farther and farther away into the open, exposing a massive breach between the rear of their tortoise formations and the fort walls. To maintain the credibility of the tactic and keep the Meluhans engaged in battle, Sati's soldiers were not running away in haste but continuing to fight, taking many casualties in the process. Sati herself had also been seriously injured, having been struck on both the shoulder and thigh. But she battled on. She knew she couldn't afford to fail. Her forces' success in their task was crucial to their overall victory.

Shiva's cavalry rode hard, in a great arc around the main battlefront. He could see the Vasudev elephants and the Meluhan chariots clashing on his right. Practically decimated, the chariots could not ride out to meet the new threat from the cavalry. Shiva rode fast, unchallenged, till he reached the unprotected rear of the Meluhan tortoise formations.

'Jai Shri Ram!' thundered Shiva.

'Har Har Mahadev!' bellowed his cavalry, kicking their horses hard.

Shiva's three thousand strong cavalry charged into the Meluhans. Locked into their formation as they faced the opposite side, weighed down by immensely heavy spears, they were unable to turn around. Shiva's mounted soldiers cut through the Meluhan tortoise corps, hacking away with their long swords. Within moments of this brutal attack, the Meluhan formations started breaking. Some soldiers surrendered while others simply ran away. By the time Vidyunmali, who was fighting at the head of his army, received the news of the decimation of his troops towards his rear, it was already too late. The Meluhans had been outflanked and defeated.

Chapter 27

The Neelkanth Speaks

The survivors had been disarmed and chained together in groups. The chains had been fixed into stakes buried deep in the ground. They were surrounded by four divisions of Shiva's finest. It was well nigh impossible for them to escape. Ayurvati had commandeered the outer port area and created a temporary hospital. The injured, of both the Meluhan as well as Shiva's armies, were being treated.

Shiva squatted next to a low bed where Sati had just received a quick surgery. The wound on her shoulder would heal quickly but the thigh injury would take some time. Kali and Gopal stood at a distance.

'I'm all right,' said Sati, pushing Shiva away. 'Go to Mrittikavati. You need to take control of the city quickly. They need to see you. You need to calm them down. We don't want skirmishes breaking out between the citizens of Mrittikavati and our army.'

'I know. I know. I'm going,' said Shiva. 'I just needed to check on you.'

Sati smiled and pushed him once again. 'I'm fine! I will not die so easily. Now go!'

'*Didi* is right,' said Kali. 'We need to do a flag march within the precincts of the city and cow them down.'

A surprised Shiva turned around. 'We are not taking our army into the city.'

Kali flailed her hands in exasperation. 'Then why did we conquer the city?'

'We haven't conquered the city. We've only defeated their army. We need to get the citizens of Mrittikavati on our side.'

'On our side? Why?'

'Because we will then be free to sail out of here with our entire army. We have ten thousand prisoners of the Meluhan army. Do you want to commit our soldiers to guarding prisoners of war? If Mrittikavati comes to our side, we can keep the Meluhan army imprisoned in the city itself.'

'They're not going to do that, Shiva. In fact, if they see any weakness in us, they will sense an opportunity to rebel.'

'It's not weakness, Kali, but compassion. People usually know the difference.'

'You've got to be joking! How in God's name are you going to show compassion after massacring their army?'

'I will do it by not marching into the city with my army. I will go there only with Bhadra, Nandi and Parshuram. And I will speak to the citizens.'

'How will that help?'

'It will.'

'You have just destroyed their army, Shiva! I don't think they would be interested in listening to anything you have to say.'

'They will be. I am their Neelkanth.'

Kali could barely contain her irritation. 'At least let me accompany you along with some Naga soldiers. You may need some protection.'

'No.'

'Shiva...'

'Do you trust me?'

'What does that have to...'

'Kali, do you trust me?'

'Of course I do.'

'Then let me handle this,' concluded Shiva, before turning to Sati. 'I'll be back soon, darling.'

Sati smiled and touched Shiva's hand.

'Go with Lord Ram, my friend,' said Gopal, as Shiva rose and turned to leave.

Shiva smiled. 'He's always with me.'

— ⋆ —

A collective buzz of a thousand voices hovered over the central square as the citizens of Mrittikavati came in droves for a glimpse of their Neelkanth. News of his presence in the city had spread like wildfire.

Was it the Neelkanth who attacked us?

Why would he attack us?

We are his people! He is our God!

Was it really him who banned the Somras and not a fraud Neelkanth? Did our Emperor lie to us? No, that cannot be...

Shiva stood tall on the stone podium, surveying the milling, excitable crowd. He allowed them to have a clear view of his uncovered *blue throat*, the *neel kanth*. Unarmed as ordered, Nandi, Veerbhadra and Parshuram stood apprehensively behind him.

'Citizens of Mrittikavati,' thundered Shiva. 'I am your Neelkanth.'

Whispers hummed through the square.

'Silence!' said Nandi, raising his hand, quietening the audience immediately.

'I come from a faraway land deep in the Himalayas. My life was changed by what I had believed was an elixir. But I was wrong. This mark I bear on my throat is not a blessing from the Gods but a curse of Evil, a mark of poison. I carry this mark,' said Shiva, pointing to his blue throat. 'But my fellow Meluhans, you bear this scourge as well! And you don't even know it!'

The audience listened, spellbound.

'The Somras gives you a long life and you are grateful for that. But these years that it gifts to you are not for free! It takes away a lot more from you! And its hunger for your soul has no limit!'

A sinister breeze rustled the leaves of the trees that lined the square.

'For these few additional transient years you pay a price that is eternal! It is no coincidence that so many women in Meluha cannot bear children. That is the curse of the Somras!'

Shiva's words found ready resonance in Meluhan hearts, many of which had been broken by the long lonely wait for children from the Maika adoption system. They knew the misery of growing old without a child.

'It is no coincidence that the mother of your country, the mother of Indian civilisation itself, the revered Saraswati is slowly drying to extinction. The thirsty Somras continues to consume her waters. Her death will also be due to the evil of the Somras!'

The Saraswati River was not just a body of water to most Indians; in fact, no river was. And the Saraswati was the holiest among them all. It was their spiritual mother.

'Thousands of children are born in Maika with painful cancers that eat up their bodies. Millions of Swadweepans are dying of a plague brought on by the waste of the Somras. Those people curse the ones who use the Somras. They are cursing you. And your souls will bear this burden for many births. That is the evil of the Somras!'

Veerbhadra looked at Shiva's back and then at the audience.

Shiva felt his blue throat and smiled sadly. 'It may appear that the Somras has my throat. But in actual fact, it has all of Meluha by the throat! And it is squeezing the life out of you slowly, so slowly, that you don't even realise it. And by the time you do, it will be too late. All of Meluha, all of India, will be destroyed!'

The citizens of Mrittikavati continued to be engrossed in his speech.

'I did try to stop this peacefully. I sent out a notice to every city, in every kingdom, all across this fair land of our India. But in Meluha, my message was replaced by another put up by your Emperor, stating that it wasn't I who banned the Somras, but some fraud Neelkanth.'

Nandi could sense the tide turning.

'Your Emperor lied to you!'

There was pin-drop silence.

'Emperor Daksha occupies the position that was Lord Ram's more than a thousand years ago. He represents the legacy of the great seventh Vishnu. He is supposed to be your Protector. And he lied to you.'

Parshuram looked at Shiva with reverence. He had swayed the Meluhans firmly to his side.

'As if that wasn't enough, he sent his army to drive a wedge between you and me. But I know that nothing can tear us apart; I know that you will listen to me. For I am fighting for Meluha. I am fighting for the future of your children!'

A collective wave of understanding swept through the crowd; the Neelkanth was fighting *for* them, not *against* them.

'You have heard myths about the tribe of Vasudev, left behind by our great lord, Shri Ram. Well, the legendary tribe does exist, the ones who carry the legacy of Lord Ram. And they are with me, sharing my mission. They also want to save India from the Somras.'

Almost every Meluhan was familiar with the fable of the Vasudevs, the tribe of Lord Ram himself. Now knowing that they not only existed in flesh and blood, but were with the Neelkanth as well, drove the issue beyond debate in their minds.

'I am going to save Meluha! I'm going to stop the Somras!' roared Shiva. 'Who is with me?'

'I am!' screamed Nandi.

'I am!' shouted every citizen of Mrittikavati.

'I love Meluha more than the Somras,' said Shiva, 'so I put up a proclamation banning the Somras. Your Emperor loves the Somras more than Meluha, so he decided to oppose me. Whose side are you on? Meluha or the Somras?'

'Meluha!'

'Then what do we do with the army that fights for your Emperor; that fights for the Somras?'

'Kill them!'

'Kill them?'

'Yes!'

'No!' shouted Shiva.

The people fell silent, dumbfounded.

'Your army was only following orders. They have surrendered. It would be against the principles of Lord Ram to kill prisoners of war. So once again, what should we do with them?'

The audience remained quiet.

'I want the soldiers to be imprisoned in Mrittikavati,' said Shiva. 'I want you to ensure that they do not escape. If they do, they will follow your Emperor's orders and fight me again. Will you keep them captive in your city?'

'Yes!'

'Will you ensure that not one of them escapes?'

'Yes!'

Shiva allowed a smile to escape. 'I see Gods standing before me. Gods who are willing to fight Evil! Gods who are willing to give up their attachment to Evil!'

The citizens of Mrittikavati absorbed the praise from their Neelkanth.

Shiva raised his balled fist high in the air. 'Har Har Mahadev!'

'Har Har Mahadev!' roared the people.

Nandi, Veerbhadra and Parshuram raised their hands and repeated the stirring cry of those loyal to the Neelkanth. 'Har Har Mahadev!'

'Har Har Mahadev!'

— ⁂ —

The governor's palace in Mrittikavati had been modified to serve as a prison for the surviving soldiers of the Meluhan army. Shiva's troops escorted the prisoners into the make-shift prison in small batches. Shiva, Kali, Sati, Gopal and Chenardhwaj were standing at a small distance from the entrance when Vidyunmali was led in. He tried to break free and lunge at Shiva. A soldier kicked Vidyunmali hard and tried to push him back in line.

'It's all right,' said Shiva. 'Let him approach.'

Vidyunmali was allowed to walk past the bamboo shields held by the soldiers, and move towards Shiva.

'You were doing your duty, Vidyunmali,' said Shiva. 'You were only following orders. I have nothing against you. But you will have to stay imprisoned till the Somras has been removed. Then you will be free to do whatever it is that you want to do.'

Vidyunmali stared at Shiva with barely concealed disgust. 'You were a barbarian when we found you and you are still a barbarian. We Meluhans don't take orders from barbarians!'

Chenardhwaj drew his sword. 'Speak with respect to the Neelkanth.'

Vidyunmali spat at the governor of Lothal-Maika. 'I don't speak to traitors!'

Kali drew her knife out, moving towards Vidyunmali. 'Perhaps you shouldn't speak at all...'

'Kali...' whispered Shiva, before turning towards Vidyunmali. 'I have no enmity with your country. I tried to achieve my purpose with peace. I had sent out a clear proclamation asking all of you to stop using the Somras, but...'

'We are a sovereign country! We will decide what we can and cannot use.'

'Not when it comes to Evil. When it comes to the Somras, you will do what is in the interest of the people and the future of Meluha.'

'Who are you to tell us what is in our interest?'

Shiva had had enough. He waved his hand dismissively. 'Take him away.'

Nandi and Veerbhadra immediately dragged a kicking Vidyunmali towards the make-shift prison.

'You will lose, you fraud,' screamed Vidyunmali. 'Meluha will not fall!'

— ⁂ —

'Shiva, I'd like you to meet someone,' said Brahaspati.

Brahaspati had just walked into Shiva's private chamber in the Mrittikavati official guesthouse, accompanied by a Brahmin. Sati, Gopal and Kali were with the Neelkanth.

'Do you remember Panini?' asked Brahaspati. 'He was my assistant at Mount Mandar.'

'Of course I do,' said Shiva, before turning to Panini. 'How are you, Panini?'

'I am well, great Neelkanth.'

'Shiva,' said Brahaspati, 'I found Panini in Mrittikavati, leading a scientific project being conducted at the Saraswati delta. He has asked me if he can join us in our battle against the Somras.'

Shiva frowned, wondering why Brahaspati was disturbing him with such an inconsequential request at this time. 'Brahaspati, he was your assistant. I completely trust your judgement. You don't have to check with me about...'

'He has some news that may be useful,' interrupted Brahaspati.

'What is it, Panini?' asked Shiva politely.

'My Lord,' said Panini. 'I was recruited by Maharishi Bhrigu for some secret work at Mount Mandar.'

Shiva's interest was immediately piqued. 'I thought the Somras factory at Mount Mandar has not been rebuilt as yet.'

'My mission had nothing to do with the Somras, My Lord. I was asked to lead a small team of Meluhan scientists personally chosen by the Maharishi to make *daivi astras* from materials that he had provided.'

'What? Was it you who made the *daivi astras*?'

'Yes.'

'Did the Vayuputras come and help you?'

'We were trained by Maharishi Bhrigu himself on how to make them from the core material that he provided us. I do know a bit about the technology of *daivi astras*, but not enough to make any usable weapons. Perhaps I was selected because even my little knowledge is more than most.'

'But weren't any Vayuputras present, in order to assist you?' asked Shiva once again. 'Did you see them with Maharishi Bhrigu perhaps?'

'I don't think the core material that the Maharishi gave us was from the Vayuputras.'

A surprised Shiva looked at Gopal, before turning back to Panini. 'What makes you say that?'

'The little that I know of the *daivi astra* technology is based on Vayuputra knowledge. Maharishi Bhrigu's processes and the materials were completely different.'

'Did he have his own core material to make the *daivi astras*?'

'It appeared so.'

Shiva turned towards Gopal once again; the implications were obvious and portentous. To begin with, the Vayuputras were not on Bhrigu's side after all. But more importantly, Bhrigu was an even more formidable opponent if he could make the core material for the *daivi astras* all by himself.

'And I also think,' said Panini, 'that Maharishi Bhrigu may have used the last of the *daivi astra* core material that he had when he asked me to prepare the weapons.'

'Why do you think so?'

'Well, he was always exhorting me to be careful with the core material and not waste even small portions of it. I remember once when we had accidentally spoilt a minuscule amount of it. He was livid and had angrily rebuked us that this was all the *daivi astra* core material that he possessed; that we should be more careful.'

Shiva took a deep breath before turning to Gopal. 'He has no more *daivi astras*.'

'It appears so,' answered Gopal.

'And the Vayuputras are not with him.'

'That would be a fair assumption to make.'

'Shiva,' said Brahaspati, 'there's more.'

Shiva raised a brow and turned towards Panini.

'My Lord,' said Panini, 'I also believe that the secret Somras factory is in Devagiri.'

'How can you be sure?' asked Shiva.

'I'm sure you're aware that the Somras needs the Sanjeevani

tree in large quantities. I was brought to Devagiri on a regular basis but only in the night, to check the quality of the Sanjeevani logs coming into the city.'

'I don't understand. Isn't it a part of your normal duties to check the consignment before it is sent off to the Somras factory?'

'That's true. But I had a friend in the customs department with whom I checked whether the Sanjeevani logs ever left the city. He was unaware of any such movement. If such huge quantities of the Sanjeevani logs are being brought into Devagiri and not being taken out, then the most logical assumption is that this is the city where the Somras is being manufactured.'

Shiva's expression reflected his gratitude towards the Brahmin. 'Panini, thank you. You have no idea how useful your information is.'

— ⁂ —

'Magadh has fallen?' asked Parvateshwar.

Parvateshwar was in the office of the Meluhan Prime Minister Kanakhala. She had finally received a bird courier from Ayodhya after many months.

'There's more,' said Kanakhala. 'The entire army of Magadh has been routed. Prince Surapadman is dead. King Mahendra has gone into deep mourning. The Brangas are now in control of Magadh.'

Parvateshwar pressed the bridge of his nose as he absorbed the implications. 'If they control Magadh, they control the chokepoint on the Ganga. They would only have to keep a few thousand soldiers within the fort of Magadh to be able to attack any Ayodhyan ship that attempts to sail past.'

'*Exactly!* That means Ayodhya cannot come to our aid

quickly enough. They will have to march through forests to their west and then move towards us.'

'If Magadh has been conquered, it means the Lord Neelkanth can leave a small force in that city, sail up the Ganga with the rest of his forces and march into Meluha from Swadweep. We can expect an attack within as little as the next three or four months. We should ask our Ayodhyan allies to leave for Meluha at once. I will speak to Lord Bhrigu.'

'There's more,' said a worried Kanakhala. 'The courier also said that the army that besieged Ayodhya and attacked Magadh was led by Ganesh, Kartik, Bhagirath and Chandraketu.'

'Then where is the Lord Neelkanth?'

'Exactly!' said Kanakhala. 'Where is the Lord Neelkanth?'

Just then an aide rushed into Kanakhala's office. 'My Lord, My Lady, please come at once to His Highness' office. Lord Bhrigu has asked that the both of you come immediately.'

As Kanakhala and Parvateshwar rushed out of the office, another aide approached them with a message for the Meluhan general. From the stamp, it was clear that the message was from Vidyunmali. Parvateshwar broke the seal, intending to read the letter on the way to the emperor's office.

Chapter 28

Meluha Stunned

'What is it, Parvateshwar?' asked Kanakhala.

She had seen the Meluhan general's face turn white as he read Vidyunmali's message. Before Parvateshwar could answer, they found themselves at the door of Daksha's office.

No sooner had Parvateshwar and Kanakhala entered the emperor's chamber, than Daksha unleashed his fury. 'Parvateshwar! Are you in control of the army or not? What in Lord Ram's name have you been up to?'

Parvateshwar knew what the emperor was talking about. He also knew that speaking with the emperor on this topic was a waste of time. He wisely kept silent, saluting the emperor with a short bow of his head and his hands folded in a Namaste.

'Bad news, General,' spoke Bhrigu. 'Mrittikavati has been attacked and conquered by Shiva.'

'What?' asked a stunned Kanakhala. 'How did they even reach Mrittikavati? How could they get through the defences of Lothal?'

Lothal was an exceptionally well-designed sea fortress. Its defences were so solid that an attacker would have to fight overwhelming odds to have any hope of conquering it. It was also known that Lothal was the gateway to south-eastern Meluha, and an attacking army would have to cross this city to be able to march up to Mrittikavati.

Bhrigu raised five sheets of papyrus. 'This is from the governor of Mrittikavati. Apparently Chenardhwaj has pledged loyalty to Shiva. The traitor!'

'That swine!' growled Daksha. 'I knew I should never have trusted him!'

'Then why did you appoint him governor of Lothal, Your Highness?' asked Bhrigu.

Daksha lapsed into a sulk.

Bhrigu turned to Parvateshwar. 'Your suspicions about Lothal were correct, Lord Parvateshwar. I should apologise for not having listened to you earlier. Had we perhaps sent Vidyunmali to Lothal promptly with a strong force we would still be in control of that city.'

'We cannot undo what has happened, My Lord,' said Parvateshwar. 'Let's concentrate on what we can do now. I've received a message from Vidyunmali.'

Bhrigu looked at the letter in Parvateshwar's hand. 'What does the Brigadier say?'

'It sounds like an intelligence failure to me,' said Parvateshwar. 'He says Lord Shiva took them by surprise as he appeared at the gates of Mrittikavati with one hundred thousand soldiers. Vidyunmali put up a brave defence with a mere twenty-five thousand, but was routed.'

Kanakhala understood the strategic significance of Mrittikavati. 'Mrittikavati houses the headquarters of the Saraswati fleet. And Vidyunmali had taken what was left of our warships as well. If the Lord controls Mrittikavati, he now controls the Saraswati River.'

'Shiva is not a Lord!' screamed Daksha. 'How dare you? Who are you loyal to, Kanakhala?'

'Your Highness,' said Bhrigu, his calm tone belying the menace beneath.

Daksha recoiled in fear.

'Your Highness, perhaps it would be better if you retired to your personal chambers.'

'But...'

'Your Highness,' said Bhrigu. 'That was not a request.'

Daksha closed his eyes, shocked at the immense disrespect being shown to him. He got up and left his office, muttering under his breath about the respect due to the Emperor of India.

Bhrigu turned to Parvateshwar, unperturbed, as if nothing had happened. 'General, what else does Vidyunmali say?'

'The entire Saraswati fleet is under the Lord Neelkanth now. But it gets worse.'

'Worse?'

'The people of Mrittikavati have now pledged loyalty to him. The survivors of Vidyunmali's army have been held prisoner in Mrittikavati. Fortunately for us, Vidyunmali managed to escape with five hundred soldiers and send this message.'

'So the Neelkanth has stationed himself in Mrittikavati for now?' asked Bhrigu, careful not to use the term 'fraud Neelkanth' in Parvateshwar's presence. 'Because he will have to commit his own soldiers to guard ours, right?'

'No,' said Parvateshwar, shaking his head. 'Our army is being held prisoner by the citizens of Mrittikavati.'

'The citizens?!'

'Yes. So the Lord Neelkanth does not have to commit any of his own soldiers for the task. He has managed to take twenty-five thousand of our soldiers out of the equation but he still has practically his whole army with him. He has commandeered our entire Saraswati fleet. I'm sure he is making plans to sail up north even as we speak. Vidyunmali also writes about a fearsome corps of exceptionally well-trained elephants in the Lord's army, which are almost impossible to defeat.'

'Lord Ram, be merciful!' said a stunned Kanakhala.

'This is worse than we'd ever imagined,' said Bhrigu.

'But I don't understand one thing,' said Kanakhala. 'How does the Lord have an army of one hundred thousand in Meluha, when a hundred and fifty thousand of his soldiers were in Ayodhya a few weeks back?'

'Ayodhya?' asked a surprised Bhrigu.

'Yes,' said Kanakhala and proceeded to tell him about the message she had just received from Ayodhya about the siege and the destruction of the Magadhan forces.

'By the great Lord Brahma!' said Bhrigu. 'This means the Ayodhya army cannot sail past Magadh. They will have to march through the forest, which means it will take them forever to come to our aid.'

'But I still don't understand how the Lord Neelkanth has so many soldiers in Meluha,' persisted Kanakhala. 'The Branga and Naga armies together don't add up to this number.'

The truth finally dawned on Bhrigu. 'The Vasudevs have joined forces with Shiva. They are the only ones outside of the Suryavanshis and the Chandravanshis who can bring in so many soldiers. This also explains the presence of the exceptionally well-trained elephants Shiva used in the Battle of Mrittikavati. I have heard stories about the prowess of the Vasudev elephants.'

Bhrigu was not aware that the strongest strategic benefit of the Vasudevs was not their elephant corps, but their secretive Vasudev pandits hidden in temples across the Sapt Sindhu. These pandits were the eyes and ears of the Neelkanth, providing him with the most crucial advantage in war: timely and accurate information.

'Lord Shiva will be here soon with a large army,' said Parvateshwar. 'And the three hundred thousand soldiers of Ayodhya will not reach us in time. He has played his cards really well.'

'I do not have a military mind, General,' said Bhrigu. 'But even I can see that we are in deep trouble. What do you advise?'

Parvateshwar brought his hands together and rubbed his chin with his index fingers. He looked up at Bhrigu after some time. 'If Ganesh decides to enter Meluha from the north, we are finished. There is no way we can defend ourselves against a two-pronged attack. Our engineers have been working hard at repairing the road that was ruined by the Yamuna floods. I'll immediately send them instructions to leave the road as it is. If Ganesh chooses to cross from there, then we must make the journey difficult for him. Marching a hundred and fifty thousand strong army on a washed-out road is not going to be easy.'

'Good idea.'

'The Lord Neelkanth could be in Devagiri in a matter of weeks.'

'It's a good thing you have engaged the army in training exercises and simulations,' said Bhrigu.

'The Lord will not win here,' said Parvateshwar. 'That is my word to you, Maharishi*ji*.'

'I believe you, General. But what do we do about the Vasudev elephants? We cannot win against Shiva's army unless we stop his elephants.'

'What do you think, Shiva?' asked Gopal.

Gopal, Sati and Kali were with Shiva in his chamber at

Mrittikavati, conferring. They were re-evaluating their strategy in the light of the news received from Panini.

Kali was clear in her mind. 'Shiva, I propose that you leave Mrittikavati and sail out to Pariha. If you can convince the Vayuputras to give you a lethal *daivi astra*, say the *Brahmastra*, this war will be as good as over.'

'We cannot actually use these *daivi astras*, Your Highness,' said Gopal. 'It will be against the laws of humanity. We can only use such weapons as deterrents to make the other side see sense.'

'Yes, yes,' said Kali dismissively, 'I agree.'

'How long will the journey to Pariha take, Pandit*ji*?' asked Shiva.

'Six months at the minimum,' said Gopal. 'It could take even nine to twelve months if the winds don't favour us.'

'Then the decision is clear,' said Shiva. 'I don't think going to Pariha at this stage makes sense.'

'Why?' asked Kali.

'We have momentum and time on our side, Kali,' said Shiva. 'Ayodhya's army cannot come into Meluha for another six to eight months at least. Ganesh and Kartik can reach the northern frontiers of Meluha within a few weeks. We will have a six-month window with two hundred and fifty thousand soldiers on our side against just seventy-five thousand on the side of Meluha. I like those odds. I say we finish the war here and now. In the time that it will take me to go to Pariha and return, the situation may have become very different. Also, don't forget, all we know is that the Vayuputras are not with Maharishi Bhrigu. That does not necessarily mean that they will choose to be with us. They may well decide to remain neutral.'

'That makes sense,' agreed Sati. 'If we conquer Devagiri and destroy the Somras factory, the war will be over regardless of what the Vayuputras choose to believe.'

'So what do you suggest, Shiva?' asked Gopal.

'We should divide our navy into two parts,' said Shiva. 'I'll move up the Saraswati and then north, up the Yamuna with a small sailing force of twenty-five ships. I'll meet Ganesh and Kartik as they march down the Yamuna road and we'll board their soldiers onto my ships. By sailing, we can get to Devagiri quicker, instead of waiting for them to march to the Meluhan capital. In the meantime, Sati will lead the other contingent of the navy, carrying our entire army from Mrittikavati up the Saraswati to Devagiri. Sati should leave three weeks after me so that we reach Devagiri around the same time. With two hundred and fifty thousand soldiers besieging Devagiri, they may actually see some sense.'

'Sounds good in theory,' said Kali. 'But coordination may prove to be a problem in practice. There could be delays. If one of our armies reaches Devagiri a few weeks earlier, it may leave them weakened against the Meluhans.'

'But Shiva is not suggesting that we mount an attack and conquer Devagiri as soon as either one of us reaches,' said Sati. 'We would just fortify ourselves and wait for the other. Once we have joined forces, only then should we attack.'

'True, but what if the Meluhans decide to attack?' asked Kali. 'Remember, anchored ships are sitting ducks for devil boats.'

'I don't see them stepping out of the safety of their fort,' said Shiva. 'The army that I will lead will have a hundred and fifty thousand soldiers who have just destroyed the mighty Magadhans; the Meluhans will not attack us with only seventy-five thousand soldiers. Sati's army will have a hundred thousand, and don't forget, she will also have the Vasudev elephants. So you see, even our separate armies are capable of taking on the Meluhans on an open field. General Parvateshwar has a calm head on his strong shoulders. He will know that it's better for them to remain in the safety of their fort, rather than marching out and attacking us.'

'But I get your point, Kali,' said Sati. 'If I reach early, I will encamp some ten kilometres south of Devagiri. There is a large hill on the banks of the Saraswati which can serve as a superb defensive position since it will give us the advantage of height. I will set up a *Chakravyuh* formation with our Vasudev elephants as the first line of defence. It will be almost impossible to break through.'

'I know that hill,' said Shiva to Sati. 'That is exactly where I will camp as well if I happen to reach before you do.'

'Perfect.'

— ⁂ —

'There is no respite from the speed, is there, My Lord?'

Shiva and Parshuram stood on the deck of his lead ship, battling to keep their eyes open against the onslaught of the wind upon a speedily moving object.

The fleet was racing up the Saraswati, skeletally staffed as it was, with just two thousand soldiers, not giving any opportunity for the Meluhans to launch small strikes. While none of the cities on the Saraswati were prepared for naval warfare – since the Meluhans never expected such an attack – Shiva had decided to not tempt fate. The Meluhans were not wanting in honour and courage. As an additional precaution, he had also inducted many of the courageous Naga soldiers into his navy. Kali, the Queen of the Nagas, was travelling in the rearguard ship of the convoy.

Shiva smiled. 'No Parshuram, there will be no respite. Speed is of the essence.'

In keeping with Shiva's orders, there had been no breaks in the rowing. Four teams had been set up on gruelling six-hour shifts. The timekeepers, beating on the drums to set the rhythm for the rowers, maintained it at battle-ramming speed. Shiva did not want to trust the unpredictable winds with determining how fast they moved. In the interest of fairness, Shiva had also added his own name to the roster for rowing duties. His six hours of rowing for the day were to come up soon.

'It's a beautiful river, My Lord,' said Parshuram. 'It's sad that we may have to kill it.'

'What do you mean?'

'My Lord, I have been researching the Somras. Lord Gopal has explained many things to me. And an idea has struck me...'

'What?'

'The Somras cannot be made without this,' said Parshuram, pointing to the Saraswati.

'Brahaspati tried that, Parshuram... He tried to find some way to make the Saraswati waters unusable. But that didn't work, remember?'

'That's not what I meant, My Lord. What if the Saraswati didn't exist? Neither would the Somras, would it?'

Shiva observed Parshuram closely with inscrutable eyes.

'My Lord, there was a time when the Saraswati, as we know it today, had ceased to exist. The Yamuna had started flowing east towards the Ganga. Saraswati cannot exist without the meeting of the Yamuna and the Sutlej.'

'We cannot kill the Saraswati,' said Shiva, almost to himself.

'My Lord, for all you know, maybe that's what Nature was trying to do more than a hundred years ago, when an earthquake caused the Yamuna to change its course and flow into the Ganga. If Lord Brahmanayak, the father of the present emperor, had not changed the Yamuna's course to flow back into the Sutlej and restore the Saraswati, history would have been very different. Maybe Nature was trying to stop the Somras.'

Shiva listened silently.

'We don't have to think the Saraswati would be dead. Its soul would still be flowing in the form of the Yamuna and the Sutlej. Only its body would disappear.'

Shiva stared at the Saraswati waters, perceiving her depths. Parshuram had a point but Shiva didn't want to admit it. Not even to himself. Not yet, anyway.

Chapter 29

Every Army Has a Traitor

'Any news, Ganesh?' asked Bhagirath.

Bhagirath and Chandraketu had just joined Ganesh and Kartik on the lead ship. The massive navy was sailing up the Ganga en route to Meluha from the north. Farther ahead, they were to take the Ganga-Yamuna road. They had slowed down only for a few hours to allow a boat to rendezvous with them. The boatman carried a message from a Vasudev pandit.

'I've just received word that my father's army has conquered Mrittikavati,' said Ganesh.

Chandraketu was thrilled. 'That is great news!'

'It is indeed,' answered Ganesh. 'And it gets even better; the citizens of Mrittikavati have been won over to my father's side. They have imprisoned what was left of the Meluhan army in the city.'

'And, have they discovered the location of the Somras factory?' asked Bhagirath.

'Yes,' said Kartik. 'It's Devagiri.'

'Devagiri? What are you saying? That is so stupid. It's their capital. One would think that the factory would be built in a secure, secret location.'

'But they could have built this factory only within cities

with large populations, right? And if so, which city would be better than Devagiri? They must have assumed that they could certainly keep their capital safe.'

'So what are our orders now?' asked Chandraketu.

'The Meluhans have only seventy-five thousand soldiers in Devagiri,' said Ganesh. 'So we're going to launch a coordinated attack.'

'What are the details of the plan?'

'We're to sail up the Ganga and reach the Ganga-Yamuna road. We will then march to Meluha. My father is going to sail up the Yamuna in a fleet to meet us as we march. Together, we will then sail down to Devagiri. My mother, in the meantime, will arrive with the hundred thousand soldiers under her command.'

'So we will have two hundred and fifty thousand soldiers, all fired up with the fervour of recent victories, against seventy-five thousand Meluhans holed up on their platforms,' said Bhagirath. 'I like the odds.'

'That's exactly what *baba* must have said!' grinned Kartik.

— ⁂ —

'You are going to give me the answer I want,' growled Vidyunmali, 'whether you like it or not.'

A Vasudev major, captured from Shiva's army, had been tied up on a moveable wooden rack with thick leather ropes. The stale air in the dark dungeon was putrid. The captured Vasudev was already drenched in his own sweat, but unafraid.

The Meluhan soldiers standing at a distance looked at Vidyunmali warily. What their brigadier was asking them to do was against the laws of Lord Ram. But they were too well-trained. Meluhan military training demanded unquestioning obedience to one's commanding officer. This training had forced the soldiers to suppress their misgivings and carry out Vidyunmali's orders until now. But their moral code was about to be challenged even more strongly.

Vidyunmali heard the Vasudev whispering something again and again. He bent close. 'Do you have something to say?'

The Vasudev soldier kept mumbling softly, drawing strength from his words. *'Jai Guru Vishwamitra. Jai Guru Vashishtha. Jai Guru Vishwamitra. Jai Guru Vashishtha...'*

Vidyunmali sniggered. 'They aren't here to help you, my friend.'

He turned and beckoned a startled Meluhan soldier. The brigadier pointed at a metallic hammer and large nail.

'My Lord?' whispered the nervous soldier, knowing full well that to attack an unarmed and bound man was against Lord Ram's principles. 'I'm not sure if we should...'

'It's not your job to be sure,' growled Vidyunmali. 'That's my job. Your job is to do what I order you to do.'

'Yes, My Lord,' said the Meluhan, saluting slowly. He picked up the hammer and nail. He walked slowly to the Vasudev and placed the nail on the captive's arm, a few inches above the wrist. He held the hammer back and flexed his shoulders, ready to strike.

Vidyunmali turned to the Vasudev. 'You'd better start talking...'

'Jai Guru Vishwamitra. Jai Guru Vashishtha...'

Vidyunmali nodded to the soldier.

'Jai Guru Vishwamitra. Jai Guru... AAAAHHHHHHHHH!'

The ear-splitting scream from the Vasudev resounded loudly in the confines of the dungeon. But this deep, abandoned underground hell-hole, somewhere between Mrittikavati and Devagiri, had not been used in centuries. There was nobody around to hear his screams except for the nervous Meluhan soldiers at the back of the room, who kept praying to Lord Ram, begging for his forgiveness.

The soldier kept robotically hammering away, pushing the nail deep into the Vasudev's right arm. The Vasudev kept screaming up to a point where his brain simply blocked the pain. He couldn't feel his arm anymore. His heart was pumping madly, as blood came out in spurts through the gaping injury.

Vidyunmali approached his ear as the Vasudev breathed heavily, trying to focus on his tribe, on his Gods, on his vows, on anything except his right arm.

'Do you need some more persuasion?' asked Vidyunmali.

The Vasudev looked away, focusing his mind on his chant.

Vidyunmali yanked the nail out, took a wet cloth and wiped the Vasudev's arm. Then he picked up a small bottle and poured its contents into the wound. It burned deeply, but the Vasudev's blood clotted almost immediately.

'I don't want you to die,' whispered Vidyunmali. 'At least not yet...'

Vidyunmali turned towards his soldier and nodded.

'My Lord,' whispered the soldier, with tears in his eyes. He had lost count of the number of sins that he was taking upon his soul. 'Please...'

Vidyunmali glared.

The soldier immediately turned and picked up another bottle. He walked up to the Vasudev and poured some of the viscous liquid into the wound he had inflicted.

Vidyunmali stepped back and returned with a long flint, its edge burning slowly. 'I hope you see the light after this.'

The Vasudev's eyes opened wide in terror. But he refused to talk; he knew he couldn't reveal the secret. It would be devastating for his tribe.

'Jai... Gu... ru... Vishwa...'

'Fire will purify you,' whispered Vidyunmali softly. 'And you will speak.'

'*...Mitra... Jai... Gu... ru... Vash...*'

The dungeon resonated once again with the desperate screams of the Vasudev, as the smell of burning flesh defiled the room.

— ⋆ —

'Are you sure?' asked Parvateshwar.

'As sure as I can ever be,' said a smiling Vidyunmali.

Parvateshwar took a deep breath.

He knew that it was Shiva who led the massive fleet of ships that had just sped past Devagiri two weeks back. Parvateshwar suspected that Shiva was sailing north to pick up Ganesh's army and bring them back to Devagiri. He had also received reports about the delays faced by Ganesh's army as they marched through the washed-out Ganga-Yamuna Road. It would probably take a month for Shiva to return to Devagiri, along with the hundred and fifty thousand soldiers in Ganesh's army.

He also knew that another contingent of the Neelkanth's army, being led by Sati, had just sailed out of Mrittikavati. They would reach Devagiri in a week or two. Knowing full well that Ganesh would be delayed, Parvateshwar expected Sati's army to reach Devagiri first. He also knew that this was a force of a hundred thousand soldiers against his own seventy-five thousand. Once Shiva and Ganesh's army sailed in, the strength of the enemy would rise to two hundred and fifty thousand. Parvateshwar knew that his best chance was to attack Sati's army before Shiva and Ganesh arrived.

The only problem was that he had no answer for the unstoppable Vasudev elephant corps under Sati's command. Until now.

'Chilli and dung?' asked Parvateshwar. 'It just seems so simple.'

'Apparently, the elephants don't like the smell of chilli, My Lord. It makes them run amuck. We should keep dung bricks mixed with chilli ready, burn them and catapult them towards the elephants. The acrid smoke will drive them crazy; and, hopefully, into their own army.'

'There are no elephants to test this on, Vidyunmali. The only way to test this would be in battle. What if this doesn't work?'

'My apologies, General, but do we have any other options?'

'No.'

'Then what's the harm in trying?'

Parvateshwar nodded and turned to stare at his soldiers practising in the distance. 'How did you get this information?'

Vidyunmali was quiet.

Parvateshwar returned his gaze to Vidyunmali, his eyes boring into him. 'Brigadier, I asked you a question.'

'There are traitors in every army, My Lord.'

Parvateshwar was stunned. The famous Vasudev discipline was legendary. 'You found a Vasudev traitor?!'

'Like I said, there are traitors in every army. How do you think I escaped?'

Parvateshwar turned and looked once again at his soldiers. No harm in trying this tactic. It just might work.

— ⁂ —

Devagiri, the abode of the Gods, had become the city of the thoroughly bewildered. Its two hundred thousand citizens could not recall a time in living memory when an enemy army had gathered the gumption to march up to their city. And yet, here they were, witness to unbelievable occurrences.

Just a few weeks earlier, they had seen a large fleet of warships race past their city, rowing furiously up the Saraswati. It was clear that these ships were a part of the Mrittikavati-based Meluhan fleet and that it was now in control of the enemy. Why those enemy ships simply sailed by without attacking Devagiri was a mystery.

News had also filtered in about a massive army garrisoning itself next to the Saraswati, about ten kilometres south of the city. The normally secure Devagiri citizens now confined themselves within the walls of the city, not venturing out unless absolutely necessary. Merchants had also halted all their trading activities and their merchant ships remained anchored at the port.

Rumours ran rife in the city. Some whispered that the enemy army stationed south of Devagiri was led by the Neelkanth himself. Others swore they saw the Neelkanth on the warships that had sailed past. However, they couldn't hazard a guess as to where Lord Shiva was headed in such a hurry. Facts had also found their way in, from other cities: that except for Mrittikavati, this mammoth army had not engaged in battle with any other Meluhan city while sailing up the Saraswati. They had not looted any city or plundered any village, nor had they committed any acts of wanton destruction, but had marched through Meluha with almost hermit-like restraint.

Some were beginning to believe that perhaps the purported gossip they had heard was in fact true; the Neelkanth was not against Meluha, but only the Somras. That the proclamation they had read many months ago was actually from their Lord and not a lie as their emperor had stated. That may be the Neelkanth's army waited at the banks of the Saraswati without attacking, because the Lord himself was negotiating possible terms of surrender with the emperor.

But there were also others, still loyal to Meluha, who refused to believe that their government could have lied. They had good reason to believe that the armies of Shiva comprised the Chandravanshis and the Nagas. That the Naga queen herself was a senior commander in the Neelkanth's army and the Neelkanth had been misled by the evil combination of the Chandravanshis and Nagas. They were willing to lay down their lives for Meluha. What they didn't understand was why their army was not engaging in battle as yet.

'Are you sure, General?' asked Bhrigu.

Parvateshwar was in Bhrigu's chamber in the Devagiri royal palace.

'Yes. It is a gamble, but we have to take it. If we wait too long, the Lord will lead Ganesh's army from the Yamuna to Devagiri. Combined with Sati's army, they will then have a vast numerical advantage and it will be impossible for us to win. Right now, our opponents are only Sati's soldiers who have garrisoned themselves close to the river. They are obviously not looking for a fight. I plan to draw them out and then try to cause some chaos amongst their elephants. If it works, their elephants may just charge back into their own army. They would have no room to retreat, with the river right behind them. If everything goes according to plan, we may just win the day.'

'Isn't Sati your God-daughter?' asked Bhrigu, looking deeply into Parvateshwar's eyes.

Parvateshwar held his breath. 'At this point of time, she is only an enemy of Meluha to me.'

Bhrigu continued to peer into his eyes, increasingly satisfied with what he read. 'If you are convinced, General, then so am I. In the name of Lord Ram, attack.'

— ⅄ꝏ∪⇑⊛ —

Sati couldn't remain holed up on her anchored ships. Ships are unassailable from land when sailing fast, but sitting ducks when they are anchored, susceptible to bombardment and devil boat assaults. So she had decided to garrison herself on land, which would offer protection to her ships as well, by deterring the Meluhans from coming too close to the river banks.

She had chosen a good location to dig in her army. It was on a large, gently-rolling hill right next to the Saraswati. The trees between the hill and the city of Devagiri had been cut down. Therefore, from the vantage point of the hill, Sati had a clear line of sight of enemy movements at the Devagiri city gates ten kilometres away. The height of the hill also gave her another advantage: charging downhill was far easier than advancing uphill, which her enemies would have to do. The elevation also increased the range of her archers significantly.

Having occupied the high ground, Sati then opted to assume the most effective of defensive military formations: the *Chakravyuh*. The core of the *Chakravyuh* comprised columns of infantrymen in the tortoise position. The tortoises themselves were protected to the rear by the river and the Saraswati fleet at anchor, in the middle of the river. They would provide protection against any Meluhan forces that might attack from the river end. Rowboats had been beached and tied in the river shallows, as a contingency for retreating, if necessary. Rows of cavalry, three layers deep, reinforced the core towards the front. Two rows of war elephants formed an impregnable semi-circular outer shell, protecting the formations within. The giant *Chakravyuh,* comprising fifty thousand soldiers, left adequate space between the lines for inner manoeuvrability and for fortification of the outer shell by the cavalry in case of a breach.

All the animals had been outfitted with thin metallic armour and the soldiers had broad bronze shields to protect against any long-range arrows.

It was a near-perfect defensive formation, designed to avoid battle and allow a quick retreat if needed.

Sati intended to remain in this formation till she heard from Shiva.

Chapter 30

Battle of Devagiri

Sati sat on a tall wooden platform that had been constructed for her, behind the cavalry line. It gave her a panoramic view of the entire field and the city of Devagiri in the distance. She watched the city where she had spent most of her life, which she had once called home. A nostalgic corner of her heart longed to be able to revel in its quiet, sober efficiency and understated culture. To worship at the temple of Lord Agni, the purifying Fire God, a ritual she had adhered to as a Vikarma, an ostracised carrier of bad fate. Despite being so close, she couldn't even enter it now to meet her mother. She shook her head. This was no time for sentimentality. She had to focus.

Sati checked her horse, which had been tethered to the platform base. Nandi and Veerbhadra waited next to the platform, mounted on their stallions. They had been designated her personal bodyguards.

Sati knew this would be a difficult period – the time till Shiva returned with Ganesh's army. She had to keep her soldiers in war readiness, and yet, avoid war. As any general knows, this can sometimes breed restless irritability amongst the troops.

Her attention was pulled away as she detected some

movement in the far distance. She couldn't believe what she saw. The main gate of the *Tamra* or *bronze* platform of Devagiri was being opened.

What are they doing? Why would the Meluhans step out into the open? They are outnumbered!

'Steady!' ordered Sati. 'Everyone remain in their positions! We will not be provoked into launching an attack!'

Messengers below immediately relayed the orders to all the brigade commanders. It was important for Sati's soldiers to remain in line. As long as they did, it was almost impossible to beat them. It was especially crucial that the elephant line, at the periphery of Sati's formation, held position. They were the bulwark of her defence.

Sati continued to watch the small contingent of Meluhan soldiers marching out of Devagiri, perhaps no more than a brigade. As soon as they were out, the city gates were shut behind them.

Is it a suicide squad? For what purpose...

The Meluhan soldiers kept marching slowly towards Sati's position. She watched their progress, intrigued. Perched at a height, she soon observed that the soldiers were being followed by carts that were being pulled laboriously by oxen.

What do these thousand foot-soldiers hope to achieve? And what is in those carts?

As the Meluhans drew close to the hill, she saw that many of the soldiers carried long weapons in their left hands.

Archers.

She instantly knew what was about to happen, as she saw them stop. They even had a strong wind supporting them. The Meluhans had clearly planned this for when the winds would work in their favour. She knew the elements well in these parts and realised immediately that her archers would not have the pleasure of giving as much as receiving.

'Shields!' shouted Sati. 'Incoming arrows!'

But the archers were too far. They had clearly overestimated the wind. The arrows barely reached Sati's forces. The strong wind, though advantageous for the Meluhans, was not working to Sati's benefit. She couldn't reply to the Meluhan volley of arrows in kind with her own archers. She saw the Meluhans inch closer, lugging ox-drawn carts behind the archers. In all her years, Sati had never seen ox-drawn carts being used in warfare.

Sati frowned. *What in Lord Ram's name can oxen do against elephants? What is* Pitratulya *doing?*

Sati was clear that she did not want to test General Parvateshwar's strategy today. It was admittedly tempting because this small contingent would be wiped out in minutes if she sent her elephants. However, she smelt a trap and did not want to leave the high ground. She knew what had to be done: hold position till Shiva returned. She did not want to fight. Not today.

Having moved even closer, the Meluhan archers loaded their arrows again.

'Shields!' ordered Sati.

This time the arrows hit the shields at the right end of Sati's formation. Having tested the range, the Meluhan archers moved once again.

The Meluhans probably have some secret weapon that they are not absolutely sure about. The ox-drawn carts may have some role to play in it. They want to provoke some of my men into charging at them so that they can test their weapon.

The upshot was obvious. If her army refused to get provoked, no battle would take place. All the animals in her army were well-armoured. The soldiers had massive shields, prepared in defence for the very arrow attack that the Meluhans were attempting right now. Despite two showers of arrows, her army had not suffered a single casualty. There was nothing to gain by breaking formation. And, nothing to lose by staying in formation.

Sati also figured that since the enemy had already come close, ordering her own archers to shoot arrows now may prove counter-productive. The ox-drawn carts were not manned. A volley of arrows may well drive the animals crazy, making them charge in any direction, perhaps even at her own army, along with whatever evil they carried in the carts. She had a better idea. She instructed her messengers to tell a cavalry squad to ride out from behind the hill she was positioned on, thus hiding their movement, and go around to an adjoining hill towards the west. She wanted them to launch a flanking attack from behind the crest of that hill, surprise and decimate the Meluhan archers as well as drive the oxen away. All she had to do was wait for the Meluhans to move a little closer to her position. Then, she could have them blind-sided with her cavalry charge.

Sati shouted out her orders once again. 'Be calm! Hold the line! They cannot hurt us if we remain in formation.'

The Meluhan archers, having moved closer, arched their bows and fired once again.

'Shields!'

Sati's army was ready. Though the arrows reached right up to the centre of her army, not one soldier was injured. The Meluhans held their bows to their sides and prepared to draw nearer once again, this time a little tentatively.

They're nervous now. They know their plan is not working.

'What the hell!' growled an angry Vasudev elephant-rider as he turned to his partner. 'They are a puny brigade with oxen, against our entire army. Why doesn't General Sati allow us to attack?'

'Because she is not a Vasudev,' spat out the partner. 'She doesn't know how to fight.'

'My Lords,' said the *mahout* to the riders, 'our orders are to follow the General's orders.'

The Vasudev turned in irritation to the *mahout*. 'Did I ask you for your opinion? Your order is to only follow my orders!'

The *mahout* immediately fell silent as the distant shout of the brigadier's herald came through. 'Shields!'

Another volley of arrows. Again, no casualties.

'Enough of this nonsense!' barked one of the elephant-riders. 'We're Kshatriyas! We're not supposed to cower like cowardly Brahmins! We're supposed to fight!'

Sati saw a few elephants on the far right of her formation, the ones that were the closest to the Meluhan brigade, begin to rumble out.

'Hold the line!' shouted Sati. 'Nobody will break formation!'

The messengers carried forward the orders to the other end of the field immediately. The elephants were pulled back into formation by their *mahouts*.

'Nandi,' said Sati, looking down. 'Ride out to that end and tell those idiots to remain in formation!'

'Yes, My Lady,' said Nandi, saluting.

'Wait!' said Sati, as she saw the Meluhan archers loading another set of arrows. 'Wait out this volley and then go.'

The order of 'shields!' was relayed again and the arrows clanged harmlessly against the raised barriers. None of Sati's soldiers were injured.

As Sati put her shield down and looked up, she was horrified. Twenty elephants on the right had charged out recklessly.

'The fools!' yelled Sati, as she jumped onto her horse from the platform.

She galloped forward to cover the breach opened up by the recklessly charging elephants, closely followed by Veerbhadra and Nandi. While passing by the cavalry line, she ordered the reserve cavalry to follow her. Within a few minutes, Sati had stationed herself in the position left open by the Vasudev elephants that had charged out of formation.

'Stay here!' Sati ordered the soldiers behind her as she raised her hand.

She could see her elephants sprinting forward in the distance, goaded on by their *mahouts*, bellowing loudly. The Meluhan archers stood their ground bravely and shot another round.

The order resonated through Sati's army. 'Shields!'

The Vasudev elephant-riders screamed loudly as they crashed into the archers. 'Jai Shri Ram!'

The elephants swung their powerful trunks, tied to which were strong metallic balls. Meluhan soldiers were flung far and wide with the powerful swings. The few who remained were crushed under giant feet. Within just a few moments of this butchery, the archers began retreating.

Though it appeared as if the twenty Vasudev elephants were smashing the Meluhan archers to bits, Sati shuddered with foreboding as she felt a chill run down her spine. She screamed loudly, even though she knew that the elephant-riders couldn't hear her.

'Come back, you fools!'

The Vasudev elephant-riders though, were on a roll. Encouraged by the easy victory, they goaded their *mahouts* to keep the elephants moving forward.

'Charge!'

The elephant-riders primed their main weapon, pulling the levers on the flame throwers. Long, spear-like flames burst forth from the *howdahs*. The riders positioned the weapon, aiming for maximum effect as they crashed into the next line of Meluhans.

The elephants continued dashing forward, seeing the ox-drawn carts farther ahead. And then the tide turned. The retreating Meluhan archers spun around with arrows that had been set on fire, aiming straight for their own carts. The dry and volatile dung cakes on the carts had been mixed with chilli, and caught fire immediately. The startled oxen, sensing the blaze somewhere behind them, ran forward in panic, towards the advancing elephants.

It was the *mahouts* who had the first inkling that something was wrong. Attuned deeply to the beasts, they could sense their innate distress. Goaded on by the fiery elephant-riders behind them though, they continued to press their elephants ahead. Soon the contents on the carts were completely aflame, letting out a thick, acrid smoke. But the elephant-riders were too committed to the charge. They rode straight into the blinding smoke.

As soon as the smoke hit them, the elephants shrieked desperately. The *mahouts* recognised the smell.

Chilli!

'Retreat!' screamed a *mahout.*

'No!' shouted back a belligerent elephant-rider. 'We have them! Crush the oxen. Move forward!'

But the elephants were already in a state of frenzied panic. They turned from the source of their discomfort and ran. The hysterical oxen, with the fires burning hard on the carts, continued their frantic sprint forward as though to elude the blaze.

Sati could see the developing situation unfolding from the distance. Whatever the oxen were carrying was making the pachyderms hysterical. Within a matter of a few minutes the oxen would reach her remaining outer elephant line and spread the panic deep into her force. She saw a fire arrow being shot from the gates of Devagiri as they opened once again. The Meluhans could see their strategy was working and were committing themselves to a full attack. Her worst fears were confirmed as she saw the Meluhan cavalry thunder out of the Devagiri gates. The city was ten kilometres away, and she knew she had the luxury of some time before they reached her position. Her immediate concern was the oncoming oxen that could make all the Vasudev elephants charge madly back into her own force.

Turning back, she shouted out to her herald, 'Tell the lines at the back to retreat to the boats. NOW!'

She ordered the remaining elephant line to disband and escape southwards immediately. If the ox-driven carts reached the line of the lumbering animals and managed to spread panic among the hundreds of elephants under her command, her army would get destroyed completely by her own pachyderms.

She then ordered her cavalry forward.

'Charge at these beasts moving towards us! We have to deflect them on to a different path! We need time for our soldiers to retreat!'

Her cavalry drew their swords and roared: 'Har Har Mahadev!'

'Har Har Mahadev!' bellowed Sati, as she drew her sword and charged forward.

Sati's skilled cavalry kept up a steady volley of arrows as they drew near the elephants and oxen. While this did deflect many of the oxen away from Sati's army, the elephants continued their headlong charge. Many of the elephant *howdahs* had transformed into hell-holes, emitting fire continuously. The shocked elephant-riders, sitting atop the berserk animals, had fallen on some of their flame-throwers, breaking the levers.

Moments later, Sati's cavalry fearlessly charged headlong into her retreating elephants, riding expertly to avoid the wildly swinging trunks and metallic balls. They needed to bring their own elephants down. This required riding up close from behind and slashing the beasts' hamstrings, thus making their rear legs collapse. But this was easier said than done, with the malfunctioning flame-throwers spewing a continuous stream of fire. Sati bravely led her section of the cavalry in pursuit of the task at hand. Since there were only twenty elephants, they were brought down quickly. But not before many of the cavalrymen had lost their lives, some crushed, many burnt by the flame-throwers. Sati herself had had her face scorched on one side.

In the meantime, the rest of Sati's cavalry had managed to redirect all the charging oxen through the skilled use of spears and arrows. The bulls were still charging, panic-stricken with the burning carts tethered to them, but to the west and safely away from the rest of Sati's elephant corps. Sati looked back to the east, where many of her foot soldiers were already sailing out to the safety of the ships. Her cautious planning had ensured that a large number of rowboats had been kept ready for just such an eventuality.

But this would prove to be a minor victory, before absolute disaster. The Meluhan cavalry had been riding hard towards the battlefield, making good time. And, as the oxen stampeded away, the Meluhan riders charged into Sati's cavalry.

Swords clashed.

Sati's cavalry had numbered three thousand riders and was evenly matched with the Meluhans. But her riders had just emerged from a bruising encounter with the panic-stricken elephants and oxen. Their numbers had come down and their strength was already sapped. However, Sati knew that retreat was not an option. She had to battle on for a little longer so that all her foot soldiers could get away to the safety of the ships.

Then Sati heard the sounds of the elephants once again.

She killed the Meluhan in front of her and looked behind.

'Lord Ram, be merciful!'

Some of the elephant corps that she had ordered south were now thundering back. The elephants were trumpeting desperately, with fire spewing in all directions. The *mahouts* had already fallen off, leaving the animals totally out of control. Behind the elephants, were charging oxen with burning carts tethered to them.

The Meluhans had, in a brilliant strategic move ordered by Parvateshwar, kept another corps of ox-driven carts, laden with chilli-laced dung cakes, to the south of Sati's position. These carts had slipped out of Devagiri the previous evening, disguised as agricultural produce transport. Since Sati had not besieged the city, but only camped close to it, they only attacked armament transport and let non-lethal materials travel freely in and out of Devagiri. The reason was very obvious: a full siege would have committed too many soldiers and possibly even provoked a battle. Sati had wanted to avoid that. Little did Sati's Chandravanshi scouts realise that even dung and agricultural produce could be lethal for them.

As the elephants had charged towards these carts, they had also been set on fire. And, as expected, these retreating elephants turned around in alarm and charged back into the battlefield.

Sati was in a bind. The Meluhan cavalry was in front and a huge horde of charging, panic-stricken elephants spewing fire was behind her.

'Retreat!' yelled Sati.

Her cavalry disengaged and galloped towards the river. Fortunately for them, the Meluhan cavalry did not give chase. Alarmed by the sight of the terrified elephants speeding towards them, they turned around and rode towards the safety of their walls.

Many among Sati's horsemen were trampled or burned down by the rampaging elephants. Some of the riders managed to reach the river and rode into the waters without a second's hesitation. The horses swam desperately towards the ships, carrying their riders with them to safety. Many though, sank into the Saraswati under the weight of their light armour. Sati, Veerbhadra and Nandi were among the lucky few who managed to reach the vessels.

While most of the foot soldiers had been saved, the elephant and cavalry corps had been decimated. Memories of the elephants' killer blows in the battle of Mrittikavati were quickly forgotten as the magnitude of the disaster the animals had wreaked sank in.

Chenardhwaj, who was in charge of the ships, quickly ordered that they retreat, as soon as the last of the surviving soldiers was onboard. Without the protection of the land army, their stationary navy was a sitting duck for further attacks.

Chapter 31

Stalemate

'Absolute decimation,' crowed Vidyunmali. 'We should now chase those imbeciles and finish off what's left of the fraud's army. They should learn that nobody invades our fair motherland.'

Vidyunmali had joined Daksha, Bhrigu, Parvateshwar and Kanakhala in the Emperor's private office. Though brigadiers did not normally participate in strategy meetings, Daksha had insisted that he be allowed to attend, keeping in mind his sterling role in providing the information about the elephants.

Parvateshwar raised his hand to silence Vidyunmali. 'Let's not get ahead of ourselves, Vidyunmali. Remember, Sati's tactics under pressure were exceptional. She managed to save most of her army. So it's not as if we'll have a huge numerical advantage if we chase them.'

Vidyunmali fumed silently, keeping his eyes pinned on the floor. *Praise for a rival general? What is wrong with Lord Parvateshwar? She may have been a Meluhan princess once, but now she's a sworn enemy of our motherland.*

'And we should not forget,' said Kanakhala, 'that the Neelkanth is sailing down from the north with a large army. The safest place for our army right now is within these fort walls.'

Neelkanth? fumed Vidyunmali silently, unwilling to argue openly with senior officers of the empire. *He is not the Neelkanth. He is our enemy. And our army should be fighting, not keeping itself safe behind high walls!*

'Kanakhala is right,' said Daksha. 'We should keep our army here and attack that fraud Neelkanth the moment his ships dock. That coward left my daughter to fight alone while he went gallivanting up the Yamuna! He should pay for his cowardice!'

Vidyunmali couldn't believe what he was hearing. *Does anyone here put Meluha's interests above all else?*

'Let's worry about Meluha instead of Princess Sati and her husband's duties towards her,' said Bhrigu. 'Lord Parvateshwar is right. We have won a great victory. But we should measure our next steps carefully. What do you suggest, General?'

'My Lord, we have taken out their elephant corps and cavalry,' said Parvateshwar. 'Sati's army is in retreat. Hence, I do not expect the Neelkanth to stop and attack us here.'

'Of course he won't,' quipped Daksha. 'He's a coward.'

'Your Highness,' said Bhrigu, barely hiding his irritation. The maharishi turned to Parvateshwar. 'Why won't he stop here, General?'

'My scouts have sent back confirmation of our earlier estimates of Ganesh's army,' said Parvateshwar. 'They do have one hundred and fifty thousand soldiers. That is a big army, but it's not enough to defeat our forces if we remain within our fort walls, given that Sati's forces are no longer available to augment them. And from our defensive positions, we can slowly wear his army down. Therefore, the Neelkanth will not want to commit to a long siege here. He'll gain nothing and will unnecessarily lose men.'

'So what do you think he will do?'

'He will sail past Devagiri and join with Sati's army, perhaps in Mrittikavati or Lothal.'

'Then we should attack their ships,' interrupted Daksha.

'That will be difficult, Your Highness,' said Parvateshwar. 'Their ships are sailing downriver. We'll have to march on road since there are no warships on the Saraswati under our control. They will have the advantage of speed. We will not be able to catch up.'

'So where should we attack them?' asked Bhrigu.

'If we *have* to attack them, I would prefer to do so at Mrittikavati.'

'Why?'

'Lothal is not a good idea. I have designed the defences of Lothal myself, and sacrificing false modesty, I will say that those defences are solid. We would need a ten to one advantage in soldiers to conquer Lothal. We don't have that. We will be pitting eighty thousand of our men against more than two hundred thousand of the joint Sati-Ganesh army. Attacking Lothal will be a disaster for us; we will lose too many men. On the other hand, Mrittikavati's defences do not require that kind of numerical advantage. Also, we have twenty thousand of our own soldiers within Mrittikavati. I agree they may be imprisoned, but if they find out that their brother Meluhan soldiers are besieging the city, they may create a lot of trouble for the Lord from within. Having said that, I would expect the Lord to retreat to Lothal and not Mrittikavati, for this very reason.'

Bhrigu had an inkling that Parvateshwar preferred an altogether different strategy. 'I get the feeling that you would choose not to attack at all.'

'Not attack at all?' asked a surprised Daksha. 'Why not? Our army has tasted victory. Parvateshwar, you should...'

'Your Highness,' interrupted Bhrigu. 'Perhaps we should

leave it to an expert like Lord Parvateshwar to suggest what we should do. Go on, General.'

'The reason I suggest we avoid aggression right now is that the Lord Neelkanth would hope that we attack,' said Parvateshwar. 'One cannot attack a well-defended fort without the advantage of numbers. We don't have that. So by attacking them, we'll gain nothing and lose too many men. So I say that we stay within the safe walls of Devagiri. If we wait for six more months, Ayodhya's army will get here. Combined with their three hundred thousand soldiers, we will have a huge numerical advantage over the Lord's army.'

'So are you suggesting that we just sit around like cowards?' asked Daksha.

'It would not be cowardly to refrain from attacking when the situation is not in our favour,' said Bhrigu, before turning back to Parvateshwar. 'Go on, General.'

'Once Ayodhya's troops come in, we should march to Karachapa,' said Parvateshwar. 'We still have control over the Indus command of our navy. Along with Ayodhya's soldiers, we will have a four hundred thousand-strong army. Combine that with the vastly superior naval fleet that we have in the Indus, and we can mount a very solid attack on Lothal.'

'What you are saying appears to make sense,' said Bhrigu, before turning to Daksha. 'I suggest that we follow Lord Parvateshwar's strategy. Your Highness?'

Daksha immediately nodded his assent.

But Vidyunmali could guess that the Emperor's heart was not in this decision. He wondered if there was an opportunity for him to convince the emperor of a more aggressive course of action.

The stunned army of Ganesh was transfixed by the devastation on the hilly battlefield south of Devagiri, as they sailed down the Saraswati. Bloated carcasses of elephants and horses littered the hill, flies buzzing around them. Crows and vultures fought viciously over the beasts' entrails, even though there were enough corpses around for them all. The squawking and cawing of the feasting birds added pathos to the macabre scene.

Of particular interest to the soldiers though, was the fact that there were no human dead bodies on the battlefield. The Meluhans, true to their honourable traditions, had in all likelihood conducted funeral ceremonies for all their enemy warriors. Also, they noticed that there was no debris in the Saraswati. That meant Sati's ships had escaped the devastation, hopefully with most of her army intact.

Shiva stood on the deck of the lead ship, surveying the battlefield along with his sons and sister-in-law. He knew that he couldn't stop now and engage in a battle at Devagiri. He simply didn't have the strength of numbers anymore. He had to retreat farther south and find what was left of Sati's army. His scouts had already told him that the devastation looked worse than it actually must have been. Most of the infantrymen in Sati's army had survived and her ships were sailing south to safety. Shiva knew that with much of Sati's army intact, he still had a fighting chance in the war, but he would have to reformulate his strategy.

All that was for later, though. His mind was seized for the moment with one thought alone: was his Sati all right? Was she hurt? Was she alive?

'Neelkanth,' said Gopal, rushing up to Shiva. He had just received word from a Vasudev pandit envoy, who was hiding on the eastern bank of the Saraswati, waiting for Shiva's ships to arrive. 'Lady Sati was still alive when she was pulled aboard one of the retreating ships.'

'Still alive? What do you mean?'

'She was badly injured, Shiva. She personally led the cavalry against the rampaging elephants and Meluha's own horsemen. Nandi and Veerbhadra managed to pull her to safety. She was unconscious by the time she reached the ship. Unfortunately, the man I talked to didn't have any further information.'

Shiva made his decision immediately. He knew that his naval formation would only be able to sail as quickly as the slowest ship. He couldn't wait that long.

'Ganesh, I'm taking the fastest ship and sailing down south. I have to find your mother's ship. Kali, Kartik and you will remain with the fleet. Avoid all battles, sail as quickly as you can and meet me at Mrittikavati.'

Ganesh and Kartik stood mute, sick with worry about their mother.

'She's alive,' said Shiva, holding his sons' shoulders. 'I know she's alive. She cannot die without me.'

— ⁂ —

Shiva's ship had raced down the Saraswati and caught up with Sati's retreating fleet. He had clambered aboard his wife's ship to discover that his Sati was out of danger now, but still bed-ridden. However, this relief was accompanied by some terrible news received from a Vasudev pandit. Reports of the devastation of Sati's army in Devagiri had given the Meluhan prisoners of war in Mrittikavati the courage to challenge their citizen captors. They had broken out of their prison and taken control of the city. Three thousand citizens, loyal to the Neelkanth, had died in the process. Shiva had no choice but to avoid Mrittikavati for now, as it was no longer safe for his army. He decided to sail down another distributary of the Saraswati and then retreat to Lothal. Orders had been conveyed through a Vasudev pandit to Ganesh's army as well.

For the moment though, Shiva remained on Sati's ship as it sailed down the Saraswati. Having checked on the naval movements with the captain, Shiva descended to Sati's cabin.

Ayurvati sat by her bedside, applying soothing herbs on Sati's burnt face. Quickly and efficiently, she tied a bandage of neem leaves. 'This will ensure that your wound doesn't get infected.'

Sati nodded politely. 'Thank you, Ayurvati*ji*.'

'Also,' continued Ayurvati, thinking Sati may be concerned about the ugly mark which covered nearly a quarter of her face, 'don't worry about the scar. Whenever you are ready, I will perform a cosmetic surgery to smoothen out your skin.'

Sati nodded, her lips pursed tight.

Ayurvati looked at Shiva and then back at Sati. 'Take care, my child.'

'Thank you once again, Ayurvati*ji*,' said Sati, unable to smile due to the scar tissue forming on her face.

Ayurvati quickly walked out of the cabin. Shiva went down on his knees and held her hand.

'I'm sorry, Shiva. I failed you.'

'Please stop saying that again and again,' said Shiva. 'I've been told about the way our elephants reacted to the burning chilli; it's a miracle that you managed to save as many of our people as you did.'

'You are just being kind because I'm your wife. We have lost our elephant corps and most of our cavalry. This is a disaster.'

'Why are you so hard on yourself? What happened at Devagiri was not your fault. We'd lost our elephant corps the moment the Meluhans discovered that the smoke from burning chillies sends them into a state of panic.'

'But I should have withdrawn earlier.'

'You withdrew as soon as you saw the effect on the elephants. You had no choice but to go in with the cavalry, otherwise our soldiers would have got massacred. Practically our entire army is still intact. You did a great job to ensure that we didn't suffer even higher casualties.'

Sati looked away unhappily, still feeling terribly guilty.

Shiva touched her forehead gently. 'Sweetheart, listen to me...'

'Leave me alone for a while, Shiva.'

'Sati...'

'Shiva, please... please leave me alone.'

Shiva kissed Sati gently. 'It's not your fault. There are usually enough tragedies in life that we are genuinely responsible for. Feel guilty about them, for sure. But there is no point in burdening your heart with guilt over events that are not your fault.'

Sati turned to Shiva with a tortured expression. 'And what about you, Shiva? Do you really think a six-year-old child could have done anything to save that woman at Kailash?'

It was Shiva's turn to be silent.

'The honest answer is, no,' said Sati. 'And yet you carry that guilt, don't you? Why? Because you expected more from yourself.'

Shiva's eyes welled up with the agony of that childhood memory. There wasn't a day in his life when he didn't silently apologise to that woman he hadn't been able to save; the woman he hadn't even tried to save.

'I expected more from myself as well,' said Sati, her eyes moist.

They empathised with each other in a silent embrace.

— ⁂ —

Shiva and Sati's convoy of ships had just reached the last navigable point on this distributary of the Saraswati. From here on, the river was too shallow for the ships. Even farther, the Saraswati ran dry on land itself, unable to push through to the sea.

Shiva had avoided the distributary which led to Mrittikavati. He was on the southern-most part of the inland mouth of the Saraswati. From here on, his army would march to the frontier stronghold of Lothal. Leaving the empty ships behind was fraught with risk. It was only a matter of time before the Meluhans would get to know about it. Shiva would, in effect, be handing over twenty-five well-fitted military ships back to the Meluhans, which would allow them to move their army up and down the Saraswati with frightening speed. The decision was obvious. The ships had to be destroyed.

Once his entire army had disembarked and the caravan that would march on to Lothal had been readied, Shiva gave orders for the ships to be burned. Fortunately there had been a break in the rains which had arrived early this year, allowing the fire to consume the ships quickly.

Shiva stood observing the massive flames. He didn't hear Gopal and Chenardhwaj as they stepped up to him.

'Lord Agni consumes things rapidly,' said Gopal.

Shiva looked at Gopal before turning back to the burning ships. 'We have no choice, Pandit*ji*.'

'No, we don't.'

'What do you suggest we do, Pandit*ji*?' asked Shiva.

'The rainy season is here,' said Gopal. 'It will be difficult to mount a campaign to attack Devagiri any time soon. Even if we could, without the advantage of our cavalry it is unlikely that we will be able to conquer a well-designed citadel like Devagiri.'

'But it will be difficult for them to attack us in Lothal as well,' said Shiva. 'Lothal, in fact, is better designed for defence than even Devagiri.'

'True,' said Gopal. 'So it is a stalemate. Which suits the Meluhans just fine since all they will have to do is wait for the Ayodhyan forces to reach Meluha. They could be here in as little as six months.'

Silently, Shiva gazed at the burning ships, contemplating this unhappy turn of events.

Chenardhwaj spoke up. 'I have a suggestion, My Lord.'

Shiva turned to Chenardhwaj with a frown.

'We can draw up a crack force of Nagas and my troops,' said Chenardhwaj. 'The commandos will attack the Somras factory stealthily. It will be a suicide mission, but we will destroy it.'

'No,' said Shiva.

'Why, My Lord?'

'Because Parvateshwar will certainly be prepared for that. He's not an idiot. It will be a suicide mission all right, but not a successful one.'

'There is one other way,' whispered Gopal.

'The Vayuputras?' asked Shiva.

'Yes.'

Shiva looked back at the burning ships, his expression inscrutable. The Vayuputras appeared to be the only recourse now.

Chapter 32

The Last Resort

Shiva had pulled a light cloth over his head and wrapped it around his face, leaving his eyes open. His *angvastram* was draped across his muscular torso, affording protection from the fine drizzle. Sati lay in a covered cart as oxen pulled it gently. She was strong enough to walk now, but Ayurvati had insisted on exercising abundant caution during the march to Lothal. Shiva parted the curtains on the cart and looked at his sleeping wife. He smiled and drew the curtain shut again.

He kicked his horse into a canter.

'Pandit*ji*,' said Shiva, slowing his horse down as he approached Gopal. 'About the Vayuputras...'

'Yes?'

'What is that terrible weapon that they possess that Kali spoke of?'

'The *Brahmastra?*' asked Gopal, referring to the fearsome *weapon of Brahma*.

'Yes. How is it different from other *daivi astras?*' asked Shiva, for he didn't understand how a *Brahmastra* was so much more terrible than other *divine weapons*.

'Most *daivi astras* only kill men. But there are some, like the *Brahmastra*, that can destroy entire cities, if not kingdoms.'

'By the holy lake! How can one weapon do that?'

'The *Brahmastra* is the weapon of absolute destruction, my friend; a destroyer of cities and a mass-killer of men. When fired on some terrain, a giant mushroom cloud will rise, high enough to touch the heavens. Everyone and everything in the targeted place would be instantly vaporised. Beyond this inner circle of destruction will be those who are unfortunate enough to survive, for they will suffer for generations. The water in the land will be poisoned for decades. The land will be unusable for centuries; no crops will grow on it. This weapon doesn't just kill once; it kills again and again, for centuries after it has been used.'

'And people actually contemplate using a weapon such as this?' asked a horrified Shiva. 'Pandit*ji*, using such a dreadful weapon is against the laws of humanity.'

'Precisely, great Neelkanth. A weapon like this can never actually be used. The mere knowledge that one's enemy has this weapon, can strike terror in one's heart. No matter what the odds, one will surrender; one cannot win against the *Brahmastra*.'

'Do you think the Vayuputras will give this weapon to me? Or am I being too presumptuous? After all, I'm not one of them. They think I'm a fraud, don't they?'

'I can think of two reasons why they may help us. First, they have not tried to assassinate you, which they would have, had a majority of them believed that you were a fraud. Maybe a strong constituency amongst them still respects your uncle, Lord Manobhu.'

'And the second?'

'Lord Bhrigu used *daivi astras* in his attack on Panchavati. It was not the *Brahmastra*, but it was a *daivi astra* nevertheless. Even if it was fabricated from Lord Bhrigu's own material, he broke Lord Rudra's laws by actually using one. That, I suspect, would have turned the Vayuputras virulently against him. And an enemy's enemy...'

'...is a friend,' said Shiva, completing Gopal's statement. 'But I'm not sure these are reasons enough.'

'We don't have any other choice, my friend.'

'Perhaps... How do we get to the land of the Vayuputras?'

'Pariha is at a substantial distance towards our west. We can march overland, through the great mountains, to get there. But that is risky and time consuming. The other option is to take the sea route. But we will have to wait for the Northeasterly winds.'

'The Northeasterlies? But they begin only when the rains stop. We'll have to wait for one or two months.'

'Yes, we will have to.'

'I have an idea. I'm sure the Meluhans will set up spies and scouts in and around Lothal once they know that we have retreated into the city. So if we take the conventional route to Pariha, they will know that I have sailed west. Lord Bhrigu may guess that I've gone to the Vayuputras to seek help, which may encourage him to send assassins in pursuit. How about sailing south in a small convoy of military ships?'

Gopal immediately understood. 'We'll make them think that we're going to the Narmada, onwards perhaps to either Ujjain or Panchavati.'

'Exactly,' said Shiva. 'We could disembark from our military ships at a secret location and then set sail in a nondescript merchant ship to Pariha.'

'Brilliant. The Meluhans can keep searching for you along the Narmada while we are on our way to Pariha.'

'Right.'

'And if we use just one merchant ship instead of an entire convoy, we could keep the voyage secretive and be quick.'

'Right again.'

— ⅄ⵀ⌥⍏⊗ —

Sati stood at a window in a lookout-shelter on the southern edge of Lothal fort, staring at the vast expanse of sea beyond its walls. The monsoon had arrived in earnest and heavy rain was pelting the city.

Shiva and his army were well fortified within the city walls. Ganesh was expected to arrive in Lothal within a week or two, along with his force.

Ayurvati rushed into the shelter with a loud whoop, propping her cane and cloth umbrella beside the entrance. 'Lord Indra and Lord Varun, be praised! They have decided to deliver the entire quota of this year's rain in a single day!'

Sati turned towards Ayurvati with a wan look.

Ayurvati sat next to her and squeezed the end of her drenched *angvastram*. 'I love the rain. It seems to wash away sorrows and bring new life with renewed hope, doesn't it?'

Sati nodded politely, not really interested. 'Yes, you are right, Ayurvati*ji*.'

Not one to give up, Ayurvati plodded on, determined to lighten Sati's mood. 'I'm quite free right now. There aren't too many injured and the monsoon diseases have, surprisingly, been very low this year.'

'That is good news, Ayurvati*ji*,' said Sati.

'Yes, it is. So, I was thinking that this would be a good time to do your surgery.'

Sati's face carried an ugly blemish on her left cheek, where scar tissue had formed over the remnants of the burns she had suffered during the Battle of Devagiri.

'There's nothing wrong with me,' said Sati politely.

'Of course there isn't. I was only referring to the scar on your face. It can be removed very easily through cosmetic surgery.'

'No. I don't want surgery.'

Ayurvati assumed that Sati was worried about the long

recovery time and the possible impact on her ability to participate in the next battle. 'But it is a very simple procedure, Sati. You will recover in a couple of weeks. We seem to be in for a good monsoon this year. This means there will be no warfare for a few months. You will not miss any battle.'

'Nothing would keep me away from the next battle.'

'Then why don't you want to do this surgery, my child? I'm sure it would make the Lord Neelkanth happy.'

A hint of a smile escaped her solemn demeanour. 'Shiva keeps telling me I'm as beautiful as ever, scar or no scar. I know I look horrendous. He's lying because he loves me. But I choose to believe it.'

'Why are you doing this?' asked an anguished Ayurvati. 'It won't hurt you at all; not that you are scared of pain...'

'No, Ayurvati*ji*.'

'But why? You have to give me a reason.'

'Because, I need this scar,' said Sati grimly.

Ayurvati paused for a moment. 'Why?'

'It constantly reminds me of my failure. I will not rest till I have set it right and recovered the ground that I lost for my army.'

'Sati! It wasn't your fault that...'

'Ayurvati*ji*,' said Sati, interrupting the former chief surgeon of Meluha. 'You of all people should not tell me a white lie. I was the Commanding Officer and my army was defeated. It was my fault.'

'Sati...'

'This scar stays with me. Every time I look at my reflection, it will remind me that I have work to do. Let me win a battle for my army, and then we can do the surgery.'

— ⅄ⵀ Ʊ ⇑ ⊗ —

'*Dada*,' whispered Kartik, gently placing his hand on his angry brother's arm.

Ganesh's army had just arrived at Lothal. They too had avoided Mrittikavati as advised by a Vasudev pandit. Just like Shiva, Ganesh had ensured that all his ships were destroyed on the Saraswati before his army marched south to Lothal.

They were received at the gates of Lothal by Governor Chenardhwaj. Ganesh and Kartik had wanted to meet their parents immediately, but were informed by Chenardhwaj that Shiva wanted to meet them beforehand. Shiva wanted to prepare them for their first meeting with their mother after her defeat at the Battle of Devagiri.

Meanwhile, the allies of the Neelkanth – Bhagirath, the Prince of Ayodhya, Chandraketu, the King of Branga, and Maatali, the King of Vaishali – were led to their respective chambers in the Lothal governor's residence by protocol officers. The Chandravanshi royalty, used to the pomp and pageantry of their own land, were distinctly underwhelmed by the austere arrangements of the Meluhan accommodation. It was difficult to believe that the governor of one of the richest provinces of the richest Empire in the world lived in such simplicity. However, they accepted their housing with good grace, knowing it was the will of Shiva.

The army was accommodated in guesthouses and temporary shelters erected within the city. It was a tribute to the robust urban planning of Meluha that such a large number of new arrivals could be so quickly accommodated in reasonable comfort. All in all, a massive army, now totalling nearly two hundred and fifty thousand soldiers, had set up residence in Lothal.

Having been briefed by Shiva, Ganesh and Kartik rushed to meet their mother. They had been told about the nature of her injuries. Shiva did not want the brothers to inadvertently upset her further. While Kartik was, as instructed by Shiva, able to control his anger and shock, Ganesh's obsessive love for his mother did not allow him that ability.

Ganesh clenched his fists, staring at his mother's disfigured face. He gritted his teeth and breathed rapidly, his normally calm eyes blazing. His long nose was stretched out, trembling in anger. His big floppy ears were rigid.

Ganesh growled, 'I will kill every single one of those b...'

'Ganesh,' said Sati calmly, interrupting her son. 'The Meluhan soldiers were only doing their duty, as was I. They have done nothing wrong.'

Ganesh's silence was unable to camouflage his fury.

'Ganesh, these things happen in a war. You know that.'

'*Dada*, *maa* is right,' said Kartik.

Sati stepped close and embraced her elder son. She pulled his face down and kissed his forehead, smiling lovingly. 'Calm down, Ganesh.'

Kartik held his mother and brother as well. '*Dada,* battle scars are a mark of pride for a warrior.'

Ganesh held his mother tight, tears streaming down his face. 'You are not entering a battlefield again, *maa.* Not unless I am standing in front of you.'

Sati smiled feebly and patted Ganesh on his back.

— ⁂ —

Shiva walked into his suite of rooms in the governor's residence at Lothal. Sati had moved some of the furniture to create a training circle, and was practicing her sword movements. Shiva leaned against a wall and observed his wife quietly, so as not to disturb her. He admired every perfect warrior move, the sway of her hips as she transferred her weight; the quick thrusts and swings of her sword; the rapid movement of her shield, which she used almost like an independent weapon. Shiva breathed deeply at yet another reminder of why he loved her so much.

Sati swung around with her shield held high, as her eyes fell on Shiva.

'For how long have you been watching?' she asked, surprised.

'Long enough to know that I should never challenge you to a duel!'

Sati smiled slightly, not saying anything. She quickly sheathed her sword and put her shield down. Shiva stepped over and helped untie her scabbard.

'Thank you,' whispered Sati as she took the scabbard from Shiva, walked up to the mini-armoury and placed her shield and sheathed sword.

'We will not be able to go to Pariha together,' said Shiva.

'I know,' said Sati. 'I was told by Gopal*ji* that Parihans only allow Vayuputras and Vasudevs to enter their domain. I am neither.'

'Well, technically, nor am I.'

Sati pulled her *angvastram* over her head so as to cover her left cheek. She held the hem of the cloth between her teeth, covering her facial scar. 'But you are the Neelkanth. Rules can be broken for you.'

Shiva came forward, and pulled Sati close with one hand. With the other, he held the *angvastram* covering her face and tried to pull it back. Even though she knew he did not care, Sati liked to hide her scar from Shiva. It didn't matter to her if others saw it, but not Shiva.

'Shiva...' whispered Sati, holding her *angvastram* close.

Shiva tugged hard and pulled the *angvastram* free from her mouth. An upset Sati tried to yank it back but Shiva managed to overpower her, holding her close.

'I wish you could see through my eyes,' whispered Shiva, 'so you could see your own ethereal beauty.'

Sati rolled her eyes and turned away, still struggling within Shiva's grip. 'I'm ugly! I know it! Don't use your love to insult me.'

'Love?' asked Shiva, pretending mock surprise, wiggling his eyebrows. 'Who said anything about love? It's lust! Pure and simple!'

Sati stared at Shiva, her eyes wide. Then she burst out laughing.

Shiva pulled her close again, grinning. 'This is no laughing matter, my princess. I am your husband. I have rights, you know.'

Sati continued to laugh as she hit Shiva playfully on his chest.

Shiva kissed her tenderly. 'I love you.'

'You're mad!'

'That I am. But I still love you.'

Chapter 33

The Conspiracy Deepens

'Brilliant idea, Your Highness,' said Vidyunmali.

Daksha sat in his private office with his new confidant, Vidyunmali. The Meluhan brigadier's increasing frustration with Parvateshwar's cautious approach had forged a new alliance. According to Vidyunmali, this wait-and-watch strategy of General Parvateshwar was giving Shiva's army time to recover from its defeat at Devagiri. He had begun to spend more and more time with the emperor. Daksha had got him reassigned to head a brigade of a thousand soldiers that guarded the emperor, his family and his palace. This gave him a simple advantage: the brigade could carry out personal missions mandated by the emperor.

Sensing increasing comfort in the relationship, Daksha had finally confided in him about his idea to end the war. Much to Daksha's delight, Vidyunmali's reaction was very different from Bhrigu's.

'Exactly!' exclaimed a happy Daksha. 'I don't know why the others don't understand.'

'Your Highness, you are the emperor,' said Vidyunmali. 'It doesn't matter if others don't agree. If you have decided to go ahead, then that is the will of Meluha.'

'You really think we should go ahead...'

'It doesn't matter what I think, Your Highness. What do you think?'

'I think it is brilliant!'

'Then that is what Meluha thinks as well, My Lord.'

'I think we should implement it.'

'What are your orders for me, My Lord?'

'I haven't worked out the details, Brigadier,' said Daksha. 'You will need to think it through. My job is to look at the big picture.'

'Of course,' said Vidyunmali. 'My apologies, Your Highness. But I don't think we can execute our plan till the maharishi and the general leave Devagiri. They may try to stop us if they get the slightest whiff of our intentions.'

'They were planning to leave for Karachapa; or at least that was Parvateshwar's latest plan. I was not supportive of the idea earlier, but now I will encourage it and hasten their departure.'

'An inspired move, Your Highness. But we must also concentrate on getting the right assassins.'

'I agree. But where do we find them?'

'They must be foreigners, Your Highness. We do not want them recognised. They will be wearing cloaks and masks, of course. You want them to look like Nagas, right?'

'Yes, of course.'

'I know some people. They are the best in the business.'

'Where are they from?'

'Egypt.'

'By the great Lord Varun, that's too far! It will take too much time to get them here.'

'I will leave immediately, Your Highness. That is, if I have your permission.'

'Of course you have it. Accomplish this, Vidyunmali, and Meluha will sing your praises for centuries.'

— ⅄⊕ᑌ⍋⊗ —

'Lord Gopal and I will leave within a week,' said Shiva.

Shiva and Gopal sat in the governor's office, surrounded by Sati, Kali, Ganesh, Kartik, Bhagirath, Chenardhwaj, Chandraketu and Maatali. The monsoons were drawing to an end, light smatterings of rain appearing occasionally, as if to bid farewell. Shiva and Gopal had decided to travel south, as planned, in their small convoy of military ships. They intended to rendezvous with a merchant ship at a secret location north of the Narmada delta. The Southwesterly winds would have receded by the time and the rains would have stopped. They would then board the merchant ship and use the Northeasterly winds to set sail towards the west, in the direction of Pariha. With luck, the deception would work and the Meluhans would be unaware of Shiva's actual destination.

'I want our destination to be kept secret,' continued Shiva. 'Victory is assured if our mission succeeds.'

'What are you planning to do, My Lord?' asked Bhagirath.

'Leave that to me, my friend,' said Shiva cryptically. 'In my absence, Sati will be in command.'

Everyone nodded in instant agreement. They were unaware though, that Sati had fought this decision. After Devagiri, she didn't think she deserved this command. But Shiva had insisted. He trusted her the most.

'Pray to Lord Ram and Lord Rudra that our mission is a success,' said Gopal.

Shiva stood on the shores of the Mansarovar lake, watching the slow descent of the sun in the evening sky. There was no breeze at all and it was eerily still. A sudden chill enveloped him, and he looked down, surprised to see that he was standing in knee-deep water. He turned around and began wading out of the lake. Thick fog had blanketed the banks of the Mansarovar. He couldn't see his village at all. As he stepped out of the lake, the mist magically cleared.

'Sati?' asked a surprised Shiva.

Sati sat calmly atop a thick pile of wood. Her metal armour had been secured around her torso, carved arm bands glistened in the dusky light, her sword lay by her side and the shield was fastened on her back. She was prepared for war. But why was she wearing a saffron angvastram, *the colour of the final journey?*

'Sati,' said Shiva, walking towards her.

Sati opened her eyes and smiled serenely. It appeared that she was speaking. But Shiva couldn't hear the words. The sound reached his ears with a delay of a few moments. 'I'll be waiting for you...'

'What? Where are you going?'

Suddenly, a hazy figure appeared bearing a burning torch. Without a moment's hesitation, he rammed it into the pile of wood that Sati sat upon. It caught fire instantly.

'SATI!' screamed a stunned Shiva as he raced towards her.

Sati continued to sit upon the burning pyre, at peace with herself. Her beatific smile presented an eerie contrast to the flames that leapt up around her.

'SATI!' shouted Shiva. 'JUMP OFF!'

But Sati was unmoved. Shiva was just a few metres away from her when a platoon of soldiers jumped in front of him. Shiva drew his sword in a flash, trying to push the soldiers aside. But they battled him relentlessly. The soldiers were huge and unnaturally hairy, like the monster from his dream. Shiva battled them tirelessly but could not push through. Meanwhile, the flames had almost covered his wife, such that he couldn't even see her clearly. And yet, she continued to sit on the pyre, without attempting to escape.

'SATI!'

Shiva woke up in a sweat as his hand stretched out desperately. It took a moment for his eyes to adjust to the darkness. He turned to his left instinctively. Sati was asleep, her burnt cheek clearly visible in the night light.

Shiva immediately bent over and embraced his wife.

'Shiva...' whispered a groggy Sati.

Shiva didn't say anything. He held her tight, as tears streamed down his face.

'Shiva?' asked Sati, fully awake now. 'What's the matter, darling?'

But Shiva couldn't say a word, choked with emotion.

Sati pulled her head back to get a better look in the dim light. She reached up and touched his cheeks. They were moist.

'Shiva? Sweetheart? What's wrong? Did you have a bad dream?'

'Sati, promise me that you will not go into battle till I return.'

'Shiva, you've made me the leader. If the army has to go into battle, I will have to lead them. You know that.'

Shiva kept quiet.

'What did you see?'

He just shook his head.

'It was just a dream, Shiva. It doesn't mean anything. You need to focus your attention on your journey. You're leaving tomorrow. You must succeed in your mission with the Vayuputras. That will bring an end to this war. Don't let anxieties about me distract you.'

Shiva remained impassive, refusing to let go.

'Shiva, you carry the future on your shoulders. I'm saying this once again. Don't let your love for me distract you. It was just a dream. That's all.'

'I can't live without you.'

'You won't have to. I'll be waiting for you when you return. I promise.'

Shiva pulled back a bit, looking deep into Sati's eyes. 'Stay away from fires.'

'Shiva, seriously, what...'

'Sati, promise me! You will stay away from fires.'

'Yes, Shiva. I promise.'

Chapter 34

With the Help of Umbergaon

Shiva was ready to leave. His bags had been sent to his ship. He had ordered all his aides out of his chamber. He'd wanted a few minutes alone with Sati.

'Bye,' whispered Shiva.

She smiled and embraced him. 'Nothing will happen to me, my good man! You will not get rid of me so easily.'

Shiva laughed softly, for Sati had used his own line on him. 'I know. It was just an overreaction to a stupid nightmare.'

Shiva pulled Sati's face up and kissed her affectionately. 'I love you.'

'I love you too.'

A couple of weeks later Shiva and Gopal stood on a beach in a hidden lagoon, a short distance to the north of the Narmada delta. The small convoy of military ships had sneaked into the lagoon the previous night. Shiva and Gopal had disembarked into rowboats, along with a skeletal crew, and stolen onto the beach. Early next morning, the merchant ship that would take them to Pariha arrived in the lagoon.

'Hmmm... good workmanship,' said an admiring Shiva.

It was, without doubt, a bulky ship, obviously designed to carry large cargo. However, any sailor could judge that with its double masts, high stern and low bow, this craft was also built for speed. In addition, the ship had been rigged with two banks of oars, to allow for 'human propulsion' if required.

'We won't really need the rowers,' said Gopal. 'Our vessel will have the Northeasterly winds in its sails.'

'Where is this beauty from?' asked Shiva.

'A small shipping village called Umbergaon.'

'Umbergaon? Where is it?'

'It's to the south of the Narmada River delta.'

'That's not a part of any empire, Swadweep or Meluha.'

'You guessed right, my friend. That makes it a perfect place to build ships that one doesn't want tracked. The local ruler, Jadav Rana, is a pragmatic man. The Nagas have helped him many times. He values their friendship. And, most importantly, his people are expert ship builders. This ship will get us to Pariha as fast as is humanly possible.'

'Interesting. We should be grateful for their invaluable help.'

'No,' said Gopal, smiling. 'It is Pariha that should be grateful to Umbergaon, for the Umbergaonis have ensured that the gift of the Neelkanth shall reach Pariha.'

'I'm no gift,' said a discomfited Shiva.

'Yes, you are. For you will help the Vayuputras achieve their purpose. You will help them fulfil their vow to Lord Rudra: to not let Evil win.'

Shiva remained silent, as always, embarrassed.

'And I'm sure,' continued a prescient Gopal, 'that one day, Pariha too shall send a gift in return to Umbergaon.'

— ⁂ —

'How're you feeling now, my friend?' asked Gopal, as soon as he entered Shiva's cabin.

The vessel bearing the two men had been sailing in the open seas for a little more than a week. They were far beyond the coastline and unlikely to run into any Meluhan military ships. They'd run into choppy waters though, in the last few days. The sailors, used to the ways of the sea, were not really troubled by it. Neither was Gopal, who had travelled on these great expanses of water many times. But Shiva had undertaken a sea voyage just once, from the Narmada delta to Lothal, where the ship had stayed close to the coast. It was, therefore, no surprise that the rough sea had given the Neelkanth a severe bout of seasickness.

Shiva looked up from his bed and cursed, his eyes half shut. 'I have no stomach left! It has all been churned out! A plague on these wretched waters!'

Gopal laughed softly, 'It's time for your medicines, Neelkanth.'

'What's the point, Pandit*ji*? Nothing stays inside!'

'For whatever little time the medicine remains, it will serve a purpose. Take it.'

Gopal gently poured a herbal infusion into a wooden spoon. Balancing it delicately, the Chief Vasudev offered it to Shiva, who swallowed it quickly and fell back on the bed.

'Holy Lake, help me,' whispered Shiva, 'let this medicine stay within me for a few minutes at least.'

But the prayer probably didn't reach Mansarovar Lake in time. Shiva lurched to his side and retched into the large pot that had been placed on the ground. A sailor standing by the bed rushed forward quickly and handed a wet towel to Shiva, who wiped his face slowly.

Shiva shook his head and looked up at the ceiling of his cabin in disgust. 'Crap!'

— ⁂ —

Bhrigu and Parvateshwar rode on horseback at the head of a massive army that had marched out of Devagiri. They were on their way to the Beas River, from which point, ships would sail them down to Karachapa.

'I was thinking that the powerful fleet in Karachapa is not the only advantage derived from our decision to shift our war command,' said Bhrigu.

Parvateshwar frowned. 'What other benefit does it serve, My Lord?'

'Well, there's also the fact that you will not have to suffer idiotic orders from your emperor. You will be free to conduct the war the way you deem fit.'

It was obvious that Bhrigu held Daksha in contempt, and did not think much of his harebrained schemes. But Parvateshwar was too disciplined a Meluhan to speak openly against his emperor. He was stoic in his silence.

Bhrigu smiled. 'You really are a rare man, General, a man of the old code. Lord Ram would have been proud of you.'

— ⁂ —

Aided by the Northeasterly winds pushing hard into its sails, the merchant ship was cutting through the waters with rapid speed. Having tossed and turned for a few days, Shiva had finally adapted to the sea. The Neelkanth was able, therefore, to enjoy the stiff morning breeze on the main deck at the bow, with Gopal for company.

'We are now crossing over from our Western Sea, through a very narrow strait,' said Gopal. 'It's just a little over fifty kilometres across.'

'What's on the other side?' asked Shiva.

'The Jam Zrayangh.'

'Sounds scary. What in Lord Ram's name does that mean?'

Gopal laughed. 'Something absolutely benign. Zrayangh simply means sea in the local language.'

'And what does Jam mean?'

'Jam means "to come to".'

'To come to?'

'Yes.'

'So this is the "sea that you come to"?'

'Yes, a simple name. This is the sea you must come to if you want to go to Elam or Mesopotamia or any of the lands farther west. But most importantly, this is the sea you must approach if you need to go to Pariha.'

'I've heard of Mesopotamia. It has strong trade relations with Meluha, right?'

'Yes. It's a very powerful and rich empire, established between two great rivers in the region, the Tigris and the Euphrates.'

'Is the empire bigger than Meluha and Swadweep?'

'No,' smiled Gopal. 'It's not even bigger than Meluha alone. But they believe human civilisation began in their region.'

'Really? I thought we Indians believed that human civilisation began here.'

'True.'

'So, who's right?'

Gopal shrugged. 'I don't know. This goes back many thousands of years. But frankly, does it matter who got civilised first so long as all of us eventually became civilised?'

Shiva smiled. 'True. And where is Elam?'

'Elam is a much smaller kingdom to the south-east of Mesopotamia.'

'South-east?' asked Shiva. 'So, Elam is closer to Pariha?'

'Yes. And Elam acts as a buffer state between Pariha and Mesopotamia, which is why the Parihans have occasionally helped the Elamites unofficially.'

'But I thought Pariha never got involved in local politics.'

'They try to avoid it. And most people in the region have not even heard of the Vayuputras. But they were concerned that an expanding Mesopotamia would encroach into their land.'

'Expanding Mesopotamia?'

'A gifted gardener had once conquered the whole of Mesopotamia.'

'A gardener? How did a gardener become a warrior? Did he train in secret?'

Gopal smiled. 'From what I've heard of the story, he wasn't trained.'

Shiva's eyes widened with amazement. 'He must have been very gifted.'

'Oh, he was talented. But not in gardening!'

Shiva laughed. 'What was his name?'

'Nobody knows his original name. But he called himself Sargon.'

'And he conquered the whole of Mesopotamia?'

'Yes, and surprisingly quickly at that. But it did not satiate his ambition. He went on to conquer neighbouring kingdoms as well, including Elam.'

'That would have brought him to the borders of Pariha.'

'Not exactly, my friend. But uncomfortably close.'

'Why didn't he move farther east?'

'I don't know. Neither he nor his successors did, though. But the Vayuputras were troubled enough to offer anonymous assistance to Elam. The Elamites were able to rebel because of this support, and the conquest of the Mesopotamians did not last for too long.'

'King Sargon seems like a very interesting man.'

'He was. He challenged the entire world, and even fate itself. He was so feisty that he dared to name his empire after the water-carrier who was his adopted father.'

'His father was a water-carrier?'

'Yes, named Akki. So they called themselves the Empire of the Akkadians.'

'And does this empire still exist?'

'No.'

'That's sad. I would have loved to meet these remarkable Akkadians.'

'The people of Elam would have thought very differently, Lord Neelkanth.'

— ⅄ ⓪ Ʊ ↟ ⊛ —

'The soldiers are bored and restless,' said Ganesh. 'They have been mobilised, but there has been no action, no battle.'

Kartik and Ganesh had just entered Sati's chamber and were happy to find Kali with their mother.

'I was discussing just that, with *didi*,' said Kali. 'The men are spending their time gambling and drinking to keep themselves occupied. Training is suffering because they don't see the point of it when there is hardly any chance of combat in the near future.'

'This is the time when stupid incidents occur which can blow up into serious problems,' said Sati.

'Let's keep them busy,' suggested Kartik. 'Let's organise some animal hunts in the forests around the city. We know that the Meluhan army has still not moved out of Karachapa, so there is no risk in letting our soldiers out in large groups. Hunting will give them some sense of action.'

'Good idea,' agreed Kali. 'We can also use the excess meat to organise feasts for the citizens of Lothal. It will help assuage some of their irritation with having to host such a large army.'

'The excitement and the blood-rush will also prevent boredom from creeping into our troops,' said Ganesh.

'I agree,' said Sati. 'I'll issue the orders immediately.'

It was nearly a month and a half since they had started their journey from the secret lagoon off the Narmada delta. Shiva's ship came to anchor off a desolate coast on the Jam Sea. There didn't seem to be any habitation of any kind at all; in fact it appeared as though this land had never been disturbed by humans. Shiva was not surprised. Just like the Vasudevs, the Vayuputras were secretive about their existence. He did not expect a welcoming port of landing. But he did expect some secret symbol, something like the emblematic Vasudev flame on the banks of the Chambal near Ujjain.

Then he thought he detected something. The coast was lined by a thick row of tall bushes, maybe three or four metres high. From the distance of the anchored ship, it seemed like these bushes had reddish-orange fruit hanging in abundance. The shrubs were covered with small dark-green leaves, except at the top, where it was bright red. These bright red leaves combined with the reddish-orange fruit to give the impression that the bush was on fire.

A burning bush...

Shiva immediately turned and began climbing the main mast, all the way up to the crow's nest. Once there, the symbol became obvious. The bushes, when combined with the white sand and brownish rocks, came together to form a symbol that Shiva recognised only too well: *Fravashi*, the holy flame, the feminine spirit.

Shiva came down to find Gopal standing below.

'Did you find something, my friend?' asked Gopal.

'I saw the holy flame; the pure being. I saw the *Fravashi*.'

Gopal was astonished at first, but not for long. 'Of course! Lord Manobhu... He would have told you about *Fravashi*.'

'Yes.'

'It's a symbol of the faith of Lord Rudra's people. The *Fravashi* represents pure spirits, the angels. They exist in large numbers, their scriptures say in the tens of thousands. They send forth human souls into this world and support them in the eternal battle between Good and Evil. They are also believed to have assisted God in creating the universe.'

Shiva nodded. 'The Vasudevs believe in the *Fravashi* as well, I assume.'

'We respect the *Fravashi*. But it is a Parihan symbol.'

'Then why do you have a *Fravashi* at the entrance to your land?'

Gopal frowned. 'A *Fravashi* symbol? Where?'

'At the clearing on the Chambal, from where we communicated with you through clapping signals.'

'Oh!' smiled Gopal, as understanding dawned upon him. 'My friend, we have a symbolic fire as well. But we don't call it *Fravashi*. We call it *Agni*, the God of Fire.'

'But the symbol is almost exactly like the *Fravashi*.'

'Yes, it is. I'm aware that the Parihans give enormous importance to fire rituals. So do we Indians. The first hymn of the first chapter in the Rig Veda is dedicated to the Fire God, Agni. The importance of the element of fire is, I believe, common across all religions of the world.'

'Fire is the beginning of human civilisation.'

'It is the beginning of all life, my friend. It is the source of all energy. For one way of looking at the stars is to see them as great balls of fire.'

Shiva smiled.

A sailor walked up to the two men. 'My Lords, the rowboat has been lowered. We are ready.'

— ⁂ —

The rowboat was a hundred metres from the coast when a tall man appeared from behind the bushes. He wore a long, brownish-black cloak and held what looked like a staff. Or, it could have been a spear. Shiva couldn't be sure. He reached for his sword.

Gopal reached out to stay Shiva's hand. 'It's all right, my friend.'

Shiva spoke without taking his eyes off the stranger. 'Are you sure?'

'Yes, he is a Parihan. He has come to guide us.'

Shiva relaxed his grip on the sword, but kept his hand close to the hilt.

He saw the stranger reach into the bushes and tug at what looked like ropes. Shiva immediately caught his breath and reached for his sword once again.

To his surprise though, four horses emerged from behind the thick row of bushes. Three of them were not carrying anything, clearly ready for their new mounts. The fourth was loaded with a massive sack. Perhaps, it was carrying provisions. Shiva moved his hand away from his sword and let it relax.

The stranger was a friend.

Chapter 35

Journey to Pariha

'I'm glad that the Vayuputras have sent someone to receive us,' said Gopal.

His sailors were offloading the provisions from the rowboat. Some of the luggage would be tied onto the three horses that would be mounted by Shiva, Gopal and the Parihan, while the rest would be loaded onto the severely-burdened fourth horse.

'How can the Vayuputras ignore the Chief Vasudev, My Lord?' asked the Parihan, bowing low towards Gopal. 'We received your message from the Vasudev pandit of Lothal well in time. You are our honoured guest. My name is Kurush. I will be your guide to our city, Pariha.'

Shiva observed Kurush intently. His long brownish-black cloak could not hide the fact that he carried a sword. Shiva wondered as to how the Parihan would draw his sword quickly in an emergency if it lay encumbered within the folds of his cloak.

The man was unnaturally fair-skinned, not seen often in the hot plains of India. While one may have expected this to make the Parihan look pale and unattractive, this was not so. The sharp long nose, combined with a full beard somehow enhanced the beauty of the man while giving him the look of a warrior nevertheless. The Parihan wore his hair long, something that was in common with the Indians. On his head was perched a square white hat, made of cotton. For Shiva, the most interesting aspect was his beard. It was just like that of Lord Rudra's image in the revered Vishwanath temple at Kashi; the distinctive beard of the previous Mahadev had many strands of hair curled into independent clumps.

'Thank you, Kurush,' said Gopal. 'Please allow me the pleasure of introducing the long-awaited Neelkanth himself, Lord Shiva.'

Kurush turned towards Shiva and nodded curtly. Clearly he was one amongst those Vayuputras who considered Shiva a usurper; a Neelkanth who had not been authorised by his tribe. Shiva did not say anything. He knew that the only opinion that mattered was that of their chief, Mithra.

Shiva mounted his horse, then turned and waved at the sailors as they rowed back to their ship. They intended to sail a little farther and anchor in a hidden cove. After a waiting period of two months, the captain would send out a rowboat once every two days to the spot where Gopal and Shiva had met Kurush, to check if they had returned.

Kurush had already begun riding in front, while also holding the reins of the horse bearing the provisions, when Gopal and Shiva kicked their horses into a trot. With the Parihan safely out of earshot, Shiva turned to Gopal. 'Why does the name Kurush sound familiar?'

'Kurush is sometimes also known as Kuru,' said Gopal. 'And Kuru, I'm sure you're aware, was a great Indian Emperor in ancient times.'

'So which name came first? Kuru or Kurush?'

'You mean who influenced whom?' asked Gopal. 'Did India influence Pariha or was it the other way around?'

'Yes, that's what I want to know.'

'I don't know. It was probably a bit of both. We learnt from their noble culture and they learnt from ours. Of course, we can go on about who learnt how much and from whom, but that is nothing but our ego, showing our desperation to prove that our culture is superior to others. That is a foolish quest. It is best to learn from everyone, regardless of the cultural source of that learning.'

The Parihan rode ahead in solitary splendour. They had been travelling for a week now, and Kurush had determinedly remained uncommunicative, giving monosyllabic answers to Shiva's companionable queries. The Neelkanth had finally stopped talking to him.

'Did the Lord grow up here?' Shiva asked Gopal.

'Yes, Lord Rudra was born around this area. He came to India when we needed him.'

'He was from the *land of fairies*. That would obviously make him our guardian spirit as well.'

'Actually, I believe he wasn't born in *Pariha*, but somewhere close to this region.'

'Where?'

'Anshan.'

'Doesn't *anshan* mean hunger in India?'

Gopal smiled. 'It means the same here as well.'

'They named their land "hunger"? Was it so bad?'

'Look around you. This is a harsh, mountainous desert. Life is perennially difficult here. Unless...'

'Unless what?'

'Unless great men are occasionally able to tame this land.'

'And Lord Rudra's tribe proved to be such men?'

'Yes, they set up the kingdom of Elam.'

'Elam? You mean the same one that the Akkadians conquered?'

'Yes.'

'That would explain the Vayuputra support, wouldn't it? The Elamites were the people of Lord Rudra.'

'No, that's not the reason why. The Vayuputras supported the Elamites because they genuinely felt the need for a buffer state between them and the Mesopotamians. In fact, Lord Rudra had made it very clear to his fellow Elamites: they could either join the Vayuputra tribe, giving up all links with any other identity that they had previously cherished, or they could choose to remain Elamites. Those who chose to follow Lord Rudra are the Vayuputras of today.'

'So Pariha is not where Anshan used to be.'

'No. Anshan is the capital of the Elamite kingdom. Pariha exists farther to the east.'

'It appears to me that the Vayuputras accepted other outsiders as well, and not just the Elamites. My uncle was a Tibetan.'

'Yes, Lord Manobhu was one. The Vayuputras accept members solely on merit, not by virtue of birth. There are many Elamites who try to become Vayuputras but do not succeed. The only people who were accepted in large numbers, because they were refugees, were a tribe from our country.'

'From India?'

'Yes, Lord Rudra felt personally guilty about what he had done to them. So he took them under his protection and gave them refuge in his land, amongst the Vayuputras.'

'Who were these people?'

'The Asuras.'

Before Shiva could react to this revelation, Kurush turned and addressed Gopal. 'My Lord, this is a good place to have some lunch. The path ahead goes through a narrow mountain pass. Shall we take a break here?'

Lunch was entirely unappetising and cold, with the harsh mountain winds adding to the discomfort. But the dry fruit that Kurush had brought along provided a boost of energy, much needed for the back-breaking ride that lay ahead.

Kurush quickly packed the remaining food, mounted his horse and kicked it into action after making sure that he had a good grip over the reins of the fourth horse. Gopal and Shiva settled into a canter behind him.

'The Asuras took refuge here?' asked Shiva, still in shock.

'Yes,' answered Gopal. 'Lord Rudra himself brought the few surviving Asura leaders to Pariha. Others, who were in hiding, were also led out of India by the Vayuputras. Some Asuras went farther west, even beyond Elam. I'm not really sure what happened to them. But many of them stayed on in Pariha.'

'And Lord Rudra accommodated these Asuras into the Vayuputra tribe, did he?'

'Not all of them. He found that a few of the Asuras were not detached enough to become members of the Vayuputra tribe. They were allowed to live in Pariha as refugees. But a vast majority of the remainder became Vayuputras.'

'A lot of them would have been the Asura royalty. Wouldn't they have wanted to attack India and take revenge on the Devas who had defeated them?'

'No. Once they entered the Vayuputra brotherhood, they ceased to be Asuras. They gave up their old identities and embraced the primary task Lord Rudra had set for the Vayuputras: to protect the holy land of India from Evil.'

Shiva inhaled deeply as he absorbed this news. The Asuras had been able to go beyond their hatred for their former enemies and work for the mission mandated by Lord Rudra.

'In a strange twist of fate, the Asuras, who to the Devas were demons, were in fact actively working behind the scenes to protect them from the effects of Evil,' said Gopal, as he guided his horse to the right and entered a narrow pass.

Shiva suddenly thought of something, and rode up to Gopal.

'But Pandit*ji*, I'm sure the Asuras would not have forgotten their old culture. They must surely have influenced the Parihan way of life. It's impossible to shed one's cultural memes even after having moved away to foreign lands generations ago. Unless, of course, one becomes as detached as the ascetics.'

'You're right,' said Gopal. 'The Asura culture did impact the Parihans. For instance, do you know the Parihan term for Gods?'

Shiva shrugged.

Gopal glanced at Shiva conspiratorially. 'Before you answer, know this, that in the old Parihan language, there was no place for the production and perception of the phonetic sound "s". It either became "sh" or "h". So, what do you think they called their Gods?'

Shiva frowned, making a wild guess. 'Ahuras?'

'Yes, Ahuras.'

'Good Lord! What were their demons called then?'

'Daevas.'

'By the great Lord Brahma!'

'It's the exact opposite of the Indian pantheon. We call our Gods Devas and demons Asuras.'

Shiva smiled slightly. 'They're different, but they're not evil.'

Chapter 36

The Land of Fairies

Shiva, Gopal and Kurush had been riding for a little over a month. Late winter made travelling through the harsh mountainous terrain a test of will. Shiva, who'd lived most of his life in the highlands of Tibet, managed the expedition quite well. But Gopal, who was used to the moist heat of the plains, was struggling due to the cold and rarefied atmosphere.

'We're here,' said Kurush out of the blue one day, as he raised his hand.

Shiva pulled his reins. They had been on a narrow pathway, no more than four or five metres wide. Shiva dismounted from his horse, tied the reins to a rocky outcrop and walked up to Gopal to assist him. He tied Gopal's horse, helped him sit with his back propped up against the mountain side, and offered his water to the Chief Vasudev. Gopal sipped the life-nurturing fluid slowly.

Having helped his friend, Shiva looked around. To the left was a sheer, rocky mountainside, almost as steep as a cliff, which extended upwards for several hundred metres. To the right was a steep drop, to a dry valley far below. As far as the eye could see, there was no sign of any life anywhere. No human habitation, no animal, not even the few valiant plants and trees that they had seen at lower heights.

Shiva looked at Gopal with raised eyebrows and whispered. 'We're here?'

Gopal gestured towards Kurush. The Parihan was carefully running his hands over the mountain wall, his eyes shut, trying to locate something. He suddenly stopped. He had found what he was seeking. Shiva had moved up in the meantime and saw the faint indentation of a symbol on the mountainside. A figurative flame he had come to recognise: *Fravashi.*

Kurush pressed the ring on his index finger into the centre of the symbol. A block of rock, the size of a human head, emerged from the right. Kurush quickly placed both his hands on the rock, stepped back to get some leverage, and pushed hard.

Shiva watched in wonder as the mountain seemed to come to life. A substantial section, nearly four metres across and three metres high, receded inward and then slid aside, revealing a pathway going deep into the mountain's womb.

Kurush turned towards Shiva and indicated that they were good to go. Shiva helped Gopal onto his horse and handed the reins to his friend. As he walked towards his horse, he noticed that while the rocky outcrop where he had tethered his animal looked natural, in fact, it was manmade. Shiva mounted his horse and quickly joined Gopal and Kurush, riding into the heart of the mountain.

— ⅄ⓞ℧⍋⊛ —

The rocky concealed entrance had closed behind them just as smoothly. It would have been pitch dark inside except for a flaming torch that was maintained by the Parihans on one of the walls, which threw its light ahead for a few metres. Beyond that, the light lost its struggle against the omnipresent darkness of the cavernous pathway. Kurush picked three unlit torches from a recess on the wall, lit them and handed one each to Gopal and Shiva. Thereupon he swiftly rode ahead, holding his torch aloft. Shiva and Gopal kicked their horses and made haste after him.

Soon the pathway split into a fork, but Kurush unhesitatingly led them up one, disregarding the other. Just like the Nagas in the Dandak forests, the Vayuputras too had ensured that in the unlikely scenario of any unauthorised person finding his way into the secret pathway, he would inevitably get lost within the mountain, unless led by a Vayuputra guide.

Shiva expected many more such misleading paths along the way. He was not disappointed.

— ⅄◎Ʊ⍏⊗ —

A half hour later, after a long monotonous ride, the travellers emerged on the other side of the mountain, almost blinded by the sudden onslaught of bright sunlight. Even as his eyes adjusted, Shiva's jaw dropped with amazement as he took in what lay ahead.

The other side of the mountain was dramatically different from what they had seen up to now. A broad, winding road had been cut into the sides of the mountain. Called the Rudra Avenue by the local Parihans, a beautifully carved railing ran along its sides, affording protection for horses or carriages from slipping off the road to certain death in the sheer ravine below. The Rudra Avenue wound its way along the steep mountain in a gentle descent to the bottom. The valley itself, naturally dry as a bone, was surrounded on all sides by steep mountains. The splendour of nature notwithstanding, what Shiva was struck by was what the Parihans had done with it. Hidden away from prying eyes, surrounded by unconquerable mountains, in this secluded spot, they had truly created a *land of fairies, Pariha.*

The Rudra Avenue ended at the base of a terrace. This platform though, unlike the ones built by the Meluhans, had not been constructed as protection against flood. The problem with water in Pariha was not one of excess but that of scarcity. The platform had been built to create a smooth base atop the rough, undulating, mountainous valley, allowing for the construction of massive structures upon it. The city of Pariha had been built on it.

Kurush, Gopal and Shiva approached the platform at the lowest point of the valley. The platform was at its tallest here, nearly twenty metres high. A massive ceremonial gate had been erected at what was obviously the only entry point into the city. The road was surrounded by high walls on both sides, and narrowed down as it led to the well barricaded gate. Looking admiringly around, the warrior in Shiva understood that the approach to the city gates perforce funnelled an attacking force into a narrow neck, thus making defence easy for the Parihans.

The massive ornate city gates had been hewn out of the local brown stone that Shiva had frequently seen en route. The gate itself was flanked on either side by large pillars, on which crouched two imposing creatures, as if ready to pounce in defence of their city. This unfamiliar creature carried the head of a man on the body of a lion and sprouted the broad wings of an eagle. Parihan pride was unmistakable in the features of the face: a sharp forehead held high, a hooked nose, neatly beaded beard, a drooping moustache and lengthy locks emerging from under a square hat. The aggressive, warrior-like visage was tempered somewhat by calm, almost friendly eyes.

Shiva noted that Kurush's conversation with the gatekeeper was done. He walked back and spoke respectfully to Gopal.

'My Lord, the formalities have been completed. Please accept my apologies that it took us so long to get here. Shall we?'

'There's no need for an apology, Kurush,' said Gopal politely. 'Let's go.'

Shiva quietly followed Kurush and Gopal, keenly aware of the gatekeeper's quizzical, perhaps even judgemental eyes.

— ⚹ —

They crossed a massive tiled courtyard, guiding their horses onto the cobbled pathway leading to the top of the platform. The gradient was gentle, making it easy to negotiate the single hair-pin bend they encountered. A few pedestrians sauntered along the accompanying steps, provided with long treads to facilitate the climb. All along the pathway, the rock face of the platform had been carved and painted. Against the relief of glazed tiles, sculpted Parihans gazed at passers-by with their distinguished features, long coats and square hats. As if from nowhere, water rippled down the centre of the rock face, leaving a lilting musical sound in its wake. Shiva made a mental note to ask Gopal the secret of this water source in the harsh desert.

Shiva's questions were quickly forgotten as he reached the top and exclaimed with wonder at the sheer beauty of all that he beheld.

'By the Holy Lake!'

He had just had his first vision of the exquisite, symmetrical gardens of Pariha. These artificial heavenly creations were so extraordinary that Parihans had named them *Paradaeza, the walled place of harmony*.

The Paradaeza extended along the central axis of the rectangular city, with buildings built around it. The park and the city extended all the way to the edge of a great mountain at the upper end of the valley, which had been named the Mountain of Mercy by the Asuras. A water channel emerged from the heart of the mountain, flowing through the garden in an unerringly straight line, filling up large square ponds intermittently. The ponds themselves had flamboyant fountains constructed in the centre, spewing water high into the air. The left and right halves of the gardens, divided by the water channel, were perfect mirror images of each other. The entire expanse was covered with a carpet of thick and carefully manicured grass, which provided the base around which flower beds and trees were arranged in perfect harmony. The flora had obviously been imported from around the world; roses, narcissus, tulips, lilacs, jasmine, orange and lemon trees dotted the landscape in poetic profusion.

Shiva was so lost in the beauty of the garden that he didn't hear his friend call.

'Lord Neelkanth?' repeated Gopal.

Shiva turned to the Chief Vasudev.

'We can always come back here, my friend. But for now, we need to retire to our guesthouse.'

Shiva and Gopal had been housed in the state guesthouse, reserved for elite visitors to Pariha. Here too, the duo encountered the Parihan obsession with beauty and elegance.

Dismounting from their horses, Shiva and Gopal strode into the building. The entrance led to a wide, comfortable veranda lined with neat rows of perfectly circular columns providing support to a great stone ceiling. The columns were coloured a vivid pink all the way to the top, at which point, near the ceiling, it contained discreet etchings of animal figurines. Shiva squinted to get a better look.

'Bulls,' remarked Shiva.

Bulls and cows were sacred amongst the Indians, central to the spiritual experience of life.

'Yes,' confirmed Gopal. 'Bulls are revered by the Parihans as well. They're symbolic of strength and virility.'

As they reached the other end of the veranda, they encountered three elegantly dressed Parihans. The one in front held out a tray with warm, moistened and scented towels. Gopal immediately picked one up and went on to wipe the accumulated dust and grime from his face and hands. Shiva followed his example.

A Parihan woman walked up to Gopal, bowed low and spoke softly. 'Welcome, honoured Chief Vasudev Gopal. We can scarce believe our good fortune in hosting the representative of the great Lord Ram.'

'Thank you, My Lady,' said Gopal. 'But you have me at a disadvantage. You know my name and I do not know yours.'

'My name is Bahmandokht.'

'The daughter of Bahman?' said Gopal, for he was familiar with their old language, Avesta.

Bahmandokht smiled. 'That is one of the meanings, yes. But I prefer the other one.'

'And, what is that?'

'A maiden with a good mind.'

'I'm sure you live by that name, My Lady.'

'I try my best, Lord Gopal.'

Gopal smiled and folded his hands into a Namaste.

Unlike most Parihans who had studiously ignored Shiva all this time, Bahmandokht addressed the Neelkanth with a polite bow. 'Welcome, Lord Shiva. I do hope we have given you no cause for complaint.'

'None at all,' said Shiva graciously.

'I know you are here on a mission,' said Bahmandokht.

'I do not make so bold as to speak for my entire tribe, but I personally hope that you succeed. India and Pariha are intertwined by ancient bonds. If something needs to be done that is in the interest of your country, I believe it is our duty to help. It is the dictate that Lord Rudra laid down for us.'

Shiva acknowledged the courtesy and held his hands together in a Namaste. 'That spirit is returned in full measure by my country, Lady Bahmandokht.'

Bahmandokht glanced at a woman standing at the back towards the end of the lobby. Shiva's eyes followed her and rested on a tall woman, dressed in traditional Parihan garb. Despite the attire, it was obvious that she wasn't native to Pariha. Bronze-complexioned with jet black hair, she had large attractive doe-eyes and a voluptuous body, unlike the slender locals. She was a gorgeous woman indeed.

'Lord Shiva,' said Bahmandokht, pulling the Neelkanth's attention back. 'My aide will show you to your chamber.'

'Thank you,' said Shiva.

As Gopal and Shiva were escorted away, the Neelkanth looked back. The mystery woman had disappeared.

— ⁂ —

Shiva and Gopal were led into a lavish suite of rooms with two separate bed chambers. The suite had been furnished with every luxury imaginable. Door-length windows at the far end opened on to a huge balcony with large recliners and a couple of cloth-covered pouffes that could double up as tables. The living room contained a mini fountain on the side, its cascading waters creating a soothing tinkle. Delicately woven wall-to-wall plush carpets covered every inch of the floor. Bolsters and cushions of various sizes were strewn on the carpets at several corners, making comfortable floor-seating areas. An ornately carved oak table was placed in one corner, accompanied with cushioned chairs on the side. Another corner was occupied by Parihan musical instruments, keeping in mind the role of leisure in hospitality. Lavish gold and silver plated accoutrements decorated the mantelpiece and shelves on the walls. This was ostentatious even by the standards of Swadweepan royalty.

The two bedrooms had comfortable soft beds with silk linen. Bowls of fruit had been thoughtfully placed on low tables next to the beds. Even clothes had been specially ordered and placed in cupboards for the two guests, including traditional Parihan cloaks.

Shiva looked at Gopal with a twinkle in his eye and chortled, 'I think these miserable quarters will have to suffice!'

Gopal joined in mirthfully.

Chapter 37

Unexpected Help

After a sumptuous dinner, Gopal and Shiva were back in their chambers, welcoming the opportunity for relaxation and inactivity. The fountain in the room having drawn his attention, Shiva quipped, 'Pandit*ji*, where do they get the water from?'

'For this fountain?' asked Gopal.

'For all the fountains, ponds and channels that we have seen. Quite frankly, building this city and these gardens would have required a prodigious amount of water. This is a desert land with almost no natural rivers. I was told that they don't even have regular rains. So where does this water come from?'

'They owe it to the brilliance of their engineers.'

'How so?'

'There are massive natural springs and aquifers to the north of Pariha.'

'That is water within the rocks and the ground, right?'

'Yes.'

'But springs can never be as bountiful.'

'True, but scarcity engenders ingenuity. When you don't have enough water, you learn to use it judiciously. All the fountain and canal water that you see in the city is recycled waste water.'

Shiva, who had dipped his hand into the fountain water, immediately recoiled.

Gopal laughed softly. 'Don't worry, my friend. That water has been treated and completely cleaned. It's even safe to drink.'

'I'll take your word for it.'

Gopal smiled as Shiva judiciously wiped his hands with a sanitised napkin.

'How far away are these springs and aquifers?'

'The ones that supply this city are a good fifty to hundred kilometres away,' answered Gopal.

Shiva whistled softly. 'That's a long distance. How do they get the water here in such large quantities? I haven't seen any canals.'

'Oh, they have canals. But you can't see them as they are underground.'

'They've built underground canals?' asked Shiva, stunned.

'They're not as broad as the canals we have back home. But they serve the purpose. They built canals that are the size of underground drains, which begin at the aquifers and springs.'

'But a hundred kilometres is a long way to transport water. How do they do that? Do they have underground pumps powered by animals?'

'No. They use one of the most powerful forces of nature to do the job.'

'What?'

'Gravity. They built underground channels with gentle gradients that slope over a hundred kilometres. The water naturally flows down due to the force of gravity.'

'Brilliant. But building something like this would require precision engineering skills of a high order.'

'You're right. The angle of the descent would have to be absolutely exact over very long distances. If the gradient is even slightly higher than required, the water would begin to erode the bottom of the channel, destroying it over time.'

'And if the slope is a little too gentle, the water would simply stop flowing.'

'Exactly,' said Gopal. 'You can imagine the flawless design and execution required, in implementing a project such as this.'

'But when did they...'

Shiva was interrupted by a soft knock on the door. He immediately lowered his voice to an urgent whisper. 'Pandit*ji*, were you expecting someone?'

Gopal shook his head. 'No. And, where is our guard? Isn't he supposed to announce visitors?'

Shiva pulled out his sword, indicating to Gopal that he should follow him, as he tiptoed to the door. The safest place for him was behind Shiva. The Vasudev chief was a Brahmin and not a warrior. Shiva waited near the door. The soft knock was heard again.

Shiva turned and whispered to Gopal. 'As soon as I pull the intruder in, shut the door and lock it.'

Shiva held his sword to the side, pulled the door open and in one smooth motion, yanked the intruder into the room, pushing the Parihan to the ground. Gopal, moving just as rapidly, shut the door and bolted it.

'I'm a friend!' spoke a feminine voice, her hands raised in surrender.

Shiva and Gopal stared at the woman on the ground, her face covered with a veil.

She slowly got up, keeping her eyes fixed on Shiva's sword. 'You don't need that. Parihans do not kill their guests. It is one of Lord Rudra's laws.'

Shiva refused to lower his blade. 'Reveal yourself,' he commanded.

The woman removed her veil. 'You've seen me earlier, great Neelkanth.'

Shiva recognised the intruder immediately. It was the dark-haired mystery woman he had seen in the lobby while he'd been talking to Bahmandokht.

Shiva smiled. 'I was wondering when I would see you next.'

'I've come to help,' said the woman, still unable to tear her eyes away from the sword. 'So I'll repeat that you really don't need that. We Parihans will never break Lord Rudra's laws.'

Shiva sheathed his sword. 'What makes you think we need your help?'

'For the same reason that you don't need your sword here: we Vayuputras never break Lord Rudra's laws. I am here to help you get what you came for...'

Shiva and Gopal joined the lady, having made her comfortable on the soft cushions.

'What is your name?' asked Shiva. 'Why do you want to help us?'

'My name is Scheherazade.'

Scheherazade was a name that harked back to ancient Parihan roots; *a person who gives freedom to cities.*

Shiva narrowed his eyes. 'That is a lie. You are not from this land. What is your real name?'

'I am a Parihan. This is my name.'

'How can we trust you if you don't even tell us your real name?'

'My name has nothing to do with your mission. What the Amartya Shpand, the Vayuputra Council, think of your mission is what truly matters.'

'And you can tell us what they think?' asked Gopal.

'That's why I am here. I can tell you what you need to do to fulfil your mission.'

The Mithra was a ceremonial title for the chief of the Vayuputra tribe. It literally translated as *'friend'*; for he was the deepest friend of the Vayuputra God, the Ahura Mazda.

Ahura Mazda was a formless God, much like the Hindu concept of *Parmatma*. And Mithra was his representative on earth. Lord Rudra had mandated that the ancient title of Mithra be used for the Chief Vayuputra. Once a man became the Mithra, all his earlier identities were erased, including his old name. He even dissociated himself completely from his former family. Everyone was to know him thereafter as Mithra.

Mithra was in the antechamber of his office, when he heard a soft noise from the veranda. The nascent moon cast a faint light, impairing vision, but Mithra knew who it was as he walked over.

He heard a soft, feminine voice call out in a whisper, 'Great Mithra, I have sent her to them.'

'Thank you, Bahmandokht. The Vayuputras will be indebted to you in perpetuity, for you have helped our tribe fulfil our mission and our vow to Lord Rudra.'

Bahmandokht bowed low. There had been a time when she had loved the man who'd become the Mithra. But once he had assumed his office as the chief, the only feelings she had allowed herself were those of devotion and respect.

She stepped away quietly.

The Mithra stared at Bahmandokht's retreating form and then returned to the antechamber. He sat on a simple chair, leaned back and closed his eyes. The ancient memory was still fresh in his mind, as if it had all happened yesterday – the conversation with his close friend and brother-in-law, Manobhu.

'Are you sure, Manobhu?' asked the Parihan, who would go on to become the Mithra.

The Tibetan feigned outrage as he looked at his friend and fellow Vayuputra.

'I mean no disrespect, Manobhu. But I hope you realise that what we're doing is illegal.'

Manobhu allowed himself a slight smile as he scratched his shaggy beard. His matted hair had been tied up in a bun with a string of beads, in the style favoured by his tribe, the fierce Gunas. His body was covered with deep scars acquired from a lifetime of battle. His tall, muscular physique was always in a state of alertness, ever ready for war. His demeanour, his clothes, his hair – all conveyed the impression of a ruthless warrior. But his eyes were different. They were a window to his calm mind, one that had found its purpose and was at peace. Manobhu's eyes had always intrigued the Parihan, compelling him to become a follower.

'If you are unsure, my friend,' said Manobhu, 'you don't have to do this.'

The Parihan looked away.

'Don't feel pressured to do this just because you're related to me,' continued Manobhu, whose brother had married the Parihan's sister.

The Parihan returned his gaze. 'How does the reason matter? What matters is the result. What matters is whether Lord Rudra's commandment is being followed.'

Manobhu continued to lock gaze with the Parihan, his eyes mirthful. 'You should know Lord Rudra's commandments better than I do. After all, he was a Parihan. Like you.'

The Parihan stole a look at the back of the room nervously, where a diabolical mixture was boiling inside a vessel, the fire below it steady and even.

Manobhu stepped forward and put his hand on the Parihan's shoulder. 'Trust me, the Somras is turning Evil. Lord Rudra would have wanted us to do this. If the council doesn't agree, then the hell with them. We will ensure that Lord Rudra's commandments are followed.'

The Parihan looked at Manobhu and sighed. 'Are you sure that your nephew has the potential to fulfil this mission? That he can one day be the successor to Lord Rudra?'

Manobhu smiled. 'He's your nephew too. His mother is your sister.'

'I know. But the boy doesn't live with me. He lives with you, in Tibet. I have never met him. I don't know if I ever will. And you refuse to even tell me his name. So I ask again: Are you sure he is the one?'

'Yes,' Manobhu was confident in his belief. 'He is the one. He will grow up to be the Neelkanth. He will be the one who will carry out Lord Rudra's commandment. He will take Evil out of the equation.'

'But he needs to be educated. He needs to be prepared.'

'I will prepare him.'

'But what is the point? The Vayuputra council controls the emergence of the Neelkanth. How will our nephew be discovered?'

'I'll arrange it at the right time,' said Manobhu.

The Parihan frowned. 'But how will you...'

'Leave that to me,' interrupted Manobhu. 'If he is not discovered, it will mean that the time for Evil has not yet come. On the other hand, if I'm able to ensure that he is discovered...'

'...then we will know that Evil has risen,' said the Parihan, completing Manobhu's sentence.

Manobhu shook his head, disagreeing partially with his brother-in-law. 'To be more precise, we would know that Good has turned into Evil.'

The conversation was interrupted by a soft hissing sound from the far corner of the room. The medicine was ready. The two friends walked over to the fire and peered into the vessel. A thick reddish-brown paste had formed; small bubbles were bursting through to the surface.

'It only needs to cool down now. The task is done,' said the Parihan.

Manobhu looked at his brother-in-law. 'No, my friend. The task has just begun.'

The Mithra breathed deeply as he came back to the present. He whispered, 'I never thought that our rebellion would succeed, Manobhu.'

He rose from his chair, walked over to the veranda and looked up at the sky. In the old days, his people believed that great men, once they had surrendered their mortal flesh, went up to live among the stars and keep watch over them all. Mithra focused his eyes on one particular star and smiled. 'Manobhu, it was a good idea to name our nephew Shiva. A good clue to help me guess that he is the one.'

— ⅄⦶Ʊ⇞⊗ —

'To begin with, let me tell you that most of the Vayuputras are against you,' said Scheherazade.

'That's not really much of a secret,' said Shiva wryly.

'Look, you can't blame the Vayuputras. Our laws state very clearly that only one of us, from amongst those who're authorised by the Vayuputra tribe, can become the Neelkanth. You have emerged out of nowhere. The laws don't allow us to recognise or help someone like you.'

'And yet, you are here,' said Shiva. 'I don't think you're working alone. You were standing right at the back, almost hidden, when I saw you in the lobby. I bet you are not a fully-accepted Parihan. I can't see someone like you having the courage to do this all by yourself. Some powerful Parihans are putting you up to it. Which makes me believe that some Vayuputras realise what I am saying is true, that Evil has risen.'

Scheherazade smiled softly. 'Yes. There are some very powerful Vayuputras who are on your side. But they cannot help you openly. Unlike most of the earlier Neelkanth pretenders, your blue throat is genuine. This leads to one inescapable conclusion; some Vayuputra has helped you many decades ago. Can you imagine the chaos this has caused? There were unprecedented accusations flying thick and fast after your emergence; people within Pariha were accusing each other of having broken Lord Rudra's laws and helping you clandestinely when you were young. It was tearing the Vayuputras apart till Lord Mithra put an end to it. He held that our tribe has not authorised you as the Neelkanth and perhaps it was the doing of someone from within your own country.'

'So, if any Vayuputra helps me, he will be seen as the traitor who started it all, many years ago.'

'Exactly,' answered Scheherazade.

'What is the way out?' asked Gopal.

'You, My Lord Chief Vasudev, must lead the mission,' said Scheherazade. 'Lord Shiva must stay in the background. Don't ask for assistance to be provided for the Neelkanth, but to *you* as a member of the Vasudev tribe, seeking justice. They cannot say no to a just demand from the representative of Lord Ram.'

'I am sorry? I didn't understand.'

'What does the Neelkanth need, Lord Gopal?' asked Scheherazade. 'He needs the *Brahmastra* to threaten Meluha...'

'How did you...'

'With due respect, don't ask superfluous questions, Lord Gopal. What Lord Shiva and you need is obvious. We have to devise the best way for you to get it. If you ask for the *Brahmastra* so that you can fight Evil, then you will open yourself to questions as to Lord Shiva's legitimacy in deciding what Evil is, for we all know that he has not been authorised or trained by the Vayuputras. Instead, seek redress for a crime committed on Indian soil by a person who the Vayuputras have supported in the past. And what crime was that? The unauthorised use of *daivi astras*.'

'Lord Bhrigu...' said Gopal, remembering the great maharishi's use of the *divine weapons* in Panchavati.

'Exactly. The laws of Lord Rudra make it clear that for

the first unauthorised use of *daivi astras*, the punishment is a fourteen-year exile into the forests. A second unauthorised use is punishable by death. Many in the council agree that Lord Bhrigu has got away lightly, despite having used *daivi astras*.'

'So the Vasudevs are to present themselves as the ones enforcing the justice of Lord Rudra?'

'Exactly. It is impossible for a Vayuputra to say no to this. You should state that the law on the *daivi astra* ban was broken and those who did this – Lord Bhrigu, the Emperor of Meluha and the King of Ayodhya – need to be punished. And, the Vasudevs have decided to mete out justice.'

'And we can tell the Vayuputras,' said Shiva, completing Scheherazade's thought, 'that they may well have more reserves of *daivi astras*. So we need the *Brahmastra* to encourage them to do the right thing.'

Scheherazade smiled. 'Use the laws to achieve your objective. Once you have the *Brahmastra*, use it to threaten the Meluhans. Evil must be stopped. But I've been asked to tell you that you shouldn't...'

'We will never use the *Brahmastra*,' said Gopal, interrupting Scheherazade.

'It's not just about the laws of Lord Rudra,' added Shiva. 'Using a weapon of such horrifying power goes against the laws of humanity.'

Scheherazade nodded. 'When you meet the council, insist on speaking with Lord Mithra in private. Tell them it is a matter of the *daivi astra* law being broken. Say that the Vasudevs cannot allow those who broke Lord Rudra's law to go unpunished. That will be enough. It will then be a private conversation between Lord Mithra and the two of you. You will get what you want.'

Shiva smiled as he understood who amongst the Vayuputras

was helping him. But he was still intrigued by Scheherazade, or whatever her real name was.

'Why are you helping us?' asked Shiva.

'Because I've been told to do so.'

'I don't believe that. Something else is driving you. Why are you helping us?'

Scheherazade smiled sadly and looked at the carpet. Then she turned towards the balcony, staring into the dark night beyond. She wiped a tear from the corner of her eye and turned back towards Shiva. 'Because there was a man whom I had loved once, who had told me that the Somras was turning evil. And I didn't believe him at the time.'

'Who is this man?' asked Gopal.

'It doesn't matter anymore,' said Scheherazade. 'He is dead. He was killed, perhaps by those who'd wanted to stop him. Ending the reign of the Somras is my way of apologising...'

Shiva leaned towards her, looked straight into Scheherazade's eyes and whispered, 'Tara?'

A stunned Scheherazade pulled back. Nobody had called her by that name in years. Shiva continued to observe her eyes.

'By the Holy Lake,' he whispered. 'It is you.'

Scheherazade did not say anything. Her relationship with Brahaspati had been kept a secret. Many amongst the Parihans believed that the Somras was still a force for Good, and that the former chief scientist of Meluha was deeply biased and misguided about it. Tara would have preferred not having to live in Pariha as Scheherazade. But her presence here had served a purpose for her guru, Lord Bhrigu. Believing Brahaspati was dead, she had found no reason to return to her homeland.

'But you are Lord Bhrigu's student,' said Shiva. 'Why are you going against him?'

'I'm not Tara.'

'I know you are,' said Shiva. 'Why are you going against your guru? Do you believe that it was Lord Bhrigu who got Brahaspati killed at Mount Mandar?'

Scheherazade stood up and turned to leave. Shiva rose quickly, stretched out and held her hand. 'Brahaspati is not dead.'

A dumbstruck Scheherazade stopped dead in her tracks.

'Brahaspati is alive,' said Shiva. 'He is with me.'

Tears poured from Scheherazade's eyes. She couldn't believe what she was hearing.

Shiva stepped forward and repeated gently. 'He is with me. Your Brahaspati is alive.'

Scheherazade kept crying, tears of confused happiness flowing down her cheeks.

Shiva gently held her hand in his own. 'Tara, you will come back with us when we're done here. I'll take you back. I'll take you back to your Brahaspati.'

Scheherazade collapsed into Shiva's arms, inconsolable in her tears. She would be Tara once again.

Chapter 38

The Friend of God

The strategy that Tara had suggested worked like a charm. The Amartya Shpand was genuinely taken by surprise when Gopal entered their audience chamber without Shiva. When he raised the issue of Maharishi Bhrigu's misuse of the *daivi astras*, they knew that they had been cornered. They had no choice but to grant Gopal an audience with the Mithra. That was the law.

The following day, Shiva and Gopal were led into the official audience hall and residence of the Mithra. It had been built at one end of the city, the last building abutting the Mountain of Mercy. Unlike the rest of Pariha, this structure was incredibly modest. It had a simple base made of stone, which covered the water channel that emerged from the mountain. On it were constructed austere pillars, which supported a wooden roof four metres high. On entry, one immediately stepped into a simple audience hall furnished with basic chairs and sombre carpets. The Mithra's personal quarters lay farther inside, separated by stone walls and a wooden door. Shiva could sense that this was almost a stone replica of a large ceremonial tent, the wooden tent-poles having been converted to stone pillars and the cloth canopy into a wooden roof. In a way, this was a link to the nomadic past of Lord Rudra's people, when everybody lived in simple, easily-built tents that could be dismantled and moved at short notice. Like a tribal leader of the old code, the Mithra lived in penurious simplicity while his people lived in luxury. The only indulgence that the Mithra had allowed himself was the beautiful garden that surrounded his abode. It was bountiful in its design, precise in its symmetry and extravagant in its colourful flora.

Shiva and Gopal were left alone in the audience hall, and the doors were shut. Within a few moments, the Mithra entered.

Shiva and Gopal immediately stood up. They greeted the Mithra with the ancient Parihan salute: the left hand was placed on the heart, fist open, as a mark of admiration. The right arm was held rigidly to the side of the body, bent upwards at the elbow. The open palm of the right hand faced outwards, as a form of greeting. The Mithra smiled genially and folded his hands together into the traditional Indian Namaste.

Shiva grinned, but remained silent, waiting for the Mithra to speak.

The Mithra was a tall, fair-skinned man, dressed in a simple brown cloak. A white hat covered his long brownish hair, with tiny beads wrapped around separated strands of his beard, much like all Parihans. Though the sack-like cloak made it difficult to judge, his body seemed strong and muscular. Of interest to Shiva were his delicate hands with long, slender fingers; like those of a surgeon rather than a warrior. But Shiva was most intrigued by the Mithra's nose: sharp and long. It reminded him of his beloved mother.

The Mithra walked up to Shiva and held the Neelkanth by his shoulders. 'What a delight it is to finally see you.'

Shiva noted that the Mithra didn't even cursorily glance at his blue neck, something most people could not resist. The Mithra's attention was focused on Shiva's eyes.

And then the Mithra said something even more intriguing. 'You have your father's eyes. And your mother's nose.'

He knew my father? And my mother?!

Before Shiva could react, the Mithra gently touched Shiva's back, as he smiled at Gopal. 'Come, let's sit.'

As soon as they had seated themselves, the Mithra turned towards the Neelkanth, 'I can see the questions that are running through your mind. How do I know your father and mother? Who am I? What was my name before I became the Mithra?'

Shiva smiled. 'This eye-reading business is very dangerous. It doesn't allow one to have any secrets.'

'Sometimes, it's important that there be no secrets,' said the Mithra, 'especially when such big decisions are being taken. How else can we be sure that we have taken the right step?'

'You don't have to answer if you don't wish to. The questions running in my mind are not important to our mission.'

'You're right. You have been trained well. These questions may trouble your mind, but they are not important. But then, can we really carry out our mission with troubled minds?'

'A troubled mind makes one lose sight of the mission,' admitted Shiva.

'And the world cannot afford to have you lose sight of your mission, great Neelkanth. You are too important for us. So let me answer your personal questions first.'

Shiva noticed that the Mithra had called him the Neelkanth, something which no Parihan had, until now.

'My name is not important,' said the Mithra. 'I don't hold that name anymore. My only identity is my title: the Mithra.'

Shiva nodded politely.

'Now, how do I know your mother? Simple. I grew up with her. She was my sister.'

Shiva's eyes opened wide in surprise. 'You are my uncle?'

Mithra nodded. 'I was your uncle before I became the Mithra.'

'Why have I not met you before?'

'It's complicated. But suffice it to say that your father's brother, Lord Manobhu, and I were good friends. I held him in deep regard. We'd decided to seal our friendship with a marriage between our two families. My sister went to live with Lord Manobhu's brother in Tibet, after their wedding. And you were born from that union.'

'But my uncle had rebellious ideas...' said Shiva, trying to guess why the Mithra had been forced to keep his distance from their family.

The Mithra shook his head. 'Manobhu didn't have rebellious ideas. He had inspiring ideas. But an inspiration before its time appears like a rebellion.'

'So you were not forced by the Vayuputras to stay away from my family?'

'Oh I was forced all right. But not by the Vayuputras.'

Shiva smiled. 'Uncle Manobhu could be stubborn at times.'

The Mithra smiled.

'When did you know that I was your long-lost relative?' asked Shiva. 'Did you have spies following me?'

'I recognised you the moment I heard your name.'

'Didn't you know my name?'

'No, Manobhu refused to tell me. Now I understand why. It was a clue he'd left for me. If you emerged at all, I would recognise you by your name.'

'How so?' asked Shiva, intrigued.

'Almost nobody, even from amongst the Vayuputras, knows that Lord Rudra's mother had had a special and personal name for him: Shiva.'

'What?!'

'Yes. Lord Rudra's name means "the one who roars". He

was named so because when he was born, he cried so loudly that he drove the midwife away!'

'I have heard that story,' said Shiva. 'But I have not heard the one about Lord Rudra's mother calling him Shiva...'

'It's a secret that only a few Vayuputras are aware of. Legend holds that Lord Rudra was actually stillborn.'

'What?' asked a genuinely surprised Gopal.

'Yes,' said the Mithra. 'The midwife and Lord Rudra's mother tried very hard to revive him. Finally, the midwife tried something very unorthodox. She tried to breastfeed the stillborn Lord Rudra. Much to his mother's surprise, the baby actually started breathing and, as history recalls, roared loudly.'

'By the Holy Lake,' whispered Shiva. 'What a fascinating story.'

'Yes, it is. The midwife walked away soon thereafter, and was never heard of again. Lord Rudra's mother, who was an immigrant and a believer in the Mother Goddess Shakti, was convinced that the midwife had been sent by the Goddess to save her son. She believed her son was born as *a body without life*, a *shava*, whom Goddess Shakti had infused with life; therefore, she felt the Goddess had converted a *Shava* to *Shiva*, or *the auspicious one*. So she started calling her son Shiva, in honour of the Mother Goddess and in acknowledgement of the state in which her son was born.'

An enthralled Shiva listened in rapt attention to the Mithra.

'So,' said the Mithra, 'the moment I heard your name, I knew that Manobhu had left a clue for me about you being the one he had trained.'

'So you knew that Lord Manobhu was planning this?'

The Mithra smiled. 'Your uncle and I made the medicine together.'

'You mean the medicine that is responsible for my throat turning blue?'

'Yes.'

'But didn't that have to be given to me at a specific time in my life?'

'I'm assuming that is what Manobhu did, for here you are.'

'But Lord Mithra, this is not the way the system was supposed to work, as an unfolding series of implausible coincidences. There are so many things that could have gone wrong. To begin with, I may not have been trained well. Or the medicine may not have been given to me at the right time. I may never have been invited to Meluha. And worst of all, I may not have stumbled upon the Somras as the true Evil.'

'You're right. This is not the way our *Vayuputra* system was designed to work. But Manobhu and I had faith that this is the way the *universe's* system is supposed to work. And it did, didn't it?'

'But is it right to leave such significant outcomes to a roll of the universe's dice?'

'You make it sound as if it was all left to dumb luck. We didn't leave it only to chance, Shiva. The Vayuputras were sure the Somras had not turned evil. Manobhu and I felt otherwise. Had Manobhu been alive, he would have guided you through this period, but in spite of his untimely death, Good prevailed. Manobhu always said let us allow the universe to make the decision, and it did. We decided to set in motion a chain of events, which would work out only if the universe willed it so. Frankly, I wasn't sure. But I didn't stop him. I just didn't think his plan would succeed. I did help him in making the medicine, though. And when I saw the plan coming to fruition, I knew that it was my duty to do whatever I could to help.'

'But what if I had failed? What if I hadn't identified the Somras as Evil? Then Evil would have won, right?'

'Sometimes, the universe decides that Evil is supposed to win. Perhaps a race or species becomes so harmful that it's better to allow Evil to triumph and destroy that species. It has happened before. But this is not one of those times.'

Shiva was clearly overwhelmed by the number of things that could have gone wrong.

'You are still troubled by something...' said the Mithra.

'I've talked to Pandit*ji* as well, about this,' said Shiva, pointing to Gopal. 'So much of what I have achieved in my mission can be attributed to pure luck; just a random turn of the universe.'

The Mithra bent forward towards Shiva and whispered, 'One makes one's own luck, but you have to give the universe the opportunity to help you.'

Shiva remained stoic, not quite convinced by the Mithra's words.

'You had every reason to turn away after arriving in Meluha for the first time. You were in a strange new land. Peculiar people, who were evidently so much more advanced than you, insisted on looking upon you as a God. You were tasked with a mission, the enormity of which would have intimidated practically anyone in the world. I'm sure that at the time, you didn't even think you could succeed. And yet, you didn't run away. You stood up and accepted a responsibility that was thrust upon you. That decision was the turning point in your journey against Evil, which had nothing to do with the twists and blessings of fate.'

Shiva looked at Gopal, whose demeanour suggested he was in full agreement with the Mithra.

'You are giving me too much credit, Lord Mithra,' said Shiva.

'I am not,' said the Mithra. 'You are on course to fulfil *my* mission, without having taken any help from me. But I will not allow you to do that. You must give me the privilege of offering some help. Otherwise, how will I face the Ahura Mazda and Lord Rudra when I meet with them?'

Shiva smiled.

The Mithra looked directly into Shiva's eyes. 'But there are some things I must be sure of. What do you plan to do with the *daivi astra*?'

'I plan to use it to threaten...' Shiva stopped speaking as the Mithra raised his hand.

'I've seen enough,' said the Mithra.

Shiva frowned.

'Thoughts move faster than the tongue, great Neelkanth. I know you will not use these terrible weapons of destruction. I can also see that the reason you will not do so is not just because of the Vayuputra ban but because you believe that these weapons are too horrifying to ever be used.'

'I do believe that.'

'But I cannot give you the *Brahmastra*.'

This was unexpected. Shiva had thought the discussion had been going his way.

'I cannot give you the *Brahmastra* because it is too uncontrollable. It destroys anything and everything. Most importantly, its effect spreads out in circles. The worst destruction is in the epicentre, where everything living is instantly incinerated into thin air. While there is less destruction in the outer circles, the damage is still significantly widespread in the vicinity. So even if those outside the primary impact zone are not immediately killed, they suffer from the immense radiation unleashed by the *astra*. With Lord Bhrigu on the other side, he is sure to bet that you are using the weapon only as a threat, because you would not want to hurt your own army, which would most certainly be in the zone of radiation exposure.'

'So what is the way forward?'

'The *Pashupatiastra*. It is a weapon designed by Lord Rudra. It has all the power of the *Brahmastra*, but with much greater control. Its destruction is concentrated in the inner circle. Life outside this zone is not impacted at all. In fact, with the *Pashupatiastra*, you can even focus the effect in only one direction, leaving everyone else in the other directions safe. If you threaten to use this weapon, Lord Bhrigu will know that you can destroy Devagiri without endangering your people or the adjoining areas. Then the threat will be credible.'

This made sense. Shiva agreed.

'But you cannot actually use the weapon, Neelkanth,' reiterated the Mithra. 'It will poison the area for centuries. The devastation is unimaginable.'

'I give you my word, Lord Mithra,' said Shiva. 'I will never use these weapons.'

The Mithra smiled. 'Then I have no problems in offering the *Pashupatiastra* to you. I will give the orders immediately.'

Shiva raised his chin as a faint smile played on his lips. 'I think you had already made your decision about this, even before you met me, uncle.'

The Mithra laughed softly. 'I am just Mithra. But you didn't expect it to be so easy, right?'

'No, I didn't.'

'I have heard stories about you, especially about the way you have fought your battles. You have behaved in an exemplary manner until now. Even when you could have gained by doing something wrong, you refrained from doing so. You didn't fall prey to the logic of doing a small wrong for the sake of the greater good; of the ends justifying the means. That takes moral courage. So yes, I had already made up my mind. But I wanted to see you in any case. You will be remembered as the greatest man of our age; generations will look up to you as their God. How could I not want to meet you?'

'I am no God, Lord Mithra,' said an embarrassed Shiva.

'Wasn't it you who had said *"Har Har Mahadev"?* That *all of us are Gods*?'

Shiva laughed. 'You've got me there.'

'We don't become Gods because we think we are Gods,' said the Mithra. 'That is only a sign of ego. We become Gods when we realise that a part of the universal divinity lives within us; when we understand our role in this great world and when we strive to fulfil that role. There is nobody striving harder than you, Lord Neelkanth. That makes you a God. And remember, Gods don't fail. You cannot fail. Remember what your duty is. You have to take Evil out of the equation. You shouldn't destroy all traces of the Somras, for it may become Good in times to come, when it might be required once again. You have to keep the knowledge of the Somras alive. You will also have to create a tribe which will manage the Somras till it is required once again. Once all this is done, your mission will be over.'

'I will not fail, Lord Mithra,' said Shiva. 'I promise.'

'I know you will succeed,' smiled the Mithra, before turning to Gopal. 'Great Chief Vasudev, once the Neelkanth creates his own tribe, the Vayuputras will not remain in charge of fighting Evil anymore. It will be the task of the Neelkanth's tribe. Our relationship with the Vasudevs will become like one between distant relatives rather than the one which has entailed a joint duty towards a common cause.'

'Your relationship with the Vasudevs and with my country will exist forever, Lord Mithra,' said Gopal. 'You have helped us in our hour of need. I'm sure that, in turn, we will help Pariha if it ever needs us.'

'Thank you,' said the Mithra.

Chapter 39

He is One of Us

The Mithra called the entire city to the town centre the following morning. Shiva and Gopal stood next to him as he addressed the crowd.

'My fellow Vayuputras, I'm sure your minds are teeming with many questions and doubts. But this is not the time for that; this is the time for action. We trusted a man who had worked closely with us; we trusted him with our knowledge. But he betrayed us. Lord Bhrigu broke the laws of Lord Rudra. Lord Gopal, the chief of the Vasudevs and the representative of Lord Ram, has come here demanding justice. But, in this moment, it is not just about retribution for what Lord Bhrigu has done. It's also about justice for India, justice to Lord Rudra's principles. There is a purpose that we all serve, Parihans; it is beyond laws; it is one that was defined by Lord Rudra himself.'

Pointing at Shiva, the Mithra continued. 'Behold this man. He may not be a Vayuputra. But he does bear the blue throat. He may not be a Parihan, but he fights like one, with honour and integrity. We may not have recognised him, but the Vasudevs consider him the Neelkanth. He may not have lived amongst us, but he respects and idolises Lord Rudra as much as we do. Above all, he is fighting for Lord Rudra's cause.'

The Vayuputras listened with rapt attention.

'Yes, he is not a Vayuputra, and yet he is one of us. I am supporting him in his battle against Evil. And so shall you.'

Many amongst the Vayuputras were swayed by the Mithra's words. Those who weren't, were nevertheless aware that it was within the Mithra's legal rights to choose whom to support within India. So, while their reasons to do so may have differed, all the Vayuputras fell in line with the Mithra's decision.

Shiva and Gopal received a large crate the following evening. An entire Parihan cavalry platoon had been arranged to transport this incredibly heavy trunk safely back to the sea. Never having seen the material of the *Pashupatiastra*, Shiva assumed from the size of the trunk that they were carrying a huge quantity; probably enough to threaten an entire city. He was therefore amazed by Gopal's clarification that they were carrying only a handful of the *Pashupatiastra* material.

'Are you serious?'

'Yes, Lord Neelkanth,' said Gopal. 'Just a handful is enough to destroy entire cities. The trunk has massive insulation, made of lead and wet clay, besides the leaves of imported bilva trees. Together, these will protect us from exposure to the *Pashupatiastra* radiation.'

'By the Holy Lake,' said Shiva. 'The more I learn about the *daivi astras,* the more I'm convinced that they are the weapons of the demons.'

'They are, my friend. That's why Lord Rudra called them evil and banned their use. That is also why we will not use the *Pashupatiastra.* We'll only threaten to use it. But to make it a credible threat to the Meluhans, we will actually have to set up the weapon outside Devagiri.'

'Do you know how to do that?'

'No, I don't. Most of the Vayuputras are not privy to that knowledge either; only a select few are authorised to be in the know. There is a combination of engineering construction, mantras and other preparations that we would have to follow in order to set up this weapon. We would have to do this properly so as to convey a credible threat to Lord Bhrigu, since he does know how the *Pashupatiastra* is prepared for use. Lord Mithra and his people will commence our training from tomorrow morning.'

— ⚹ —

Parvateshwar moved his attention away from those sitting with him and cast a look outside the window of the Karachapa governor's residence. They were on the *dwitiya* or second platform of the city, and from this height, Parvateshwar had a clear view of the Western Sea, which stretched far into the horizon.

'The sea is the only way we have,' said Parvateshwar.

Bhrigu and Dilipa turned towards Parvateshwar. Dilipa's Ayodhyan army had finally arrived in Meluha, many months after the Battle of Devagiri. They had sailed on to Karachapa to join Parvateshwar's Suryavanshi forces.

'But General, isn't that the entire idea behind coming to Karachapa?' asked Dilipa. 'To attack Lothal by sea? What's new about that idea?'

'I'm not talking about attacking the city, Your Highness.'

While there were now four hundred thousand troops based in Karachapa under the command of Parvateshwar, he knew that it was not really enough to defeat a well-entrenched force of two hundred and fifty thousand in the well-designed citadel of Lothal. And despite all attempts at provocation, Sati had resolutely refused to step out of Lothal, thus giving Parvateshwar no opportunity to bring his numerical superiority into play in an open battlefield. The war had, for all practical purposes, ground to a stalemate.

'Please explain, General,' said Bhrigu, hoping the Meluhan army chief had come up with some brilliant idea to end the stalemate. 'What is your plan?'

'I think we should send forth a fleet towards the Narmada River, making sure that these ships are visible.'

Dilipa frowned. 'Have your spies discovered the route that Lord Shiva took?'

The Meluhans were aware that Shiva and Gopal had sailed to the Narmada, but they had lost track of them thereafter. They assumed that the duo may have used the Narmada route to steal into Panchavati or Ujjain. To what purpose, was still a mystery to the Meluhans.

'No,' answered Parvateshwar.

'Then what's the point of making our ships sail out in that direction? The Neelkanth's scouts and spies will surely get to know that our ships are sailing to the Narmada. We'll lose the element of surprise.'

'That is precisely what I want,' said Parvateshwar. 'We don't want to hide.'

'By the great Lord Brahma!' exclaimed an impressed Bhrigu. 'General Parvateshwar, have you discovered the Narmada route to Panchavati?'

'No, My Lord.'

'Then I don't understand... Oh right...' Bhrigu stopped mid-sentence as he finally understood what Parvateshwar had in mind.

'I'm not aware of the Narmada route to Panchavati,' said Parvateshwar. 'But the Lord Neelkanth's army doesn't know that I don't know. They may assume that we have discovered this precious route and that the Lord's life is in danger. Furthermore, the Nagas are a substantial segment of the warriors in that army. Will they keep quiet in the face of an imminent danger to their capital Panchavati, the city established by their Goddess Bhoomidevi?'

'They will be forced to sail out of Lothal,' said Dilipa.

'Exactly,' said Parvateshwar. 'Since our contingent will be approximately fifty ships, they will have to match our numbers. We will make our ships wait in ambush in a lagoon far beyond the Narmada delta.'

'And once they've begun sailing up the Narmada, we'll charge in from behind and attack them,' said Dilipa.

'No,' said Parvateshwar.

'No?' asked a surprised Dilipa.

'No, Your Highness. I intend to send out a crack team of commandos in advance, to the Narmada. They will wait for the Naga ships to race upriver, till they have travelled a considerable distance away from the sea. Naval movements in a river are constricted, no matter how large the river. Their fleet will be sailing close to each other. Our commandos will have devil boats with firewood and flints ready for our enemies. Our task will be to take out the first as well as last line of ships simultaneously.'

'Brilliant. They will lose their fleet, their soldiers will be adrift. Then our own fleet can charge in from the hidden lagoon and cut their soldiers down.'

'No, Your Highness,' said Parvateshwar, thinking he wouldn't have needed to explain all this to someone with the strategic brilliance of Shiva. 'Our fleet is not going to engage in battle at all. It's only a decoy. Our main attack will be carried out by the commandos. If the first and last line of the enemy ships are set on fire, there's a pretty good chance that all the ships in between too will eventually catch fire.'

'But won't that take too long?' asked Bhrigu. 'Many of

their soldiers would be able to abandon ship and escape onto land.'

'True,' said Parvateshwar. 'But they will be stranded far from their base with no ships. I had learnt at Panchavati that there is no road between Maika-Lothal and the Narmada. It will take them at least six months to march back to Lothal through those dense impenetrable forests. I'm hoping that on seeing the size of our decoy fleet, Sati will commit at least one hundred thousand men to attack us. And with those hundred thousand enemy soldiers stuck in the jungles of the Narmada, our army would become vastly superior numerically; a ratio of almost four to one. We could then attack and probably take Lothal.'

Dilipa still hadn't understood the entire plan. 'But many of our own soldiers will also be in the decoy fleet, right? So we'll have to wait for them to come back to Karachapa and then...'

'I'm not planning on using our decoy fleet to engage in battle,' said Parvateshwar. 'So we're not going to load them up with soldiers. We'll only keep a skeletal staff, enough to set sail. We will not commit more than five thousand men. Imagine what we can achieve. Only five thousand of our men, including the commandos, will leave Karachapa but we would have removed nearly one hundred thousand of the enemy men, leaving them stranded in the jungles around the Narmada, at least six months away from Lothal. And not a single arrow would have been fired. We can then go ahead and easily march in to capture Lothal.'

'Brilliant!' said Bhrigu. 'We will move towards Lothal as soon as our ships leave for the Narmada.'

'No, My Lord,' said Parvateshwar. 'I'm sure Sati has scouts lurking in and around Karachapa. If they see four hundred thousand of our troops marching out of the city, they will know that our ships are thinly manned and will therefore understand our ruse. Our army will have to remain hidden within the walls of Karachapa to convince them that our attack on Panchavati is genuine.'

— ⅄ ◎ Ʊ ⍏ ⊛ —

The customs officer at Karachapa frowned at the merchant ship manifest. 'Cotton from Egypt? Why would any Meluhan want cotton from Egypt? They are no match for our own cotton.'

The customs procedure in Meluha was based on a system of trust. Ship manifests would be accepted at face value and the relevant duty applied. It was also accepted that, on random occasions, a customs officer could cross-check the ship load if he so desired. This was possibly one of those random occasions.

The officer turned to his assistant. 'Go down to the ship hold and check.'

The ship captain looked nervously to his right, at the closed door of the deck cabin, and turned back to the customs officer. 'What is the need for that, Sir? Do you think that I would lie about this? You know that the amount of cotton I have declared matches the maximum carrying capacity of this ship. There is no way you can charge me a higher custom duty. Your search will serve no purpose.'

The Meluhan customs officer looked towards the cabin that the captain had surreptitiously glanced at. The door suddenly swung open and a tall, well-built man stepped out and stretched his arms as he lazily yawned. 'What's the delay, Captain?'

The customs officer held his breath as he recognised the man. He instantly executed a smart Meluhan military salute. 'Brigadier Vidyunmali, I didn't know you were on this ship.'

'Now you know,' said Vidyunmali, yawning once more.

'I'm sorry, My Lord,' said the customs officer, as he immediately handed the manifest back to the captain and ordered his assistant to issue the receipt for the duty payment.

The paperwork was done in no time.

The customs officer started to leave, but then turned back and hesitatingly asked Vidyunmali, 'My Lord, you are one of our greatest warriors. Why isn't our army deploying you at the battlefront?'

Vidyunmali shook his head with a wry grin. 'I'm not a warrior now, officer. I'm a bodyguard. And also, as it now appears, a transporter of royal fashions.'

The customs officer smiled politely, and then hurried off the ship.

— ⁂ —

'Why the delay?' asked the Egyptian.

Vidyunmali had just entered the hold below the lowermost deck, deep in the ship's belly. The only porthole, high in one corner, had been shut tight and it was unnaturally dark. As his eyes adjusted, he was able to see the countenance of about three hundred assassins sitting with cat-like stillness in a huddle.

'Nothing important, Lord Swuth,' said Vidyunmali to the Egyptian. 'A stupid customs officer got it in his head to check the ship's hold. It's been taken care of. We're sailing past Karachapa now. We will be in the heart of Meluha soon. There's no turning back.'

Swuth nodded silently.

'My Lord,' said the captain, as he entered quietly with a shielded torch.

Vidyunmali took the torch from the captain, who was

followed by two men carrying large jute bags. They left the bags next to Vidyunmali.

'Wait outside,' said Vidyunmali.

The captain and his men obeyed. Vidyunmali turned towards the Egyptian.

Swuth was the chief of the shadowy group of Egyptian assassins that Vidyunmali was escorting back to Devagiri. The sweaty heat of the closed ship hold had made Swuth and his assassins strip down to their loincloths. Vidyunmali could see the several battle scars that lined Swuth's body in the dim light of the flaming torch. But it was the numerous tattoos on him that drew his attention. The Meluhan brigadier was familiar with one of them: a black fireball on the bridge of his nose, with rays streaming out in all directions. It was usually the last thing that his hapless victims saw before being butchered. The fireball represented the God that Swuth and his assassins believed in: Aten, the Sun God.

'I thought that Ra was the Sun God for the Egyptians,' said Vidyunmali.

Swuth shook his head. 'Most people call him Ra. But they're wrong. Aten is the correct name. And this symbol,' said Swuth, pointing to the fireball on his nose, 'is his mark.'

'And the jackal tattoo on your arm?' asked Vidyunmali.

'It's not a jackal. It's an animal that looks like a jackal. We call it Sha. This is the mark of the God I am named after.'

Vidyunmali was about to move on to the other tattoos, but Swuth raised his hand.

'I have too many tattoos on my body and too little interest in small talk,' said Swuth. 'You're paying me good money, Brigadier. So I will do your job. You don't need to build a relationship with me to motivate me. Let's talk about what you really want.'

Vidyunmali smiled. It was always a pleasure to work with

professionals. They focused all their attention on the work at hand. The mission that Emperor Daksha had tasked him with was difficult. Any brute could kill, but to kill with so many conditions attached, required professionals. It needed artists who were dedicated to their dark art.

'My apologies,' said Vidyunmali. 'I'll get down to it right away.'

'That would be good,' said Swuth, sarcastically.

'We don't want anybody recognising you.'

Swuth narrowed his eyes, as though he'd just been insulted. 'Nobody ever sees us killing, Brigadier Vidyunmali. More often than not, even our victims don't see us while they're being killed.'

Vidyunmali shook his head. 'But I want you to be seen, only not recognised.'

Swuth frowned.

Vidyunmali walked over to one of the jute bags, opened it and pulled out a large black cloak and a mask. 'I need all of you to wear this. And I want you to be seen as you kill.'

Swuth picked up the cloak and recognised it instantly. It was the garment that the Nagas wore whenever they travelled abroad. He stared at the mask. He was aware that these were worn during Holi celebrations.

Swuth looked at Vidyunmali, his eyes two narrow slits. 'You want people to think the Nagas did it?'

Vidyunmali nodded.

'These cloaks will constrain our movements,' said Swuth. 'And the masks will restrict our vision. We're not trained with these accoutrements.'

'Are you telling me that the warriors of Aten can't do this?'

Swuth took a deep breath. 'Please leave.'

Vidyunmali stared at Swuth, stunned by his insolence.

'Leave,' clarified Swuth, 'so that we can wear these cloaks and practice.'

Vidyunmali smiled and rose.

'Brigadier,' said Swuth. 'Please leave the torch here.'

'Of course,' said Vidyunmali, fixing the torch on its clutch before walking out of the ship hold.

Chapter 40

Ambush on the Narmada

'They aren't coming here?' exclaimed a surprised Sati.

Together with Kali, Ganesh and Kartik, she had been enjoying a family moment accompanied by rounds of sweet saffron milk. They were soon joined by Bhagirath, Chandraketu, Maatali, Brahaspati and Chenardhwaj with some fresh news. The information received earlier from the Vasudevs had suggested that a fleet of nearly fifty ships had sailed out of Karachapa a few weeks back. They had expected them to head for Lothal. But the latest news was that the ships had turned south.

'It looks like they're heading towards the Narmada,' said the Vasudev pandit who had just walked in with the information.

'That can't be!' A panic-stricken Kali looked at Ganesh.

Kali had not agreed with Shiva's tactic of misleading the Meluhans by pretending to go to the Narmada and from there, sailing on to Pariha. She was afraid that this would give the Meluhans a clue as to the possible route to Panchavati. Shiva had dismissed her concerns, saying that Bhrigu knew that the river near Panchavati flowed from west to east, whereas the Narmada flowed east to west; clearly Panchavati was not on the Narmada itself. The Meluhans would know that, even if they sailed up the Narmada, they would have to pass the dense Dandak forests to be able to reach Panchavati. And doing so was fraught with danger without a Naga guide.

Therefore, the news of the Meluhan navy sailing towards the Narmada left Kali with only one logical conclusion: they had discovered the route to Panchavati.

'How would they know the Narmada path to Panchavati?' asked a bewildered Ganesh.

Kali turned on Sati. 'Your husband did not listen to me and stupidly insisted on sailing towards the Narmada.'

'Kali, the Meluhans are in the know of all our goings and comings on the Narmada,' said Sati calmly. 'It is no secret. But they would have no idea how to travel from the Narmada to Panchavati. Shiva has not given anything away.'

'Bullshit!' shouted Kali. 'And it's not just Shiva's fault, it's yours as well. I had told you to kill that traitor, *didi*. You and your misplaced sense of honour will lead to the destruction of my people!'

'*Mausi*,' said Ganesh to Kali, immediately springing to his mother's defence. 'I don't think we should blame *maa* for this. It is entirely possible that it's not General Parvateshwar but Lord Bhrigu who has discovered the Narmada route. After all, he did know the Godavari route, right?'

'Of course, Ganesh,' said Kali sarcastically. 'It's not General Parvateshwar. And it obviously cannot be your beloved mother's fault, either. Why would the most devoted son in the history of mankind think that his mother could make a mistake?'

'Kali...' whispered Sati.

Kali continued her rant. 'Have you forgotten that you are a Naga? That you are the Lord of the People, sworn to protect your tribe to the last drop of your blood?'

Bhagirath decided to step in before things got out of hand. 'Queen Kali, there is no point in going on about how the

Meluhans discovered the Narmada route. What we should be discussing is what are we going to do next? How do we save Panchavati?'

Kali turned to Bhagirath and snapped, 'We don't need to be maharishis to know what needs to be done. Fifty ships will set sail tomorrow with all the Naga warriors on it. The Meluhans will regret the day they decided to attack my people!'

— ⁂ —

Kali, Ganesh and Kartik had assembled at Lothal's circular port along with a hundred thousand men, comprising all the Nagas and many Branga warriors, clambering aboard their ships rapidly. They knew that time was at a premium.

Sati had come to the port to see her family off. She was going to stay in Lothal. She suspected the Meluhans might mount a siege on their city at the same time, to try and take advantage of her divided army.

'Kali...' approached Sati softly.

Kali gave her a withering look and then turned her back on her sister, screaming instructions to her soldiers. 'Board quickly! Hurry up!'

Ganesh and Kartik stepped forward, bent to touch her feet and take their mother's blessings.

'We'll be back soon, *maa*,' said Ganesh, smiling awkwardly.

Sati nodded. 'I'll be waiting.'

'Do you have any instructions for us, *maa*?' asked Kartik.

Sati looked at her sister, who still had her back turned stiffly towards her. 'Take care of your *mausi*.'

Kali heard what Sati said, but refused to respond.

Sati stepped up and touched Kali on her shoulder. 'I'm sorry about General Parvateshwar. I only did what I thought was right.'

Kali stiffened her shoulders. '*Didi,* one who clings to moral arrogance even at the cost of the lives of others, is not necessarily the most moral person.'

Sati remained quiet, staring sadly at Kali's back. She could see Kali's two extra arms on top of her shoulders quivering, a sure sign that the Naga queen was deeply agitated.

Kali turned and glared at her sister. 'My people will not suffer for your addiction to moral glory, *didi*.'

Saying this, Kali stormed off, verbally lashing out at her soldiers to board the ships quickly.

— ⁂ —

Kanakhala couldn't believe what she was hearing. A real shot at peace!

'This is the best news I have heard in a long time, Your Highness,' said Kanakhala.

Daksha smiled genially. 'I hope you understand this has to be kept secret. There are many who do not want peace. They think that the only way to end this is an all-out war.'

Kanakhala looked at Vidyunmali, standing next to Daksha. She had always assumed he was a warmonger. She was surprised to see him agreeing with the Emperor.

Perhaps, thought Kanakhala, *the Emperor is referring to Lord Bhrigu as the one who doesn't want peace with the Neelkanth.*

'We've seen the loss of life and devastation caused by the minor battle that was staged outside Devagiri,' said Daksha. 'It was only Sati's wisdom that stopped it from descending into a massacre that would have hurt both Meluha and the Lord Neelkanth.'

Maybe it's his love for Sati that is forcing the Emperor's hand. He would never allow any harm to come to his daughter. Whatever the reason, I will support him in his peace initiative.

'What are you thinking, Kanakhala?'

'Nothing important, My Lord. I'm just happy that you are willing to discuss peace.'

'You have your work cut out,' said Daksha. 'An entire peace conference has to be organised at short notice. We will name it, in keeping with tradition, after our Prime Minister: the *yagna* of Kanakhala.'

An embarrassed Kanakhala smiled. 'You're most kind, My Lord. But the name doesn't matter. What matters is peace.'

'Yes, peace is paramount. That is why you must take my instruction of secrecy seriously. Under no circumstances should the news of the peace conference reach Karachapa.'

Karachapa was where Lord Bhrigu had stationed himself, along with King Dilipa of Ayodhya and General Parvateshwar.

'Yes, My Lord,' said Kanakhala.

A happy Kanakhala rushed to her office to get down to immediate work.

Daksha waited for the door of his private office to shut before turning to Vidyunmali. 'I hope Swuth and his people will not fail me.'

'They will not, My Lord,' said Vidyunmali. 'Have faith in me. This will be the end of that barbarian from Tibet. Everyone will blame the Nagas. They are perceived as bloodthirsty, irrational killers in any case. No reasonable citizen here has been able to swallow that fraud Neelkanth's championing of the Nagas; just like they didn't accept the freeing of the Vikarmas, regardless of the greatness of Drapaku. The people will readily believe that the Nagas killed him.'

'And my daughter will return to me,' said Daksha. 'She'll have no choice. We will be a family again.'

Delusions create the most compelling of beliefs.

— ⅄ꝏ℧⇞⊗ —

Shiva, Gopal and Tara stood on the foredeck of their merchant ship. The Parihans had helped in loading their precious merchandise onto the vessel. With everyone having said their goodbyes, the Neelkanth had just ordered his ship to set sail on the Jam Sea.

'Scheherazade,' said Gopal, 'how long...'

'Tara, please,' she interrupted the Chief Vasudev.

'Sorry?'

'My name is Tara now, great Vasudev,' said Tara. 'Scheherazade was left behind in Pariha.'

Gopal smiled. 'Of course. My apologies. Tara it is.'

'What was your question?'

'I was wondering how long you'd lived in Pariha.'

'Too long,' said Tara. 'Initially, I had gone on an assignment that Lord Bhrigu had given me. I had thought that it would be a short stay. He had assigned me to work on the *daivi astras* with the Vayuputras and said I could return only when he gave his permission. But after I heard of Brahaspati's death, I saw no reason to return.'

'Well, Brahaspati is not too far off now,' said Gopal kindly. 'Just a couple of weeks more on the Jam Sea and then we will be sailing east on the Western Sea to Lothal and to Brahaspati.'

Tara smiled happily.

'Yes,' said Shiva, playfully cracking a joke on the meaning of Jam. 'But it's all very confusing. The sea that "you come to", will be the sea that "we go from" now! And then we have to travel east on the Western Sea! Only the Holy Lake knows where we'll finally land up!'

Tara raised her eyebrows.

'I know,' said Shiva. 'It's a terrible joke. I guess the law of averages catches up with everyone.'

Tara burst out laughing. 'It's not your joke that astonished me. Though I agree, it really was a terrible joke.'

'Thank you!' laughed Shiva softly. 'But what exactly were you surprised by?'

'I'm assuming you think "Jam" means "to come to".'

Shiva turned to Gopal with a raised eyebrow, for it was the Chief Vasudev who had told him the meaning.

'Doesn't "Jam" mean "to come to"?' asked Gopal.

'That is what everybody thinks,' said Tara. 'Except for the Parihans.'

'What do they believe?' asked Shiva.

'Jam is the Lord of Dharma. So, this sea is actually the Sea of the Lord of Dharma.'

Shiva smiled. 'But in India, the Lord of Dharma...'

'...is Yam,' said Tara, completing Shiva's statement. 'Also the Lord of Death.'

'Exactly.'

'Is there a relationship between the two names: Yam and Jam? Was there a great leader or God called Jam in Pariha?'

'I don't know about any relationship between the names. But in ancient times there was a shepherd called Jam who, blessed by the Ahura Mazda, went on to become a great king, one of the earliest in this area. He spread prosperity and happiness throughout the land. When a great catastrophe was to strike, that would have destroyed the entire world, he is believed to have built an underground city which saved many of his people. The citizens of his realm later began to call him Jamshed.'

'Why "shed"?'

'"Shed" means radiant. So Jamshed means the radiant Lord of Dharma.'

Chapter 41

An Invitation for Peace

Sati, Bhagirath, Chandraketu, Maatali and Brahaspati had collected in the Lothal governor Chenardhwaj's private office. They had just received a visitor from Devagiri with a message from Kanakhala. A message that had left them stunned.

'Peace conference?' asked Bhagirath. 'What deception are they planning?'

'Prince Bhagirath,' rebuked the Lothal governor, Chenardhwaj. 'This is Meluha. Laws are not broken here. And the laws of a peace conference are very clear; they were designed by Lord Ram himself. There is no question of there being any deception.'

'But what about the attack on Panchavati?' asked Maatali, the King of Vaishali. 'They have clearly found the Narmada route to the Naga capital and have sent their ships on an attack mission even as they try to sidetrack us.'

'How is that subterfuge, King Maatali?' asked Chenardhwaj. 'They are at war with us. They found a weak spot and decided to attack. That is how wars are conducted.'

'I don't have a problem with the Meluhans choosing to attack, Governor Chenardhwaj,' said Chandraketu, the King of Branga. 'What is worrying is that they chose to attack Panchavati and call a peace conference at the same time. That sounds fishy to me.'

'I agree,' said Bhagirath. 'Maybe it is a ruse to draw us out of the city with the call for a peace conference and then attack us. Without the protective defences of the Lothal fort, we may well be beaten by the Meluhans.'

'Prince Bhagirath,' said Brahaspati, 'we've also received word that the Meluhan army has still not marched out of Karachapa. If their plan was to trick us out of Lothal, why wouldn't they mobilise their army at the same time?'

Chandraketu nodded. 'That is confusing.'

'Maybe there are divisions within Meluha,' suggested Brahaspati. 'Maybe some people want peace while others want war?'

'We cannot trust this initiative blindly,' said Sati. 'But we cannot ignore it either. If there's a possibility that the Somras can be stopped without any more killing, it is worth grabbing, right?'

'But the message is for Lord Shiva,' said Bhagirath. 'Shouldn't we await his return?'

Sati shook her head. 'That may take months. We don't even know if he has succeeded in convincing the Vayuputras. What if he hasn't? We would then be in a very weak position to negotiate a ban on the Somras. It's a stalemate right now. Even the Meluhans know that. Who knows, we might be able to negotiate good terms at the conference.'

'We could,' said Chandraketu. 'Or we might just march straight into a trap and have our entire army destroyed.'

Sati knew that this was a difficult decision. It couldn't be made in a hurry.

'I need to think about this some more,' she said, ending the discussion.

Sati walked into the heavily guarded room. The visitor from Devagiri, who had carried Kanakhala's message, had been detained in a comfortable section of the Lothal governor's office. While the messenger had been treated well, the windows of his room had been boarded up and the doors kept locked at all times, as abundant caution. He had been blindfolded while being allowed into the city and was led straight to this room. His men had been made to wait outside the city. Sati did not want the peace envoy to take note of the defensive arrangements within the city.

'Your Highness,' said the Meluhan as he rose and saluted Sati. She was still the Princess of Meluha for him.

'Brigadier Mayashrenik,' said Sati with a formal Namaste. She had always thought well of the Arishtanemi brigadier.

Mayashrenik looked towards the door with a frown. 'Isn't the Neelkanth joining us?'

Bhrigu had decided against sharing intelligence with Daksha at Devagiri. It would only cause Daksha's unwelcome interference in war strategies to continue, which Parvateshwar, being a disciplined Meluhan, would find difficult to constantly withstand. Therefore Mayashrenik, like every Meluhan in Devagiri, did not know what Parvateshwar in Karachapa suspected: that Shiva may have sailed up the Narmada and then marched on to Panchavati.

Sati, obviously, didn't want to reveal to Mayashrenik that Shiva was not in Lothal. But she didn't want to lie either. 'No.'

'But...'

'When you speak with me,' said Sati, interrupting him, 'it's as good as speaking with him.'

Mayashrenik frowned. 'Is it that the Lord Neelkanth doesn't want to meet me? Doesn't he want peace? Does he think that destroying Meluha is the only way forward?'

'Shiva does not think that Meluha is evil. Only the Somras

is evil. And of course, he is very willing to sue for peace if Meluha meets just one simple demand: abandon the Somras. '

'Then he must come for the peace conference.'

'That's where the problem lies. How can we believe that Kanakhala's invitation is genuine?'

'Your Highness,' said a stunned Mayashrenik. 'Surely you don't think Meluha would lie about a peace conference. How can we? Lord Ram's laws forbid it.'

'Meluhans may always follow the law, Brigadier. My father doesn't.'

'Your Highness, the Emperor's efforts are genuine.'

'And why should I believe that?'

'I'm sure your spies have already told you that Maharishi Bhrigu is in Karachapa.'

'So?'

'Maharishi Bhrigu is the one who doesn't want any compromise, Your Highness. Your father wants peace. He has an opportunity for it while the Maharishi is away. You know that once your father signs a peace treaty, it will be very difficult for Maharishi Bhrigu to overrule it. Meluha recognises only the Emperor's orders. Even now, while Maharishi Bhrigu may give the orders, they are all issued in the name of the Emperor.'

'You want me to believe that my father has suddenly developed enough character to stand up for what he thinks is right?'

'You are being unfair...'

'Really? Don't you know that he killed my first husband? He has no respect for the law.'

'But he loves you.'

Sati rolled her eyes in disgust. 'Please, Mayashrenik. Do you really expect me to believe that he's pushing for peace because he loves me?'

'He saved your life, Your Highness.'

'What utter nonsense! Have you also fallen for that ridiculous explanation? Do you really believe that my father threw out my Naga child and kept him hidden from me for nearly ninety years so he could "save my life"? No, he didn't. He did it because he wanted to protect his own name; he didn't want people to know that Emperor Daksha has had a Naga grandchild. That is the reason why he broke the law.'

'I'm not talking about what happened ninety years ago, Your Highness. I'm talking about what happened just a few years ago.'

'What?'

'How do you think the alarm went off at Panchavati?'

Sati remained silent, stunned by the revelation.

'The timely triggering of that alarm saved your life.'

'How do you know about that?'

'Lord Bhrigu had sent the ships to destroy Panchavati. But your father sent me to sabotage that operation. I triggered the alarm that saved all of you. I did it on your father's orders. He harmed his empire and his interests in order to protect you.'

Sati stared at Mayashrenik, gobsmacked. 'I don't believe you.'

'It is the truth, Your Highness,' said Mayashrenik. 'You know I don't lie.'

Sati took a deep breath and looked away.

'Even if His Highness is thinking of peace only because of his love for you and not because of his duty towards Meluha, wouldn't our country benefit all the same? Do we really want this war to continue till Meluha is destroyed?'

Sati held her counsel, as she turned towards Mayashrenik.

'Please speak to the Neelkanth, My Lady. He listens to you. The peace offer is genuine.'

Sati didn't say anything.

'May I please have an audience with the Neelkanth, Your Highness?' asked Mayashrenik, still unsure of whether Sati had committed herself to peace.

'No, you may not,' said Sati. 'One of my guards will guide you to the city gates. Go back to Devagiri. I will give serious thought to what you have said.'

— ⁂ —

'We should consider attending the peace conference,' said Sati.

She was in conference with Bhagirath, Brahaspati, Chenardhwaj, Chandraketu and Maatali, at the governor's residence.

'That is not a wise idea, My Lady,' said Bhagirath. 'Only Lord Ram can know what traps they may have set for us.'

'On the contrary, I think it may be very wise. Is there a good possibility that the army in Karachapa doesn't know what my father is doing in Devagiri?'

'It's possible,' said Brahaspati. 'But do you actually think your father is driving the peace conference? Does he have the strength to push his way through?'

'Perhaps it's not him alone. Prime Minister Kanakhala is certainly involved, for one,' said Sati. 'The invitation is in her name.'

'Kanakhala has influence over the Emperor, no doubt,' agreed Chenardhwaj. 'And she is certainly not a warmonger. Her instincts are usually towards peace. Also, she is a devoted follower of the Neelkanth.'

'Does she have the capability to enforce the peace accord?' asked Bhagirath.

'Yes, she does,' said Sati. 'The Meluhan system works on

the principle of written orders. The supreme written order is the one that comes from the Emperor. Lord Bhrigu does not issue orders himself. He asks my father to ratify what he deems fit. If my father issues an order on peace before Lord Bhrigu gets to know of it, all Meluhans will be forced to honour it. So if Prime Minister Kanakhala can get my father to issue the order, she can enforce the peace accord.'

'If we can achieve the objective of removing the Somras without any further bloodshed, it will be a deed that Lord Rudra would be proud of,' said Maatali.

'But we should respond carefully,' persisted a cautious Bhagirath. 'If it is true that peace is being pursued only by Emperor Daksha and Prime Minister Kanakhala, we will put our army at risk if we march out. Karachapa is not very far.'

'Right,' said Sati, with healthy respect for the tactical brilliance of General Parvateshwar. 'If *Pitratulya* in Karachapa hears about our army moving out, he'll assume that we're attacking Devagiri. He'll race out of Karachapa to intercept us at the Saraswati River.'

'Damned if we respond and damned if we don't,' said Chandraketu.

'So what do we do?' asked Chenardhwaj.

'I'll go,' said Sati. 'The rest of you, including the army, should stay within the walls of Lothal.'

'My Lady,' said Maatali. 'That is most unwise. You will need the army's protection to prevent any possible harm to your person in Devagiri.'

'The Meluhans may fight with my army outside Devagiri,' said Sati. 'But they'll not fight me alone. It's my father's house.'

Bhagirath shook his head. 'My apologies, My Lady, but your father has not proved himself to be a paragon of virtue so far. I would be wary of your travelling to Devagiri without protection. We cannot discount the remote possibility that the peace conference is a ruse to draw our leaders to Devagiri and then assassinate them.'

Chenardhwaj was genuinely offended now. 'Prince Bhagirath, I say this for the last time, these things do not happen in Meluha. Arms cannot be used at a peace conference under any circumstances. Those are the rules of Lord Ram. No Meluhan will break the laws of the seventh Vishnu.'

Sati raised her hand, signalling a call for calm, and then turned towards Bhagirath. 'Prince, trust me. My father will never harm me. He loves me. In his own twisted way, he really does care for me. I'm going to Devagiri. This is our best shot at peace. It is my duty to not let it slip by.'

Bhagirath could not shake off his sense of foreboding. 'My Lady, I insist you allow me and an Ayodhyan brigade to travel with you.'

'Your men will be put to better use here, Prince Bhagirath,' said Sati. 'Also, you and your soldiers are Chandravanshis. Please don't misunderstand me, but I would much rather take some Suryavanshis along. After all, I'm going to the Suryavanshi capital. I'll go with Nandi and my personal bodyguards.'

'But, my child,' said Brahaspati, 'that is only one hundred soldiers. Are you sure?'

'It's a peace conference, Brahaspati*ji*,' said Sati. 'Not a battle.'

'But the invitation was for the Lord Neelkanth,' said Chandraketu.

'The Lord Neelkanth has appointed me as his representative, Your Highness,' said Sati. 'I can negotiate on his behalf. I have made up my mind. I am going to Devagiri.'

— ⅄ⵔ⋃⇡⊗ —

'I have a bad feeling about this, My Lady,' pleaded Veerbhadra. 'Please don't go.'

Also assembled in Sati's private chamber were Parshuram and Nandi, whose expressions were equally anguished.

'Veerbhadra, don't worry,' said Sati. 'I will return with a peace treaty that will end the war as well as the reign of the Somras.'

'But why aren't you allowing Veerbhadra and me to accompany you, My Lady?' asked Parshuram. 'Why is only Nandi being given the privilege of travelling with you?'

Sati smiled. 'I would have loved to have the both of you with me; it's just that I'm only taking Suryavanshis, that's all. They're familiar with the Meluhan customs and ways. This is going to be a sensitive conference, anyway. I wouldn't want anything going wrong inadvertently even before it begins.'

'But, My Lady,' continued Parshuram, 'we have sworn to protect you. How can we just let you go without us?'

'I will be with her, Parshuram,' said Nandi. 'Don't worry. I will not let anything happen to Lady Sati.'

'There is absolutely no reason why anything untoward should happen, Nandi. It's a peace conference. If we don't arrive at a peace settlement, the Meluhans will have to allow us to return unharmed. That is Lord Ram's law.'

Veerbhadra continued to brood silently, clearly unconvinced.

Sati reached out and patted Veerbhadra on his shoulder. 'We must make an attempt at peace, you know that. We can save the lives of so many. I have no choice. I must go.'

'You do have a choice,' argued Veerbhadra. 'Don't go yourself. I'm sure you can nominate someone to attend the conference on your behalf.'

Sati shook her head. 'No. I must go. I must... because it was my fault.'

'What?'

'It was my fault that so many of our soldiers died in Devagiri and our elephant corps was destroyed. I'm to blame for the loss of almost our entire cavalry. It is because of me that we do not have enough strength to beat them in an open battle now. Since it is my fault, it is now my responsibility to set it right.'

'The loss in Devagiri was not your fault, My Lady,' said Parshuram. 'Circumstances were aligned against us. In fact, you salvaged a lot from a terrible situation.'

Sati narrowed her eyes. 'If an army loses, it is always because of the general's poor planning. Circumstance is just an excuse for the weak to rationalise their failures. However, I have been given another chance to make up for my blunder. I cannot ignore it. I will not.'

'My Lady,' said Veerbhadra. 'Please listen to me...'

'Bhadra,' said Sati, using the name her husband did for his best friend. 'I am going. I will return unharmed. *And* with a peace treaty.'

Chapter 42

Kanakhala's Choice

The invitation for the peace conference had been accepted.

Kanakhala rushed to Daksha's private office the minute she received a bird courier from Lothal. The door attendant tried to stop her, saying the Emperor had asked him not to let anyone enter.

Kanakhala brushed him aside. 'That order would not have included me. He asked me to meet him as soon as I received this,' said Kanakhala, pointing to a folded letter.

The door attendant moved aside and Kanakhala heard whispers as soon as she opened the door. Vidyunmali and Daksha were speaking softly with each other. She gently shut the door behind her.

'Are you sure they are ready?' asked Daksha.

'Yes, My Lord. Swuth's men have been practising in Naga attire. That fraud Neelkanth won't know what hit him,' said Vidyunmali. 'The world will blame the terrorist Nagas for their beloved Neelkanth's assassination.'

Daksha suddenly stopped him as he noticed a shocked Kanakhala rooted at the entrance. Vidyunmali drew his sword.

Daksha raised his hand. 'Vidyunmali! Calm down. Prime Minister Kanakhala knows where her loyalties lie.'

'Your Highness...' whispered Kanakhala, her eyes wide with terror.

'Kanakhala,' said Daksha with eerie calm, walking up and placing his hands on her shoulders. 'Sometimes an Emperor has got to do what has to be done.'

'But we cannot break Lord Ram's laws,' said Kanakhala, her breathing quickening with nervousness.

'Lord Ram's laws on a peace conference apply to a king, not to his prime minister,' said Daksha.

'But...'

'No buts,' said Daksha. 'Remember your oath. This is war time. You have to do whatever your Emperor asks of you. If you reveal his secrets without his permission, the punishment is death.'

'But, Your Highness... This is wrong.'

'What will be wrong is for you, Kanakhala, to break your vow.'

'Your Highness,' said Vidyunmali. 'This is too risky. I think the Prime Minister should be...'

Daksha interrupted Vidyunmali. 'We're doing no such thing, Vidyunmali. If we don't have her here to organise the conference, Shiva's men will get suspicious the moment they arrive. It is, after all, the "Conference of Kanakhala".'

Kanakhala was speechless with horror.

'You have been loyal to me for decades, Kanakhala,' said Daksha. 'Remember your vows and you will live. You can continue to be prime minister. But if you break them, not only will you be given the death sentence, you will also be damned by the *Parmatma*.'

Kanakhala couldn't utter a word. She knew that the prime ministerial oath also said that if she betrayed her liege, no funeral ceremonies would be conducted for her. According to ancient superstitions, this was a fate worse than death.

Without funeral rituals, her soul would not be able to cross the mythical Vaitarni River to *Pitralok, the land of one's ancestors.* The onward journey of her soul, either towards liberation or to return to earth in another body, would be interrupted. She would exist in the land of the living as a *Pishach,* a *ghost.*

'Remember your vows and do your duty,' said Daksha. 'Focus on the conference.'

— ⁂ —

Kanakhala stood quietly on the terrace outside her home-office. She loved the sound of trickling water from the small fountain in the centre of the chamber. This sound was wafting gently towards her, all the way to the open balcony. It kept her mind focused and calm. She looked up; the sun was already on its way down.

She took a deep breath and looked towards the street. The soldiers weren't even trying to hide. Kanakhala did not feel any anger towards the men who kept watch outside her house. They were good soldiers. They were simply following orders given to them by their commander.

Kanakhala knew it was pointless to try and send a message to Lothal and warn the Neelkanth. She was sure Vidyunmali would have positioned expert archers along the route to bring down any bird courier. Furthermore, it was very possible that the Neelkanth's convoy had already left Lothal. Her only recourse was Parvateshwar. If Lord Bhrigu and he managed to reach Devagiri in time, this travesty that her Emperor and Brigadier Vidyunmali were planning could be stopped. But getting a message to Karachapa wouldn't be easy.

Kanakhala looked at the small message in her hand. She had personally addressed it to the Neelkanth. She rolled the message tightly and slipped it into a small canister attached to a pigeon's leg. She shut the canister, closed her eyes and whispered, 'Forgive me, noble bird. Your sacrifice will aid a greater cause. *Om Brahmaye Namah.'*

Then she threw the bird into the air.

She could immediately sense the soldiers below go into a tizzy. She saw an archer emerging from the rooftop of a building some distance away. He quickly loaded an arrow on to his bow and shot at the pigeon, hitting the bird unerringly. The stricken pigeon dropped like a stone, with the arrow pierced through its body. The soldiers quickly scattered to find the pigeon. The message would be taken to Vidyunmali instantly. It would appear genuine since it was in Kanakhala's handwriting and had been addressed to the Neelkanth.

Kanakhala looked towards the street once again. From the corner of her eye, she saw her servant slip quietly out of the side door, using the temporary distraction of the soldiers with the fallen bird. The servant would release a pigeon outside the city walls, a homing bird set for Karachapa. Kanakhala hoped Bhrigu and Parvateshwar would be able to arrive in Devagiri in time to stop this madness; to prevent this subversion of Lord Ram's laws. Subsequently, the servant had been instructed to ride hard southwards, towards Lothal, and attempt to stop the Neelkanth and his peace negotiators from walking into a trap. Kanakhala had done all that she possibly could.

The Prime Minister sighed. She had broken her vow of loyalty to the Emperor, but she sought solace from an ancient scriptural verse: *Dharma matih udgritah;* dharma is that which is well judged by your mind; think deeply about dharma and your mind will tell you what is right.

In this case, it appeared to Kanakhala that breaking her vows was the right thing to do. For that was the only way to stop an even bigger crime from being committed. But she was no fool. She knew her punishment. She would not give Daksha that pleasure, though.

Kanakhala smiled sadly and walked back into her office. She stopped at her writing desk and picked up a bowl, which contained a clear, greenish medicine that had been prepared recently. She swallowed it quickly. It would numb her pain and make her feel drowsy; exactly what she needed. She ambled up to the fountain. The small pool at the base of the fountain was perfect; deep enough to keep her hand submerged. Clotting would be arrested if the wound was continually washed by flowing water.

She picked up the sharp ceremonial knife that she carried on her person. For one brief moment, she wondered whether she would roam the earth forever as a ghost, if her funeral ceremony was not conducted in accordance with the prescribed rituals. Then she shook her head and dismissed her fears.

Dharmo rakshati rakshitaha; dharma protects those who protect it.

She shut her eyes, balled her left hand into a fist and submerged it in the water. She then took a deep breath and whispered softly, 'Jai Shri Ram.'

In a swift move, she slashed deep, slicing through the veins and arteries on her wrist. Blood burst out in a rapid flood. She rested her head on the side of the fountain and waited for death to take her away.

'It doesn't change the plans at all, Your Highness,' said Vidyunmali.

A stunned Daksha was sitting in his private office, having just received word of Kanakhala's suicide.

'Your Highness,' said Vidyunmali, when he didn't get a response.

'Yes...' said Daksha, still reeling from shock, looking distracted.

'Listen to me,' said Vidyunmali. 'We will go ahead with the plans as before. Swuth's men are ready.'

'Yes...'

'Your Highness!' said Vidyunmali loudly.

Daksha's face suddenly showed some focus as he stared at Vidyunmali.

'Did you hear me, Your Highness?' asked Vidyunmali.

'Yes.'

'Everyone will be told that Kanakhala died in an accident. The peace conference will continue in her memory.'

'Yes.'

'Also, I have to go.'

'What?' Daksha seemed to panic.

'I told you, Your Highness,' said Vidyunmali patiently, as if he was talking to a child. 'One of Kanakhala's servants is missing. I fear he may have set out to warn the fraud Neelkanth. He has to be stopped. I'm going to ride out myself, towards the south, with a platoon.'

'But how will I manage all this?'

'You don't have to do anything. Everything is under control. My soldiers will find a way to bring Princess Sati into the palace. Nobody else from her party will be allowed to accompany her. The moment she is with you, signal my man who will wait at your window. He will shoot a fire arrow high in the air, which will signal to Swuth's assassins that the coast is clear. They will then quickly move in and kill the fraud Neelkanth. They will also leave a few of Shiva's people alive so that they can testify that they were attacked by Nagas.'

Daksha still looked nervous.

Vidyunmali stepped up and spoke gently. 'You don't have to worry. I have planned everything in detail. There will be no mistakes made. All you have to do is signal my man when Princess Sati enters your room. That's it.'

'That's it?'

'Yes, that's it. Now I really need to go, Your Highness. If Kanakhala's man manages to reach the fraud Neelkanth, it will be the end of our plans.'

'Of course. Go.'

— ⁂ —

'Those sons of bitches!' scowled Kali.

Jadav Rana, the ruler of Umbergaon had just rowed up to the Naga fleet in a fast cutter. His small kingdom lay to the south of the Narmada. The Nagas had helped him on many occasions. And, Jadav Rana was not an ungrateful man.

When the fishermen in his kingdom informed him of a large Meluhan fleet stationed in a hidden lagoon nearby, he had gone personally to investigate. Keeping himself concealed, Jadav had seen the massive fleet and immediately surmised that this had something to do with the war raging in the north between the Neelkanth's forces and the Meluhans. He had also received news that the Nagas themselves were racing down the western coast, towards the mouth of the Narmada. He'd immediately got into a fast cutter to intercept the Nagas before they entered the river that marked the southern boundary of the Sapt Sindhu. He was convinced the Meluhans intended to take the Nagas by surprise and attack them from the rear.

'Your Highness,' said Jadav Rana. 'I assumed the Meluhans would enter the Narmada after you and assault your rear guard. They could devastate your entire fleet before you even realised what had happened.'

'I wouldn't be surprised if they have a forward ambush planned for us as well,' said Kartik.

'We'll attack them in their hidden lagoon,' said Kali. 'We'll burn their ships down and hang their rotten carcasses on the coastal trees.'

Ganesh had remained silent till now. Something was amiss. 'Your Highness, how many Meluhans are there?'

'Fifty ships, Lord Ganesh,' said Jadav Rana. 'It's a reasonably large force. But you have more than enough ships to take them on.'

'I didn't ask you about the ships, Your Highness,' said Ganesh. 'I asked how many men...'

Jadav Rana frowned. 'I don't know, Lord Ganesh.' He then turned to his men. 'Do you people have any idea?'

'It's difficult to be sure, My Lord, since they have largely remained on ship,' said one of Jadav Rana's lieutenants. 'But judging by the amount of food they have been foraging, I don't think there would be more than five thousand. You have many more men, Lord Ganesh. You can win very easily.'

Ganesh held his head. 'Bhoomidevi, be merciful.'

A stunned Kali stared at Jadav Rana's lieutenant. 'Are you sure? Just five thousand?'

Jadav Rana was surprised. He didn't understand why the Nagas looked so upset. Logically, they should have been happy. They outnumbered the Meluhans dramatically.

'My men are well acquainted with these coasts, Your Highness,' said Jadav Rana. 'If they're saying that the Meluhans number only five thousand, I would go with that number.'

'We've been taken for a ride,' said Ganesh. 'There's no

attack planned on Panchavati. They were trying to divide our forces. And they succeeded.'

A worried Kartik looked at his elder brother. 'They're probably attacking Lothal even as we speak.'

'And we took a hundred thousand men away from *maa*,' said a distraught Ganesh.

Kali turned and yelled the order at her prime minister, Karkotak. 'Turn around, now! We're going back to Lothal! Double rowing till we get there! MOVE!'

Chapter 43

A Civil Revolt

Bhagirath and Brahaspati had come to the Lothal port, having been informed by an advance boat that Shiva's ship would be arriving soon. They could now see Shiva's merchant ship sailing in from the east, from the vantage position of the port walls. To the south, they could also see the naval contingent that had left under Kali's command, steaming forward. All the ships would probably dock at Lothal at the same time.

Brahaspati took a sharp intake of breath as he saw a woman on the foredeck of Shiva's ship.

Bhagirath couldn't help notice the dramatic transformation in Brahaspati. He turned towards Shiva's ship. They were still quite far, but he could make out the countenance of Shiva and Gopal. Standing next to them was a woman, an Indian-looking woman. But the Ayodhyan prince didn't have the foggiest clue about her identity.

'Who is she, Brahaspati*ji*?' asked Bhagirath.

Brahaspati was crying. 'Oh Lord Brahma! Oh Lord Brahma!'

'Who is she?'

Brahaspati seemed to be delirious now. Delirious but happy! He turned around, rushing down the steps towards the docks. He was rambling in pure delight. 'They let her go! Shiva freed her! Lord Ram be praised, he freed her!'

— ⅄ⓞ𐌵ᛏ⊛ —

'Isn't that Shiva's ship?' said Kali, pointing ahead.

Kali, Ganesh and Kartik had rushed back to Lothal and were surprised to discover that there was no siege on the city at all. They saw the merchant ship just ahead, pulling into the circular port. Fifteen minutes later Kali's ship docked at a berth as well. Shiva's ship was anchored just ahead of theirs. As soon as they got off the gangway plank, they rushed towards Shiva. They could see that Bhagirath and Brahaspati had come to receive the Neelkanth and Gopal. A stunned Brahaspati had just embraced a woman. Both of them were crying profusely.

'Shiva!' shouted Kali from a distance, sprinting towards him.

Shiva turned and smiled at Kali. 'I saw the Naga ships behind us. Where had you gone?'

'We were led on a wild goose chase,' said Kali. 'We were led to believe that Panchavati was under attack.'

'The Meluhan ships were a decoy?' asked Bhagirath.

'Yes, Prince Bhagirath,' said Kartik. 'The ships had only five thousand men. They had no intention of attacking Panchavati.'

'That is good news,' said Bhagirath.

'Where's Sati?' asked Shiva, looking around.

'There's some good news regarding her as well,' said Bhagirath.

'Good news?' asked Ganesh.

'Yes, we may have found a solution to end the war,' said Bhagirath.

'We've come back with a solution as well,' said Gopal, pointing to the large trunk that was being lowered carefully onto the docks from their ship.

Shiva looked again at an obviously delighted Brahaspati who was refusing to let go of Tara. She was crying inconsolably, her head gently nestled against Brahaspati's chest. They appeared like teenagers in the first heady flush of love.

'Looks like there is good news all around,' said Shiva, smiling.

— ⸙ —

'How in the Holy Lake's name can this be good news?'

Bhagirath maintained a nervous silence, fearful of Shiva's wrath.

'But, My Lord,' said Chandraketu, 'Lady Sati believed this was our best chance at peace. And it looks like Emperor Daksha himself wants it. If he signs a peace treaty, then the war is over. And we do not want to destroy Meluha, do we? All we want is the end of the Somras.'

'I don't trust that goat of a man,' said Kali. 'If he hurts my sister, I will burn his entire city to a cinder, with him in it.'

'He won't hurt her, Kali,' said Shiva, shaking his head. 'But I'm afraid that he may make her a prisoner and use that to negotiate with us.'

'But, My Lord,' said Chenardhwaj, 'that is impossible. The rules governing a peace conference are very clear. Both parties are free to return, unharmed, if a solution or compromise is not found.'

'What's to stop my grandfather from not following the laws?' asked Ganesh. 'It will not be the first time he's broken a law.'

'My Lord,' said a Vasudev pandit entering the chamber and addressing Gopal. 'I have urgent news.'

'I think we can talk later, Pandit*ji*,' said Gopal.

'No, My Lord,' insisted the pandit in charge of the Lothal temple. 'We must speak now.'

Gopal was surprised but he knew his Vasudev pandits did not panic unnecessarily. It had to be something important. He rose and walked up to the pandit.

'Lord Ganesh,' said Chenardhwaj, resuming his conversation with Ganesh. 'The peace conference rules were laid down by Lord Ram himself. They are amongst the fundamental rules that can never be amended. They have to be rigorously followed, on pain of a punishment worse than death. Even a man like Emperor Daksha will never break these rules.'

'I pray to the *Parmatma* that you are right, Chenardhwaj,' snarled Kali.

'I have no doubt, Your Highness,' said Chenardhwaj. 'The worst that can happen is that no deal will be struck. Then Lady Sati will return to us.'

'Lord Ram, be merciful,' exclaimed Gopal loudly.

Everyone turned sharply to look at the Chief Vasudev. Gopal was still standing close to the door, along with the Lothal Vasudev pandit.

'What happened, Pandit*ji*?' asked Shiva.

An ashen-faced Gopal turned to Shiva. 'Great Neelkanth, the news is disturbing.'

'What is it?'

'Parvateshwar's army finally mobilised and marched out of Karachapa three days back.'

A loud murmur erupted in the chamber. *They would have to prepare for battle...*

'Silence,' snapped Shiva, before turning to Gopal. 'And?'

'Surprisingly, they turned back within a few hours,' said Gopal.

'Turned back? Why?'

'I don't know,' said Gopal. 'My Vasudev pandit tells me the army has been sent back to the barracks. But Lord Parvateshwar and Lord Bhrigu have pressed on. They set sail up the Indus in a lone fast-ship, with just their personal bodyguards.'

'Where are they going?' asked an alarmed Shiva.

'I have been told that they're rushing towards Devagiri.'

Shiva felt a chill run up his spine.

'And a flurry of birds have been flying out of Karachapa,' said Gopal. 'All of them towards Devagiri. My pandit at Karachapa doesn't know the contents of those messages. But he says he has never seen so much communication between Karachapa and Devagiri.'

There was deathly silence in the chamber. All those present were aware of Parvateshwar's spotless reputation for honourable conduct. If he was rushing to Devagiri without a large army that would slow him down, it only meant that something terrible was going on in the Meluhan capital. And he was rushing to stop it.

Shiva was the first to recover. 'Get the army mobilised immediately. We're marching out.'

'Yes, My Lord,' said Bhagirath, rising quickly.

'And, Bhagirath, I want to leave within hours, not days,' said Shiva.

'Yes, My Lord,' said Bhagirath, hurrying out.

Chandraketu, Chenardhwaj, Maatali, Ganesh and Kartik hastily followed the Ayodhyan prince.

— ⁂ —

'*Maa* will be all right, *baba*,' said Kartik, allowing hope to triumph over confidence.

Shiva and his entourage had stopped for a quick meal, just a few hours outside of Lothal. The Neelkanth had marched out immediately with Kartik, Ganesh, Kali, Gopal, Veerbhadra, Parshuram, Ayurvati and an entire brigade. Their main army, led by Bhagirath, would move out the next morning. Shiva's entire being was wracked with worry. He couldn't wait till the entire army was mobilised. He had taken the *Pashupatiastra* with him, as insurance.

'Kartik is right, great Neelkanth,' said Gopal. 'It's possible that Emperor Daksha may break the rules of a peace conference, but he will not hurt Princess Sati. He may try to imprison her to improve his negotiating position. But we have the *Pashupatiastra*. That changes everything.'

Shiva nodded silently.

Kali listened intently to Gopal. But the words did not give her any solace. She did not trust her father. She was deeply troubled about the safety of her sister. She was consumed with guilt about the petulant way in which she had parted with Sati. The two extra arms on her shoulders were in a constant quiver.

Shiva held Kali's hand and smiled faintly. 'Relax, Kali. Nothing will happen to her. The *Parmatma* will not allow such an injustice.'

Kali was too pained to respond.

'Finish your food,' said Shiva. 'We have to leave in the next few minutes.'

As Kali began gulping down her food, Shiva turned towards Ganesh. The Neelkanth's elder son was staring into the forest, his eyes moist. Ganesh had not touched the food in front of him. Shiva could see he was praying under his breath, his hands clasped tightly, repeating a chant in rapid succession.

'Ganesh,' said Shiva. 'Eat.'

Ganesh was pulled back from his trance. 'I'm not hungry, *baba*.'

'Ganesh!' said Shiva firmly. 'We may have to engage in battle the moment we reach Devagiri. I will require all of you to be strong. And for that you need to eat. So if you love your mother and want to protect her, keep yourself strong. Eat.'

Ganesh nodded and looked at his banana-leaf plate. He had to eat.

Shiva turned towards Veerbhadra, who had already finished and was wiping his hands on a piece of cloth that Krittika had handed to him.

'Bhadra, order the heralds to make an announcement,' said Shiva. 'We'll leave in ten minutes.'

'Yes, Shiva,' said Veerbhadra and rose up immediately.

Shiva pushed his empty banana-leaf plate aside and walked away. He reached the wooden drum where the water was stored, scooped some water out with his hands and gargled.

A chill ran up his spine again. He looked up at the sky, towards the north, about to make a prayer to the Holy Lake. Then he shook his head. It wasn't required.

'He'll not hurt her. He cannot hurt her. If there's one person in this world that that fool loves, it is my Sati. He'll not hurt her.'

— ⅄ⵀ⋃⇡⊛ —

'You are behaving like traitors!' shouted Vraka.

Brigadier Vraka had been ordered by Parvateshwar to mobilise the army quickly and leave for Devagiri. Parvateshwar hadn't told them anything about why they were required in the Meluhan capital and the general himself had rushed out earlier with Maharishi Bhrigu. It had taken Vraka two days to get his soldiers boarded onto ships and begin their journey up the Indus. However, they had been waylaid at Mohan Jo Daro by a non-violent protest.

The governor of the city remained loyal to the emperor, but his people worshipped the Neelkanth. When they heard that their army was sailing up the Indus to battle with the Neelkanth, they decided to rebel. Almost the entire population of Mohan Jo Daro had marched out of the city, boarded their boats and anchored all across the river. The line of boats extended across the massive breadth of the Indus and covered nearly a kilometre in length. It was impossible for Vraka to ram his ships through such an effective blockade.

'We will be traitors to Emperor Daksha,' said the leader of the protestors, 'but we will not be traitors to the Neelkanth!'

Vraka drew his sword. 'I will kill you all if you don't move,' he warned.

'Go ahead. Kill us all. We will not raise our hands. We will not fight against our own army. But I swear by the great Lord Ram, we will not move!'

Vraka snorted in anger. By not fighting with him, the citizens were not giving him a legal reason to attack them. He had been stymied.

Slowly regaining consciousness, Vidyunmali saw that he was lying on a cart that was ambling along on the riverside road. He raised his head. The fresh stitches on his stomach hurt.

'Lie back down, My Lord,' said the soldier. 'You need to rest.'

'Is that traitor dead?' asked Vidyunmali.

'Yes,' said the soldier.

Vidyunmali and his platoon had raced down the riverside road leading from Devagiri to Lothal. They had managed to waylay Kanakhala's servant, who was rushing to Lothal to warn Shiva of the planned perfidy at Devagiri. The servant had been killed, but not before he had managed to stab Vidyunmali viciously in his stomach.

'How far are we from Devagiri?' asked Vidyunmali.

'At the pace we're going, another five days, My Lord.'

'That's too long...'

'You cannot ride a horse, My Lord. The stitches may burst open. You have to travel by bullock cart.'

Vidyunmali cursed under his breath.

Chapter 44

A Princess Returns

Sati and her entourage surveyed the scene from the docked ship in Devagiri. They had commandeered a fast merchant ship and sailed up the Saraswati speedily to reach in time for the peace conference.

Nandi stood beside Sati and gestured at the sky.

'Look,' he said, pointing to a small bird winging its way overhead. 'Another homing pigeon.'

It was not the first that they had spotted. Sati's warriors had seen more than a few pigeons flying in the direction of Devagiri.

'Lord Ganesh believes that eavesdropping can give us good intelligence on the enemy's plan,' said Nandi. 'Shall we shoot one of them and see what is being discussed?'

Sati shook her head. 'We will obey the laws Lord Ram set for us, Nandi, and negotiate in good faith. Lord Ram said that there is no such thing as a small wrong. Understanding your opponent's strategy prior to peace negotiations, through the use of subterfuge, will give us only a small advantage. But to behave without honour is against Lord Ram's way.'

Nandi bowed his head in Sati's direction. 'I'm Lord Ram's servant, Princess.'

Sati turned away, and Nandi glanced one last time at the tiny speck of a bird disappearing into Devagiri.

The docks of the port had been completely cleared out, with no sign of commerce or any other activity. From the vantage point of her ship deck, Sati could see the walls of Devagiri in the distance. She remembered that there were those who lovingly called the city Tripura, in honour of its three platforms named after Gold, Silver and Bronze. But the name had never really caught on. The citizens of Devagiri couldn't imagine tampering with the name that Lord Ram himself had given it.

With a loud thud, the gangway plank was lowered onto the dock.

Sati signalled to Nandi and whispered, 'Let's go.'

As she began leading her men out, a Meluhan protocol officer walked up to her, a broad smile plastered on his face. The Meluhan noticed Sati's disfigured left cheek, but wisely refrained from commenting on it. 'My Lady, it's an honour to meet you once again.'

'It's a pleasure to be back in my city, Major. And in better circumstances this time.'

The Meluhan acknowledged the reference with a solemn nod.

'I hope you will succeed in negotiating a lasting peace, My Lady,' said the Meluhan. 'You can't imagine how distressed we Meluhans are that our country is at war with our living God.'

'With Lord Ram's blessing, the war will end. And we shall have lasting peace.'

The Meluhan joined his hands together and looked up at the sky. 'With Lord Ram's blessing.'

Sati stepped out of the port area to find a large circular building that had been quickly constructed for the proceedings of the peace conference. One of the rules laid down for a peace conference was that it couldn't take place within the host city itself. The current venue was at a healthy distance from the city walls, almost adjacent to the port. The peace conference building had been constructed on a large rectangular base of standard Meluhan bricks, almost a metre high. Tall wooden columns had been hammered into holes on top of this base. The columns served as the skeleton for the structure. Smaller bamboo sticks had been tied together and stretched across these poles, creating an enclosed circular wooden building that was surprisingly strong despite no mortar having been used in its construction.

Sati looked up at the high ceiling as soon as she entered the structure and spoke loudly to check the acoustics. 'Good construction.'

The sound did not reverberate. Sati smiled. Meluhan engineers had not lost their talent.

A large idol of Lord Ram and Lady Sita had been placed near the entrance of this cavernous chamber. From the flowers and other oblations scattered around the idols, Sati knew that the chief priest of Devagiri had conducted the *Pran Prathishtha* ceremony; *the life force of the two deities had been infused into the idols.* A true Hindu would, therefore, believe that Lord Ram and Lady Sita themselves were residing in the idols and were supervising the proceedings. Nobody would dare to break the law in their presence. A separate enclosure had been walled off at one end; there was a large wooden door in the middle. The room within had been completely sound-proofed so that even the most raucous sounds would not be able to travel beyond its walls. It had been set aside for private internal discussions for either party during the course of the conference.

Sati nodded. 'The arrangements are precisely in keeping with the ancient laws.'

'Thank you, My Lady,' said the Meluhan.

'Now the armoury,' said Sati.

'Of course, My Lady,' said the Meluhan. 'We can leave right away.'

As she stepped out of the conference hall, she saw her horse tethered outside. It had been unloaded from her ship and was saddled up and ready. The horses of her companions had been similarly saddled, girthed and groomed.

'My Lady,' said the Meluhan. 'You do know that according to the laws, the animals will also need to be locked up next to the armoury. All your horses will be taken away.'

'All except mine,' said Sati. Very few were more well-versed with the laws of Lord Ram than her. The leader of the visitors was allowed to keep his or her horse. 'My horse remains with me.'

'Of course, My Lady.'

'And the horses of my men will be returned as soon as the conference is over.'

'That is the law, My Lady.'

'And the animals within Devagiri would also be locked up.'

'Of course, My Lady,' said the Meluhan. 'That has already been done.'

'All right,' said Sati. 'Let's go.'

— ⋯ —

The temporary armoury had been built outside the city walls under the connecting bridge between the Svarna and Tamra platforms, once again, to exact specifications. A massive door with a double lock had been built at the entryway, making it almost impossible to break into. One of the keys was handed over to Sati, who personally checked that the door was locked. The Meluhan protocol officer used his key to double-lock the door, allowed Sati to check it again, and then fixed a seal on top of the lock. All the weapons in Devagiri had been effectively put out of reach.

Sati handed over her key to Nandi. 'Keep this carefully.'

Bowing and turning to leave, the officer hesitated, as if remembering something. 'My Lady, your weapons? Aren't they supposed to be locked in here as well?'

'No,' said Sati.

'Umm, My Lady, but the rules state that...'

'What the rules say, Major,' interrupted Sati, 'is that the armies have to be disarmed. But the personal bodyguards and the leaders at the peace conference are allowed to retain their weapons. I'm sure my father's bodyguards have not been disarmed, have they?'

'No, My Lady,' replied the Meluhan protocol officer, 'they still hold their weapons.'

'As will my bodyguards,' said Sati, pointing to Nandi and her other soldiers.

'But, My Lady...'

'Why don't you check with Prime Minister Kanakhala? I'm sure she will know the law...'

The Meluhan protocol officer didn't say anything further. He knew that Sati was legally correct. He also knew that Prime Minister Kanakhala could not be called upon for any clarifications. Meanwhile, Sati was looking at the giant animal enclosure a few hundred metres away. The horses of her men were being led in there for a temporary sequester.

'Also, My Lady,' said the protocol officer, 'Emperor Daksha has made a request for your presence at his palace for lunch.'

Sati turned towards Nandi. 'I'll ride ahead. You check the lock on the animal enclosures and then join me in...'

'My Lady,' said the officer, interrupting Sati. 'The instructions were very clear. He wanted you to come alone.'

Sati frowned. This was unorthodox. She was about to reject the suggestion when the officer spoke up again. 'My Lady, I don't think this has anything to do with the conference. You are His Highness' daughter. A father has the right to expect that he can have a meal with his daughter.'

Sati took a deep breath. She was in no mood to break bread with her father. But she would dearly like to meet her mother. In any case, the conference was scheduled for the following day. There was nothing much to do today. 'Nandi, once you have checked the enclosure, go back to the conference building and wait for me. I'll be back soon.'

'As you command, My Lady,' said Nandi. 'But may I have a word with you before you leave?'

'Of course,' said Sati.

'In private, My Lady,' said Nandi.

Sati frowned, but left the reins of her horse in the hands of a soldier standing discreetly at the back, and then walked aside.

When they were out of earshot, Nandi whispered, 'If I may be so bold as to make a suggestion, My Lady, please don't think you are going to meet your father. Think instead that you are going to meet the emperor with whom you will be negotiating. Please use this lunch as an opportunity to set the right atmosphere for the peace conference tomorrow.'

Sati smiled. 'You are right, Nandi.'

Sati tied her horse at the stables near the palace steps, refusing the proffered assistance of the attendant. Owing to the peace conference, there were no animals in Devagiri so Sati's was the only horse present. As she approached the main steps of her father's palace, the guards in attendance executed a smart military salute. Sati saluted back politely and continued walking.

She had grown up in this palace, sauntered around its attached gardens, run up and down the steps a million times, practised the fine art of swordsmanship on its grounds. Yet, the building felt alien to her now. Maybe it was because she had been away for so many years. Or more likely, it was because she didn't feel any kinship with her father anymore.

She knew her way around the palace and did not need the aid of the various soldiers who kept emerging to guide her onward. She was surprised though that she couldn't recognise any of them. Perhaps Vidyunmali had changed the troops after taking over her father's security. She waved the soldiers away repeatedly, walking unerringly towards her father's chamber.

'Her Highness, Princess Sati!' announced the chief doorman loudly as one of his lieutenants opened the door to the royal chamber.

Sati walked in to find Daksha, Veerini and a man she didn't recognise, who stood at the far end of the chamber. Judging by his arm band, he was a colonel in the Meluhan army.

As she turned towards her parents, the Meluhan colonel looked out of the window and imperceptibly nodded at someone standing outside.

'By the great Lord Ram, what happened to your face?' exclaimed Daksha.

Sati folded her hands together into a Namaste and bowed low, showing respect, as she must, to her father. 'It's nothing, father. Just a mark of war.'

'A warrior bears her scars with pride,' said the Meluhan colonel congenially, his hands held together in a respectful Namaste.

Sati looked at the Meluhan quizzically as she returned his Namaste. 'I'm afraid I don't know you, Colonel.'

'I've been newly assigned, My Lady,' said the Meluhan colonel. 'I have served as second-in-command to Brigadier Vidyunmali. My name is Kamalaksh.'

Sati had never really liked Vidyunmali. But that was no reason to dislike Kamalaksh. She nodded politely at the Meluhan colonel, before turning to her mother with a warm smile. 'How are you, *maa*?'

Sati had never addressed Veerini by the more affectionate '*maa*'. She'd always used the formal term 'mother'. But Veerini liked this change. She walked up and embraced her daughter. 'My child...'

Sati held her mother tight. Years spent with Shiva had broken the mould. She could now freely express her pent-up feelings.

'I've missed you, my child,' whispered Veerini.

'I've missed you too, *maa*,' said Sati, her eyes moist.

Veerini touched Sati's scar and bit her lip.

'It's all right,' said Sati, with a slight smile. 'It doesn't hurt.'

'Why don't you get Ayurvati to remove it?' asked Veerini.

'I will, *maa*,' said Sati. 'But the beauty of my face is not important. What is important is to find a way towards peace.'

'I hope Lord Ram helps your father and the Neelkanth to do so,' said Veerini.

Daksha smiled broadly. 'I have already found a way, Sati. And we'll all be together once again; a happy family, like before. By the way, I hope the Neelkanth didn't mind waiting in the camp outside. After all, it would not be considered a good omen for us to meet before the peace conference.'

Sati frowned at her father's strange suggestion that all of them would be living together 'as a family' once again. She was about to clarify that Shiva had not come with her to Devagiri, but Daksha turned to Kamalaksh.

'Order the attendants to bring in lunch. I'm famished. As I'm sure are the women in my family,' said Daksha.

'Of course, My Lord.'

Veerini was still holding Sati's hand. 'It is sad that Ayurvati wasn't here last week.'

'Why?' asked Sati.

'Had she been here, she would certainly have saved Kanakhala. Nobody has the medical skills that she possesses.'

From the corner of her eye, Sati could see Daksha's body stiffen. 'Veerini, you talk too much. We need to eat and...'

'One moment, father,' said Sati, turning back to her mother. 'What happened to Kanakhala?'

'Didn't you know?' asked a surprised Veerini. 'She died suddenly. I believe there was some kind of accident in her house.'

'Accident?' asked a suspicious Sati, whirling around to face Daksha. 'What happened to her, father?'

'It was an accident, Sati,' said Daksha. 'You don't need to make a mountain of every mole hill...'

On seeing Daksha's evasive reaction to Sati's question, Veerini got suspicious as well. 'What's going on, Daksha?'

'Will you two please give it a rest? We've come together for a meal after a very long time. So let us just enjoy this moment.'

'Everything will be fine soon, Princess,' said Kamalaksh, in a soft voice.

Sati did not turn her attention to Kamalaksh. But there was something creepy in his voice. Her instincts kicked in.

'Father, what are you hiding?'

'Oh, for Lord Ram's sake!' said Daksha. 'If you are so worried about your husband, I'll have some special food sent out for him as well!'

'I did not mention Shiva,' said Sati. 'You are avoiding my question. What happened to Kanakhala?'

Daksha cursed in frustration, slamming his fist on a desk. 'Will you trust your father for once? My blood runs in your veins. Would I ever do anything that is not in your interest? If I say Kanakhala died in an accident, then that is what happened.'

Sati stared into her father's eyes. 'You're lying.'

'Kanakhala got what she deserved, Princess,' said Kamalaksh, from directly behind her. 'As will everyone who dares to oppose the true Lord of Meluha. But you don't need to worry. You are safe because your father adores you.'

A stunned Sati glanced back briefly towards Kamalaksh and then turned to her father.

Daksha's eyes were moist as he spoke with a wry smile. 'If only you'd understand how much I love you, my child. Just trust me. I will make everything all right once again.'

Almost imperceptibly, Sati tensed her muscular frame and shot her right elbow back into Kamalaksh's solar plexus. The surprised colonel staggered back as he bent over with pain, thus bringing his head within her range. Losing no time, Sati sprung onto her left foot and swung her right leg in a great arc, a lethal strike that she had learnt from the Nagas. Her right heel crashed with brutal force into Kamalaksh's head, right between his ear and temple. It burst his ear drum and rendered him unconscious. The giant frame of the Colonel came crashing down onto the floor. Sati swung full circle in the same smooth motion and faced Daksha again. Quick as lightning, she drew her sword and pointed it at her father.

It all happened so quickly that Daksha had had no time to react.

'What have you done, father?' screamed Sati, her anger at boiling point.

'It's for your own good!' shrieked Daksha. 'Your husband will not trouble us anymore.'

Sati finally understood. 'Lord Ram, be merciful... Nandi and my soldiers...'

'My God!' cried Veerini, moving towards him. 'What have you done, Daksha?'

'Shut up, Veerini!' screamed Daksha, as he shoved her aside and rushed towards Sati.

Veerini was in shock. 'How could you break the laws of a peace conference? You have damned your soul forever!'

'You can't go out!' shouted Daksha, trying to get a hold of Sati.

Sati pushed Daksha hard, causing the emperor to fall on the floor. She turned and ran towards the door, her sword held tight in her hand, ready for battle.

'Stop her!' yelled Daksha. 'Guards! Stop her!'

The doorman opened the door, stunned to see the princess sprinting towards him. The guards at the door were immobilised by shock.

'Stop her!' bellowed Daksha.

Before the guards could react, Sati crashed into them, pushed them aside and burst through the door. She raced down the main corridor. She could still hear her father screaming repeatedly for his guards to stop her. She had to get to her horse. No one else was in possession of one in Devagiri at this time. Were she able to do so, she could easily speed past all the guards and ride out of the city.

'Stop the Princess!' screamed a guard from behind.

Sati saw a platoon of guards taking position up ahead. They held their spears out, blocking the way. She looked behind her without slowing down. Another platoon of soldiers was running towards her from the other end. She was trapped.

Lord Ram, give me strength!

Sati heard Daksha's distant voice. 'Don't hurt her!'

A window to the left was open, up ahead. She was on the third floor. It would be foolish to jump. But she knew this palace well; it had been home. She knew that there was a thin ledge above the window. A short jump from there would land her on the palace terrace. Thereafter, she could race away from a side entrance towards the palace gate before anyone would be able to reach her.

Sati sheathed her sword and raised her hands, as if in surrender. The soldiers thought they had her and moved forward, slowing their gait so as to calm the princess' nerves. Sati suddenly jumped to her side, and was out of the window in a flash. The soldiers gasped, thinking the princess had fallen to a certain death into the courtyard below. But Sati had stretched her hands out simultaneously and used the momentum to jump up, grab the edge of the protruding ledge, swing upwards, and then land safely on top of the ledge in a half-flip. She took a moment to balance herself. She then took a couple of quick steps and leapt onto the terrace.

'She's on the terrace!' screamed a soldier.

Sati knew the path the soldiers would take. She quickly ran the other way, towards the far end of the terrace, jumping onto another ledge. She crept along the ledge till she reached another terrace, leapt onto it and sprinted towards the staircase on the far side. She charged down the stairs, three steps at a time, till she reached the landing above the first floor, which led to a side entrance. While this entrance was usually not guarded, she didn't want to take a chance. She leapt out of the balcony into the small garden at the side. There was a tree right next to the wall. She clambered onto the tree, reached its highest branch and used the elevation to jump over the boundary wall. She landed right next to her horse. In one leap, she mounted her horse, freed its reins and kicked the animal into motion.

'There she is!' shouted a guard.

Twenty guards rushed towards Sati, but she pushed through, refusing to slow down. Her horse galloped out of the palace enclosure and within seconds she was out into the city. She could hear the distant shouts of the guards screaming and swearing behind her.

'Stop her!'

'Stop the Princess!'

Startled Meluhans scrambled out of the way to escape the flaying hooves of Sati's steed. She turned into a small lane to avoid a big crowd of citizens up ahead, and came out of a different access road which led straight to the city's main gates. She rode hard, pushing her horse to its limit and was through the iron gates in no time. As soon as she crossed to the other side, her horse reared ferociously onto its hind legs, disturbed by loud noises of battle in the distance.

From the vantage point of the Devagiri city platform, Sati had a clear view of the venue of the peace conference, right next to the Saraswati, nearly four kilometres away. Her people were under attack. A large number of cloaked and hooded men were battling Nandi and his vastly outnumbered soldiers, many of whom already lay on the ground.

'Hyaaah!' Sati kicked her horse hard, goading it into a swift gallop.

She raced down the central steps of the Svarna platform of Devagiri, straight towards the battling men, screaming the war cry of those loyal to the Neelkanth.

'Har Har Mahadev!'

Chapter 45

The Final Kill

As she sped towards the battleground, Sati could estimate that there were almost three hundred cloaked assassins. They wore masks, just like the Nagas. But their battle style was nothing like the warriors from Panchavati. They were obviously some other group, being made to look like the Nagas. Nearly half of Sati's one hundred bodyguards were already on the ground, either grievously injured or dead.

Since the assassins and her soldiers were completely locked in combat, there was no clear line of enemies whom she could ride her horse into and mow down. She knew she'd have to dismount and fight. As she neared the battle scene, she rode towards the area where Nandi was combating three assassins simultaneously.

She heard Nandi's loud scream as he brutally drove his sword into his enemy's heart. He turned to his left, easily lifted the diminutive assassin impaled on his sword, and flung the hapless soul's body onto an oncoming attacker. Another assassin had moved up to Nandi, ready to slash him from behind.

Sati pulled her feet out of the stirrups, jumped up and leveraged herself to crouch on top of her saddle, even as she drew her sword out. As she neared the assassin who was about to slash Nandi from the rear, she flung herself from her horse and swung her sword viciously at the same time, decapitating the assassin in one fell swoop. Sati landed on her side and smoothly rolled over to stand behind Nandi as the quivering body of the beheaded assassin collapsed to the ground, blood bursting through, his adrenalised heart pumping the life-giving fluid furiously out of his gaping neck.

'My Lady!' yelled Nandi over the din, slashing hard at another assassin in front. 'Run!'

Sati stood steadfast, defensively back-to-back with Nandi, covering all angles. 'Not without all of you!'

An assassin leapt at Sati from the side, as she pulled her shield forward. He reached into the folds of his robe and threw something at her eyes. Instinctively, she pulled her shield up. A black egg splattered against her shield, deflecting its contents – shards of metal – safely away from her eyes. Some of the shrapnel cut through her left arm.

Sati had heard of this combat manoeuvre; it was Egyptian. Eggs were drained of their contents through a small hole and then filled with bits and pieces of sharp metal. These were flung at the eyes of enemies, thus blinding them. Usually the next move was a low sword thrust. Though her vision was blocked by her shield, Sati moved instinctively and swerved to her side, to avoid the expected low blow. Then she pressed a lever on her shield, extending a short blade which she rammed into her opponent's neck, ferociously driving the blade through his windpipe. As the assassin began to choke on his own blood, Sati ran her sword through his heart.

Nandi, meanwhile, was effortlessly killing all those in front of him. He was a big man, and he towered over the diminutive Egyptians like a giant. Not one of the assassins could even come close as he hacked through anyone who dared to challenge him. They threw knives and the modified eggs at him. But nothing got through to any vital part of his body. With a knife buried in his shoulder and numerous metallic shrapnel pierced all over his body, a bloodied Nandi fought relentlessly against his enemies. But both Nandi and Sati could see that the odds were stacked heavily against them. Most of their soldiers were falling, overwhelmed by the surprise attack and the sheer numbers. Escape wasn't an option either, as they were now surrounded on all sides. Their only hope was that other Suryavanshis in Devagiri, who were not part of Daksha's conspiracy, would come to their aid.

An assassin swung at Sati from a high angle on the right. She swung back with vicious force, blocking his blow. The man turned and swerved from the left this time, hoping to push Sati on her back foot. Sati met his strike with equal ferocity. The assassin then attempted to drop low and stab Sati through her abdomen, but he was unaware of her special technique.

Most warriors can only swing their sword in the natural direction, away from their body. Very few can swing it towards their own body, because of a lack of strength and skill. Sati could. Hence, both the inner and the outer sides of her sword were sharpened, unlike the vast majority of swords which only have sharpened outer edges. Sati swung back, and with a near impossible stroke, masterfully pulled her sword arm towards herself with tremendous force. The surprised assassin had his throat cut cleanly before he could respond. The wound was deep, almost beheading the man. The Egyptian's head fell backwards, dangling tenuously from his body by a shred of tissue, his eyes still rolling in his head. Sati kicked his body away as it collapsed.

She saw movement on her left and realised her mistake too late. She tried to block the sword stroke from the second assassin but it glanced off her sword, and went up into her scarred left cheek, cutting through her eye and grating off her skull. Her left eye collapsed in its socket, and blood poured from the wound, obscuring the vision in her other eye. Blinded, she executed a desperate defensive block, hoping to ward off any blows while she tried to wipe the blood from her face. She heard a woman panting, almost sobbing and realised that it was she herself. She braced as the man moved forward for a second attack.

She detected a movement from the right, and through her pinkish blurred vision, she saw Nandi swing from his massive height, beheading the assassin in one fell swoop.

'My Lady!' screamed Nandi, pulling his shield forward to protect himself from another assassin's blow. 'Run!'

The world had slowed around her, and his voice came to her as if from a great distance. She could hear her own heart beating; hear her breath gasping as she gazed at the carnage. The bodies of her guards lay bloodied and broken at her feet. Some of the fallen still lived, reaching and clawing at the legs of the attackers in desperation, until they were kicked aside in annoyance, their lives finished with half-distracted sword-strokes of irritation.

My arrogance, a voice whispered in her head. *I have failed them. Again.*

Her brain had blocked out the throbbing in her mutilated eye. She spat out the blood streaking down her face and into her mouth. Using her good right eye, she swung back into battle. Stepping back to avoid a brutal stab from another assassin, she slashed her sword from the right and sliced through his hand. As the Egyptian howled in pain, Sati rammed her shield into his head, cracking open his skull. She stabbed the staggering assassin in his eye, pulled her sword back quickly and turned to face another.

The assassin flung a knife across the distance. It cut through Sati's upper left arm, getting stuck in her biceps, restricting the movement of her defensive limb. Sati snarled in fury and swung her sword viciously across the assassin's body, cutting through the cloak and slashing deep into his chest. As the man staggered back, Sati delivered the killer blow, a stab straight through his heart. But the flow of assassins was unrelenting. Another one ran in to battle Sati. Using sheer will to overpower her tiring body, Sati raised her blood-drenched sword once again.

Swuth was observing the battle from a short distance away. His orders had been to ensure the death of the one they called Neelkanth. Surely he was the tall one, the powerful warrior, cutting down all his opponents with such ease. Swuth moved into the fray, striding towards the embattled Nandi.

Nandi looked up and turned to face his new opponent, swinging his sword fiercely at Swuth's blade. The Egyptian stepped back, his hand stinging with the force of Nandi's blow. Swuth dropped his sword and drew out two curved blades, something he kept for special occasions. Nandi had never seen swords such as these. They were short, a little less than two-thirds the length of his own sword. They curved in sharply at their edges, almost like hooks. The hilts of the swords were also peculiar, since most of it was made of uncovered metal, instead of being enveloped in leather or wood. A sword fighter would have to be very skilled not to cut himself while holding such swords, for the handles were also unsheathed sharp metal.

Swuth was no amateur. He swung both swords in a circular motion skilfully and with frightening speed. Nandi, never having seen swords and a battle style such as this, was naturally cautious and kept his shield held high. He waited for the Egyptian to move in, while keeping a safe distance at the same time. Using the attention that Nandi had focused on Swuth, and Sati's distraction with battling the assassin on her side, an Egyptian moved in suddenly and slashed Nandi's back viciously with his sword. Nandi roared with fury as his body lurched forward in reaction to the excruciatingly painful wound.

Swuth used this moment to suddenly hook his left sword onto his right blade, thus extending its reach two-fold, and swung hard from a low angle, aiming a little below Nandi's defensive shield. The sharp edge on the metallic hilt sliced through Nandi's left arm, severing it cleanly, a few inches above his wrist. The Suryavanshi bellowed in pain as blood burst from his slashed limb, the shock of the massive blow causing his heart to pump furiously. Swuth stepped close to a paralysed Nandi and slashed at his right arm, hacking the sword-bearing limb just below the elbow. The mighty Suryavanshi, with blood bursting forth from both his severed limbs, collapsed on the ground. Swuth spat as he kicked both of Nandi's hacked hands away.

'Damn!' cursed Swuth as he wiped some of his spittle that had got stuck on the Naga mask that he wasn't used to wearing. But he was careful enough to curse in Sanskrit. He had strictly forbidden his people from speaking in their native Egyptian tongue. The charade of their being Nagas had to be strictly maintained.

'Nandi!' screamed Sati, as she swirled around and thrust her sword at Swuth.

Swuth moved aside, easily avoiding her attack. Another assassin swung his sword from behind Sati, cutting through her upper back and left shoulder.

'Wait!' said Swuth, as two of his men were about to plunge their swords into her heart.

The assassins immediately held Sati's arms, awaiting Swuth's instructions. The leader did not want to sully his tongue by speaking to a woman; a sex that he believed was far beneath men, only a little better than animals.

'Ask her who the blue-throated Lord is.'

One of his assistants looked at Sati and repeated Swuth's question.

A shocked Sati did not hear them. She continued to stare at Nandi, lying prone on the ground, losing blood at an alarming rate from his severed limbs. But the unconscious Suryavanshi was still breathing. She knew that since the wounds were only on the limbs, the blood loss would not be so severe as to cause immediate death. If she managed to keep him alive for some more time, expert medical help could still save him.

'Is this the blue-throated Lord?' asked Swuth, pointing at Nandi.

Swuth's assistant repeated his question to Sati. But Sati was looking towards the gates of Devagiri from the corner of her eye. She could see people at the top of the platform running towards her. They would probably reach in another ten to fifteen minutes. She had to keep Nandi alive for that much time.

Swuth shook his head when he did not get any response from Sati. 'A curse of Aten on these stupid baby-producing machines!'

Sati stared at Swuth, catching on to his mistake in swearing in his own God's name, sure at last of his identity. He was an Egyptian; an assassin of the cult of Aten. She had learnt about their culture in her youth. She knew immediately what she had to do.

Swuth pointed at Nandi and turned to his men. 'Behead this fat giant. He must be the blue-throated Lord. Leave the other injured alive. They will bear witness that they were attacked by the Nagas. And collect our dead. We'll leave immediately.'

'He's not the blue-throated one,' spat Sati. 'Can't you see his neck, you Egyptian idiot?'

The Egyptian holding Sati hit her hard across her face.

Swuth sniggered.

'Leave the giant alive,' said Swuth, before turning to one of his fighters. 'Qa'a, torture this hag before you kill her.'

'With pleasure, My Lord,' smiled Qa'a, who was not the best of assassins, but an expert in the fine art of torture.

Swuth turned to his other men. 'How many times do I have to repeat myself, you putrid remains of a camel's dung? Start gathering our dead. We leave in a few moments.'

As Swuth's assassins started implementing his order, Qa'a moved towards Sati, returning his blood-streaked sword to its scabbard. He then pulled out a knife. A smaller blade always made torture much easier.

Sati suddenly straightened up and shouted loudly, 'The duel of Aten!'

Qa'a stopped in his tracks, stunned. Swuth stared at Sati, surprised beyond measure. The duel of Aten was an ancient code of the Egyptian assassins, wherein anyone could challenge them to a duel. They were honour-bound to engage in the duel. It could only be a one-on-one fight; multiple assassins could not attack or they would suffer the wrath of their fiery Sun God – an everlasting curse from Aten.

Qa'a turned towards Swuth, unsure.

Swuth stared at Qa'a. 'You know the law.'

Qa'a nodded, throwing his knife away. He drew his sword, pulled his shield forward, and waited.

Sati wrenched herself free from the assassins who were holding her. She bent down and ripped out some cloth from a fallen assassin's cloak, tying the strip of cloth across her face, covering her mutilated eye in an effort to stem the blood from flowing across her face. She hoped this would give her unimpeded vision and not disturb the good eye. Then she slowly pulled out the knife buried in her upper arm and tied another strip of cloth around the injury, using her teeth to tighten the bind.

She then drew her sword and held her shield high. Ready. Waiting.

Qa'a suddenly threw his shield away. All the assassins standing around burst out laughing and began to clap. Clearly, Qa'a was taunting Sati, suggesting that he didn't even need his shield to combat a stupid woman. Much to Qa'a's surprise, Sati threw her shield away as well.

Qa'a bellowed loudly and charged, swinging his sword at a high angle. Sati smoothly leaned back and swerved to the left as she avoided the strike. Qa'a turned swiftly and swung his sword high again, catching Sati by surprise. The Egyptian's sword cut through Sati's left hand, slicing off four fingers. Much to his surprise, Sati didn't flinch from the injury but swung her sword from a height at Qa'a. Qa'a swerved and defended Sati's blow with an elevated strike.

Sati, meanwhile, had surmised that the swinging strike was Qa'a's standard attack. She played to that as she kept swinging at Qa'a from a high angle and the Egyptian kept striking back. Both of them kept changing the direction repeatedly to surprise the other, but the strikes were almost typical and therefore, no serious injury was caused. Suddenly, Sati dropped to one knee and swung hard. The strike hit home. Her blade hacked brutally through Qa'a's abdomen, cutting deep. He collapsed as his intestines spilled on to the ground.

Sati stood up, towering over a kneeling Qa'a, who had been paralysed by the intense pain. She held her sword high vertically, and thrust it through Qa'a's neck, straight down, deep into his body right up to his heart, killing him instantly.

Swuth stared at Sati, dumbfounded. It wasn't just her skill

with the sword that had surprised him; it was also her character. She hadn't beheaded Qa'a when she could easily have done so. She let him keep his head. She gave him an honourable death; a soldier's death. She had followed the rules of the duel of Aten, even though the rules were not her own.

Sati pulled aside and ran her bloodied sword into the soft muddy ground. She bent over and ripped another piece of cloth from the now dead Qa'a's cloak and tied it around her left palm, covering the area where her fingers had been amputated.

She stood tall, pulled up her sword from the ground and held it aloft, careful not to look at Nandi. *Just a few more minutes.*

'Who's next?'

Another assassin stepped forward, reached for his sword and then hesitated. He had seen Sati battle brilliantly with the long blade. He drew out a knife from his shoulder belt instead.

'I don't have a knife,' said Sati, putting her sword back in its scabbard, wanting to fight fair.

Swuth pulled out his knife and flung it high in Sati's direction. She reached out and caught the beautifully-balanced weapon easily. In the meantime, the assassin had removed his mask and pulled back his hood. He didn't want to suffer the disadvantage of a restricted vision against a skilled warrior.

Having lost four fingers of her left hand, Sati couldn't battle this assassin the way she had battled Tarak in Karachapa many years ago, where she had hidden the knife behind her back with the aim of confusing her opponent about the direction of attack. So she held the knife in front, in her right hand. But she kept the hilt forward with the blade pointing back, towards herself, much to the surprise of the gathered assassins.

The Egyptian adopted the traditional fighting stance, and

pointed the knife directly at Sati. He moved forward and slashed hard. Sati jumped back to avoid the blow, but the blade sliced her shoulder, drawing some blood. This emboldened the assassin to move in further, swinging the knife left and then right as he charged in. Sati kept stepping back, allowing the assassin to draw closer into the trap. The assassin suddenly changed tack and thrust forward with a jabbing motion. Sati swerved right to avoid the blow, raising her right hand. She now held the knife high above her left shoulder. But she hadn't moved back far enough. The assassin's knife sliced through the left side of her abdomen, lodging deep within her, right up to the hilt.

Without flinching at the horrifying pain, Sati brought her hand down hard from its height, stabbing the Egyptian straight through his neck. The blow had so much force that the knife cut all the way through, its point sticking out at the other end of the hapless Egyptian's throat. Blood burst forth from the assassin's mouth and neck. Sati stepped back as the Egyptian drowned in his own blood.

Swuth was staring at this strange woman, the sneer wiped off his face. She had killed two of his assassins one-on-one, in a free and fair fight. She was bleeding desperately, and yet she stood tall and proud.

Sati, meanwhile, was breathing slowly, trying to calm her rapidly beating heart. She had been cut up in too many places. A pulsating heart would work against her, pumping more blood out of her body. She also needed to conserve her energy for the duels that were to come. She looked at the knife buried deep in her abdomen. It hadn't penetrated any vital organ. The only danger was the continuous bleeding. She spread out her feet, took a deep breath, held the knife's handle and yanked it out. She didn't flinch or make any sound of pain while doing so.

'Who is this woman?' asked a stunned assassin standing next to Swuth.

Sati bent down, ripped a part of the bloodied cloak of the assassin she had just killed, and bandaged it tightly around her abdomen. It staunched the blood flow. While doing so, she'd seen from the corner of her eye that the Meluhans who were running towards her were probably a third of the way through. She knew she couldn't stop the duels now. She had seen the killers. They couldn't leave her alive. Her only chance was to continue duelling and hope that she would still be breathing when the Meluhans reached her.

Sati drew her sword. 'Who's next?'

Another assassin stepped forward.

'No!' said Swuth.

The assassin stepped back.

'She's mine,' said Swuth, drawing one of his curved swords.

Swuth didn't approach Sati with both his curved swords. That would have been unfair according to the rules of Aten, since Sati had only one sword hand. He held the sword forward in his right hand. As he neared Sati, he started swinging the sword around, building it into a stunning circle of death just ahead of him, moving inexorably towards her. Even as Swuth's sword whirred closer, Sati began to step back slowly. She suddenly thrust her sword forward quickly, deep into the ring of the circling blade of Swuth, inflicting a serious cut on the Egyptian's shoulder. She pulled her sword back just as rapidly, before Swuth's circling blade could come back to deflect her sword.

The wound must have hurt, but Swuth didn't flinch. He smiled. He'd never met anyone with the ability to penetrate his sword's circle of death.

This woman is talented.

Swuth stopped circling his sword and held it in a traditional sword-fighter stance. He stepped forward, swinging viciously from the right. Sati bent low to avoid the blow and thrust her blade at Swuth's arm, causing a superficial cut. But Swuth suddenly reversed the direction of his blade, slashing hard across Sati's shoulder.

Sati swerved back just in time, reducing the threat of what could have been a devastating blow. Swuth's sword grazed her right arm and shoulder. Sati growled in fury and stabbed with such rapid force that a surprised Swuth had to jump back.

Swuth stepped back even further. This woman was a very skilled warrior. His standard tactics would not work. He decided to keep his distance, pointing his sword forward, thinking of what could be a good move against her. Sati remained stationary, conserving her strength. She couldn't afford to move too much for fear of increasing the blood loss from her numerous wounds. Also, she was playing for time. She didn't mind a few moments of reprieve.

An idea struck Swuth. Sati was primarily injured on her left side. This would impair her movements in that direction. He quickly took a giant step forward and swung viciously from his right. Sati twisted to the left and swung her blade up to block Swuth's strike. The Egyptian could see that the movement had made blood spurt out of her wounded abdomen. As Sati stabbed at Swuth again, she stepped a little to the left to improve her angle. But Swuth had anticipated her move. He stepped further to his right and kept on swinging again and again from that awkward angle.

The intense pain of continuously turning leftwards forced Sati to take a gamble. She pirouetted suddenly and swung her sword in a great arc from her right, hoping to decapitate him. But this was exactly what Swuth had expected. He ducked low and stepped forward rapidly, easily avoiding Sati's strike. At the same time, he brought his sword up in a low, brutal jab. His curved sword with its serrated edges went right through Sati's abdomen, ripping almost every single vital organ; her intestines, stomach, kidney and liver were slashed through viciously. A paralysed Sati, her face twisted in agony, lay impaled on Swuth's curved sword. Her own blade fell from her hand. The Egyptian bent back, used the leverage and rammed his sword in even further, till its point burst through to the other side, piercing her shattered back.

'Not bad,' said Swuth, twisting his blade as he pulled it out of Sati, ripping her organs to ribbons. 'Not bad for a woman.'

Sati collapsed to the ground, her body shivering as dark blood began to pool on the ground around her. She knew she was going to die. It was only a matter of time. The blood flow couldn't be staunched now. Her vital internal organs and the massive numbers of blood vessels in them had been mortally damaged. But she also knew something else very clearly. She wouldn't die lying on the ground, slowly bleeding to death.

She would die like a Meluhan. She would die with her head held high.

She lifted her quivering right hand and reached for her sword. Swuth stared at Sati in awe, transfixed as he watched her struggling to reach her blade. He knew that she must know she was going to die soon. And yet, her spirit hadn't been broken.

Could she be the final kill?

The cult of Aten had a belief that every assassin would one day meet a victim so magnificent, so worthy, that it would be impossible for the man to kill ever again. His duty would then be to give his victim an honourable death and give up his profession to spend the rest of his life worshipping that last victim.

As Sati's arm flopped to her side after another vain attempt to reach her sword, Swuth shook his head. *It can't be a woman. This cannot be the moment. The final kill cannot be a woman!*

Swuth turned around and screamed at his people. 'Move out, you filthy cockroaches! We're leaving!'

The man standing next to Swuth didn't obey his order. He continued to stare beyond Swuth, stupefied by the awe-inspiring sight.

Swuth whirled around, stunned. Sati was up on one knee. She was breathing rapidly, forcing some strength into her debilitated body. She had dug her sword into the ground and her right hand was on its hilt as she tried to use the leverage to push herself up. She failed, took quick breaths, fired more energy into her body, and tried once more. She failed again. Then she stopped suddenly. She felt eyes boring into her. She looked up and locked eyes with Swuth.

Swuth stared at Sati, dumbstruck. She was completely soaked in her own blood, there were cavernous wounds all over her body, and her hands were shivering with the tremendous pain she was in. Her soul must know that death was just minutes away. And yet, her eyes did not exhibit even the slightest hint of fear. She stared directly at Swuth with only one expression. An expression of pure, raw, unadulterated defiance.

Tears sprang into Swuth's eyes as his heart felt immeasurably heavy. His mind grasped his heart's message instantly. This indeed was his final kill. He would never, ever, kill again.

Swuth knew what he had to do. He drew both his curved swords, held them high by the hilt and thrust them in a downward motion. In a flash, the swords were buried in the ground. For the last time, he looked at both the half-buried, bloodied swords that had served him so well. He would never use them again. He went down on one knee, pulled his shoulders back to give himself leverage and then slammed the hilts with his palms in an outward motion, snapping both blades in two.

He then got up, pulled back his hood and removed his mask. Sati could see the tattoo of a black fireball with rays streaming out on the bridge of his nose. Swuth reached behind and pulled out a sword from a scabbard tied across his back. Unlike all his other weapons, this sword was marked. It was marked with the name of their God, Aten. Below that had been inscribed the name of the devotee, Swuth. The blade had never been used before. It had but one purpose alone: to taste the blood of the final victim. Thereafter, the sword would never be used again. It would be worshipped by Swuth and his descendants.

Swuth bowed low before Sati, pointed at the black tattoo on the bridge of his nose and repeated an ancient vow.

'The fire of Aten shall consume you. And the honour of putting out your fire shall purify me.'

Sati didn't move. She didn't flinch. She continued to stare silently at Swuth.

Swuth went down on one knee. He had to give Sati an honourable death; beheading her was out of the question. He pointed his sword at her heart, holding the hilt with his thumb facing up. He pressed his other hand into the back of the hilt to provide support.

Ready in every way, Swuth stared back at Sati, at a face that he knew would haunt him for the rest of his life, and whispered, 'Killing you shall be my life's honour, My Lady.'

'NOOOOOOOO!'

A loud scream came wafting in from the distance.

An arrow whizzed past and pierced Swuth's hand. As his sword dropped to the ground, a surprised Swuth turned to find another arrow flying straight into his shoulder.

'Run!' screamed the assassins.

One of them picked up Swuth and started dragging him along.

'Noooo!' roared Swuth, struggling against his people, who were bodily carrying him back. Not killing the final victim was one of the greatest sins for the followers of Aten. But his people wouldn't leave him behind.

Nearly a thousand Meluhans had reached Sati, a desperately distraught Daksha and Veerini in the lead.

'S-A-T-I-I-I-I,' screamed Daksha, his face twisted in agony.

'DON'T TOUCH ME!' bellowed Sati as she collapsed to the ground.

Daksha buckled, crying inconsolably, digging his nails into his face.

'Sati!' screamed Veerini as she lifted her daughter into her arms.

'*Maa...*' whispered Sati.

'Don't talk. Relax,' cried Veerini, before frantically looking back. 'Get the doctors! Now!'

'*Maa...*'

'Be quiet, my child.'

'*Maa*, my time has come...'

'No! No! We'll save you! We'll save you!'

'*Maa*, listen to me!' said Sati.

'My child...'

'My body will be handed over to Shiva.'

'Nothing will happen to you,' sobbed Veerini. The Queen of Meluha turned around once again. 'Will someone get the doctors?! Now!'

Sati held her mother's face with surprising strength. 'Promise me! Only to Shiva!'

'Sati...'

'Promise me!'

'Yes, my child, I promise.'

'And, both Ganesh and Kartik will light my pyre.'

'You're not going to die!'

'Both Ganesh and Kartik! Promise me!'

'Yes, yes. I promise.'

Sati slowed her breathing down. She had heard what she needed to. She blocked out the weeping she could hear all around her. She rested her head in her mother's lap and looked towards the peace conference building. The doors were open. Lord Ram and Lady Sita's idols were clearly visible. She could feel their kind and welcoming eyes upon her. She would be back with them soon.

A sudden wind picked up, swirling dust particles and leaves lying around her on the ground. Sati gazed at the swirl. The particles appeared to form a figure. She stared hard as Shiva's image seemed to emerge. She remembered the promise she had made to him; that she would see him when he returned.

I'm sorry. I'm so sorry.

The wind died down just as suddenly. Sati could feel her vision blurring. Blackness appeared to be taking over. Her vision seemed to recede into a slowly reducing circle, with darkness all around it. The wind burst into life once again. The dust particles and leaves rose in an encore and showed Sati the vision she wanted to die with: the love of her life, her Shiva.

I'll be waiting for you, my love.

Thinking of her Shiva, Sati let her last breath slip quietly out of her body.

Chapter 46

Lament of the Blue Lord

To reach the Meluhan capital as quickly as possible, Shiva had commandeered a merchant ship, which docked at Devagiri a little more than a week later.

'That must be the ship Sati commandeered,' said Shiva, pointing towards an anchored empty vessel.

'It means she's still in Devagiri,' said Ganesh. 'Bhoomidevi, be praised.'

Kali clenched her fist. 'If they've imprisoned her and hope to negotiate, I will personally destroy everything that moves in this city.'

'Let's not assume the worst, Kali,' said Shiva. 'We all know that whatever may be his faults, the Emperor will not harm Sati.'

'I agree,' said Kartik.

'And don't forget, Queen Kali,' said Gopal, 'We have the fearsome *Pashupatiastra*. Nobody can stand up to it. Nobody. The mere threat of this terrifying weapon would be enough to achieve our purpose.'

Their conversation came to a stop with the sound of the gangplank crashing on the deck.

'Where is everyone?' asked Shiva, frowning as he stepped onto the gangplank.

'How can the port be left abandoned?' asked a surprised Ayurvati, who had never seen something like this in all the years that she had lived in Meluha.

'Let's go,' said Shiva, unease trickling down his spine.

The entire brigade marched out in step with the Neelkanth. As Shiva's men stepped out of the port area their eyes fell on the large peace conference building. Inexplicably, a colony of tents had been set up outside the building.

'This area has been thoroughly cleaned recently,' said Gopal. 'Even the grass has been dug out.'

'Of course, it would be,' said Shiva, quietening his fears. 'They would need a pure area for the conference.'

A phalanx of Brahmins was conducting a *puja* next to the closed door of the peace conference hall.

'What are they praying for, Pandit*ji*?' asked Shiva.

'They're praying for peace,' said Gopal.

Shiva found nothing amiss in that.

'But... They're praying for peace for the souls,' said a surprised Gopal. 'The souls of the dead...'

Shiva instinctively reached to his side and pulled out his sword. His entire brigade did the same.

As they approached the colony, Parvateshwar and Anandmayi stepped out from one of the tents. Behind them was a short man in a simple white dhoti and *angvastram*, his head shaved clean except for a traditional tuft of hair at the crown signifying his Brahmin lineage, and sporting a long, flowing white beard.

'Lord Bhrigu,' whispered Gopal, immediately folding his hands together in a Namaste.

'Namaste, great Vasudev,' said Bhrigu politely, walking up to Gopal.

Shiva held his breath as he stared at his real adversary. A man he was meeting for the first time.

'Great Neelkanth,' said Bhrigu.

'Great Maharishi,' returned Shiva, his grip over his sword tightening.

Bhrigu opened his mouth to say something, hesitated and then looked at Parvateshwar, who had now walked up to stand next to him. Parvateshwar and Anandmayi bent low in respect to their living God. As Parvateshwar rose, Shiva got his first close look at his friend-turned-foe's face. He was stunned. The Meluhan general's eyes were red and swollen, like he hadn't slept in weeks.

'Isn't the Emperor allowing you into the city?' asked Shiva.

'We have chosen not to enter, My Lord,' said Parvateshwar.

'Why?'

'We don't recognise him as our Emperor anymore.'

'Is it because you don't agree with what the conference is trying to achieve? Is that why you are waiting here for us, with your Brahmins chanting death hymns?'

Parvateshwar could not speak.

'If you want a battle, Parvateshwar, you shall have it,' announced Shiva.

'The battle is over, My Lord.'

'The entire war is over, great Neelkanth,' added Bhrigu.

Shiva frowned, astonished. He turned towards Gopal.

'Has Princess Sati managed to convince the Emperor?' asked Gopal. 'We want nothing but the end of the Somras. So long as Meluha agrees to those terms, the Neelkanth is happy to declare peace.'

'My Lord,' said Parvateshwar as he touched Shiva's elbow, his eyes brimming with tears. 'Come with me.'

'Where?'

Parvateshwar glanced at Shiva briefly, and then looked at the ground again. 'Please come.'

Shiva sheathed his sword in its scabbard and followed

Parvateshwar as he walked towards the peace conference building. He in turn was followed by the others: Bhrigu, Kali, Ganesh, Kartik, Gopal, Veerbhadra, Krittika, Ayurvati, Brahaspati and Tara. Anandmayi remained outside her tent. She couldn't bear to see what was about to happen.

The Brahmins continued their drone of Sanskrit *shlokas* as Parvateshwar came up to the building's entrance. The general took a deep breath and pushed the large doors open. As Shiva walked in he was stunned by what he saw.

Twenty beds had been laid out in the massive hall. Each bed was occupied by an injured soldier, being tended to by a Brahmin doctor. On the first bed lay one of Shiva's most ardent devotees, the one who had found him in Tibet.

'Nandi!' screamed Shiva, racing to the bed in a few giant strides.

Shiva went down on his knees and touched Nandi's face. He was unconscious. Both his arms had been severed; the left one close to his wrist and the right close to the elbow. There were numerous tiny scars all over his body, perhaps the result of small projectiles. His face was pockmarked with wounds. The bed had been especially designed to keep a part of Nandi's back untouched. He'd probably suffered a serious injury on his back as well. Shiva could see that the wounds were healing, but it was equally obvious that the injuries were grave and his body would take a long time to recover.

'The wounds have been left open so they can be aired, great Neelkanth,' said the Brahmin doctor, avoiding his eyes. 'We will put in a fresh dressing soon. Major Nandi will heal completely. As will all the other soldiers here.'

Shiva continued to stare at Nandi, gently touching his face, anger rising within him. He got up suddenly, drew his sword out and pointed it straight at Parvateshwar.

'I should murder the Emperor for this!' growled Shiva.

Parvateshwar stood paralysed, staring at the ground.

'If the Emperor thinks he can force my hand by doing this and capturing Sati,' said Shiva, 'he is living in a fool's paradise.'

'Once *didi* knows we are here,' hissed Kali to Parvateshwar, 'she will escape. And believe me, our wrath will then be terrible. Tell that goat who rules your Empire to release my sister. NOW!'

But Parvateshwar remained still, silent. Then he started shaking imperceptibly.

'General?' said Gopal, trying to sound reasonable. 'There doesn't have to be any violence. Just let the Princess go.'

Bhrigu attempted to speak to Gopal, but was unable to find the strength to say what he had to.

'Lord Bhrigu,' said Gopal, keeping his voice low but stern. 'We have the *Pashupatiastra*. We will not hesitate to use it if our demands are not met. Release Princess Sati at once. Destroy the Somras factory in Devagiri. Do it now and we shall leave.'

Bhrigu seemed stunned by the news of the *Pashupatiastra*. He turned briefly towards Parvateshwar. But the general had failed to even register the risk from the terrible *daivi astra*. He was crying now, his whole body shaking with misery. He cried for the loss of the woman he had loved like the daughter he'd never had.

'Parvateshwar,' snarled Shiva, moving his sword even closer. 'Don't test my patience. Where is Sati?'

Parvateshwar finally looked at Shiva as tears streamed down his face.

Shiva stared at him, a horrific foreboding entering his heart. The space between his brows began to throb frantically.

'My Lord,' sobbed Parvateshwar. 'I'm so sorry...'

Shiva's sword slipped from his weakened grip as an excruciatingly painful thought entered his mind.

With terror-struck eyes, Shiva stepped towards the general. 'Parvateshwar, where is she?'

'My Lord... I did not reach in time...'

Shiva pulled Parvateshwar by his *angvastram* and grabbed his neck hard. 'PARVATESHWAR! WHERE IS SATI?'

But Parvateshwar could not speak. He continued to cry helplessly.

Shiva noticed that Bhrigu had glanced for one brief moment at a direction behind him. He let go of Parvateshwar and spun around instantly. He saw a large wooden door at the far end of the hall.

'S-A-T-I-I-I-I,' screamed Shiva as he ran towards the room.

The Brahmin doctors immediately stepped out of the raging Shiva's path.

'SATI!'

Shiva banged on the door. It was locked. He stepped back, gave himself room, and rammed his shoulder into the door. It yielded an inch before the strong lock snapped it back into place.

In that instant, through the crack, Shiva saw a tower made of massive blocks of ice, before the door slammed back. His brow was burning now, a pain impossible for most mortals to tolerate.

One of the Meluhans went running for the keys to the room.

'SATI!' cried Shiva and slammed into the door again, splinters sticking into his shoulder, drawing blood.

The door held strong.

Shiva stepped back and kicked hard. It finally fell open with a thundering crash.

The breath was sucked out of the Neelkanth.

At the centre of the room, within the tower of ice, lay the mutilated body of the finest person he had ever known. His Sati.

'SATIIIII!'

The Neelkanth stormed into the room. His brow felt like something had exploded within. Fire was consuming the area between his eyes.

He banged his fists repeatedly against the large ice block covering Sati's body, desperately trying to push it away. Blood burst forth from Shiva's shattered knuckles as he pounded against the immovable block. He kept hammering against the ice, breaking bits of it, trying to shove it away, trying to reach his Sati. His blood started seeping into the frozen water.

'SATIII!'

Some Meluhans came running in from the other side of the room, sinking hooks into the block of ice covering Sati. They pulled hard. The block gave way and started sliding back. Shiva continued to hit hard, desperately pushing against it.

The block was barely half-way out when Shiva leapt onto the tower. A small depression had been carved in the ice, like a tomb. Within that icy coffin lay Sati's body, her hands folded across her chest.

Shiva jumped into the tomb and pulled her body up, holding it tight in his arms. She was frozen stiff, her skin dulled to a greyish blue. There was a deep cut across her face, and her left eye had been gouged out. Her left hand had been partially sliced off. There were two gaping holes in her abdomen. Frozen blood, which had seeped out of her multiple injuries, lay congealed all across her mutilated body. Shiva pulled Sati close as he looked up, crying desperately, screaming incoherently, his heart inundated, his soul shattered.

'SATIIII!'

It was a wail that would haunt the world for millennia.

Chapter 47

A Mother's Message

The setting sun infused the sky with a profusion of colours, casting a dull glow on the peace conference building. Parvateshwar's camp had been cleared out. A raging Kartik had threatened to kill every single man present. Not wanting to further excite the justified fury of the Neelkanth's son, Bhrigu had ordered the retreat of Parvateshwar, Anandmayi and their men into Devagiri, a city they had refused to enter thus far.

Gopal was outside the peace conference building, in the temporary camp that had been set up for Shiva's brigade. The Vasudev chief was in discussion with the brigade commander on the best course of action. Everyone wanted vengeance, but attacking Devagiri with just one brigade was unwise. Though the main Meluhan army and its allies were waylaid in faraway Mohan Jo Daro by its citizens, Devagiri still had enough troops to defend itself. The defensive features of the capital, moreover, could not be scaled with an offensive force as small as the one under Shiva's command. Some of them suggested using the *Pashupatiastra*. Gopal immediately rejected it. There was no question of using the weapon. Both Shiva and he had given their word.

Ayurvati had busied herself in the outer room of the peace

conference building, supervising the recovery of Sati's injured bodyguards. As she attended to the medical infusions being administered to a patient, her eyes strayed towards the locked door of the inner room. Sati's dead body lay there, with her family mourning quietly behind closed doors. Ayurvati wiped a tear and got back to work. Keeping herself busy was the only way in which she could cope with her grief.

The inner room, where Sati's body had been kept temporarily, had been built by the Meluhans to fulfil the princess' last wish of preserving her body till Shiva arrived. Tiny holes had been drilled high in the inner chamber walls with many huge blacksmith's bellows fitted into them to push in air regularly. A massive wooden circular gear had been constructed outside the peace conference building with twenty bulls harnessed to it. The non-stop circular movement of the beasts made the gear move constantly. This in turn powered the steady squeezing and releasing of the blacksmith bellows, through a system of smaller gears and pulleys, thus pushing in air regularly into the inner room that stored Sati's body. A screen of jute, cotton and a special cooling material had been hung in front of the bellows. Through a system of pipes and capillaries, water dripped down the screen in a constant stream. The air pushed through the bellows would pass through this screen, and cool down rapidly before flowing into the room. The integrity of the ice tower had been maintained with this classic Meluhan technology, but now the ice within the heart of the tower had begun to gradually melt due to the heat emanating from Shiva's body and his rapid breathing. This had caused Sati's corpse to thaw slowly, making her frozen blood melt. A pale, colourless fluid oozed out, appearing almost to weep from her wounds ever so gently.

Shiva sat there, immobile, shivering due to the cold

and his grief, stunned into absolute silence, staring into nothingness, holding Sati's lifeless body in his arms. Despite sitting on ice, Shiva's brow throbbed desperately, as if a great fire raged within. An angry blackish-red blotch had formed between his brows. He had been sitting thus for many hours. He hadn't moved. He hadn't eaten. He had stopped crying. It was almost as if he had chosen to be as lifeless as the love of his life.

Kali sat near the door of the inner room, sobbing loudly, cursing herself for her behaviour during her last meeting with Sati. It was a guilt that she would carry for the rest of her life. Uncontrollable rage was rising within her slowly but steadily. At this point, though, it was still swamped by her grief.

Krittika sat next to the tower of ice, shaking uncontrollably. She had cried till she had no tears left. She kept touching the ice tower every few seconds. Veerbhadra, his eyes swollen red, sat quietly next to her. One arm was around his wife Krittika, drawing as well as giving comfort. But his other arm was stiff, its fist clenched tight. He wanted vengeance. He wanted to torture and annihilate every single person who'd done this to Sati; who had done this to his friend Shiva.

Brahaspati and Tara sat quietly at another end of the room. The former Meluhan chief scientist's face was soaked with tears. He respected Sati as an icon of the Meluhan way of life. He also knew that Shiva would never be the same again. Ever. Tara kept staring at Shiva as her heart went out to the unfortunate Neelkanth. He was a mere shadow of the confident and friendly man she had met at Pariha.

Kartik and Ganesh sat impassively next to each other on the icy floor, their backs resting against the wall. Their eyes were fixed on the tower, on their father's paralysed figure on top, holding their mother's mutilated body. The tears had almost blinded their eyes. The deluge of sorrow had stunned their hearts. They sat quietly, holding hands, desperately trying to make sense of what had happened.

Ganesh thought he saw some movement on top of the ice tower. He looked up to a bewildering sight. His mother seemed to have risen from her body and floated high up in the air. Ganesh moved his gaze back to his father to see another body of his mother, lying still in his father's arms. Ganesh looked up again at his mother's apparition, his mouth agape.

Sati flew in a great arc and landed softly in front of Ganesh. Her feet didn't touch the ground, remaining suspended in the air, just like those of mythical Goddesses. She wore a garland of fresh flowers, again like mythical Goddesses. But mythical Goddesses didn't bleed. Sati, on the other hand, was bleeding profusely. Ganesh could see her mutilated body as she stood in front of him, her left eye gouged out with a deep cut across her face, leaking blood slowly. The burn scar on her face was flaming red, as though still burning. Her left hand had been sliced through brutally, blood spurting out of the wound in sudden jerks, timed with her heartbeat. There were two massive wounds in her abdomen from which blood was streaming out with the ferocity of a young mountain river. There were several small serrations all across her body, each of them seeping out even more blood. Sati's right fist was clenched tight, her body shaking with fury. Her right eye was bloodshot, focused directly on Ganesh. Her blood-soaked hair was loose; fluttering, as if a great wind had been assaulting it.

It was a fearsome sight.

Maa...

Maa...

'Avenge me!' hissed Sati.

Maa...

'Avenge me!'

Ganesh pulled his hand away from Kartik's and clenched it tight. He gritted his teeth and whispered within the confines of his mind. *I will, maa!*

'Remember how I died!' snarled Sati.

I will! I will!

'Promise me! You will remember how I died!'

I promise, maa! I will always remember!

Sati suddenly vanished. Ganesh reached out with his hand, weeping desperately. 'Maa!'

At exactly the same time as Ganesh, Kartik too saw his mother's apparition.

Sati's spirit appeared to escape from her body and hovered for some time before landing in front of Kartik. Her feet were suspended a little above the ground, a garland of fresh flowers around her neck. But unlike the vision that Ganesh had seen, the apparition in front of Kartik was whole and complete.

There was no wound. She looked exactly the way Kartik remembered seeing her last. Tall of stature and bronze-skinned, she wore a beautiful smile which formed dimples on both her cheeks. Her bright blue eyes shone with gentle radiance, her black hair was tied demurely in a bun. Her erect posture and calm expression reminded Kartik of what she'd symbolised: an uncompromising Meluhan who always put the law and the welfare of others before herself.

Kartik burst out crying.

Maa...

'My son,' whispered Sati.

Maa, I will torture everyone! I will kill every single one of them! I will drink their blood! I will burn down this entire city! I will avenge you!

'No,' said Sati softly.

A dumbfounded Kartik fell silent.

'Don't you remember anything?'

I will remember you forever, maa. And I will make all of Devagiri pay for what they did to you.

Sati's face became stern.

'Don't you remember anything I've taught you?'

Kartik remained silent.

'Vengeance is a waste of time,' said Sati. 'I am not important. The only thing that matters is dharma. Do you want to prove your love for me? Do so by doing the right thing. Don't surrender to anger. Surrender only to dharma.'

Maa...

'Forget how I died,' said Sati. 'Remember how I lived.'

Maa...

'Promise me! You will remember how I lived.'

I promise, maa... I will always remember...

Chapter 48

The Great Debate

The ones amongst Shiva's brigade who were seeking vengeance got a boost the next morning. Against all expectations, Bhagirath sailed in at the head of the entire army of two hundred and fifty thousand troops. The Ayodhyan prince had been worried about what would happen to his Lord if the Meluhans tried some trickery at Devagiri. He had marched the troops all the way from Lothal to the Saraswati, through the broad Meluhan highways without a halt, breaking only for brief food breaks and minuscule rest sessions. At the Saraswati, he had commandeered as many merchant ships as possible and raced up the great river, to Devagiri.

'Oh Lord Ram!' whispered a stunned Bhagirath.

Gopal had just told Bhagirath about what had occurred at Devagiri and the brutal manner in which Sati had been killed.

'Where is the Princess' body?' asked Chenardhwaj, tears welling up in his eyes.

'In the peace conference building,' said Gopal. 'The Lord Neelkanth is with her. He hasn't moved from there in the last twenty-four hours. He hasn't eaten. He hasn't spoken. He's just sitting there, holding Princess Sati's body.'

Chandraketu looked up at the sky. He turned around and

wiped away a tear. Those pearls of emotion were signs of weakness in a Kshatriya.

'We'll kill every single one of those bastards!' growled Bhagirath, his knuckles whitening on his clenched fists. 'We'll obliterate this entire city. There will be no trace left of this place. They have hurt our living God.'

'Prince Bhagirath,' said Gopal, his palms open in supplication. 'We cannot punish the entire city. We must keep a clear head. We should only punish those who're responsible for this assassination. We should destroy the Somras factory. We must leave the rest unharmed. That is the right thing to do...'

'Forgive me, great Vasudev,' interrupted Chandraketu, 'but some crimes are so terrible that the entire community must be made to pay. They have killed Lady Sati; and, in such a brutal manner.'

'But not everyone came out to kill her. A vast majority was not even aware of what the Emperor was up to,' argued Gopal.

'They could have come out to stop the killing once it had begun, couldn't they?' asked Chandraketu. 'Standing by and watching a sin being committed is as bad as committing it oneself. Don't the Vasudevs say this?'

'This is an entirely different context, King Chandraketu,' said Gopal.

'I disagree, Pandit*ji*,' said Maatali, the King of Vaishali. 'Devagiri must pay.'

'I think Lord Gopal is right, King Maatali,' said Chenardhwaj, the Lothal governor. 'We cannot punish everyone in Devagiri for the sins of a few.'

'Why am I not surprised to hear this?' asked Maatali.

'What is that supposed to mean?' asked Chenardhwaj, stung to the quick.

'You are a Meluhan,' said Maatali. 'You will stand up for your people. We are Chandravanshis. We are the ones who are truly loyal to the Lord Neelkanth.'

Chenardhwaj stepped up close to Maatali threateningly. 'I rebelled against my own people, against my country's laws, against my vows of loyalty to Meluha because I am a follower of the Neelkanth. I am loyal to Lord Shiva. And, I don't need to prove anything to you.'

'Calm down everyone,' said Chandraketu, the Branga king. 'Let's not forget who the real enemy is.'

'The real enemy is Devagiri,' said Maatali. 'They did this to Lady Sati. They must be punished. It's as simple as that.'

'I agree,' said Bhagirath. 'We should use the *Pashupatiastra*.'

Gopal flared with anger. 'The *Pashupatiastra* is not some random arrow that can be fired without any thought, Prince Bhagirath. It will leave total death and devastation behind in this area for centuries to come.'

'Maybe that is what this place deserves,' said Chandraketu.

'These are *daivi astras*,' said an agitated Gopal. 'They cannot be used casually to settle disputes among men.'

'Lord Shiva is not just another man,' said Bhagirath. 'He is divine. We must use the weapon to...'

'We cannot use the *Pashupatiastra*. That is final,' said Gopal.

'I don't think so, Pandit*ji*,' said Chandraketu. 'Lady Sati was a great leader and warrior, with the highest moral standards. The Lord Neelkanth loved Lady Sati more than I've seen any man love his wife. I'm sure Lord Shiva wants vengeance. And frankly, so do we.'

'It's not vengeance that we need, King Chandraketu,' said Gopal. 'But justice. The people who did this to Lady Sati must face justice. But only those who were responsible for this perfidy. Nobody else should be punished. For that would be an even bigger injustice.'

'Yours is the voice of reason, Pandit*ji*,' said Maatali. 'But this is not the time for reason. This is the time for anger.'

'I don't think the Neelkanth will make a decision in anger,' said Gopal.

'Then, why don't we ask Lord Shiva?' asked Bhagirath. 'Let him decide.'

— ⅄ⓞⓤ↑⊛ —

'Kill them all!' growled Kali. 'I want this entire city to burn with every one of its citizens in it.'

All the commanders of Shiva, including his family members, were seated in a secluded area on the peace conference platform, outside the main building. Brahaspati and Tara had also joined in, but remained mostly silent. The area had been cordoned off by soldiers to prevent anyone from listening in on the deliberations. Gopal had tried to get Shiva to attend, but the Neelkanth did not respond to any of his entreaties. He remained alone, within the freezing inner chamber, holding Sati.

'Queen Kali,' argued Gopal, 'my apologies for disagreeing with you, but we cannot do this. This is morally wrong.'

'Didn't the Meluhans give their word that this is a peace conference? Nobody is supposed to use arms at a peace conference, right? They did something that is very morally wrong. How come you didn't notice that, Pandit*ji*?'

'Two wrongs don't make a right.'

'I don't care,' said Kali, waving her hand dismissively. 'Devagiri will be destroyed. They will pay for what they did to my sister.'

'Queen Kali,' said Chenardhwaj carefully. 'I respect you immensely. You are a great woman. You have always fought for justice. But does punishing an entire city for the crimes of a few serve justice?'

Kali cast him a withering look. 'I saved your life, Chenardhwaj.'

'I know, Your Highness. How can I forget that? That is the reason...'

'You will do what I tell you to do,' interrupted Kali. 'My sister will be avenged.'

Chenardhwaj tried to argue. 'But...'

'MY SISTER WILL BE AVENGED!'

Chenardhwaj fell silent.

Bhagirath was carefully avoiding this discussion. While walking towards the peace conference building, he had learnt that his sister Anandmayi was in Devagiri. The city would be destroyed, but he had to save his sister first.

'I agree with Queen Kali,' said Chandraketu. 'Devagiri must be destroyed. We must use the *Pashupatiastra*.'

At the mention of the devastating *daivi astra*, Kartik spoke up for the first time. 'The *astra* cannot be used.'

Gopal looked at Kartik, grateful to have at least one member of the Neelkanth's family on his side.

'Justice will be done,' said Kartik. '*Maa's* blood will be avenged. But not with the *Pashupatiastra*. It cannot be done with that terrible weapon.'

'It must not,' agreed Gopal immediately. 'The Neelkanth has given his word to the Vayuputras that he will not use the *Pashupatiastra*.'

'If that is the case, then we cannot use it,' said Bhagirath.

Gopal breathed easy, glad to have pulled at least some of them back from the brink. 'The question remains, how do we give justice to Princess Sati?'

'By killing them all!' roared Kali.

'But is it fair to kill children who had nothing to do with this?' asked Bhagirath.

'You are assuming, Prince Bhagirath,' said Kali, 'that Meluhans care for their children.'

'Your Highness,' said Bhagirath. 'Please try to understand that children who had nothing to do with this crime should not be punished.'

'Fine!' said Kali. 'We will let their children out.'

'And non-combatants as well,' said Kartik.

'Particularly the women,' said Bhagirath. 'We must let them go. But once they are out, we should destroy the entire city.'

'Is there anyone else you would like to save?' asked Kali sarcastically. 'What about the dogs in Devagiri? Should we lead them out too? Maybe the cockroaches as well?'

Bhagirath did not respond. Anything he said would only inflame Kali further.

Kali cursed. 'All right! Children and non-combatants will be allowed out. Everyone else will remain prisoner in the city. And they will all be killed.'

'Agreed,' said Bhagirath. 'All I'm saying is that we should be fair.'

'That is not all there is to it, Prince Bhagirath,' erupted Kartik. 'The Somras is not to be destroyed. My father had been very clear about that. It is only supposed to be taken out of the equation. We do have to destroy the Somras factory. But we also have to ensure that the knowledge of the Somras is not lost. We have to save the scientists and take them to a secret location. They will be a part of the tribe that my father will leave behind. These people will keep the knowledge of the Somras alive. Today it is Evil, but there may come a time in the future when the Somras may be Good again.'

Gopal nodded. 'Kartik has spoken wisely.'

'This means that even if some of these scientists had something to do with my mother's death,' said Kartik, 'we have to set aside our pain and save them. We have to save them for the sake of India's future.'

Ganesh glared at Kartik with dagger eyes.

'Set aside our pain?'

Kartik became silent.

Ganesh was breathing heavily, barely able to keep a hold on his emotions. 'Don't you feel any anger about *maa's* death? Any rage? Any fury?'

'*Dada,* what I was trying to say...'

'You always received *maa's* love on a platter, from the day you were born. That's why you don't value it!'

'*Dada...*'

'Ask me about the value of a mother's love... Ask me how much you hanker for it when you don't have it!'

'*Dada,* I loved her too. You know I...'

'Did you see her body, Kartik?'

'*Dada...*'

'Did you? Have you looked at her body?'

'*Dada*, of course, I have...'

'There are fifty-one wounds on her! I counted them, Kartik! Fifty-one!'

'I know...'

Furious tears were pouring down Ganesh's face. 'Those bastards must have continued hacking at her even after she was dead!'

'*Dada*, listen...'

Ganesh's body was shaking with anger now. 'Didn't you feel any rage when you saw your mother's mutilated body?'

'Of course I did, *dada*, but...'

'But?! What but can there be? She was attacked by many of those Somras-worshipping demons simultaneously! It is our duty to avenge her! Our duty! It is the least we can do for the best mother in the world!'

'*Dada*, she was the best mother... But she taught us to always put the world before ourselves.'

Ganesh didn't say anything. His long floppy nose had

stiffened, like it did on the rare occasions when he was enraged.

Kartik spoke softly. '*Dada,* if we were any other family I would give in to my rage... But we are not.'

Ganesh looked away, too livid to even respond.

'We are the family of the Neelkanth,' said Kartik. 'We have a responsibility to the world.'

'Responsibility to the world?! My *parents* are my world!'

Kartik fell silent.

Ganesh pointed his finger threateningly towards Kartik. 'Not one of those Somras-worshipping bastards will get out of here alive.'

'*Dada...*'

'Every single one of them will be killed; even if I have to kill them myself.'

Kartik fell silent.

Gopal sighed as he looked at Kali, Ganesh and Kartik. There was too much anger. He couldn't figure out a way to save the Somras scientists from Ganesh and Kali's rage. But at least he had managed to take the conversation away from the dangerous talk of using the *Pashupatiastra.* And maybe there was still hope that, over the next few hours, he would convince the Neelkanth's family of the necessity of saving the Somras scientists.

Shiva had been sitting quietly in the icy tomb, holding Sati's body. His eyes were sunken and expressionless, with no light of hope in them, with no reason to even exist. The blackish-red blotch on his brow was visibly throbbing; he was shivering due to the cold. A single droplet of fluid had escaped from Sati's good eye, now closed, and ran down her face like a tear. There was an unearthly silence in the room, except for the soft hissing of the cold air being pumped in at regular intervals. A sudden sharp noise startled Shiva, perhaps from the bulls harnessed to the Meluhan cooling system.

He looked around with cold, emotionless eyes. There was nobody in the chamber. He looked down at his dead wife. He pulled her body close and kissed her gently on her forehead. Then he carefully placed her back on the ice.

Caressing her face tenderly, Shiva whispered, 'Stay here, Sati. I'll be back soon.'

Shiva jumped off the ice tower and walked up to the door of the inner chamber. As soon as he opened it, Ayurvati stood up. Accompanied by her medical team, she had been tending to Nandi and the other soldiers for the last twenty-four hours.

'My Lord,' said Ayurvati, her eyes red and swollen from accumulated misery and lack of sleep.

Shiva ignored her and continued walking. Ayurvati looked at Shiva with foreboding and terror. She had never seen the Neelkanth's eyes look so hard and remote. He looked like he had gone beyond rage; beyond ruthlessness; beyond insanity.

Shiva opened the main door. He heard voices to his right. He turned to see his commanders in deep discussion. Tara was the first to notice him.

'Lord Neelkanth,' said Tara, immediately rising to her feet.

Shiva stared at her blankly for a few seconds, then took a deep breath and spoke evenly. 'Tara, the *Pashupatiastra* trunk is in my ship. Bring it here.'

A panic-stricken Gopal rushed towards Shiva. He knew that Shiva hadn't eaten in twenty-four hours. He hadn't slept. He had been sitting on top of an inhumanly cold tower. Grief had practically unhinged him. He knew the Neelkanth wasn't himself. 'My friend... Listen to me. Don't make a decision like this in haste.'

Shiva looked at Gopal, his face frozen.

'I know you are angry, Neelkanth. But don't do this. I know your good heart. You will repent it.'

Shiva turned around to walk back into the conference building. Gopal reached out and held Shiva's arm, trying to pull him back.

'Shiva,' pleaded Gopal, 'you've given your word to the Vayuputras. You've given your word to your uncle, Lord Mithra.'

Shiva gripped Gopal's hand tightly and removed it from his arm.

'Shiva, the power of this weapon is terrible and unpredictable,' pleaded Gopal, grasping at any argument to stop this tragedy. 'Even if the *Pashupatiastra's* destruction is restricted to the inner circle, any attempt to destroy all three platforms of Devagiri will widen this circle. It will not just destroy Devagiri, it will also destroy all of us. Do you really want to kill your entire army, your family and your friends?'

'Tell them to leave.'

Shiva's voice was soft, barely audible. His eyes remained remote and unfocused, staring into space. Gopal paused for a moment, watching Shiva with a glimmer of hope. 'Should I tell our people to leave? With the *Pashupatiastra*?'

Shiva did not move. There was no reaction on his face. 'No. Tell the people of this city to leave. All except those who have protected or made the Somras, and those directly responsible for Sati's death. For when I am done, there will be no more Daksha. There will be no more Somras. There will be no more Evil. It will be as if this place, this Evil, never existed. Nothing will live here, nothing will grow here, and no two stones will be left standing upon each other to show that there ever was a Devagiri. It all ends now.'

Gopal was grateful that at least the innocent people of

Devagiri would be saved. But what about Lord Rudra's law banning the use of *daivi astras*?

'Shiva, the *Pashupatiastra*...' whispered Gopal with hope.

Shiva stared at Gopal unemotionally and spoke in a voice that was eerily composed. 'I will burn down this entire world.'

Gopal stared at Shiva with foreboding. The Neelkanth turned around and walked back into the building, to his Sati.

Tara rose.

'Where are you going?' whispered Brahaspati.

'To get the *Pashupatiastra*,' answered Tara softly.

'You cannot! It will destroy us all!'

'No, it won't. These weapons can be triangulated in such a way that the devastation will remain confined within the city. We will not be affected if we remain more than five kilometres away.'

Tara began to walk away.

Brahaspati pulled her back and whispered urgently, 'What are you doing? You know this is wrong. I feel for Shiva, but the *Pashupatiastra*...'

Tara stared at Brahaspati without a hint of doubt in her eyes. 'Lord Ram's sacred laws have been shamelessly broken. The Neelkanth deserves his vengeance.'

'Of course, he does,' said Brahaspati, meeting her gaze without flinching. 'But not with the *Pashupatiastra*.'

'Don't you feel his pain? What kind of friend are you?'

'Tara, I had once considered doing something wrong. I had wanted to assassinate a man who was to duel Sati. Shiva stopped me. He stopped me from taking a sin upon my soul. If I have to be a true friend to him, I have to stop him from tarnishing his soul. I can't let him use the *Pashupatiastra*.'

'His soul is already dead, Brahaspati. It's lying on top of that ice tower,' said Tara.

'I know, but...'

Tara pulled her hand away from Brahaspati. 'You expect him to fight in accordance with the laws when his enemies have not. They have taken everything from him, his life, his soul, his entire reason for existence. He deserves his vengeance.'

Chapter 49

Debt to the Neelkanth

Shiva's army had been divided into three groups, led by Bhagirath, Chandraketu and Maatali. Each group was stationed outside the gates of the three platforms of Devagiri. Maatali's troops blocked the Svarna platform, Chandraketu's forces guarded the exit from the Rajat platform and Bhagirath's troops were at the steps of the Tamra platform. Shiva's instructions had been followed. Ignoring Kali's protests, Shiva's forces informed those within the city that they would be allowed to leave, all except those Kshatriyas who had fought to protect the Somras and those Brahmins who had worked to create the Somras. Daksha and his personal bodyguards, including Vidyunmali, had also been specifically excluded from the amnesty. An evacuation had begun. What amazed the Chandravanshis among Shiva's troops was the number of citizens who chose to stay on and die with Devagiri.

There were many who came in a disciplined line to the city gates, said a dignified goodbye to their families and walked silently back to their homes to await death. There was no acrimony; no fighting at the gates or attempts to save the city. Not even melodramatic farewells.

Gopal and Kartik had stationed themselves at the Tamra platform, along with Bhagirath's troops. The soldiers on this side were primarily Brangas. A tired Bhagirath, having just supervised the construction of the perimeter barricades, rejoined them.

The Ayodhyan prince nodded towards the odd movements of citizens at the gate, half of them leaving and the other half returning to the city. 'What's going on here?'

Kartik dropped his eyes and said nothing, while Gopal's eyes welled up.

'It is becoming a movement amongst the Meluhans,' said the chief of the Vasudevs. 'An act of honour. A cause that demands your life. Stay and die with your city. Have your soul purified by allowing yourself to be killed by the Neelkanth...' He stopped himself, obviously overcome with emotion.

Bhagirath raised his eyebrows. 'What do you mean?'

Gopal gestured towards the crowd, where yet another woman had said goodbye to a couple, before calmly turning back towards the city. 'See for yourself,' he said.

Bhagirath paused for a moment, brows knitted, to study Gopal's face before turning back to the woman.

'Excuse me, madam,' Bhagirath called out to her, and she stopped, turning to face him. 'Why are you returning to the city? Why are you not evacuating with the others?'

The folds of her *angvastram* wafted gently in the breeze around her. She had a kind face with dark, quiet eyes and a soft voice. She spoke calmly, as if she was discussing the weather. 'I am a Meluhan. To be Meluhan is not about the country you live in – it is about how you live, what you believe in. What is the purpose of a long life, if not to strive for something higher? Lord Ram's most sacred law has been broken. We have fallen. All that we are has already been destroyed. What can we now hope to strive for in this life, if this is our karma?'

Bhagirath couldn't believe his ears.

The Meluhan woman continued. 'I believe in the Neelkanth. I have waited for him for so many years, worshipped him. And this is what Meluha has done to him. To our Princess – the most exemplary Meluhan of us all, who lived every breath of her life strictly according to Lord Ram's code. This is what Meluha has done to our Laws that make us who we are.' She was quiet for a moment, her eyes searching his. 'I am guilty. I took the Somras. I followed the Emperor and, through my complacency and silence, was party to everything that conspired to bring this about. If this is Meluha's evil, then it is my evil too. My karma. I will pay my debt to the Neelkanth this day, and pray that it may allow me to be reborn with a little less sin upon my soul.'

Bhagirath was stunned. What logic was this? She inclined her head in a half nod towards him, and again began walking with perfect composure back into the city.

Gopal's voice came from behind him. 'I know. They all say the same thing. I am Meluhan. The Law has been broken. It is my karma.'

They stood in silence together and watched the woman go.

'Prince Bhagirath.' The two of them started slightly, pulled out of their silent contemplation.

'Yes, Kartik?' said Bhagirath, turning to face him.

'I want you to call General Parvateshwar.'

'I have already sent in a messenger to get Anandmayi,' said Bhagirath. 'But neither she nor her husband has come as yet. She will not leave without Parvateshwar. I'm still trying to convince the both of them.'

'Tell them,' said Gopal, 'Lord Kartik and I have invited them here. We need to talk about something that is important for India's future.'

Bhagirath frowned. He knew that what Gopal and Kartik were suggesting was the only way to get his sister and her husband out of Devagiri, tenuous though it may be.

'I will go into the city myself,' said Bhagirath.

'And, Prince Bhagirath...' Gopal hesitated.

'I understand, Pandit*ji*. I will not breathe a word of this to anyone.'

They stood in silence together, looking at a city that would no longer exist tomorrow.

'Excuse me,' said a voice. They turned around to see a small group of Meluhans.

'Yes?' asked Kartik.

'We left the city this morning but have changed our minds now. We would like to stay. May we go back in?'

Gopal stared at them in disbelief, and Bhagirath dropped his eyes, praying that he would be able to convince his sister to leave.

— ⁂ —

It was late into the third prahar and the sun was on its way down. This would be the last time that the sun would set on Devagiri. Veerini looked up at the sky as she walked out of the Devagiri royal palace.

'Your Highness,' saluted a guard smartly, falling into step behind her.

Veerini absently waved her hand and walked towards the gate.

'Your Highness? Are you leaving?' asked the shocked guard.

He seemed genuinely stunned that the Meluhan queen was abandoning them and taking up the Neelkanth's offer of amnesty.

Veerini didn't bother with a reply but continued walking down the road, towards the Svarna platform gate.

— ⁂ —

'Has this been ordered by the Neelkanth?' asked Anandmayi, before looking at her husband.

Parvateshwar and she were in a secluded section outside the Tamra platform, speaking with Gopal, Kartik and Bhagirath.

'It's what he would want,' said Gopal. 'He just doesn't know it at this point of time.'

Parvateshwar frowned. 'If the Neelkanth has said no, then it means no.'

'General, I appreciate your loyalty,' said Gopal. 'But there is also the larger picture. The Somras is evil now. But it's not supposed to be completely destroyed. You know as well as I do, it's only supposed to be taken out of the equation. We have to keep the knowledge of the Somras alive, for it may well be required again. It's the future of India that we are talking about.'

'Are you suggesting that the Lord Neelkanth doesn't care about India?' asked Parvateshwar.

'I'm saying no such thing, General,' said Gopal. 'But...'

Kartik suddenly stepped in. 'I appreciate your loyalty to my father. And, I'm sure you're aware of my love for him as well.'

Parvateshwar nodded, not saying anything.

'My father is distraught at this point in time,' said Kartik. 'You know of his devotion to my mother. The grief of her death has clouded his mind. He is furious, and rightly so. But you also know that his heart is pure. He would not want to do anything that is against his dharma. I only intend to keep the technology of the Somras alive till my father's rage subsides. If, after calm reflection, he still decides that everything associated with the Somras should be destroyed, I will personally see to it.'

Parvateshwar stared into space, his eyes brooding and dark.

'And in order to do that you must ensure the survival of the Brahmins, together with their Somras libraries,' he sighed.

'Many of those Somras-worshipping intellectuals would grab the opportunity to live. But there are some who have heard the call of honour. Kartik, you cannot coerce a man to forsake his honour. You cannot force him to live, particularly if it is to continue the Somras which his Neekanth has declared Evil, and which is causing the destruction of his homeland.'

Kartik held Parvateshwar's hand. 'General, my mother appeared in a dream to me. She told me to do the right thing. She told me to remember how she lived, and not how she died. Even you know she would have done exactly what I'm trying to do.'

Parvateshwar looked up at the sky and quickly wiped a tear. He was quiet for a long time. 'All right, Kartik,' he said at last. 'I will bring those people out. I will talk them out where I can, and force them out where I cannot. But remember, they are your responsibility. They cannot be allowed to propagate Evil any longer. Only the Lord Neelkanth can decide the fate of the Somras. Not you, not Lord Gopal, nor anyone else.'

***

Veerini rapidly walked down the Svarna platform steps as all the assembled people made way for their queen. Maatali's forces were in charge here, checking the papers and antecedents of everyone who sought to leave the city. The soldiers saluted Veerini. She acknowledged them distractedly but kept walking towards the massive wooden tower being constructed a good four kilometres from the city. That was the base from which the *Pashupatiastra* missile would be launched.

As she neared the tower, Veerini could see Shiva issuing instructions. She immediately recognised the woman who stood next to him: Brahaspati's love, Tara. Ganesh was working with Tara, his brilliant engineering skills coming in handy in building the solid tower. Kali sat a little distance away on a rock, seemingly lost in thought.

Kali was the first to see her. *'Maa!'*

Veerini walked up to Shiva as Kali and Ganesh stepped up.

Shiva looked at Veerini with glazed eyes, the now-constant throbbing pain in his brow making it difficult for him to focus. Veerini had always been struck by Shiva's eyes; the intelligence, focus and mirth that resided in them. She believed that it was his eyes rather than his blue throat that were the foundation of his charisma. But they now reflected nothing but pain and grief, giving a glimpse into a soul that had lost its reason to live.

Shiva had not for a moment suspected that Veerini was involved with Sati's assassination in any way. He bowed his head and brought his hands together in a respectful Namaste.

Veerini held Shiva's hand, her eyes drawn to the throbbing blackish-red blotch on his brow. 'My son, I can't even imagine the pain that you are going through.'

Shiva was quiet, looking lost and broken.

'I gave my word to Sati, a promise she extracted from me just before her death. I am here to fulfil it.'

Shiva's eyes suddenly found their focus. He looked up at Veerini.

'She insisted that she be cremated by both her sons.'

Ganesh, who was standing next to Veerini, sucked in his breath as tears slipped from his eyes. Tradition held that while the eldest child cremated the father, it was the youngest who conducted the funeral proceedings of the mother. Also, it was considered inauspicious for Nagas to be involved in any funeral ceremony. So Ganesh had not expected the honour of lighting his mother's pyre.

Kali turned and held Ganesh.

'But traditionally only the youngest child can perform the mother's last rites,' said Veerini to Shiva. 'If there is anyone who can challenge that tradition, it is you.'

'I don't give a damn about that tradition,' said Shiva. 'If Sati wanted it, then it will be done.'

'I'll tell Kartik as well,' said Veerini. 'I've been told he's at the Tamra platform.'

Shiva nodded silently before looking back towards the building where Sati's body lay entombed in ice.

Veerini stepped forward to embrace Shiva. He held his mother-in-law lightly.

'Try to find some peace, Shiva,' said Veerini. 'It's what Sati would have wanted.'

'Have *you* been able to find peace?'

Veerini smiled wanly.

'We will only find peace now when we meet Sati again,' said Shiva.

'She was a great woman. Any mother would be proud to have a daughter like her.'

Shiva kept quiet, wiping a tear from the corner of his eye.

Veerini held Shiva's hand. 'I have to tell you this. She could have been alive. When she found out about the conspiracy, she was in Devagiri, in our palace. She could have chosen to stay out of it. But she fought her way out of the city and rushed into the battle to save Nandi and her other bodyguards. And she did save many. She died a brave, honourable, warrior's death, fighting and challenging her opponents till her last breath. It was the kind of death she always wished for herself; that any warrior wishes for himself.'

Shiva's eyes welled up again. 'Sati set very high standards for herself.'

Veerini smiled sadly.

Shiva took a deep breath. He needed to focus on the *Pashupatiastra*. He folded his hands together into a polite Namaste. 'I should...'

'Of course,' said Veerini. 'I understand.'

Shiva bent and touched his mother-in-law's feet. She touched his head gently and blessed him. He turned and walked back to supervise the work on the weapon. This was the only thing that stopped his spirit from imploding.

Veerini turned and embraced her daughter Kali and grandson Ganesh.

'I have been unfair to the both of you,' said Veerini.

'No you haven't, *maa*,' said Kali. 'It was father who committed the sins. Not you.'

'But I failed in my duty as a mother. I should have abandoned my husband when he refused to accept you.'

Kali shook her head. 'You had your duty as a wife as well.'

'It is not a wife's duty to support her husband in his misdeeds. In fact, a good wife corrects her husband when he is wrong, even if she has to ram it down his throat.'

'I don't think he would have listened, *naani*,' said Ganesh to his *grandmother*, 'no matter how hard you tried. That man is...'

Veerini looked at her grandson as Ganesh checked himself from insulting his grandfather to her face. She noticed his eyes. They weren't calm and detached, like they had been the last time she had met him. They were full of rage; repressed fury over his mother's death.

'*Naani*, if you will excuse me. I need to work on the tower.'

'Of course, my child.'

Ganesh bent down, touched his grandmother's feet and walked back to Tara.

'*Maa*, wait for a bit and Ganesh will take you to our ship,' said Kali. 'You can stay there till this is over and then return with us to Panchavati. It would be so wonderful to have you in my home, even if it is a hundred years after it was meant to be. Having you with us will help us all cope with our grief and the vacuum left behind by Sati.'

Veerini smiled and embraced Kali. 'I'll have to wait for my next birth to live in your home, my child.'

Kali was taken aback. '*Maa!* You don't have to be punished for that old goat's crimes! You will not return to Devagiri!'

'Don't be ridiculous, Kali. I'm the Queen of Meluha. When Devagiri dies, so shall I.'

'Of course not!' cried Kali. 'There's no reason...'

'Would you leave Panchavati on the day of its destruction?'

Kali was stumped. But the Naga queen was not one who gave in easily. 'That's a hypothetical question, *maa*. What is important is that...'

'What is important, my child,' interrupted Veerini, 'is the identity of the man who helped your father execute the conspiracy. Many of the conspirators have escaped, as have the assassins. They will not die here tomorrow. You need to find them. You need to punish them.'

Chapter 50

Saving a Legacy

The sun had long set across the western horizon. Kartik, Gopal and Bhagirath were stationed at the far corner of the Tamra platform. Neither the other two Devagiri platforms nor Shiva's army encampment had a clear view of this area. It was the best place for Kartik to carry out his mission.

Twenty Branga soldiers from the command of Divodas, who had become fanatically loyal to Kartik after the Battle of Bal-Atibal Kund, were with him. These soldiers held on tightly to a rope, gently allowing it to roll away from them at a gradual pace. Divodas worked along with them. The rope was attached to a pulley that had been rigged on top of the Tamra platform wall. Circling the pulley, the rope went down to where it had been tied to a wooden cage, which could carry ten Brahmins at a time. Ten of them, together with their books and essential equipment, were descending towards Kartik's refuge. Secrecy was essential, for it was forbidden to remove any knowledge of the Somras from the city, the penalty being death.

As a failsafe, another rope had been tied to the wooden cage. This particular rope was also circled around a pulley that was rigged onto the fort wall. But the grasping end of this rope was in the hands of Suryavanshi soldiers at the top of the platform. They were being supervised by Parvateshwar. Both groups of soldiers worked in tandem to release their end of the ropes at the same pace, so that the cage could descend gently to the ground. The angle of the wall made it impossible for Parvateshwar to look over and judge the movement of the wooden cage as well as its distance from the ground. And if the Suryavanshis holding the rope on top did not synchronise their movement with Divodas' team below, it could lead to the cage becoming unbalanced, resulting in a possible accident.

To prevent this from happening, Bhagirath had been made to stand at a distance, far enough to be able to view both Divodas' team as well as the Suryavanshis above. The new moon helped aid Bhagirath's vision. His task was to keep whistling the way birds do, but in a steady rhythm, till the wooden cage touched the ground. He played the role of a time-keeper, setting the pace for the movements of the soldiers.

Kartik whirled around when Bhagirath's whistling stopped. Divodas and his team had not paused but continued releasing the rope at the same pace. The Suryavanshis on top of the fort walls however, used to following orders, had instantly come to a halt when Bhagirath stopped whistling. Immediately, the wooden cage became unbalanced and tilted heavily to one side.

'Stop!' hissed Kartik.

Divodas and his team stopped. The cage containing ten Brahmins of the Somras factory remained suspended dangerously in the air. To the admiration of Gopal, the Brahmins in the cage remained quiet despite the possibility of falling to their death. Any sharp noise would have alerted others to what was going on.

Kartik rushed towards Bhagirath, who seemed lost in his own world.

'Prince Bhagirath?'

Bhagirath immediately came out of his stupor and began to whistle. The Suryavanshis started releasing the rope at a steady pace and the wooden cage descended softly to the ground. The Brahmins caged within stepped out quickly in an orderly fashion.

As the two teams began pulling the empty cage back up, the whistling was no longer required. In the upward movement, what was necessary was speed, and not steadiness.

'Prince Bhagirath, please pay attention. The lives of many people are at stake.'

Kartik was aware of the reason behind Bhagirath's distress. Parvateshwar had refused to leave Devagiri. The Meluhan general had decided he would perish along with his beloved city. And to Bhagirath's utter dismay, Anandmayi had decided to stay with her husband.

Bhagirath had fought passionately with her over her decision. He had pleaded with her, had begged her to reconsider. 'Do you think Parvateshwar wants you to die? And what about me? Why are you trying to hurt me? Do you hate me so much? I am your brother. What have I done to deserve this?'

Anandmayi had only smiled, her eyes glistening with love and tears. 'Bhagirath, you love me and want me to live, with every fibre of your soul. So let me live. Let me live every last second of my life, in the way that I believe life should be lived. Let me go.'

Bhagirath shook his head as if to clear his mind. 'My apologies, Kartik.'

Kartik stepped forward and held Bhagirath's arm. 'Prince, your sister was right about you. You will make a far better king than your father.'

Bhagirath snorted. He already knew the Chandravanshi

army that had been ordered to march to Devagiri under the command of the Meluhan brigadier Vraka had rebelled against his father, Emperor Dilipa. The soldiers believed that the Ayodhyan emperor had led them into an ill-conceived battle where they were fighting on the side of their former enemies, the Meluhans, against their Neelkanth. Bhagirath knew that a section of the troops had already set out for Devagiri to convince him to ascend the throne. But he didn't care. He was tormented by the impending loss of his beloved sister.

'But do you know what the mark of a great king is?' asked Kartik.

Bhagirath looked at Kartik.

'It's the ability to remain focused, regardless of personal tragedy. You will have time to mourn your sister and brother-in-law, Prince Bhagirath. But not now. You are the only one here who can whistle like a night bird and make it sound natural. You cannot fail.'

'Yes, Lord Kartik,' said Bhagirath, addressing the young man as his Lord for the first time.

Kartik turned around. 'Come here.'

A Branga soldier marched up.

'Prince Bhagirath,' said Kartik, 'this man will remain here to support you in your task.'

Bhagirath didn't object. Kartik quickly walked back to Gopal.

Seeing the pensive look of the Vasudev chief, Kartik asked, 'What happened, Pandit*ji*?'

Gopal pointed to the Suryavanshi soldier. 'Lord Parvateshwar has sent a message. Maharishi Bhrigu has refused to leave the city.'

Kartik shook his head. 'Why are the Meluhans so bloody eager to die?'

'What do I do, Lord Kartik?' asked the Suryavanshi.

'Take me to Maharishi Bhrigu.'

A flickering sacrificial flame spread its light as best as it could in the night. Its reflection on the nearby Saraswati River aided its cause. Ganesh sat quietly on a *patla, a low stool,* with his legs crossed and his fleshy hands placed on his knees, his long fingers extended out delicately. He wore a white dhoti.

A barber was shearing Ganesh's hair, while Ganesh kept chanting a *mantra* softly and dropping some ghee into the sacrificial flame.

Having removed all of Ganesh's hair, the barber put his implement down and wiped his head with a cloth. Then he picked up a small bottle he had taken from Ayurvati, poured the disinfectant into his hands and spread it on Ganesh's head.

'It's done, My Lord.'

Ganesh didn't reply. He looked directly at the sacrificial flame and spoke softly. 'She was the purest among them all, Lord Agni. Remember that as you consume her. Take care of her and carry her straight to heaven, for that is where she came from. She was, is and forever will be a Goddess. She will be the Mother Goddess.'

It was late in the night when a tired Shiva trudged back to his Sati. The *Pashupatiastra* was ready. There were just a few more tests that needed to be conducted. Tara was at it. The peace conference area was within the external blast radius of the *Pashupatiastra*, so Sati's body would be moved from her icy tomb the next morning.

What nobody dared verbalise was that, without the Meluhan cooling mechanism, her body would start decomposing, and she would need to be cremated. That was something Shiva refused to contemplate.

Shiva opened the door of the inner chamber in the building, shivering at the sudden blast of cold air. He could see Ganesh, his son, standing next to the ice tower, holding his dead mother's hand. His head had been shaven clean. The Lord of the Nagas was on his toes, his mouth close to his mother's ear. Following an ancient tradition, he was whispering hymns from the Rig Veda into her ear.

Shiva walked up to Ganesh and touched his shoulder lightly. Ganesh immediately pulled up his white *angvastram* and wiped his eyes before turning to face his father.

Shiva embraced his son.

'I miss her, *baba*.' Ganesh held Shiva tightly.

'I miss her too...'

Ganesh began to cry. 'I abandoned her in her hour of need.'

'You weren't the only one, my son. I wasn't there either. But we will avenge her.'

Ganesh kept sobbing helplessly.

'I want to kill them all. I want to kill every single one of those bastards!'

'We will kill the Evil that took her life.' Shiva held his son quietly while he sobbed. He closed his eyes and pulled Ganesh in tighter, and whispered hoarsely, 'Whatever the cost.'

— ⅄ⵀ ⱴ ⴷ ⊗ —

Veerbhadra and Krittika had come to the Rajat platform. Krittika had lived in Devagiri for a long time and knew most people, so she had been trying to speak to those who were choosing to stay back, trying to convince them to leave.

'Veerbhadra, I need to talk to you.'

Veerbhadra turned around to see Kali and Parshuram standing behind him.

'Yes, Your Highness,' said Veerbhadra.

'In private,' said Kali.

'Of course,' said Veerbhadra, touching Krittika lightly before walking away.

— ⅄◎Ṵ⇡⊛ —

'Vidyunmali?' spat out Veerbhadra, his face hardening with fury.

'He's the main conspirator,' said Kali. 'He's hidden in the city, badly injured from some recent skirmish.'

Parshuram touched Veerbhadra's shoulder. 'We have to enter the city in a small group and locate him.'

Kali touched her knife, a serrated blade that delivered particularly painful wounds. 'We need to encourage him to talk. We need to know the identity of the assassins who escaped.'

'That son of a bitch deserves a slow, painful death,' growled Veerbhadra.

'That he does,' said Kali. 'But not before we've made him talk.'

Parshuram stretched his hand out, palm facing the ground. 'For the Lord Neelkanth.'

Veerbhadra placed his hand on Parshuram's. 'For Shiva.'

Kali placed her hand on top. 'For Sati.'

Chapter 51

Live On, Do Your Karma

'You want to enter Devagiri?' screeched Krittika. 'Are you mad?'

'I will be back soon, Krittika,' argued Veerbhadra. 'There is no lawlessness in the city. You've seen the way the Meluhans are behaving.'

'That may be so. But Vidyunmali's men will surely be prowling the streets. What do you think they're going to do? Welcome you with flowers?'

'They will not notice me, Krittika.'

'Nonsense! Most people in Devagiri recognise you as the Lord Neelkanth's friend.'

'They will recognise me only if they see me. It's late at night. I'm going to be hidden from view. Nobody will notice me.'

'Why can't you send someone else?'

'Because this is the least I can do for my friend. We need to find out who Princess Sati's actual killers are. Vidyunmali knows. He is the one who organised and implemented this peace farce.'

'But we are destroying the entire city. All the conspirators will be dead in any case!'

'Krittika, many of the killers got away,' said Veerbhadra.

'Except for Vidyunmali, nobody knows who they are. If we don't get to know their identities now, we will never know.'

Krittika looked away, having run out of arguments but still deeply troubled. 'I'm as angry as you are about Princess Sati's death. But the killing has to stop some time.'

'I have to go, Krittika.'

Veerbhadra tried to kiss her goodbye but she turned her face away. He could understand her anger. She had lost the woman she had idolised all her life. Her hometown, Devagiri, was about to be destroyed. She did not want to risk losing her husband as well. But Veerbhadra had to do this. Sati's killers had to be punished.

— ⅄ⵋⵡ⇡⊛ —

'Pandit*ji*,' said Kartik, his hands folded in a Namaste and his head bowed low.

Bhrigu opened his eyes. The maharishi had been meditating in the grand Indra temple next to the Public Bath.

'Lord Kartik,' said Bhrigu, surprised to see Kartik in Devagiri at this time of night.

'I'm too young for you to address me as Lord, great Maharishi,' said Kartik.

'Noble deeds make a man a Lord, not merely his age. I have heard about your efforts to ensure the Somras is not completely destroyed. History will thank you for it. Your glory will be recounted for ages.'

'I'm not working for my own glory, Pandit*ji*. My task is to be true to my father's mission. My task is to do what my mother would have wanted me to do.'

Bhrigu smiled. 'I don't think your mother would have wanted you to come here. I don't think she would have wanted you to save me.'

'I disagree,' said Kartik. 'You are a good man. You just picked the wrong side.'

'I didn't just pick this side, I *led* it into battle. And the dictates of dharma demand that I perish with it.'

'Why?'

'If the side I led committed such crimes, I must pay for it. If fate has determined that those that supported the Somras have sinned, then the Somras must be evil. I was wrong. And, my punishment is death.'

'Isn't that taking the easy way out?'

Bhrigu stared at Kartik, angered by the implied insult.

'So you think you have done something wrong, Pandit*ji*,' said Kartik. 'What is the way out? Escaping through death? Or, actually working to set things right by balancing your karma?'

'What can I do? I've conceded that the Somras is evil. There's nothing left for me to do now.'

'You have a *vast storehouse of knowledge* within you Pandit*ji*,' said Kartik. 'The Somras is not the only subject you excel at. Should the world be deprived of Lord Bhrigu's *Samhita*?'

'I don't think anyone is interested in my knowledge.'

'That is for posterity to determine. You should only do your duty.'

Bhrigu fell silent.

'Pandit*ji*, your karma is to spread your knowledge throughout the world,' said Kartik. 'Whether others choose to listen or not is their karma.'

Bhrigu shook his head as a wry smile softened his expression. 'You speak well, son of the Neelkanth. But I chose to support something that turned out to be evil. For this sin, I must die. There is no karma left for me in this life. I will have to wait to be born again.'

'One cannot allow a bad deed to arrest the wheel of karma. Don't banish yourself from this world as a punishment for your sin. Instead, stay here and do some good, so that you can cleanse your karma.'

Bhrigu stared at Kartik silently.

'One cannot undo what has happened. But the inexorable march of time offers the wise opportunities for redemption. I entreat you, do not escape. Stay in this world and do your karma.'

Bhrigu smiled. 'You are very intelligent for such a young boy.'

'I'm the son of Shiva and Sati,' smiled Kartik. 'I am the younger brother of Ganesh. When the gardeners are good, the flower will bloom.'

Bhrigu turned towards the idol of Lord Indra within the sanctum sanctorum. The great God, the killer of the primal demon Vritra, stood resplendent as he held his favourite weapon, *Vajra, the thunderbolt.* Bhrigu folded his hands into a Namaste and bowed, praying for the God's blessing.

The maharishi then turned back to Kartik and whispered, '*Samhita...*'

'The *Bhrigu Samhita,*' said Kartik. 'The world will benefit from your vast knowledge, Pandit*ji*. Come with me. Don't sit here and wait for death.'

— ⅄◎Ʊ⍏⊗ —

The sun rose on the day that would be Devagiri's last. The *Pashupatiastra* was ready. After barring the gates, Shiva's soldiers had been asked to retreat beyond the safety line, out of the range of the expected radius of exposure. The relatives of those remaining within Devagiri too waited patiently, as they were herded back by Chandraketu's Brangas. They kept up a constant prayer for the souls of their loved ones who were left behind in the city.

Maharishi Bhrigu and another three hundred people, who knew the secrets of the Somras, had been successfully spirited out of Devagiri the previous night. They were now kept imprisoned in a temporary stockade ten kilometres north of Devagiri under the watchful eye of Divodas and his soldiers. Kartik intended to wait for his father's anger to subside before talking to him about Bhrigu and the others.

The peace conference building had been abandoned. Nandi and the other surviving bodyguards had been carefully evacuated onto Shiva's ship, where a medical team under the supervision of Ayurvati maintained a constant vigil.

Ayurvati was worried about the blackish-red mark on Shiva's brow. It had made its appearance many times before, especially when Shiva was angry. But very rarely had it stayed for so long. Shiva had brushed aside Ayurvati's concerns.

Shiva, Kali, Ganesh and Kartik carried Sati's body gently to a specially prepared cabin on the ship. Her corpse was laid with great care within another tomb of ice.

Shiva gently ran his hand across Sati's face and whispered, 'Devagiri will pay for its crimes, my love. You will be avenged.'

As Shiva stepped back, the soldiers placed another block of ice on top, enveloping Sati's body completely.

Shiva, Kali, Ganesh and Kartik took one last look at Sati before turning around and walking out of the ship. Gopal and the kings in Shiva's army waited at the port.

Shiva turned and nodded towards the ship captain. Soldiers marched into the rowing deck of the ship to row it back a fair distance down the Saraswati River, far away from the external blast radius of the *Pashupatiastra*.

'The weapon is armed, Lord Neelkanth,' said Tara.

Shiva cast an expressionless look at an unhappy Gopal and then turned back towards Tara. 'Let's go.'

— ⁂ —

It was the fourth hour of the second prahar, just a couple of hours before Devagiri was to be destroyed. Veerini knocked on Parvateshwar's door. There was no answer. Parvateshwar and Anandmayi were probably alone at home.

Veerini pushed open the door and stepped into the house. She walked past the lobby into the central courtyard.

'General!' called out Veerini.

No response.

'General!' said Veerini again, a little louder this time. 'It is I, the Queen of Meluha.'

'Your Highness!'

Veerini glanced up to see a surprised Parvateshwar looking down from the balcony on the top floor. His hair was dishevelled and an *angvastram* had been hastily thrown over his shoulders.

'My apologies if I have come at a bad time, General.'

'Not at all, Your Highness,' said Parvateshwar.

'It's just that we don't have much time left,' said Veerini. 'There is something I needed to tell you.'

'Please give me a moment, Your Highness. I'll be down shortly.'

'Of course,' said Veerini.

Veerini walked into the large waiting room next to the courtyard, settled on a comfortable chair and waited. A few minutes later Parvateshwar, clad in a spotless white dhoti and *angvastram*, his hair neatly in place, walked into the room. Behind him was his wife, Anandmayi, also clad in white, the colour of purity.

Veerini rose. 'Please accept my apologies for disturbing you.'

'Not at all, Your Highness,' said Parvateshwar. 'Please be seated.'

Veerini resumed her seat, as Parvateshwar and Anandmayi sat next to her.

'What did you want to talk about, Your Highness?' asked Parvateshwar.

Veerini seemed to hesitate. Then she looked at Anandmayi and Parvateshwar with a smile. 'I wanted to thank you.'

'Thank us?' asked a surprised Parvateshwar, casting a look at Anandmayi before turning back to Veerini. 'Thank us for what, Your Highness?'

'For keeping the legacy of Devagiri alive,' said Veerini.

Parvateshwar and Anandmayi remained silent, their expressions reflecting their confusion.

'Devagiri is not just a physical manifestation,' said Veerini, waving her hand around. 'Devagiri exists in its knowledge, its philosophies and its ideologies. You have managed to keep that alive by saving our intellectuals.'

An embarrassed Parvateshwar didn't know how to react. How could he openly acknowledge having broken the law to save the scientists who worked at the Somras factory? 'Your Highness, I didn't...'

Veerini raised her hand. 'Your conduct has been exemplary all your life, Lord Parvateshwar. Don't spoil it by lying on your last day.'

Parvateshwar smiled.

'The people you've saved are not merely the repositories of the knowledge of Somras, but also of the accumulated knowledge of our great land. They are the custodians of our philosophies, of our ideologies. They will keep our legacy alive. For that, Devagiri and Meluha will forever be grateful to you.'

'Thank you, Your Highness,' said Anandmayi, accepting the gratitude on behalf of her discomfited husband.

'It's bad enough that the both of you are dying for my

husband's sins,' said Veerini. 'It would have been really terrible had Maharishi Bhrigu and our intellectuals suffered for it as well.'

'I think what's really unfair is your suffering for your husband's sins, Your Highness,' said Anandmayi. 'Your husband may not have been a good emperor, but you have been an excellent queen.'

'No, that's not true. If it were, I would have stood up to my husband instead of standing by him.'

They sat quietly together for a moment, then Veerini straightened her shoulders and rose to leave. 'Time grows short,' she said, 'and there are preparations we still have to make for our final journey. Thank you, both of you, and let us say our farewells. For one last time.'

Chapter 52

The Banyan Tree

Daksha sat quietly in his chamber, staring out of the window, waiting for his death. He looked towards the door, wondering where Veerini had gone so early in the morning.

Has she abandoned me as well?

As death approached, he was honest enough at least with himself, to not blame her if she had.

Daksha took a deep breath, wiped a tear and turned his gaze back at the window, towards the banyan tree in the distance. It was a magnificent tree, centuries old, even older than Daksha. He had known this tree for as long as he could remember. He recalled its size when he was young and the fact that he always marvelled at how the tree never seemed to stop growing. Its branches spread themselves out over vast distances, and when they extended too far, they dropped thin reed-like roots into the ground. The drop-roots then matured, anchoring themselves deep, drawing nourishment and growing enough in bulk to eventually resemble another trunk, thus supporting the further extension of the branch that gave them birth. After a few decades, there were so many new trunks that it was impossible to tell which the original one was. It had been a single tree when Daksha was born. It still was, but now it was so massive, that it appeared like a jungle.

Daksha knew all Indians looked upon the grand banyan tree with utmost respect and devotion. It was considered holy in India; a tree that unselfishly gave its all to others, building an ecosystem that sustained many birds and animals. Innumerable plants and shrubs found succour and shade under its protective cover. It remained firm and solid, even in the face of the most severe storm. Indians believed that ancestral spirits, even the Gods, inhabited the banyan tree.

For most citizens of Devagiri, this massive tree represented the ideal of life. They worshipped it.

Daksha's perspective though, was very different.

At a very young age, he had noted that no offspring of a banyan was able to flourish, or even grow, around its parent. The roots of the tree were too strong; they twisted and pushed away any attempt by another banyan sapling to grow roots in the vicinity. For a young sapling to survive, it would have to move very far away from its parent.

I should have run away.

The banyan tree is pollinated by a particular species of wasp. But the tree extracts a terrible price from the tiny insect that aids its reproduction. It kills the wasp, kills it brutally, ripping the insect to shreds. Daksha's interpretation of this fact was very simple: the banyan hated its own progeny so much that it would murder the kindly wasp that tries to bring its offspring to life.

To a neglected child's imagination, the banyan tree's munificence was reserved for others. It did not care for its own. In fact, it went out of its way to harm its own.

So while everyone else looks upon the banyan tree with reverential eyes, Daksha viewed it with fear and hatred.

He was fearful because this was not the only banyan tree in his life. He had had another: his father.

He hated his father with venomous intensity; but at a

deeper level, perhaps loved and admired his abilities. Just like the desperate offspring of the banyan, he had always tried to prove that he could be as great as his father. He had carried this burden all his life. But there had been this one time when he had unshackled himself from his father's grip; when he had been free for a few magical moments. He remembered that day so clearly. It had been a long time ago; more than a hundred years.

Sati had just returned from the Maika gurukul, a headstrong, idealistic girl of sixteen. In keeping with her character, she had jumped in to save an immigrant woman from a vicious pack of wild dogs. Daksha remembered well that Parvateshwar and he had rushed in to her rescue. He also remembered that, despite not being an accomplished warrior, he had, with Parvateshwar's help, courageously fought back the dogs that were out to kill his daughter. He had been seriously injured in that terrible fight.

Fortunately, the medical teams had reached quickly. Parvateshwar and Sati's injuries were superficial and had been quickly dressed. Daksha knew that since he had been in the thick of the battle, his injuries were the most serious. The medical officers had decided to take him to the *ayuralay* so that senior doctors could examine him. However, due to massive blood loss, he had lost consciousness on the way.

When he had regained consciousness, he had found himself in the *ayuralay*. He remembered that he'd scolded Sati for risking her own life to save an insignificant immigrant woman. Later, when recuperating in his room, he had asked Veerini to bring Sati to him, in order to make peace with her now. But before Sati could be brought in, Daksha's father Brahmanayak had stormed into the chamber, accompanied by the doctor who had treated Daksha.

Brahmanayak, being one of the foremost warriors in

Meluha, had mocked Daksha about how he could have got himself so badly injured while fighting mere dogs. The doctor had pulled Brahmanayak out of the room using the excuse of a private conversation, wanting to save Daksha from any further mental anguish. As soon as Brahmanayak had left the room, Veerini had repeated the plea she had made many times earlier, that they should escape from Meluha and live in Panchavati with both their daughters, Kali and Sati.

'Daksha, trust me,' said Veerini. 'We'll be happy in Panchavati. If there was any other place where we could live with both Kali and Sati, I'd suggest it. But there isn't.'

Maybe Veerini's right. I can escape the old man. We can be happy. Also, Sati is the only pure one in my bloodline. Veerini's corrupt soul has led to Kali's birth. It's difficult to help them. But I have to protect Sati from the terrible fate of seeing her father being insulted every day. My elder daughter is the only one worthy of my love.

Daksha breathed deeply. 'But how...'

'You leave that to me. I'll make the arrangements. Just say yes. Your father is leaving tomorrow for Karachapa. You are not so badly injured that you can't travel. We'll be in Panchavati before he knows you're gone.'

Daksha stared at Veerini. 'But...'

'Trust me. Please trust me. It will be for our good. I know you love me. I know you love your daughters. Deep inside, I know you don't really care about anything else. Just trust me.'

Perhaps this is what we need.

Daksha nodded.

Veerini smiled, bent close and kissed her husband. 'I'll make all the arrangements.'

Veerini turned and walked out of the room.

In this moment of solitude, Daksha glanced at the ceiling, feeling light and relaxed; feeling free.

Everything happens for a reason, perhaps even this battle with the dogs. We can be happy in Panchavati. We will be away from my father. We will be free of that monster. To hell with Meluha. To hell with the throne. I don't want any of it. I just want to be happy. I just want to be with my Sati and be able to take care of her. I will also look after Veerini and Kali. Who do they have besides me?

He noticed Veerini's prayer beads on the chair. Next to the prayer beads was the tiger claw that Sati wore as a pendant. It must have fallen off during the battle with the dogs and Veerini must have recovered it to return it to their young daughter. Daksha stared at the blood stains on the tiger claw; his daughter's blood. His eyes became moist again.

I will be nothing like my father. I'll take care of Sati. I will love her like every father should love his child. I will not ridicule her in public. I will not deride her for the qualities she doesn't possess. Instead, I will cherish everything that she does have. She will be free to live her own dreams. I will not force my dreams upon her. I will love her for who she is; not for what I'd like her to be.

Daksha looked at his own injured body and shook his head.

All of this to save an immigrant woman! Sati can be so naive at times. But she is a child. I shouldn't have screamed at her. I should have explained things calmly to her. After all, who does she have to look up to besides me?

Just then the door opened and Sati walked in, looking grouchy; almost angry.

Daksha smiled.

She's only a child.

'Come here, my child,' said Daksha.

Sati stepped forward hesitantly.

'Come closer, Sati,' laughed Daksha. 'I'm your father. I'm not going to eat you up!'

Sati stepped closer. But her face still reflected the righteous anger she felt within.

Lord Ram, be merciful! This girl still thinks that she did the right thing in risking all our lives to save an unimportant immigrant woman.

Daksha reached out and held Sati's hand, speaking patiently. 'My child, listen to me. I care for you. I only had your best interests at heart. It was stupid of you to risk your life for that immigrant. But I admit I shouldn't have shouted at...'

Daksha fell silent as the door swung open suddenly and Brahmanayak strode in.

Sati suddenly withdrew her hand and turned around to look at Brahmanayak, her back towards her father.

'Aah!' said Brahmanayak as his face broke into a broad smile. He walked up to Sati and embraced her. 'At least one of my progeny has my blood coursing through her veins!'

Sati looked at Brahmanayak adoringly, pure hero-worship in her eyes. Daksha stared at him with impotent rage.

'I've heard about what you did,' said Brahmanayak to Sati. 'You risked your own life to protect a woman whom you didn't even know; a woman who was only a lowly immigrant.'

Sati smiled in embarrassment. 'It was nothing, Your Highness.'

Brahmanayak laughed softly and patted Sati's cheek. 'I am not "Your Highness" for you, Sati. I'm your grandfather.'

Sati nodded, smiling.

'I'm proud of you, my child,' said Brahmanayak. 'I am honoured to call you a Meluhan, honoured to call you my granddaughter.'

Sati's smile broadened as her heart felt light. She had done the right thing after all. She embraced her grandfather once again.

Brahmanayak bent down and kissed his adolescent granddaughter on her forehead. He then turned to Daksha, the smile immediately disappearing from his face. With barely concealed contempt, he told his son, 'I'm leaving for Karachapa tomorrow morning and will be gone for many weeks. Perhaps you will need that much time to recover from your so-called injuries. We'll talk about your future when I return.'

A seething Daksha refused to answer Brahmanayak, turning his face away.

Brahmanayak shook his head and rolled his eyes. He then patted Sati on her head. 'I'll see you when I return, my child.'

'Yes, grandfather.'

Brahmanayak opened the door and was gone.

Daksha glared at the closed door.

Thank God I'm going to be rid of you, you beast! Insulting me in front of my favourite daughter? How dare you! Take the throne away, take all the riches away, take the world away if you wish. But don't you dare take my good daughter away from me! She's mine!

He looked at Sati's back. She was still staring at the door, her body shaking.

Is she crying?

Daksha thought that perhaps Sati was angry with Brahmanayak for insulting her father. She was his daughter after all.

Daksha smiled. 'It's all right, my child. I'm not angry. Your grandfather doesn't matter anymore because...'

'Father,' interrupted Sati as she turned around, tears streaming down her cheeks. 'Why can't you be more like grandfather?'

Daksha stared at his daughter, dumbstruck.

'Why can't you be more like grandfather?' whispered Sati again.

Daksha was in shock.

Sati suddenly turned around and ran out of the room.

Daksha kept staring at the door as it slammed shut behind Sati. Fierce tears were pouring from his eyes.

More like grandfather?

More like that monster?

I am better than him!

The Gods know that! They know I will make a far better king! I will show you!

You will love me! I am your creator!

You will love me! Not him! Not that monster!

The sound of the door being opened broke his train of thought, bringing Daksha back to the present from that ancient memory.

He saw Veerini walk into the bed chamber. She glanced at Daksha for an instant, then shook her head, walked up to her private desk and rummaged through it to find what she was looking for: her prayer beads. She brought them up to touch her forehead reverentially, then both her eyes and then her lips. She held the beads tightly and turned to take one last look at her husband. The disgust she felt couldn't be expressed in words. She had no intention of desecrating her ears by listening to his voice. She hadn't spoken to him since Sati's death.

Daksha's eyes followed Veerini's passage. He couldn't muster the courage to speak, even if it was only to apologise for all that he'd done.

She walked into the private prayer room next to her bed chamber and shut the door. She bowed before the idol of Lord Ram, which was, as usual, surrounded by the idols of his favourite people, his wife, Lady Sita, his brother, Lord Lakshman and his loyal devotee, Lord Hanuman, the Vayuputra.

Veerini sat down cross-legged. She held the beads high, in front of her eyes and began chanting as she waited for her death. 'Shri Ram Jai Ram Jai Jai Ram; Shri Ram Jai Ram Jai Jai Ram...'

The faint echo of this chanting reached Daksha's ears. He

stared at the closed door of the attached chamber, his angry wife closeted within.

I should have listened to her. She was right all along.

'Shri Ram Jai Ram Jai Jai Ram; Shri Ram Jai Ram Jai Jai Ram....'

He continued to hear the soft chanting of his wife in the prayer room. Those divinely serene words should have brought him peace. But there was no chance of that. He would die a frustrated and angry man.

Daksha clenched his jaw and looked out of the window. He stared at the banyan tree in the distance, tears streaming down his face.

Damn you!

The banyan shook slightly and its leaves ruffled dramatically with the strong wind. It appeared as if the giant tree was laughing at him.

Damn you!

Chapter 53

The Destroyer of Evil

'The wind is too strong,' murmured a worried Tara, looking at the windsock that had been set up close to the *Pashupatiastra* missile tower.

Tara and Shiva were mounted on horses, stationed far from the *Pashupatiastra* launch tower. It was almost the end of the second prahar and the sun was just a few moments away from being directly overhead. Shiva's entire army and the refugees from Devagiri had been cordoned off seven kilometres from the launch tower, safely outside the *Pashupatiastra's* blast radius.

Shiva glanced at Tara and then up at the sky, trying to judge the wind from the movement of dust particles. 'Not a problem.'

Saying this, Shiva's attention returned to stringing his bow. Parshuram had been working on making this composite bow for months. Its basic structure was made of wood, reinforced with horn on the inside and sinew on the outside. It was also curved much sharper than normal, with its edges turning away from the archer. Due to the mix of different elements and the curve at the edges, the bow had exceptional draw strength for its small size. It was ideal for an archer to shoot arrows from, while riding a horse or a chariot. Parshuram had named the bow *Pinaka*, after the fabled great ancient longbow of Lord Rudra.

Though Parshuram didn't know this while designing the bow, the Pinaka would prove ideal for Shiva's purpose, as firing the *Pashupatiastra* was not easy.

The *Pashupatiastra* was a pure nuclear fusion weapon, unlike the *Brahmastra* and the *Vaishnavastra* which were nuclear fission weapons. In a pure nuclear fusion weapon, two *paramanoos*, the *smallest stable division of matter*, are fused together to release tremendous destructive energy. In a nuclear fission weapon, *anoos*, *atomic particles*, are broken down to release *paramanoos*, and this is also accompanied by a demonic release of devastating energy.

Nuclear fission weapons leave behind a trail of uncontrollable destruction, with radioactive waste spreading far and wide. A nuclear fusion weapon, on the other hand, is much more controlled, destroying only the targeted area with minimal radioactive spread.

So the *Pashupatiastra* would be the obvious weapon of choice for those who intended to destroy a specific target with the precision of a surgeon. The problem though, was its launch.

These *daivi astras* were usually mounted on launching towers, packed with a mixture of sulphur, charcoal, saltpetre and a few other materials which generated the explosive energy that propelled the *astra* towards the target. Once the *astra* was close to its target, another set of explosions would trigger the weapon.

The launch material within the tower had to be triggered from a safe distance or else the people firing the *astra* would be incinerated in the initial launch explosion. Keeping this in mind, archers were called upon to shoot flaming arrows from a distance to trigger the launch explosion. These archers usually used long bows with a range of more than eight hundred metres. To hit a target accurately from this distance required archers of great skill.

The *Brahmastra* and *Vaishnavastra* did not need a precise landing as their destruction spread far and wide. Since accuracy was not of the essence, the launch towers that cradled these weapons had huge firing targets.

The *Pashupatiastra* or *Weapon of the Lord of Animals* was a precise missile. It had to land at the exact spot. What complicated the issue even more at this particular time was that the attempt was to fire three missiles concurrently. The trajectory of the three missiles had been planned such that they would detonate over the Svarna, Rajat and Tamra platforms of Devagiri simultaneously, guaranteeing the complete and instantaneous destruction of the entire city. The risk with trying to destroy three platforms at the same time was that the inner circle of devastation would expand, since the weapons would have to be triggered from a greater height. Tara had planned the angles of descent of each missile such that, together, their simultaneous explosions would ensure the annihilation of Devagiri while their excess energies would be trapped within each other, thus preventing any fallout destruction outside the inner circle.

A precise descent needed a perfect take-off. Therefore, the *Pashupatiastra* missiles had been set at precise angles within the tower. The target area on the tower where the fiery arrow would be shot was small. Shiva had to fire an arrow to hit the target, placed more than eight hundred metres away. Moreover, he had to do this while seated on a horse, so that he could escape immediately after firing the arrow.

'Remember, great Neelkanth,' said Tara, 'the moment your arrow hits the target, you have to ride away. You will have less than five minutes before the *Pashupatiastra* explodes over Devagiri. You have to cover at least three kilometres within that time. Only then will you be out of the range of the minuscule number of neutrons from the *Pashupatiastra* which may escape that far.'

Shiva nodded distractedly, still testing his bow's draw strength.

'Neelkanth? It is crucial for you to ride as fast as you can. The blast can be fatal.'

Shiva didn't respond. He pulled out the arrows from the quiver. He smelt them and then rubbed the tip of one of the arrows against the rough leather of the pommel. The tip immediately caught fire. Perfect. Shiva threw the burning arrow away and returned the rest to the quiver.

'Did you hear me? You need to move away immediately.'

Shiva wiped his hand on his *dhoti* and turned to Tara. 'Ride beyond the safety line now.'

'Shiva! You shoot the arrow and move.'

Shiva looked at Tara, his gaze glassy. Tara could see the blackish-red blotch on his brow throbbing frantically.

'You will ride away immediately!' emphasised Tara. 'Promise me!'

Shiva nodded.

'Promise me!'

'I have already promised you. Now go.'

Tara stared at Shiva. 'Neelkanth...'

'Go, Tara. The sun is about to reach overhead. I need to fire the missiles.'

Tara pulled her horse's reins and spun it around.

'And Tara...'

Tara pulled up her horse and looked back over her shoulder.

'Thank you,' said Shiva.

Tara was still, watching the face of the Neelkanth with clouded eyes. 'Ride back quickly beyond the safety line. Remember, all those who love you are waiting for you.'

Shiva held his breath.

Yes, my love is waiting for me.

Tara kicked her horse into action and rode away.

Shiva pressed his forehead, right above the blackish-red mark. The pressure seemed to ease the horrendous burning sensation. The pain had been immense and continuous for the last few days, ever since he had seen Sati's body.

Shiva shook his head and focused his attention on the tower. He could see the target in the distance. It had been marked a bright red.

He took a deep breath and looked towards the ground.

Holy Lake, give me strength.

Shiva breathed once again and looked up.

Lord Ram, be merciful!

Arrayed in front of him was an army of clones, blocking his view of the *Pashupatiastra* launch tower; clones of the giant hairy monster who had tormented him in his nightmares since his childhood. Shiva looked carefully and noticed that none of the monsters had faces. There was a smooth, white slate where their faces should have been. All of them had their swords drawn, blood dripping from every single blade. He could clearly hear their ghastly roar. For a moment Shiva imagined he was a terrified little boy once again.

Shiva looked up at the sky and shook his head, as if to clear it.

Help me!

Shiva heard his uncle Manobhu's voice call out. 'Forgive them! Forget them! Your only true enemy is Evil!'

Shiva brought his eyes down and locked his gaze on the launch tower. The monsters had disappeared. He stared directly at the red spot, right at the centre of the tower.

Shiva pulled his horse's reins and turned it right, singing softly in its ear to calm it down. The horse stayed still, offering Shiva the stable base he needed to hit a target. He turned his head to his left, creating the natural angle for a right-handed archer to get a straight shot. He pulled his bow forward and tested the string once again. He liked the twang of the bowstring when it was pulled and released rapidly. It was as taut as it could be. He bent forward and pulled an arrow from the quiver. He held it to his side and looked up, judging the wind.

The art of shooting arrows from this huge distance was all about patience and judgement. It was about waiting for the right wind conditions; the ability to judge the parabolic movement of the arrow; determining the ideal angle of release; controlling the speed of the arrow at release; deciding the extent to which the string should be pulled. Shiva kept his eyes fixed on the windsock, keeping his breathing steady, trying to ignore the burning sensation between his eyes.

The wind is changing direction.

Pointing the bow towards the ground Shiva nocked an arrow, the shaft firmly gripped between his hooked index and middle finger.

The wind is holding.

He ignited the tip by rubbing it against the leather pommel. Taut muscles raised the bow and drew the string in one fluid motion, even as his warrior mind instinctively calculated the correct angle of flight. Master archer that he was, he kept his dominant eye focused on the target. His left hand held the bow rock-steady, ignoring the searing heat from the tip of the arrow.

The wind is perfect.

He released the arrow without hesitation.

He saw the arrow move in a parabola, as if in slow motion. His eyes followed its path till it hit the red target, depressing it with its force. The fire immediately spread to the waiting receptacle behind the target. The *Pashupatiastra's* initial launch had been triggered.

'Ride away!' screamed Tara from the distance.

'*Baba*, turn your horse around!' shouted Kartik.

But Shiva could not hear either of them. They were too far away.

Shiva kept staring at the rapidly spreading fire behind the target, the pain within his brow ratcheting up once again. He felt as if the insides of his forehead were on fire as well, just like the launch tower. He pulled the reins of his horse and turned it around.

He could see his troops far away. Beyond them, he could see his ship, anchored on the Saraswati. Sati's body was stored in there.

She's waiting for me.

Shiva kicked his horse. The animal didn't need much coaxing as it quickly broke into a gallop.

The fire within the launch tower finally triggered the initial explosion. The three *Pashupatiastras* shot out of their pods, the two that were directed at the Tamra and Swarna platforms taking off just a few milliseconds after the third. That was because the target of the third missile, the Rajat platform, was farther away.

Shiva kept kicking his horse as it galloped faster and faster. He was just a few seconds away from the safety line. The missiles flew in a great arc, leaving a trail of fire behind them. Seconds later, they began their simultaneous descent into the city, like giant harbingers of absolute destruction.

'S-H-I-V-A!'

Shiva could have sworn he heard the voice that he loved beyond all reason. But it couldn't have been for real. He kept riding on.

The *Pashupatiastra* missiles were descending rapidly.

'S-H-I-V-A! S-H-I-V-A!'

Shiva looked back.

A bloodied and mutilated Sati was running after him. Her left hand was spewing blood in bursts, in tune with each beat of her pounding heart. Two massive wounds on her abdomen gaped open as blood streamed out from them in a torrent. Her left eye was gouged out. Her burn scar seemed like it was on fire once again. She was struggling desperately, but she kept running towards Shiva.

'S-H-I-V-A! HELP ME! DON'T LEAVE ME!'

An army of soldiers chased Sati, holding bloodied swords aloft. Each warrior was the exact likeness of Daksha. The area between Shiva's brows began throbbing even more desperately. The fire within was struggling to burst through.

'SATI!' screamed Shiva, as he pulled the reins of his horse. He was not going to lose her again.

The horse balked at Shiva's anxious command and refused to slow down.

'SATI!'

Shiva desperately yanked at the reins. But the horse had a mind of its own. He was not going to either slow down or turn. The beast could sense the stench of death behind it.

Shiva pulled both his feet out of the stirrups and jumped to the ground, the speed of his fall making him lurch dangerously. He rolled quickly and was up on his feet in a flash.

'SATI!'

The horse kept galloping ahead towards the safety line as Shiva turned around, drew his sword and ran to protect the mirage of his wife.

'*Baba!*' shouted Ganesh. 'Come back!'

The blackish-red mark at the centre of Shiva's forehead burst open and blood spewed out. He ran desperately towards his wife, roaring at the army of Dakshas who chased her.

'LEAVE HER ALONE, YOU BASTARDS! FIGHT ME!'

The three *Pashupatiastra* missiles simultaneously exploded as planned, some fifty metres above the three platforms. A blinding burst of light erupted. Shiva's army and the Devagiri refugees shielded their eyes, only to be stunned by what they saw of their own bodies. Glowing and translucent, blood, muscle and even bone were visible. They even saw a demonic flash within their bodies, an echo of the devastating blasts over Devagiri. Sheer terror entered their hearts.

Almost immediately thereafter, three bursts of satanic fire descended from the heights where the three *Pashupatiastras* had exploded. They tore into *Devagiri* fiendishly, instantaneously incinerating all three platforms. The great *City of the Gods*, built and nurtured over centuries, was reduced to nothingness in a fraction of a second.

'Lord Ram, be merciful,' whispered Ayurvati in absolute horror as she saw the massive explosion from aboard the ship that was carrying Sati.

As the fire ripped through Devagiri, giant pillars of smoke shot up from the site of the explosions. As Tara had predicted, the energy blasts of the three missiles seemed to attract each other. All the three pillars of smoke crashed into each other with diabolical rage, as thunder and lightning cracked through the destructive field. The unified pillar of smoke now shot higher; higher than anything that any living creature watching the explosion had ever seen. The smoke column rose like a giant and steeply inclined pyramid and then it exploded into a massive cloud about one kilometre high in the air. And just as instantaneously, the pyramid of smoke collapsed into itself, closeted permanently within the ruins of Devagiri.

Shiva, unmindful of the terrible devastation taking place in front of him, kept running forward, his sword drawn, his brow spouting blood at an alarming rate.

As soon as the pyramid of smoke collapsed, another silent blast occurred. As this blast of neutrons raced out, the sound of the initial explosion reached Shiva's army cowering behind the safety line.

'*Baba!*' screamed Ganesh, as he jumped from the platform he was on and raced towards his horse.

The neutron blast was invisible. Shiva couldn't see it. But he could feel a demonic surge rolling towards him. He had to save his wife. He kept running forward, screaming desperately.

'SATI!'

His body was lifted high by the neutron blast wave. For a moment he felt weightless, and then the wave propelled him back brutally. His brow and throat were on fire, while blood spewed out from his mouth. He landed hard on the ground, flat on his back, his head jerking as he felt a sharp sensation on the crown of his head.

And yet, he felt no pain. He just kept screaming.

'SA...TI...!'

'SA...TI...!'

Suddenly, he saw Sati bending over him. There was no blood on her. No wounds. No scars. She looked just like she had on the day he'd met her, all those years ago at the Brahma temple. She bent forward and ran her hand along Shiva's face, her smiling visage suffused with love and joy; a smile that always set the world right for him.

She touched the crown of Shiva's head. The sharp sensation receded and was replaced by a calm that was difficult to describe. He felt like he had been set free. Strangely, his blue throat was not cold anymore. Equally strange was the realisation that his brow had stopped burning from within.

Shiva opened his mouth, but no sound emerged. So he thought of what he wanted to say.

Take me with you, Sati. There's nothing left for me to do. I'm done.

Sati bent forward and kissed Shiva lightly on his lips. She smiled and whispered, 'No, you are not done yet. Not yet.'

Shiva kept staring at his wife. *I can't live without you...*

'You must,' said Sati's shimmering image.

Shiva couldn't keep his eyes open anymore. Sati's beautiful and calm face began to blur. He collapsed into a peaceful dream-like state. As he was descending the depths of consciousness though, he thought he heard a voice, almost like a command.

'No more killing from now on. Spread life. Spread life.'

Chapter 54

By the Holy Lake

Thirty years later, Mansarovar Lake (at the foot of Mount Kailash, Tibet)

Shiva squatted on the rock that extended over the Mansarovar. Behind him was the Kailash Mountain, each of its four sides perfectly aligned with the four cardinal directions. It stood sentinel over the great Mahadev, the one who had saved India from Evil.

The long years and the tough Tibetan terrain had taken its toll on his body. His matted hair had greyed considerably, though it was still long and wiry enough to be tied in a traditional bun with beads. His body, honed with regular exercise and yoga, was still taut and muscular, but the skin had wrinkled and lost its tone. His *neel kanth,* the *blue throat* had not lost colour at all over the years. But it didn't feel cold anymore. Not since the day he had been hit by the neutron blast from the *Pashupatiastra* that had destroyed Devagiri. The area between his brows didn't burn or throb either; perhaps also due to the neutron blast. But it had taken on a darker hue, almost black, that contrasted sharply with his fair skin. It wasn't an indistinct, indeterminate mark either. It looked like the tattoo of an eye; an eye with the lids shut. Kali had named it Shiva's third eye, which stood vertical on his forehead, between his natural eyes.

Shiva looked across the lake at the setting sun. In the distance he spotted a pair of swans gliding over the shimmering waters. It appeared to Shiva as if the birds beheld the sight together; the setting sun cannot be enjoyed unless shared with the one you love.

He breathed deeply and picked up a pebble. When he was young, he could throw one such that it skipped off the surface of the lake. His record had been seventeen bounces. He flung the pebble, but he failed; it sank immediately into the lake with a plop.

I miss you.

Not a day passed in his life without his mind dwelling on his wife. He wiped a tear from his eye before turning back to look at the bonfires outside his village compound. A large crowd had gathered around the fires, eating, drinking and making merry.

Some members of his Guna tribe had followed him when he had returned to Kailash Mountain many years ago. In addition, nearly ten thousand people from across India had decided to leave their homes and migrate to the homeland of their Mahadev. Chief amongst them were Nandi, Brahaspati, Tara, Parshuram and Ayurvati. The deposed Ayodhyan ruler, Dilipa, who was still alive thanks to Ayurvati's medicines; former Maika-Lothal governor Chenardhwaj and former Naga Prime Minister Karkotak had also migrated to the shores of the Mansarovar. Shiva's followers had established new villages in close proximity to his. Seeing the massive contingent Shiva now commanded, even the Pakratis, the local Tibetans who had maintained a long-standing enmity with the Gunas, had made peace with the Neelkanth.

The fires reminded Shiva of one of the worst days of his life, the day he had destroyed Devagiri. Sati had been cremated on the same day, later on in the evening. But Shiva did not have memories of that event. He had been unconscious, having been battered by the neutron blast of the *Pashupatiastra.* He had been fighting for his life under Ayurvati's care. What he knew about Sati's cremation was from what Kali, Ganesh and Kartik had told him.

He had been told that a calm breeze had blown across the land, picking up the ashes from the ruins of Devagiri and scattering them around slowly. It was almost as if the ashes were trying to reach the waters of the Saraswati, to give some closure to the souls of the departed. Hazy specks had coloured the entire landscape around the Saraswati to a pale shade of grey.

The sandalwood pyre, lit by both Ganesh and Kartik, had taken some time to light, but once it did, it had raged like an inferno. It seemed as if even *Lord Agni*, the *God of Fire*, needed some coaxing to consume the body of the former Princess of Meluha. But once the task had begun, it must have been so painful for Lord Agni that he wanted to finish it as soon as possible.

Shiva had regained consciousness three days later, to find an anxiety-filled gathering of Kali, Ganesh and Kartik sitting next to him. After he had regained his strength, a tearful Ganesh had handed him an urn containing Sati's ashes.

A few drops of water splashed on Shiva, perhaps from a fish swimming vigorously below. They pulled him back from the thirty-year-old memory to the present.

Shiva tarried for some more time, allowing his gaze to dwell on the lake waters. As always, he could have sworn that he saw Sati's ashes swirling in it. Of course, it was a mirage. Her ashes had been immersed in the holy Saraswati, a day after Shiva had regained consciousness.

He remembered struggling weakly onto the boat thirty years ago, helped by Ganesh and Kartik. The Neelkanth had been rowed to the middle of the river, where Kali and he had jointly scattered some of Sati's ashes into the water. Shiva had refused to immerse all of it, regardless of what tradition held. He needed to keep some portion of Sati for himself.

Indians believe that the body is a temporary gift from Mother Earth. She lends it to a living being so that one's soul has an instrument with which to carry out its karma. Once the soul's karma is done, the body must be returned, in a pure form, so that the Mother may use it for another purpose. The ashes represent a human body that has been purified by the greatest purifier of them all: Lord Agni, the God of Fire. By immersing the ashes into holy waters, the body is offered back, with respect, to Mother Earth.

He recalled the Brahmins in an adjacent boat, chanting Sanskrit hymns throughout the ceremony. One specific chant from the *Isha Vasya Upanishad* had caught Shiva's attention and had been committed to memory.

Vayur anilam amritam; Athedam bhasmantam shariram

Let this temporary body be burned to ashes. But the breath of life belongs elsewhere. May it find its way back to the Immortal Breath.

'My Lord!' shouted Nandi loudly.

Shiva turned to see Nandi standing at a distance, two hooks where his arms used to be.

'My Lord, everyone is waiting,' said Nandi, keeping his voice loud enough to reach his ears.

Shiva held his hand up, signalling for Nandi to wait. He needed some more time with his memories. They had sent Nandi to call him as they knew that he had become Shiva's favourite; he had fought bravely alongside Sati thirty years ago, losing both his hands in his doomed attempt to save Shiva's wife.

Shiva glanced beyond Nandi and saw Maharishi Bhrigu, sitting away from the others, talking to Ganesh and Kartik. The sage seemed to be explaining something from a palm-leaf book. Both his sons listened attentively. Chandraketu, the King of Branga and Maatali, the King of Vaishali, were also listening intently to Maharishi Bhrigu.

He looked back towards the lake and took another deep breath.

Kartik saved my honour.

Kartik had chosen the moment wisely to tell Shiva how he had saved the Devagiri scientists who had the knowledge of the Somras. The Neelkanth had received the news with equanimity. Shiva was also happy that Bhrigu had been saved, as the great maharishi had had no role to play in Sati's death. Furthermore, the India of the future would be the proud inheritor of the legacy of his immense knowledge.

Shiva had decreed that the Somras scientists be given lands in central Tibet, far beyond the expanse of Indian empires; in fact, beyond the reach of any empire. The Somras scientists had established their home with the help of Suryavanshi and Chandravanshi troops. These survivors named their new dwelling place after their original city, *Devagiri*, the *Abode of the Gods*. This new city established in Tibet was given a name with the same meaning, albeit in the local Tibetan language: Lhasa. The knowledge of the Somras, the elixir of immortality, was to be the sacred secret of the citizens of Lhasa, till such a time as India needed that knowledge again.

Shiva had also decreed that his two sons would set up the tribe that would protect Lhasa. The tribe that Ganesh and Kartik established was drawn from an eclectic mix of Chandravanshis, Suryavanshis and Nagas. They had also inducted most of the Gunas, Shiva's tribesmen, and many other local Tibetan tribes. Veerbhadra, Shiva's friend and loyal follower, was appointed chief of this tribe. He was given the title of Lama, the Tibetan word for guru or master. The people of Lhasa and the followers of the Lama would protect India's ancient knowledge. Their sworn duty was to rise up and save India whenever it faced the onslaught of Evil again.

The Somras waste dump site that had been set up in Tibet, on the Tsangpo River, was dug out and its contents were removed. This waste was taken farther north, into an inhospitable, remote and mostly uninhabited part of the Tibetan plateau. It was buried there, deep into the ground, enclosed within sludgy cases made of wet clay and bilva leaves, which were further encased within boxes of thick lead. These boxes had been buried deep under vast quantities of earth, snow and permafrost. It was hoped that this poison would remain undisturbed forever. Fortunately, there would be no new toxic waste to be taken care of since the manufacturing of Somras had stopped with the destruction of Devagiri.

Shiva had also realised that, just removing the knowledge of the *Somras* was not enough to stop the *drink of the Gods*. If it had to be wiped out from India, its very foundation needed uprooting. In that sense, the idea that Parshuram had had was sound: without the Saraswati, the Somras couldn't be manufactured. Furthermore, the river's present course was picking up radioactive waste at Devagiri and poisoning the lands farther downstream. The Saraswati emerged from the confluence of the Sutlej and the Yamuna. If these two tributaries were separated, the Saraswati water itself would not be available for the manufacture of the Somras or for picking up radioactive waste.

Shiva had decided that, in the interest of India, the Sutlej and the Yamuna would part company forever. It was decreed that the Yamuna's course would be changed once again, back to the temporary course that it had taken more than a century before the destruction of Devagiri, when it had merged into the Ganga. But this was easier said than done. If the course of a river as mighty as the Yamuna was changed suddenly, the resultant flooding would cause havoc. The change had to be controlled.

Bhagirath, with the help of Meluhan engineers, had come up with a brilliant plan. The sides of the Yamuna were dug up and giant sluice gates were built along them. These gates, serving as locks, would be opened slowly to guide the Yamuna onto its new course in a deliberate and controlled manner, over many months. Bhagirath had named these sluice gates the 'Locks of Shiva'. The Yamuna was thus slowly diverted onto its new course, to unite with the Ganga at Prayag. The Locks of Shiva had thereby allowed the Ganga to take its new form, gradually, without the chaos of an uncontrolled flood.

The addition of the massive Yamuna, along with the already worthy presence of the enormous Brahmaputra, had enhanced the mighty Ganga into the biggest river system in India. It also came to be believed that the Yamuna carried the soul of the Saraswati into the Ganga, thus transforming it into the holiest river in India. In a sense, the devotion associated with the hallowed river Saraswati had been transferred onto the Ganga. Furthermore, the burst of fresh clean water from the Yamuna had cleansed the poisonous waters in Branga, freeing the great rivers in that land of the Somras poison. The Brangas living at Gangasagar, the place where the resurgent Ganga met the sea, began to believe in a legend over time: that the Ganga had purified their land. It was a myth that was not far from the truth.

Meluha, without the centralising presence of Devagiri, had devolved into its different provinces which became independent kingdoms. Without the incompetent rule of

Daksha and with the fresh breath of freedom, there had been a burst of creativity and an efflorescence of varied but equally beautiful cultures.

Shiva heard a loud laugh, which he knew could belong only to Bhagirath. He turned and looked at him, standing near a bonfire, talking animatedly to Gopal and Kali. Dilipa had been deposed by his army before the destruction of Devagiri. He was succeeded by Bhagirath, who had ruled Ayodhya wisely, heralding a new era of peace and prosperity. Judging by the expression on Dilipa's face as he stood close to Bhagirath, the former emperor seemed to have made peace with his fate.

Shiva turned his attention to the tall, lanky figure speaking with Bhagirath and Kali. The great Vasudev perhaps sensed that somebody was looking at him. He turned to look at Shiva, smiled, folded his hands into a Namaste and bowed low. Shiva returned Gopal's greeting with a formal Namaste. Gopal had made his peace with Shiva.

The outcome at Devagiri was certainly not what the Vasudev chief had desired. But what had given him peace was the realisation that Evil had been removed and the knowledge of the Somras saved. India had rejuvenated itself as the malevolent effects of Evil were removed. The Neelkanth had succeeded in his mission, and in that lay the success of the Vasudevs. Gopal had also established formal relations with Veerbhadra and the citizens of Lhasa, the new tribe of the Mahadev. The Vasudevs and the Lhasans would maintain their watch over India in tandem, ensuring that this divine land continued to prosper and grow with balance.

Seeing his friend Gopal also reminded Shiva of the Vayuputras. They had never forgiven Shiva for having used the *Pashupatiastra.* It had been a source of particular embarrassment for the Mithra since he had personally backed the announcement of Shiva as the Neelkanth, against some virulent opposition. The punishment for the unauthorised use of a *daivi astra* was a fourteen-year exile. As a form of atonement for breaking his word to them, and for having been the cause of the death of his mother-in-law Veerini and his friends Parvateshwar and Anandmayi, Shiva had punished himself with exile from India; not just for fourteen years, but for the entire duration of his remaining life.

'*Baba...*'

Shiva hadn't noticed Ganesh, Kartik and Kali sneak up on him.

'Yes, Ganesh?'

'*Baba*, it's the feast of the Night of the Mahadev,' said Ganesh. 'And the Mahadev needs to be a part of the celebration instead of brooding next to the lake.'

Shiva nodded slowly. His neck had begun to hurt a bit; the perils of old age.

'Help me up,' said Shiva, as he made an effort to rise.

Kartik and Ganesh immediately leaned forward, helping their father to his feet.

'Ganesh, you get fatter every time I see you.'

Ganesh laughed heartily. He had suffered intensely and taken a long time to recover from his mother's death, but had ultimately reconciled himself with that loss, choosing to learn from her life instead. He had taken it upon himself to spread the word of Shiva and Sati throughout India. That sense of purpose in his life had helped him return to his calm state of being; in fact, he was even jovial at times.

'Thanks to your wisdom, peace prevails all over India, *baba*,' said Ganesh. 'There are no more wars, no conflicts. So I do very little physical activity and eat a lot. Ultimately, the way I see it, it's your fault that I'm getting fatter.'

Kali and Kartik laughed loudly. Shiva nodded faintly, his eyes not losing their seriousness.

'You should smile sometimes, *baba*,' said Kartik. 'It will make us happy.'

Shiva stared at Kartik. It had been a long time since Sati's death, and even young Kartik was now beginning to acquire a smattering of white hair. Shiva knew that Kartik had travelled a very long distance to come to Kailash. After most of Shiva's tasks had been completed and he had decided to return to Kailash-Mansarovar, Kartik had migrated to the south of the Narmada, going deep into the ancient heartland of India; the land of Lord Manu.

History had recorded that Lord Manu was a prince of the Pandya dynasty. This dynasty had ruled the prehistoric land of Sangamtamil. That nation and its fine Sangam culture had been destroyed as sea levels had risen with the end of the last Ice Age. Kartik had discovered that many people continued to live in this ancient Indian fatherland, breaking Lord Manu's law that banned people from travelling south of the Narmada. Kartik had established a new Sangam culture on the banks of the southern-most major river of India, the Kaveri.

'I will smile when the three of you will reveal your secret,' said Shiva.

'What secret?' asked Kartik.

'You know what I'm talking about.'

Shiva did discover in due course that on the night before the destruction of Devagiri, Kali, Parshuram and Veerbhadra had kidnapped Vidyunmali. Under pain of vicious torture, Vidyunmali had revealed the names of Sati's assassins. He had then been tormented with a brutal and slow death.

A few years after the destruction of Devagiri, Kali, Ganesh, Kartik, Parshuram and Veerbhadra had slipped out of India. Nobody really knew where they had disappeared. They had consistently refused to tell Shiva, perhaps because he had prohibited any further reprisals for Sati's death. But Shiva had his suspicions...

Those suspicions were not unfounded, because around the same time, rumours had arisen in Egypt about the near complete destruction of the secretive tribe of Aten. It was said that the death of each of the tribe's leaders had been long, slow and painful, their blood-curdling screams echoing through the hearts of their followers. What Kali and the rest didn't know was that a few months earlier Swuth had exiled himself. He had gone south, to the source of the Nile River, and had spent the rest of his years bemoaning the fact that he had been unable to complete his holy duty of executing the final kill. But the magnificence of Sati had been branded upon his soul. He didn't know her name. So he worshipped her as a nameless Goddess till his last days. His descendants continued the tradition. The few remaining survivors of the tribe of Aten would have to wait for centuries before a revolutionary Pharaoh, the ruler of Egypt, reformed and revived the cult. That Pharaoh would be remembered as the great Akhenaten, the living spirit of Aten. But that is another story.

'*Baba*, we had gone to...'

Kali placed her hand on Kartik's lips. 'There's nothing to reveal, Shiva. Except that the food is extremely delicious. You need to eat. So follow me.'

Shiva shook his head. 'You still haven't lost your regal airs.'

Kali didn't have a kingdom anymore. Within a few years of her return from Egypt, she had renounced her throne and supported the election of Suparna as the new queen of the Nagas. Leaving her kingdom in capable hands, Kali, accompanied by Shiva, Ganesh and Kartik, had toured the land of India. The family of the Neelkanth had established fifty-one Shakti temples across the length and breadth of the country. Kali had also convinced Shiva to part with the portion of Sati's ashes that he had kept for himself. She had told him that Sati belonged to the whole of India and not just to Shiva. Therefore, small portions of Sati's ashes were consecrated at each of these fifty-one temples so that Indians would forever remember their great Goddess, Lady Sati.

Kali had finally settled down in north-eastern Branga, close to the Kamakhya temple, and devoted her life to prayer. Her spiritual presence had made the Kamakhya temple one of the foremost Shakti temples in India. Many Suryavanshis, Chandravanshis and Nagas who were inspired by the Naga queen, had followed her to her new abode. Over time, they set up their own individual kingdoms. The Suryavanshis had named their kingdom *Tripura*, the *Land of the Three Cities,* after the three platforms of their destroyed capital. The Chandravanshis, worshippers of the seventh Vishnu, Lord Ram, had called their land *Manipur*, the *Land of the Jewel*; for the seventh Vishnu was, no doubt, a crown jewel of India. Many of Kali's Naga followers established their own empire farther to the east. All of these different peoples followed the path of Kali; proud warriors forged from the womb of Mother India. Therefore, if treated with respect, these people would be your greatest strength. If you disrespected them, then no power on earth would be able to save you.

'I may not have a kingdom anymore, Shiva,' said Kali, her eyes dancing with mirth, 'but I will always be a queen!'

Ganesh and Kartik smiled broadly. Shiva just stared at Kali's face, a splitting image of Sati's; it reminded him of how happy his life had once been.

'Come, let's go eat,' said Shiva.

As the family of the Mahadev walked back towards the bonfires, Ganesh and Kartik started speaking to Shiva about the brilliant composition that Bhrigu had just shown them; it would be known over the millennia as the greatest classic on the ancient science of astrology, the *Bhrigu Samhita*.

Over the subsequent years, Shiva became increasingly ascetic. He began spending many days, even months, in isolation within the claustrophobic confines of mountain caves, performing severe penance. The only one allowed to meet him at such times was Nandi. Legends emerged that the only way to reach Shiva's ears was through Nandi.

Shiva also devoted long hours to the study of yoga. The knowledge that he developed helped create a powerful tool for finding physical, mental and spiritual peace through unity with the divine. Shiva also added many fresh thoughts and philosophies to the immense body of ancient Indian knowledge and wisdom. Many of his ideas were captured in the holy scriptures of the *Vedas, Upanishads* and the *Puranas*, benefiting humanity for millennia.

Notwithstanding the prodigious productivity of Shiva's mind, his heart never really found happiness ever again. Legend has it that despite repeated attempts by his family, nobody ever saw Shiva smile again after that terrible day in Devagiri. Nobody saw his ethereal dances or heard his soulful singing and music again. Shiva had given up everything that offered even a remote possibility of bringing him happiness. But legends also hold that Shiva did smile once, just once, only a moment before he was to leave his mortal body to merge once again with the God whom he had emerged from. He smiled, for he knew that the love of his life, his Sati, was just one last breath away.

Kartik's wisdom and courage ensured that the Sangam culture in South India continued to flourish and its power spread far and wide. While Kartik continued to be adored in northern India, especially in Kashi where he was born, his influence in southern India was beyond compare. He is remembered to this day as the Warrior God, the one who can solve any problem and defeat any enemy.

Meanwhile, the adoration for Kartik's elder brother, the wise and kind-hearted Ganesh, grew to astronomical heights in India. People revered him as a living God. A belief spread throughout the country that he should be the first God to be worshipped in all ceremonies, before all others. It was held that worshipping Ganesh would remove all obstacles from one's path. Thus, he came to be known as the God of Auspicious Beginnings. His profound intellect also led to him gradually becoming the God of Writers; thus his name acquired immense significance for authors, poets and other troubled souls.

The Somras had had an especially strong effect on Ganesh, so he lived for centuries, beyond all his contemporaries. And Ganesh did not mind this. He loved interacting with people from across India, helping them, guiding them. But there did come a time when, enfeebled by old age, Ganesh began to think that perhaps he had lived in this mortal body for too long.

For he would have to suffer the mortification of seeing the ancient Vedic Indians turn on each other in a catastrophic civil war. A minor dispute within a dysfunctional royal family escalated into a mighty conflict which sucked in all the great powers of the day. The calamitous blood-letting in that war destroyed not just all the powerful empires of the time but also the way of life of the ancient Vedic Indians. What was left behind was utter devastation. From these ruins, as is its wont, civilisation did rise again. But this new culture had lost too much. They knew only snippets of the greatness of their ancestors. The descendants were, in many ways, unworthy.

These descendants beheld Gods in what were great men

of the past, for they believed that such great men couldn't possibly have existed in reality. These descendants saw magic in what was brilliant science, for their limited intellect could not understand that great knowledge. These descendants retained only rituals of what were deep philosophies, for it took courage and confidence to ask questions. These descendants divined myths in what was really history, for true memories were forgotten in chaos as vast arrays of *daivi astras* used in the Great War ravaged the land. That war destroyed almost everything. It took centuries for India to regain its old cultural vigour and intellectual depth.

When the recreated history of that Great War was written, built through fragments of surviving information, the treatise was initially called *Jaya* or *victory*. But even the unsophisticated minds of the descendants soon realised that this name was inappropriate. That dreadful war did not bring victory to anyone. Every single person who fought that war, lost the war. In fact, the whole of India lost.

Today, we know the inherited tale of that war as one of the world's greatest epics: *The Mahabharat*. If the Lord Neelkanth allows it, the unadulterated story of that terrible war shall also be told one day.

Om Namah Shivāya

The universe bows to Lord Shiva. I bow to Lord Shiva.

Glossary

Agni: God of fire

Agnipariksha: A trial by fire

Angaharas: Movement of limbs or steps in a dance

Ankush: Hook-shaped prods used to control elephants

Annapurna: The Hindu Goddess of food, nourishment and plenty; also believed to be a form of Goddess Parvati

Anshan: Hunger. It also denotes voluntary fasting. In this book, Anshan is the capital of the kingdom of Elam

Apsara: Celestial maidens from the court of the Lord of the Heavens – Indra; akin to Zeus/Jupiter

Arya: Sir

Ashwamedh yagna: Literally, the Horse sacrifice. In ancient times, an ambitious ruler, who wished to expand his territories and display his military prowess, would release a sacrificial horse to roam freely through the length and breadth of any kingdom in India. If any king stopped/captured the horse, the ruler's army would declare war against the challenger, defeat the king and annexe that territory. If an opposing king did not stop the horse, the kingdom would become a vassal of the former

Asura: Demon

Ayuralay: Hospital
Ayurvedic: Derived from Ayurved, an ancient Indian form of medicine
Ayushman bhav: May you have a long life
Baba: Father
Bhang: Traditional intoxicant in India; milk mixed with marijuana
Bhiksha: Alms or donations
Bhojan graham: Dining room
Brahmacharya: The vow of celibacy
Brahmastra: Literally, the weapon of Brahma; spoken of in ancient Hindu scriptures. Many experts claim that the description of a Brahmastra and its effects are eerily similar to that of a nuclear weapon. I have assumed this to be true in the context of my book
Branga: The ancient name for modern West Bengal, Assam and Bangladesh. Term coined from the conjoint of the two rivers of this land: *Bra*hmaputra and Ga*nga*
Brangaridai: Literally, the heart of Branga. The capital of the kingdom of Branga
Chandravanshi: Descendants of the moon
Chaturanga: Ancient Indian game that evolved into the modern game of chess
Chillum: Clay pipe, usually used to smoke marijuana
Choti: Braid
Construction of Devagiri royal court platform: The description in the book of the court platform is a possible explanation for the mysterious multiple-column buildings made of baked brick discovered at Indus Valley sites, usually next to the public baths, which many historians suppose could have been granaries
Dada: Elder brother

Daivi Astra: Daivi = Divine; Astra = Weapon. A term used in ancient Hindu epics to describe weapons of mass destruction

Dandakaranya: Aranya = forest. Dandak is the ancient name for modern Maharashtra and parts of Andhra Pradesh, Karnataka, Chhattisgarh and Madhya Pradesh. So Dandakaranya means the forests of Dandak

Deva: God

Dharma: Dharma literally translates as religion. But in traditional Hindu belief, it means far more than that. The word encompasses holy, right knowledge, right living, tradition, natural order of the universe and duty. Essentially, dharma refers to everything that can be classified as 'good' in the universe. It is the Law of Life

Dharmayudh: The holy war

Dhobi: Washerman

Divyadrishti: Divine sight

Dumru: A small, hand-held, hour-glass shaped percussion instrument

Egyptian women: Historians believe that ancient Egyptians, just like ancient Indians, treated their women with respect. The anti-women attitude attributed to Swuth and the assassins of Aten is fictional. Having said that, like most societies, ancient Egyptians also had some patriarchal segments in their society, which did, regrettably, have an appalling attitude towards women

Fire song: This is a song sung by Guna warriors to agni (fire). They also had songs dedicated to the other elements viz: *bhūmi* (earth), *jal* (water), *pavan* (air or wind), *vyom* or *shunya* or *akash* (ether or void or sky)

Fravashi: Is the guardian spirit mentioned in the *Avesta*, the sacred writings of the Zoroastrian religion. Although, according to most researchers, there is no physical description of Fravashi, the language grammar of *Avesta* clearly shows it to be feminine. Considering the importance given to fire in ancient Hinduism and Zoroastrianism, I've assumed the Fravashi to be represented by fire. This is, of course, a fictional representation

Ganesh-Kartik relationship: In northern India, traditional myths hold Lord Kartik as older than Lord Ganesh; in large parts of southern India, Lord Ganesh is considered elder. In my story, Ganesh is older than Kartik. What is the truth? Only Lord Shiva knows

Guruji: Teacher; ji is a term of respect, added to a name or title

Gurukul: The family of the guru or the family of the teacher. In ancient times, also used to denote a school

Har Har Mahadev: This is the rallying cry of Lord Shiva's devotees. I believe it means 'All of us are Mahadevs'

Hariyupa: This city is currently known as Harappa. A note on the cities of Meluha (or as we call it in modern times, the Indus Valley Civilisation): historians and researchers have consistently marvelled at the fixation that the Indus Valley Civilisation seemed to have for water and hygiene. In fact historian M Jansen used the term 'wasserluxus' (obsession with water) to describe their magnificent obsession with the physical and symbolic aspects of water, a term Gregory Possehl builds upon in his brilliant book, *The Indus Civilisation — A Contemporary Perspective.* In the book, *The Immortals of Meluha*, the obsession with water is shown to arise due to its cleansing of the toxic sweat and urine triggered by consuming the Somras. Historians have also marvelled at the level of sophisticated standardisation in the Indus Valley Civilisation. One of the examples of this was the bricks, which across the entire civilisation, had similar proportions and specifications

Holi: Festival of colours

Howdah: Carriage placed on top of elephants

Indra: The God of the sky; believed to be the King of the Gods

Jai Guru Vishwamitra: Glory to the teacher Vishwamitra

Jai Guru Vashishtha: Glory to the teacher Vashishtha. Only two Suryavanshis were privileged to have had both Guru Vashishtha and Guru Vishwamitra as their gurus (teachers) viz. Lord Ram and Lord Lakshman

Jai Shri Brahma: Glory to Lord Brahma

Jai Shri Ram: Glory to Lord Ram

Janau: A ceremonial thread tied from the shoulders, across the torso. It was one of the symbols of knowledge in ancient India. Later, it was corrupted to become a caste symbol to denote those born as Brahmins and not those who'd acquired knowledge through their effort and deeds

Ji: A suffix added to a name or title as a form of respect

Kajal: Kohl, or eye liner

Karma: Duty and deeds; also the sum of a person's actions in this and previous births, considered to limit the options of future action and affect future fate

Karmasaathi: Fellow traveller in karma or duty

Kashi: The ancient name for modern Varanasi. Kashi means the city where the supreme light shines

Kathak: A form of traditional Indian dance

Kriyas: Actions

Kulhads: Mud cups

Maa: Mother

Mandal: Literally, Sanskrit word meaning circle. Mandals are created, as per ancient Hindu and Buddhist tradition, to make a sacred space and help focus the attention of the devotees

Mahadev: Maha = Great and Dev = God. Hence Mahadev means the greatest God or the God of Gods. I believe that there were many 'destroyers of evil' but a few of them were so great that they would be called 'Mahadev'. Amongst the Mahadevs were Lord Rudra and Lord Shiva

Mahasagar: Great Ocean; Hind Mahasagar is the Indian Ocean

Mahendra: Ancient Indian name meaning conqueror of the world

Mahout: Human handler of elephants

Manu's story: Those interested in finding out more about the historical validity of the South India origin theory of Manu should read Graham Hancock's pathbreaking book, *Underworld*

Mausi: Mother's sister, literally translating as *maa si* i.e. like a mother

Maya: Illusion

Mehragarh: Modern archaeologists believe that Mehragarh is the progenitor of the Indus

	Valley civilisation. Mehragarh represents a sudden burst of civilised living, without any archaeological evidence of a gradual progression to that level. Hence, those who established Mehragarh were either immigrants or refugees
Meluha:	The land of pure life. This is the land ruled by the Suryavanshi kings. It is the area that we in the modern world call the Indus Valley Civilisation
Meluhans:	People of Meluha
Mudras:	Gestures
Naga:	Serpent people
Namaste:	An ancient Indian greeting. Spoken along with the hand gesture of open palms of both the hands joined together. Conjoin of three words. 'Namah', 'Astu' and 'Te' – meaning 'I bow to the Godhood in you'. Namaste can be used as both 'hello' and 'goodbye'
Nirvana:	Enlightenment; freedom from the cycle of rebirths
Oxygen/ anti-oxidants theory:	Modern research backs this theory. Interested readers can read the article 'Radical Proposal' by Kathryn Brown in the *Scientific American*
Panchavati:	The land of the five banyan trees
Pandit:	Priest
Paradaeza:	An ancient Persian word which means 'the walled place of harmony'; the root of the English word, Paradise
Pariha:	The land of fairies. Refers to modern Persia/Iran. I believe Lord Rudra came from this land
Parmatma:	The ultimate soul or the sum of all souls

Parsee immigration to India: Groups of Zoroastrian refugees immigrated to India perhaps between the 8th and 10th century AD to escape religious persecution. They landed in Gujarat, and the local ruler Jadav Rana gave them refuge

Pashupatiastra: Literally, the weapon of the Lord of the Animals. The descriptions of the effects of the Pashupatiastra in Hindu scriptures are quite similar to that of nuclear weapons. In modern nuclear technology, weapons have been built primarily on the concept of nuclear fission. While fusion-boosted fission weapons have been invented, pure fusion weapons have not been invented as yet. Scientists hold that a pure nuclear fusion weapon has far less radioactive fallout and can theoretically serve as a more targeted weapon. In this trilogy, I have assumed that the Pashupatiastra is one such weapon

Patallok: The underworld

Pawan Dev: God of the winds

Pitratulya: The term for a man who is 'like a father'

Prahar: Four slots of six hours each into which the day was divided by the ancient Hindus; the first prahar began at twelve midnight

Prithvi: Earth

Prakrati: Nature

Puja: Prayer

Puja thali: Prayer tray

Raj dharma: Literally, the royal duties of a king or ruler. In ancient India, this term embodied pious and just administration of the king's royal duties

Raj guru: Royal sage

Rajat:	Silver
Rajya Sabha:	The royal council
Rakshabandhan:	Raksha = Protection; Bandhan = thread/ tie. An ancient Indian festival in which a sister ties a sacred thread on her brother's wrist, seeking his protection
Ram Chandra:	Ram = Face; Chandra = Moon. Hence Ram Chandra is 'the face of the moon'
Ram Rajya:	The rule of Ram
Rangbhoomi:	Literally, the ground of colour. Stadia in ancient times where sports, performances and public functions would be staged
Rangoli:	Traditional colourful and geometric designs made with coloured powders or flowers as a sign of welcome
Rishi:	Man of knowledge
Sankat Mochan:	Literally, reliever from troubles. One of the names of Lord Hanuman
Sangam:	A confluence of two rivers
Sanyasi:	A person who renounces all his worldly possessions and desires to retreat to remote locations and devote his time to the pursuit of God and spirituality. In ancient India, it was common for people to take sanyas at an old age, once they had completed all their life's duties
Sapt Sindhu:	Land of the seven rivers – Indus, Saraswati, Yamuna, Ganga, Sarayu, Brahmaputra and Narmada. This was the ancient name of North India
Saptrishi:	One of the 'Group of seven Rishis'
Saptrishi Uttradhikari:	Successors of the Saptrishis
Shakti Devi:	Mother Goddess; also Goddess of power and energy
Shamiana:	Canopy
Shloka:	Couplet
Shudhikaran:	The purification ceremony

Sindhu:	The first river
Somras:	Drink of the Gods
Sundarban:	Sundar = beautiful; ban = forest. Hence, Sundarban means beautiful forest
Svarna:	Gold
Swadweep:	The Island of the individual. This is the land ruled by the Chandravanshi kings
Swadweepans:	People of Swadweep
Swaha:	Legend has it that Lord Agni's wife is named Swaha. Hence it pleases Lord Agni, the God of Fire, if a disciple takes his wife's name while worshipping the sacred fire. Another interpretation of Swaha is that it means offering of self
Tamra:	Bronze
Thali:	Plate
Varjish graha:	The exercise hall
Varun:	God of the water and the seas
Vijayibhav:	May you be victorious
Vikarma:	Carrier of bad fate
Vishnu:	The protector of the world and propagator of good. I believe that it is an ancient Hindu title for the greatest of leaders who would be remembered as the mightiest of Gods
Vishwanath:	Literally, the Lord of the World. Usually refers to Lord Shiva, also known as Lord Rudra in his angry avatar. I believe Lord Rudra was a different individual from Lord Shiva. In this trilogy, I have used the term Vishwanath to refer to Lord Rudra
Yagna:	Sacrificial fire ceremony

Other Titles by Amish

The Shiva Trilogy

The fastest-selling book series in the history of Indian publishing

THE IMMORTALS OF MELUHA
(Book 1 of the Trilogy)

1900 BC. What modern Indians mistakenly call the Indus Valley Civilisation, the inhabitants of that period knew as the land of Meluha – a near perfect empire created many centuries earlier by Lord Ram. Now their primary river Saraswati is drying, and they face terrorist attacks from their enemies from the east. Will their prophesied hero, the Neelkanth, emerge to destroy evil?

THE SECRET OF THE NAGAS
(Book 2 of the Trilogy)

The sinister Naga warrior has killed his friend Brahaspati and now stalks his wife Sati. Shiva, who is the prophesied destroyer of evil, will not rest till he finds his demonic adversary. His thirst for revenge will lead him to the door of the Nagas, the serpent people. Fierce battles will be fought and unbelievable secrets revealed in the second part of the Shiva trilogy.

Indic Chronicles

LEGEND OF SUHELDEV

Repeated attacks by Mahmud of Ghazni have weakened India's northern regions. Then the Turks raid and destroy one of the holiest temples in the land: the magnificent Lord Shiva temple at Somnath. At this most desperate of times, a warrior rises to defend the nation. Read this epic adventure of courage and heroism that recounts the story of King Suheldev and the magnificent Battle of Bahraich.

www.authoramish.com

The Ram Chandra Series

The second fastest-selling book series in the history of Indian publishing

RAM – SCION OF IKSHVAKU
(Book 1 of the Series)

He loves his country and he stands alone for the law. His band of brothers, his wife, Sita, and the fight against the darkness of chaos. He is Prince Ram. Will he rise above the taint that others heap on him? Will his love for Sita sustain him through his struggle? Will he defeat the demon Raavan who destroyed his childhood? Will he fulfil the destiny of the Vishnu? Begin an epic journey with Amish's latest: the Ram Chandra Series.

SITA – WARRIOR OF MITHILA
(Book 2 of the Series)

An abandoned baby is found in a field. She is adopted by the ruler of Mithila, a powerless kingdom ignored by all. Nobody believes this child will amount to much. But they are wrong. For she is no ordinary girl. She is Sita. Through an innovative multi-linear narrative, Amish takes you deeper into the epic world of the Ram Chandra Series.

RAAVAN – ENEMY OF ARYAVARTA
(Book 3 of the Series)

Raavan is determined to be a giant among men, to conquer, plunder, and seize the greatness that he thinks is his right. He is a man of contrasts, of brutal violence and scholarly knowledge. A man who will love without reward and kill without remorse. In this, the third book in the Ram Chandra Series, Amish sheds light on Raavan, the king of Lanka. Is he the greatest villain in history or just a man in a dark place, all the time?

www.authoramish.com

Non-fiction

IMMORTAL INDIA

Explore India with the country's storyteller, Amish, who helps you understand it like never before, through a series of sharp articles, nuanced speeches and intelligent debates. In *Immortal India*, Amish lays out the vast landscape of an ancient culture with a fascinatingly modern outlook.

DHARMA – DECODING THE EPICS FOR A MEANINGFUL LIFE

In this genre-bending book, the first of a series, Amish and Bhavna dive into the priceless treasure trove of the ancient Indian epics, as well as the vast and complex universe of Amish's Meluha, to explore some of the key concepts of Indian philosophy. Within this book are answers to our many philosophical questions, offered through simple and wise interpretations of our favourite stories.